TAINTED BY LOVE

by

GILLIAN JONES

Julie,
we all deserve love!

Inquiries please email gillianjonesauthor@gmail.com

First print edition: February 2017

Edited by Quoth the Raven Writing Co.
Cover design © Book Covers by Ashbee Designs
www.ashleybaumann.com
"Eyes That See" poem ©: S. Louise
Formatting by Paul Salvette

About the Book

My name is Hendrix Hills.

When I was twenty-nine, I fell in love with a girl.

We loved fast. We loved hard.

But our love was tainted.

My name is Trinity Adams.

When I was twenty-seven, I fell in love with a boy.

We loved fast. We loved hard.

It's too bad my blood was tainted.

Dedication

For Kym.

This one's yours.

You rooted for this story since its inception.

I hope it's how you pictured it, even if it was you who decided to change it!

XOX

And for Paige.

I don't think you realize how much of an integral role you play in these stories.

For that, I thank you.

XOX

Warning: Not your traditional HEA (Happily Ever After). May contain emotional triggers for some. There will be things that you won't like—and some that you will—but I hope you have fun finding out!

"I don't understand
What destiny's planned
I'm starting to grasp
What is in my own hands…"
—Depeche Mode, "Clean"

"I alone cannot change the world, but I can cast a stone across the waters to create many ripples."
—Mother Teresa

"AIDS is such a scary thing and it's also the kind of thing that you think won't happen to you. It can happen to you and it's deadly serious."
—Ice T

"If I could give you one thing in life, I would give you the ability to see yourself through my eyes. Only then would you realize how special you are to me."
—Author unknown

Eyes That See

This. Right here, this poem, *Eyes That See,* written by an amazing friend of mine—one I've never met except online, but adore like a friend who lives nearby. S. Louise tilted the axis of my emotions with her beautiful words, and as soon as she trusted me with this poem, I knew it was meant to preface this book. I felt it reflected the theme of my story, and the ways society can be cruel. These words are beautiful, the message powerful, and I'm completely humbled that she would allow me to share this piece of herself with my readers. I'm so bloody proud of my friend.

Be kind to one another.

Eyes that see,
Make them stop.
For eyes that see,
A mouth full of words is born.

Tick tock.

If only the world were blind, we would live by touch, sensation and love only.
Not by pretty, strong or the ideal body.
If only the world were blind,
Hate and discrimination would eventually cease to exist.

For every pair of eyes that peruse the world,
A mouth full of words dripping with venom comes alive.
Words that have the power to destroy.
I do not want to be destroyed by what I love the most.

Tick Tock.
If the world were only blind,

I would finally be free.

Tick.

Tock.

—by S. Louise x

Playlist

(Available on Spotify)

Real Love – Tom Odell

Start Beginning – Nizlopi

Clarity – Zedd, Foxes

All I See Is You – Meaku

By Your Side – Remastered – Sade

Starving – Hailee Steinfeld, Grey, Zedd

Cold Water – Major Lazer, MØ, Justin Bieber

Let Me Love You – DJ Snake, Justin Bieber

Chains – The Sweeplings

Breathe Me – Sia

Tonight I Wanna Cry – Keith Urban

Stay – Rihanna, Mikky Ekko

Best of You – Foo Fighters

All We Know – The Chainsmokers, Phoebe Ryan

Love On Me – Galantis, Hook N Sling

The Little Things – Kasbo Remix – Big Gigantic, Angela McCluskey, Kasbo

Unsteady – X Ambassadors

Let It Go – James Bay

Say You Won't Let Go – James Arthur

Scars To Your Beautiful – Alessia Cara

Warrior – Demi Lovato

In The Name Of Love – Martin Garrix, Bebe Rexha

Learning to Fly – Pink Floyd, James Guthrie

Try – P!nk

Dark Necessities – Red Hot Chili Peppers

Blown Wide Open – Big Wreck

Cut – Plumb

Born – Over The Rhine

I Gave You All – Mumford & Sons

Oblivion – Bastille

With Me – dvsn

Bloodstream – Stateless

Let Me In – Grouplove

Run – Revised Album Version – Snow Patrol

The Background – Third Eye Blind

Only Time – Original Version – Enya

Address In The Stars – Caitlin & Will

Here Without You – 3 Doors Down

In Loving Memory – Alter Bridge

Save A Place For Me – Matthew West

Who Knew – P!nk

Heaven – Beyoncé

Who Do You Love – Marianas Trench

Collide – Acoustic Version – Howie Day

When You Say Nothing At All – Ronan Keating

Wasn't Expecting That – Jamie Lawson

You Said You'd Grow Old With Me – Michael Schulte

When You're Gone – Avril Lavigne

Clean – 2006 Remastered Version – Depeche Mode

You & I (Nobody in the World) – John Legend

Can You Hold Me – NF, Britt Nicole

The Fighter – Keith Urban, Carrie Underwood

Love Me Now – John Legend

Can't Slow Down – Hedley

Comfortably Numb – Pink Floyd

Nothing Like Us – Bonus Track – Justin Bieber

She Is Love – Parachute

Young And Beautiful – Lana Del Rey

Sad Song (feat. Elena Coats) – We The Kings, Elena Coats

Tainted Love – Soft Cell

Table of Contents

PROLOGUE

Trinity

"SHIT, TRINITY, YOU taste good. I can't wait to finally be inside you," my boyfriend Blake whispers, looking up from between my legs, his blue eyes dilated with lust. "You're so fucking tight, wet, so ready."

He slides a second finger inside me, stretching and filling me, doing that fluttery curve thing with his fingers, the one that hits my G-spot perfectly every time. "The idea of getting to be the first one to slip my cock inside you makes me goddamn crazy and so fucking hard, Trin. I can't wait to feel you wrapped around my cock."

He's right. He will be the first. I'm not sure how it happened, but I came to Queen's University a virgin. Sure, I'd had boyfriends, but never anyone I felt confident enough to go all the way with, never anyone I trusted or loved like I do Blake. On top of being an almost-twenty-year-old virgin, I'm a first-year commerce student here at Queen's (having taken a year off to make some money for school) while Blake's a third-year business major specializing in marketing. We met during Frosh week, and we've been inseparable ever since.

"Yes, right there. Don't, don't stop, ohhhh..." I moan, as his fingers play me perfectly.

"You're beautiful like this. Legs spread open, pussy in my face, those steel grey eyes taking me in like you can't get enough of me...and fuck if you don't taste like heaven," he says, his voice husky.

"I can't get enough, Blake," I tell him as I gaze down at his face, which is glistening with my excitement and hovering between my legs. His blonde hair is mussed, his blue eyes dark pools of desire. I feel myself melting even more. "It feels good, Blake, keep going," I moan loudly, my body quivering beneath him, needing him to stop talking now. "Please, don't stop. Just keep going, no more words, no talking," I plead, pushing the back of his head toward where I want it most, and I hear him chuckle.

"Love it when you beg," he grins, his eyes reflecting the same lust I feel. "You being bossy tonight, Trinity? Gonna take what you want?"

I nod yes.

"This tight pussy likes all the attention, doesn't it? You ready to come, Sunshine? Play with your tits. Let me see the way you make those nipples ready for me," he says, pausing, waiting for me to comply and beg him some more. He always likes it when I beg. We've been doing the oral sex thing now for a few months. With me being a virgin, Blake was determined to take things slow between us, to let me set the pace.

I'm happy I waited for him to come along. I had a few boyfriends in the past, but none as patient as Blake. I was in a couple of relationships where I was pressured to give it up, but, thankfully, I never caved. I would have lived with that regret, especially when I have Blake now, and I'm happy to have this gift to give him. One boy went as far as breaking up with me because I wouldn't put out by our third date, and he went around spreading rumours about how I was a cocktease. Then I met Blake, and he's shown me that this is about more than sex for him, it's about knowing each other, having someone to confide and trust in. But tonight, however, I'm beyond ready to not be the resident virgin anymore; tonight, it's about sex and it's my decision.

"Yes. So ready, please. I want to come, Blake. I—I'm close."

"That's my girl." He reaches up, pinching my hard nipples before finally moving his face back to my pussy where it belongs. He slides his tongue over my clit and between my slick lips, then slips his fingers in and out while sucking my clit between his lips, bringing me closer to the brink with each motion. My moans of excitement coupled with our heavy breathing become our only soundtrack. His two fingers slip deep inside, flickering at a frenzied pace. My legs begin to shake and his tongue is everywhere I need it to be while his fingers fuck me in perfect synchronization. Waves of pleasure crash against my body as Blake continues driving me towards nirvana, then suddenly it peaks and becomes so intense that my world explodes, and I see colours and flashing lights and feel like I'm melting all over the bed as an orgasm takes over.

"Thank you. Oh, shit, that was good…" I pant, as Blake moves up beside me. He holds me while my body continues to come down from the most epic orgasm I've ever had. Thank the dorm gods that Tara, my not-so-friendly roommate, has gone home for the weekend, although it wouldn't surprise me if my sexcapades weren't heard by everyone living on the third floor of Chown Hall.

"Holy shit, baby. That was a big one. And I've just started with you tonight," he says, nuzzling into the crook of my neck and kissing my collarbone, down to my nipples.

"You ready for more, Sunshine?"

"Yes, definitely could go for a few more of those," I giggle, leaning into Blake's kisses. I begin running my hands along his chiseled chest before grabbing his cock, stroking it and lightly smearing the pre-cum over the smooth tip.

"Fucking hell, that feels amazing Trin. You ready for Round Two?" he asks, rubbing my clit with the pad of his thumb, the move causing my barely extinguished fire to reignite, and soon I'm at the precipice again. I feel a hunger deep inside for Blake to fill me up. Despite how nervous I am about it hurting, I want him badly.

"More than ready. Blake, please, it's time. Fuck me. I need to feel *you,*" I say, lifting my hips in reaction. Pulling on his blond hair, I force him to look up at me.

"Jesus, Trin. You're going to kill me…do you know how many times I've pictured this exact moment? Getting to slip deep inside you, to connect to you like this?" He strokes my long brown hair, giving it a tug before kissing me. "So sweet."

"Please. I'm close. I hunger to feel you inside me. I want to feel you come inside me, for us to come together. I'm more than ready," I add, reaching into my bedside table drawer for the box of condoms I'd bought earlier today, hoping he'd see I was ready to take this next step, to know that I was ready for him to finally make love to me. *To know that I loved him.*

"No. I…I don't want anything between us, Trinity. No barriers. I only want to feel *you.*" He reaches for my hand, pressing it hard into his chest. He meets my gaze, his stare intense, and then starts kissing me like we can't get close enough to one another, our tongues battling. "You make me happy," Blake whispers, once he pulls away. "So sexy." He makes his way down my body, kissing my chest, each nipple, and then coming up and taking my lips again as his hands reach down between us. I squirm from the contact, loving how he makes me feel, needing to feel his hardness inside me all that much more.

"You're on the Pill. And I'm clean, Sunshine. Please, no condom. Let me do this right. Let me make this the best night for us."

I contemplate for a moment, but he's back sucking on my neck and licking my earlobe, his breath warm in my ear as he whispers how amazing I am, how incredible we'll feel together, driving me crazy with desire before moving to kiss me tenderly once again.

All logic and any protests die on my lips. We've been together for eight months now, we've talked about me moving into his apartment, and he's right—I am on the Pill, and it's my first time therefore I know

I'm clean, and he says he's clean. *I trust him, so we're good.*

"Okay. No condom," I agree, dropping the box of Trojans onto the tabletop. I feel him smile against my lips before he finally eases his way deep inside me, moving slowly. It's beautiful and feels so good, the little bit of pain is worth the pleasure it chases.

"So…fucking…tight," he moans a short time later, as he bucks and jerks inside me. Then, a moment later: Everything's changed now, Trin. Can you feel it?"

Truer words have never been spoken.

1

Trinity

Taking a huge gulp of wine, I sit back on my cozy corduroy couch.

I balance my MacBook on my lap, readying myself to type the three letters into the Google search bar.

I'm sitting alone, stunned, in my downtown Toronto apartment. The silence around me is deafening. The city's currently experiencing its first snowstorm of the season, a fitting scenario, really, as I sit here facing a storm of my own.

"Breathe, just breathe," I say, trying to calm myself.

It's crazy how three tiny letters can have such a major impact.

HIV.

I'm twenty-five.

I've only had one sexual relationship where we didn't use condoms—Blake was my first. We were together on and off for four years. After him, I'd dated a few men and had sex with two of them but, thankfully, always used protection. I thought I'd been responsible and safe.

But today I learned that I have Human Immunodeficiency Virus. *HIV.*

My doctor called my cell phone when I was on a lunch date with a colleague. I'd excused myself to take the call. I agreed to stop by her clinic on my way home, I assumed just to pick up a prescription, something to finally make me feel better. I'd been feeling unwell for a while now.

"I'm sorry, Trinity. Your last blood test revealed that you've tested positive..."

I tuned the doctor out. I think I might have even had an out-of-body experience.

"...with a proper treatment plan..."

There must be some kind of mistake. The doctor and I had never even discussed that I could have HIV. I didn't even know she was testing me for that.

"...symptoms are similar to...don't always surface right away...it takes years for some..."

I'd been having headaches.

"...live a normal life..."

I'd had the flu a few times.

"...it's not like it used to be. We've made significant advances..."

I'd been more tired than normal.

"I'm sorry, Trinity."

Finding out that this was possibly only the beginning of feeling unwell was terrifying.

Hovering my cursor over the message in my Facebook Messenger inbox, I can see the first words of the answer to the question I'd just sent Blake. Without having to open the chat—without having to let him see that I've read it—I see the beginning of his response to the question I already knew the answer to, even before I typed it hours earlier.

"I'm so sorry, Sunshine. I didn't know. I..."

I've seen all I need to, no reason to read the rest. And I vow to never fully open that message.

Tonight, I'll have a Pity Party.

Tonight, I'll cry and fall apart.

Tomorrow, I will pick myself up.

Tomorrow, I'll start living the life I love again.

Just three tiny letters…

2

Trinity

"ARE YOU EXCITED for your big date?" Shannon Maracle—my best friend and hair dresser—asks, her green eyes reflecting her own excitement.

Tucking her long black hair behind her ear, she continues to probe me with questions as she flitters around me in her tiny bathroom, armed with a way-too-hot straightener she's using as a curling iron. I'm twenty-six, and apparently in her eyes I don't know how to do my own hair, so she's helping me get ready. It's an important date, and I want to look my best, so I indulge her. *And I do want him to think I'm worth it.*

"I'm *extremely nervous.* I really like Jared, but I can't shake the feeling that he's going to be pissed I didn't tell him sooner. I feel like he's looking for the whole package, and I'm not sure I can offer that," I answer honestly, shrugging my shoulders as she works her way around, curling the long strands of my ombre-style hair. It goes from a red velvet colour at the roots to platinum blonde on the ends. Call it an act of rebellion, but I love it.

So does Jared, the man I've been seeing for about a month. The same man I'm completely stressing over about how he'll react tonight. I really like him and so far I think we've clicked. Despite the fact that he travels a lot for work (he sells automotive parts), we've managed to talk on the phone, text and Skype almost every night. I want very much to see where this relationship could go. We're very compatible and he's a great guy; I just need to get past tonight.

I have to tell him before I get my hopes up. I know it's going to be a shock, I can only pray that he's the man I want him to be. My wish is that Jared will see past the stigmas that having HIV can hold. I want nothing more than for him to see me as the same girl after our date.

The Third Date.

Therefore, tonight's a huge deal.

Tonight's the night I tell him that I'm HIV-positive.

For Shannon, and many in the dating world, the third date is considered the Have Sex Date: the hot, passionate, sex-on-fire date. The one with the promise of a relationship—or, at least, more sex—date.

In my world, it means disclosure. It means being vulnerable and sharing with someone outside my close-knit circle that I'm HIV-positive.

It means admitting that I'm not a guaranteed happily ever after.

That I'm...*tainted.*

Putting myself back out there after a long road of depression, anxiety, and—honestly—just learning how to live again knowing that not everyone will accept the Trinity I am today, has been tough. It's taken over a year. There's been a lot of reflection and education to get myself where I am today, happy again. I've accepted myself as the Trinity I am now. One who's determined to fight and continue living a long and healthy life despite having HIV.

I'm finally dating, and tonight I'm ready to let myself be seen openly. I just hope I've met the right man, one who can accept all the facets of who I am, one who can see past the disease that by no means defines who I am.

"There. All done," she says. "You're ready for your big night."

"Shannon, I'm terrified. A part of me wants to cancel and just tell him over the phone that I'm HIV-positive. That way I can save face. I want him to still want me, but there's this pit in my stomach that's lingering like a warning." I wipe away a tear that I hadn't realized had escaped.

"Trin. Be positive. I mean, look at you. You're gorgeous, fun, kind and wicked smart. He's an idiot if he can't accept a little virus. It's not what defines you." She grabs my chin, forcing me to meet her gaze. "And if he uses that as his definition of you, then fuck him. It's his loss."

Placing my hands over hers, I pause. "I know you get it, see past it. But you also don't want to have sex with me. It's a moot point between us. Not everyone has the capacity to."

"I have a feeling Jared will. He seems like a good one, Trin."

"Let's hope so."

It turns out it's easier to judge me than it is to love me.

3

Trinity

"Please say something," I whisper. I fiddle with my red cocktail napkin, wringing the shit out of it as the tension between us causes me to recede into myself. "Say *anything*, Jared..."

He's silent, but his glare—penetrating me from across the table in the dimly lit bar—speaks volumes.

We're sitting in a back booth at The Fox, a local pub I suggested going to for a nightcap and, well, to talk, because it's taken me until after dinner to build up the nerve to say what I need to say to him.

I'm completely smitten. He's brilliant, and I really, really like him. I think part of my hesitancy to reveal my secret tonight is due to the fact that we've been having such a great time all evening, laughing and sharing anything and everything about ourselves, our jobs, and whatever else we could think of. *Except the one thing I need to tell him.* I just don't want our night to end.

But it all changes the instant I take a sip of my Guinness and blurt, I'm HIV-positive."

His glass hovers between the table and his mouth then stops, his arm frozen in mid-air.

"I wanted you to know that, before things go any farther," I say, "...which is completely where I want them to go. Farther. I really like you. This is such a hard thing to share. I hope you'll still want to date me, to see where this goes?" It pours out of my mouth like a verbal waterfall.

As I predicted, things are not going to go my way. It's been five minutes since I made my confession, and five minutes of total silence from Jared.

Funny. I've gone to therapy, joined support groups, asked questions and practiced this exact conversation over and over again with my reflection in my bathroom mirror, but no matter how prepared I think I am, it's all bullshit. You cannot prepare for the emotional or psychological impact of telling someone that you're infected with a communicable disease—one they risk contracting should they chose to be with you. Or for the rejection. You can never really entirely prepare for that.

I try again. "Please."

"How *could* you?" he whispers, his eyes cold when he finally speaks. "How could you string me along…make me think you're *normal?*"

I flinch at his comment along with the snide tone in which he delivers it. I swear I can see the disdain dripping off his face as he takes me in.

"I *am* normal. It's still me, Jared," I say, after a few beats of silence. Shaking my head in disbelief, I repeat it again, as though I think it will change anything. "It's still me."

"Bullshit," he hisses. "You let me get close to you when you're fucking contagious. Here I thought we'd be having sex tonight. I didn't expect this shit." He shakes his own head now. I try to reach for his hand, but he rips it away. "Don't touch me," he deadpans, "you're…*sick.*"

How can he say that to me? Why can't he realize that I'm still me; the same woman he's gotten to know in person and over hours spent on the phone? "I'm not sick," I blurt. I know a lot of people might consider me ill, however to me, I'm here, I'm feeling good, and I'm fighting to stay healthy and live as much of a normal life as possible.

"But you *are,*" Jared says. "And what's worse, you kept it a god-damn secret. Like some kind of shitty surprise, to share once you felt like it. Once *you* thought it was the right time." Contempt and judgment cross his usually jovial face, and his blue eyes look at me like I'm a stranger. "The right time should have been our first date."

"I'm sorry, please let me explain..." I say.

Shaking his head, his lips curl as he spits out his next words. "Before we kissed, you should have told me. I hate fucking surprises. I mean...*fuck!* We've *kissed!*" he says, in disbelief. "You have AIDS, for Christ's sake! I could have it now..." Jared sits stone-faced as he makes a point of wiping his sleeve over his mouth, as if he's cleaning off some invisible threat.

"No, Jared. I have HIV. It's different, and this isn't the '80s. We're educated. Everyone knows—or should know—that you can't get HIV or AIDS from kissing. It's not transmitted through saliva, so it's a low-risk activity. I mean, unless you kissed me and had gaping open wounds in your mouth, I'd say you're safe," I tell him, a bit cheekily. Unfortunately, though, my burst of bravado doesn't last. Reality hits again. *This man seriously thinks this little of me.* The realization that Jared honestly believes that I'd be reckless and unsafe where his safety was concerned unnerves me. Suddenly, a feeling of worthlessness hits me like a freight train. *I'll never be seen as normal.*

Wiping tears that are falling despite trying my damnedest to keep them at bay, I reach for my napkin and mutter, while meeting his gaze. "Despite what you may think of me, I never would have kissed you if I thought I was putting you at risk," I say, barely audibly, the shame overtaking me. "I'm sor—"

"I've read about people like you. You're as bad as a serial killer. Fucking whore." He points his finger at me. "I can't believe you were willing to risk my life to get yourself off. I'm fucking done here, done with this." He stands abruptly, his chair clattering to the floor behind him. "Lose my number. I'm erasing yours. And you."

With that, he drops a twenty on the table, leaving me sitting alone in The Fox, tears streaming down my face.

I was right. I knew he wouldn't see me.

4

HENDRIX

KNOW WHAT THE best feeling on Earth is?

Pussy.

Yep. Nothing beats the feeling of a hot and wet pussy gripping my cock, guiding me in, welcoming me deep inside into that incessant heat. Watching my cock as it drives in and out is what really drives me wild. I'm an admitted pussy voyeur. Seeing my cock coated in a woman's excitement—knowing she's all wet for me—is the ultimate turn on.

And right now, I'm hard as granite as I pound into Nikki, my current fuck buddy.

Nikki and I have been fucking on and off for a few weeks. I don't call it dating because I don't date unless it's a means to an end, one that will get me laid. Then I might buy a chick a meal or take her for a drink if the situation calls for it.

Nikki's my usual type: thin, big tits and a greedy little pussy, one that fits me just right. Uncomplicated fucking at its finest is my style. I'm simply looking for an arrangement that gets us both off, and nothing more.

Finding chicks who are down to fuck is easy enough, thanks to the company I keep and the places I hang. Like all things, though, these arrangements tend to run their course, some quicker than others, and there's always a clear expiration date. I have yet to find a girl who truly understands my full definition of "nothing more".

And tonight, Nikki's crossed that line. She's getting attached. The signs of her wanting us to be a real couple are becoming more and more blatant each time we get together. The façade of being merely fuck buddies is slipping on her end. She's texting, stopping by the garage, wanting to go out to dinner and all that clingy shit. Things that don't fit into the dos and don'ts of the Fuck Buddy System. Exclusive sex—with a bit of light conversation before and after—is all I want. Feelings, long-term commitment and love were never part of the deal. And trust me, this is no good at all, because she sucks me off like a champ and she's always down to fuck, giving me the release I'm chasing.

"Fuck, you feel good, Hendrix. Fuck, yes. Right there. Oh, oh. Yes, yes, yes…right there, big boy. Yes, right there…"

I move my mouth over Nikki's collagen-plumped lips, not so much to kiss her, but to quiet her down. Sure, she's hot and she fucks like an animal, but the porn star routine is a bit much for me tonight. I'm here, too. I know it's good. I don't need that much audio to oversell it. I'd just called her over for a bit of stress relief. I have a huge day tomorrow and needed to take the edge off.

It was working at first, and then she tried to get me to go bareback (relationship red flag number one). I never go bareback. The last thing I need is some kid binding me to a casual lay for the rest of my life. *No, thanks.*

Then she invited me to Thanksgiving dinner, which is over a month from now (another red flag, a definite sign that this isn't only fucking anymore).

Then tonight—along with these ridiculous porn star sounds—she also brought an overnight bag, which included tomorrow's clothes and a toothbrush. *Pretty fuckin' presumptuous, don't ya think? Sleepovers aren't my thing. Ever.*

Tonight is definitely our last roll in the sheets; it's time to move on. Sure, I'm a dick for fucking her before I tell her, but I really needed the relief. *Won't be the first time or last time I'm an asshole...*

"You gonna come for me, Nik? Gonna come all over my huge throbbing cock?" I thrust in and out, increasing the pace. I'm close, so I lay on a little of the porn talk myself, wondering if she'll realize I'm doing it ironically. I do love the feel of her lips wrapped around my dick, though, milking me while I fuck her hard and deep. *Such a shame...*

"God. Yes. Now. Now. Nowwwww..."

And with that, her hot cunt pulses around my cock. One more quick thrust and I shoot my load into the condom, then roll shakily onto my side to catch my breath.

"That was so good, honey," she purrs. "It's always been good between us. We're a perfect fit, don't you think?"

And here we go.

"Yeah, Nik, it was good. I needed that tonight." I rub her arm for a few seconds and then she snuggles closer to me, her auburn hair sticking to my sweaty skin. After waiting for her breathing to even out, I release myself from her hold, stand, remove and tie off the rubber before heading to the bathroom where I toss it into the small trash bin, then clean myself off in the sink.

Coming back to my room, I see she's passed out. Not one for spooning—especially with what's coming—I head into the kitchen, deciding to let her rest before I offer to drive her home. I figure the least I can do is give her half an hour or so.

Grabbing a beer, I enter my office and boot up my Chromebook. I've got some work to do before tomorrow, I figure I might as well get it over with while I'm waiting.

I'm reading over my proposal for the deal I hope to close tomorrow, one that will mean big changes for me if it goes through, when I hear her calling from the hallway. I'd been caught up, I'd lost track of the time.

"Hendrix, baby? You in there?" I hate that she calls me that. It's too intimate for what this is. In the bedroom, fine. But not here and not when sex is the farthest thing from my mind. *Another sign this needs to end.*

"Yeah, I'm in here," I say, peering over my laptop.

"Baby, I missed you. I woke up and I was all alone," she pouts, wrapping her arms around my neck. Sighing, I shut down my laptop and take a deep breath. "Come back to bed. Let your girl make you feel good again. I'll help tire you out," she smirks, giggling.

"You're not my girl, Nik. I've told you, it's just fucking. It's only ever just fucking."

"Whatever, Hen. You know I'm your girl." She rubs her tits on my back, completely ignoring what I've just said. *Why do chicks do this? Does she think I'll just give in and go along with what she wants?*

"No, Nik. You're not. I was clear about what this was." I get up from the chair, forcing her to take a step back. Turning, I meet her eyes and register the hurt starting to form. *Maybe she's actually getting it after all?* "I'm sorry to say this, Nik, but I warned you not to fall for me. I told you I'm not looking for anything other than a casual fuck buddy. You told me that's what you wanted, too. Then, tonight, the bag, Thanksgiv—"

"Well, I—I thought…I thought I was different. We've been good together, honey. I just know we'd make an awesome couple." She steps in closer, her hands resting on my bare chest.

"Sorry, but I don't want more. I think it would be best if I took you home now." I start to walk out of the room.

But instead of following, she yells at me.

"You're an asshole, Hendrix Hills! A complete douchebag. How *didn't* you think I'd fall for you?"

"I didn't want that, Nikki. The last thing I wanted was for you to be hurt. But you flipped the script here, not me. I've been upfront since the start."

"Well, fuck you, anyway, Hendrix! You know that? Fuck you. I'm outta here."

And she rushes past me.

Hanging my head, I close the office door and go to the living room to grab a hoodie and my keys, intent on taking her home.

I can hear her on her cell as she stomps out of my bedroom, dressed and in full-on anger mode, her bag in hand.

"Thank you, yes. I'll meet it outside."

"I'll take you home," I tell her, once she's ended the call.

"Don't worry about it. I called a cab. I never want to see you again, Hendrix."

She jabs her finger into my chest before slamming my front door behind her.

5

Hendrix

PULLING INTO THE Brightspot Diner's small parking lot, I'm nervous as fuck. My knuckles ache from gripping the steering wheel too tight on the drive here.

I don't know why I agreed to meet at the small diner. It's not like I can stomach food right now. Not even sex helped.

"Fuck." I tap the steering wheel, letting out a deep breath. "Relax, man. It's gonna work out. This Flynn guy wants to sell. No reason he won't go for the offer," I tell myself.

I pull the keys out of the ignition and prepare to meet the man who could be the stepping-stone I need to change my future for the better, to help me succeed in achieving my biggest goal.

Owning my own garage has been my goal since my dad died when I was eighteen. *Fucking heart disease.* One day he was working at the shop, the next day he keeled over the hood of a navy '65 Cadillac Coupe De Ville from a massive heart attack.

I'd grown up under the hood—learned everything I know from him. I spent every day after school, my weekends and my summers soaking in my dad's knowledge, learning the tricks of the trade. Owning my own place would be my way to make him proud beyond the grave. The only reason I don't have my dad's shop is because, at eighteen, there was no way I could have handled the responsibility, so my mum sold it and invested the money for my future. It took me a long time to see her decision as being in my best interest, but eventually I did. It had taken me a while to get my act together after my dad died. I spent some time rebelling with the wrong crowd, and with booze, drugs and women. Now, at twenty-nine, I figure it's time I grow up and get serious about life, start laying down some roots (business ones, anyway, 'cause the whole marriage- and kid-thing isn't my style). I feel like I've finally pulled my head out of my ass, and I'm ready to start being a man my dad would be proud of.

When I saw the listing for Flynn's garage, I knew right away it was perfect, down to the location, size and price. It's not too often I get sentimental and feel that "it was meant to be" crap, but this might just be one of those times. *Now, to convince Mr. Flynn that he should sell his baby to me…*

Pull it together. Relax and be yourself. I replay my mum's words from our phone call earlier this morning as I thumb through my business proposal and an agreement to purchase one last time.

My mum, Kara, moved back to England when I was twenty-five. She and my dad had fallen in love when he was over in Bromsgrove visiting family when he was twenty-three, and they apparently were inseparable from the start. I guess when it came time for my dad to leave, they couldn't stand to part, so he bought Mum a ticket and the rest is history.

When my dad passed, I encouraged my mum to move back to her family in the UK. I even offered to move with her, but she wouldn't have it. But once I turned twenty-five, we sat down and discussed her moving back again. Despite being torn about leaving me here, she decided that she did really want to go back, at least for a few years. I was happy that she'd made the decision for herself and I knew it would be something that would make her happy again. I promised I'd be fine, and encouraged her decision by promising to Skype, text and talk whenever she needed if it would make her decision easier. That was four years ago. She's since remarried, and is the happiest I've seen her in a long time. I visit her and my stepfather, Arran, in Bromsgrove at least once a year. She's been my biggest supporter, especially with this venture.

"Let's do this," I say, exiting my silver '69 Chevy Camaro, smoothing my black dress shirt and straightening my tie one last time. I feel like a damned monkey in this getup. *I'm a mechanic, why the hell I decided to dress like I'm looking for a desk job is beyond me.* "Fuck." I rub my fingers through my short brown hair and pull open the door to the restaurant.

"Welcome to the Brightspot. Table for one, handsome?" a bubbly blonde asks, grabbing a menu and giving me a sexy smile. She's cute. Her nametag reads "Katie", and she's got nice eyes and perky tits, too. I might just have to grab her number if all goes well here today. *Nothing like a celebratory fuck.*

"I'm meeting someone, babe," I say, and a look of disappointment crosses her face before I add, "I think he might be here already?"

I scan the place, taking in the outdated décor of black-and-white checkered flooring, worn red leather swivel chairs by the long counter, and rows of leather booths lining the perimeter. The smell of greasy food is thick in the air, making my already queasy stomach revolt even more. "Table's under 'Flynn'. He messaged me, said he's here already," I say, holding up my phone where the message is.

"Oh, okay, perfect." Katie's eyes light up like everything's right in her world again, having registered that I'm meeting a guy. "Follow me," she says, turning her back to me, clutching the menu and sashaying her slim hips. "Mr. Flynn is waiting; I just sat him a few minutes ago." I follow the petite blonde, checking out her ass as she moves to the back of the diner, where I spot a large man whom I assume is Flynn.

"Here ya go, hon. Enjoy your meal. Maybe I'll see you soon," she giggles flirtatiously. *Yeah, I'm definitely thinking I'll be seeing her later.*

"Hey, there." Flynn stands, extending his hand. "Nice to meet you, Mr. Hills," the tall grey-haired man who looks to be in his mid-sixties says through his beard. "I'm Flynn. Glad you could meet me here. I'm not one for office hoity-toity. We got business; we'll hash it out ourselves. Better that way, and cheaper too. No sense paying a lawyer to listen to us as we sort our shit out. We know what we're looking to get out of this."

Laughing, I agree, and feel my nerves dissipate with his easygoing demeanour as I settle back into the seat across from him.

"Thank you," I say to the server, who's arrived offering coffee.

She smiles. "I'll give youse a few minutes with your menus," she says, walking away.

"Please, sir, call me Hendrix. 'Mr. Hills' was my father. It's good to meet you."

"Flynn's good, too. Everyone but my family calls me that. No need for the 'mister' stuff with me, either," he chuckles, his eyes taking in my appearance. I note the pull of his lips as he looks at my tie. "You're a little dressed up. You sure you know what you're getting yourself into, wantin' to buy a dirty old garage? It ain't no pretty-boy shop I got. We aren't afraid of the big jobs, of gettin' dirty." He eyes me skeptically.

I bark out a laugh as my nerves immediately settle, allowing me to continue the meeting with ease and confidence.

"Thank fuck," I blurt, reaching for my tie, loosening it and removing it from around my neck. I finish by rolling up the sleeves of my dress shirt, allowing my tatted-up arms to reveal themselves. "Yeah, I was going for a good first impression. My mum is big on 'em," I laugh, taking in Flynn's grease-stained hands, worn flannel shirt, and Dickies work pants.

"No need, son," he says.

Hearing that term pulls at something inside me. Memories of my dad calling me "son" flood my mind, and I find myself grinning. I like Flynn, and hope we can make this work.

"Your resume, references and background with cars speak volumes. You could've shown up in a tux and I'd still have been impressed."

"Well, thanks. That means a lot coming from you. You're one of the best in the biz," I say honestly, because it's true. Flynn's reputation is very well known here in Stoney Creek, Ontario. I could learn a lot from him.

"Alright, let's iron out the details and see if we can make this shit happen," Flynn gruffs, closing his menu, "Let me start by sayin' I'm a tired old man and I'm looking forward to lightening up my workload. What's ideal for me is to partner up with someone who will work alongside me, learn the business and everything we specialize in, then buy me out in a year's time. I figure I got a good year left in me. It'll give me time to settle in the new owner, help train them and ease the regulars into the idea of dealing with a new boss."

"That sounds fair. I—"

He cuts me off. "I do, however, have a few stipulations that I will not concede on, so let's order," he says, nodding to the server, "then we'll get down to the nitty-gritty. Let me say, though, I have a good feeling about this, son."

"Me too, sir. Me too."

"You boys ready to order?" the waitress asks while topping up our coffee.

"Sure thing, darlin', I'll have the special, over easy, with white toast and extra bacon, please," Flynn orders, patting his belly. "I'm starvin'."

I laugh. "I'll have the bacon and eggs, sunny-side-up, and extra crispy please." My appetite has suddenly come back now that I've relaxed.

An hour-and-a-half later, I've heard Flynn's stipulations about keeping his staff, him staying on part-time, and a few other things that made not a lick of difference to me. There was nothing he said that had me changing my mind. And I'm fucking pumped that there were no red flags that came up for either of us to make me think this deal won't happen.

I leave Flynn (and my number with Katie) and feel the best that I've felt in a long time. *This is happening.* Taking out my phone, I shoot a text to my buddy, Cannon.

Me: *Voltage tonight?*

Cannon: *You know it. It went well?*

Me: *Feels like it did.*

Cannon: *Great. Drinks on you then fucker*

Me: *Aren't they always, you cheap fuck? Later.*

I tuck my phone away before folding myself back into my car and peeling out of the parking lot, Pink Floyd's "Learning to Fly" blaring from the speakers.

Damn, I want this. A wave of excitement washes over me. *Things are finally falling into place, and fuck, I'm ready for it.*

6

Hendrix

"YOU TAKING HER home?" Cannon—my best friend and the best automotive custom paint specialist I know—asks, nodding towards my lap.

Cannon Locke and I met on the first day of Grade 9 when some asshole shoved him into the girls' bathroom, a stupid way of welcoming us Minor Niners to four years of hell. We met because I, of course, followed him right in since the Grade 12 quarterback Jason Blackburn tossed my ass through the door about one second after Cannon. The impact of our bodies colliding knocked us both on our asses in front of the hottest chick in school, Willow Frayer, who was standing at the mirror fixing her hair. She turned when she heard the commotion then completely lost her shit as she saw not one—but two—of us boys come barreling into the girl's washroom. Fuck, she was pretty (even though she was screaming and flailing). To top it all off, both Cannon and I landed like two weak bags of shit right at her feet. That day, Cannon and I agreed to stick together and to start working out. We've been best friends ever since.

Smiling down, I nod an affirmative back to Cannon, watching Katie laugh with her friend as she subtly grinds on my cock with that tight ass of hers. She's got me rock hard beneath my jeans. I'm not sure how much longer my zipper will be able to contain the boner I've got going on. The bastard is a needy fuck with Katie being all flirty and ready like she is. I knew before I left the diner that Katie was going to call; it only took fifteen minutes after I walked out of the joint before I had a text from her. *I love me an eager beaver.* We'd made plans for her and her girlfriend Brittany to meet us at Voltage, a local bar where Cannon and I hang out a few times a week.

With the bass from the Red Hot Chili Peppers' "Dark Necessities" pounding through the speakers, I lean over so only Cannon can hear me.

"Thinking I just might. Figure I deserve a reward after today. She's got great tits and her lips are a dick's dream. They'll look great with my cock between 'em when I fuck her face."

He shakes his head. "With a mouth like that, how you get all these chicks is baffling to me."

"What? Like you're not gonna take Britt home and fuck her? It's what we do. You should be thanking me that Katie's friend is as hot as she is. Remember the chick you brought me the last time? I'd say you're going to owe me after this one."

"Yeah, but…you're such a dog, man."

"Nope. I'm honest, and I was honest with her on the phone. She knows the score, knows it's just casual, that the last thing I'm looking for is a relationship. Especially not now, with the prospect of having the garage."

"Whatever, man. One word: Nikki. They always say it's fine, then they can't handle it. I can't wait for the day some chick comes along and owns your ass. Can't deke a relationship and love forever, man."

"Whoa! Easy with that voodoo shit. Keep that crap to yourself." I shake and shudder as if I'm creeped out, and Cannon laughs.

"On that note, I'm gonna take Britt home now, but she wanted to make sure Katie was in good hands."

"Oh, she's in real good hands, brother. You know it." I take a pull from my beer before offering a mischievous smirk.

"Jesus, these two are hot," Cannon whistles, drawing my attention over to where Katie and Britt are up dancing to some Drake song.

"Shit, yeah, they are." I'm rooted in place as I take in their little routine. They're grinning and moving up and down each other as if they were going to get it on. *Shit, what I wouldn't give to be in the middle of that sandwich. They're sexy as fuck.*

"Yeah, I think we're leavin' now, too." I stand, clasping Cannon on the shoulder as we make our way to the girls.

Sneaking my hands around her waist, I pull Katie's ass back into my groin. "Time to go, sweetheart."

My heart speeds up at the images of things to come with Katie, and I'm also getting this giddy feeling deep in my gut thinking back on today's meeting. I'm fucking happy and I'm ready to celebrate. I push my face into her neck.

"I wanna see you dance with your pussy on my face."

7

Trinity

I'M STANDING IN the wings of the stage waiting for my cue, and I swear I'm going to be sick. Thankfully, I know I won't. This is just a silly game my nerves like to play. It's our own version of chicken, the face-off we have every time I'm about to give a speech. Besides, that would be highly embarrassing in front of all these people, and I'm sort of a pro now, right? As always, my mind runs through its array of doubts. *What if they look at me and see me as sick? Contagious? Dirty? Or worse, what if all I see are faces full of pity staring back at me? Is my speech lame? Does it need more humour? Will they even listen…?*

That's the thing I hate the most. *Pity.*

Never, ever, pity me. I'm a survivor. I am living. And all I want is to be seen—I want people to see *me*, not just see what they will soon discover resides in my blood.

I am me. I am not HIV.

I get myself all riled up at the idea of how much I hate that as I listen to the principal talk to the senior classes at Westdale High School. Working to relax, I wipe my now-sweaty palms down the front of my skinny jeans while shifting nervously side to side in my orange Chucks.

The gentle touch of Uncle Dexter's hand immediately puts me at ease.

Uncle Dex. He's been my biggest supporter, worrywart and advocate since the day I told him about my HIV diagnosis. He comes with me to every speaking engagement I do, even though I'm a grown woman who can handle this on her own. Despite my protests and assurances, he takes the day—or half of the day off (depending how far we need to drive)—leaving the other guys in charge. He says it's good training for them for when he retires, a notion he's been bringing up more and more, but I'll believe it when I see it. Dex loves Ignition Inc. way too much.

"Kiddo, you're gonna crush it. You always do. You know better than to worry, the kids always love you," he says, breaking me away from my thoughts. "They eat up every word you say. Relax. It's in the bag, a piece of cake."

I nod. "I know. It's just nerves."

"Take a deep breath before you puke on those new shoes of yours," he smiles.

"You're right. I always do this to myself. It's not like this is my first rodeo."

"Exactly. You're a professional. This is what you love doing. Now, go out there and just be you—the kick-ass girl everyone loves."

"You're right, Uncle Dex. This is what I love. I get inside my own head sometimes, you know? Because I want them to see *me*, not just some tainted girl they pity."

"You get that shit outta your head right this instant, you hear me, darlin'? No-one sees that. They see a fighter, an educator, a rockstar." He nudges me and I smile. He's called me the "Rockstar of Speeches" ever since I decided to share my story once I finally came to terms with my own diagnosis, which makes it just over a year ago. The first time he, my aunt and cousins came to watch, he said he was in awe of my ability to connect with the audience. Dex said it was like watching his idol Robert Plant putting his fans in a trance, as soon as I started talking. I think he was completely exaggerating but who was I to knock my number one fan down? Besides, isn't it every girl's dream to be a rock goddess?

"I love you, too, you hairy, burly wrench-wielder," I giggle, and Dex pushes me away from him in jest. I always tease him like that, both because he's a talented mechanic and also because he's somewhat of a hefty fellow. Also, the majority of his face is hidden behind an unruly beard, a beard I've watched change from brown to grey over the past few years.

"That's 'Silver Fox', I'll have you know. Your Aunt Tillie confirmed it just last night," he winks, puffing out his chest at the innuendo.

"Eww. Too much information," I whisper back. "Next thing I know, you'll be telling me that you're a 'lumbersexual'! Yuck. Not a good visual, Dex—you and Tillie. I could have done without *that*."

"A lumber-what now? What the hell is that shit?"

"Exactly," I hiss, stifling a laugh and tugging on the end of his beard. "Let's just pretend this whole conversation didn't happen," I pause for effect, "okay, Silver Fox?"

"Yeah, yeah, okay. But I'm asking your cousins when we get back to the shop about that lumber-shit."

"Whatev—"

"Students of Westdale High, please join me in giving a warm welcome to today's special guest speaker as we welcome her to the stage: Ms. Trinity Adams."

Hearing my name, I lean up and give Dex a quick peck on the cheek, whispering,

"Thanks for always getting me outta my head. I couldn't do this without you."

"Love ya, kiddo. Go woo 'em."

With that, I take my cue and stride out to centre stage, ready to share my story, ready to help fight the stigma associated with HIV and AIDS that still exists today.

And ready to let them see me.

8

Trinity

"Hi!" I wave. "I'm Trinity. Thank you for having me as a speaker today for your Healthy Life Week. I'm excited to be here," I say, and begin to relax a little, the mic feeling at home in my hand.

"Before we start, I want you to do something for me, a warm up exercise. I'd like you to look at me for ten seconds. Yes, stare right at me. Then think of the first word that comes to mind. And don't worry about hurting my feelings, I'm super tough. I only hope I'm pulling off my new short do," I say, fluffing my newly-dyed pastel pink pixie cut, earning a few laughs, "and these shoes that maybe aren't typical for a twenty-seven year old accountant, but I'm a bit of a rebel like that," I say, lifting my orange Converse-clad foot. "Okay everyone the ten seconds starts…now." I set the timer on my phone and begin pacing and turning from one end of the stage to the next.

"Alright, and…time." I return to the auditorium's centre stage at the beep sound. "Okay, who's brave enough to share their thoughts?"

This is my hook. The way I reel them in and make them want to hear the rest of what I have to say. As always, a bunch of hands bolt up into the air. Looking around, I spot a young girl with glasses to my right in the front row.

"Hi. You in the pink t-shirt. Tell me what you see."

"You've got really pretty eyes," she says, and sits back down.

"Thank you. Okay, how about you?" I ask a boy a few rows back.

"You've got a nice body. You're pretty hot, actually, for being older."

Laughter erupts from the crowd. "Oh my God, Shane!" a few people call out.

"Well, thanks. I work out and watch what I eat—most of the time—so I'll take it," I nod. "How about you over there in the red hoodie?"

"Well...you're kinda *short.* And I think that the shoes are a bit much on you," a cute brunette says, as if embarrassed.

"I *love* your shoes!" a boy calls out from the back row.

"Okay. I am only 5'3", so, yeah, you're right. I'm kinda short," I repeat, using her words. "One more," I say, scanning the theatre where about two hundred high school seniors and faculty members sit listening to me intently, which makes me feel good, reminding me why I love doing this as much as I do.

"How about you?" I ask a boy sitting alone to one side. He didn't have his hand up, but he caught my eye. "What do you see when you look at me?"

"I dunno. This being Healthy Living Week, I guess you look...healthy. Maybe a bit tired, but other than that, you look good." He shrugs his shoulders, having no idea how he just proved the age-old saying that looks can be deceiving, that looking "healthy" can be deceiving. I'm a prime example of this. On the outside I look and seem like everyone else, but on the inside, my body is fighting daily against the virus that lives dormant in my blood, with medications to keep the proverbial monster at bay.

"'*Healthy*'. Perfect answer. Thanks for letting me call on you even though you didn't have your hand up."

Moving back to centre stage, I place the microphone back in its stand. I take a deep breath and say: "My name is Trinity Paige Adams. I'm twenty-seven years old. And two years ago, when I was twenty-five, I was diagnosed with Human Immunodeficiency Virus."

I hear scattered gasps of *"Oh my god!"* and students whispering, but I don't stop to acknowledge their shock.

It's like this every time.

"Yes. I have HIV."

I carry on, sharing my story. "I lost my virginity when I was in university. I was nineteen, and it was with my first real boyfriend. We dated for four years after that, before we broke up and he moved to Hong Kong for work. I loved him. He was the one and only man I didn't use protection with, a guy I trusted to be clean because he looked clean and told me he was, who also convinced me that sex would be best with nothing between us. I believed him. Shame on me, right? But, like he said, I was on the Pill. What could go wrong?" I pause, letting it sink in for a minute. "If only I could go back and give my naïve self a smack upside the head. I don't know which time I contracted HIV, exactly, because we never used condoms. I don't know how he contracted it, either. We'll leave it at that for now."

Looking around the room, I see the following expressions spread across some of the students' faces: *I've done that, too; Holy shit; Oh my God; I need to get tested*, plus panic and fear. And, of course, I see the other looks, too. The judgment. The pity.

"Okay, now that the cat's out of the bag, let me ask you one favour. I need you to get rid of those faces you're looking at me with. Don't drop your smiles. I'm alive. I'm living my life to the fullest. I might have to take my medication at the same time every day like clockwork to help keep me going, but I'm otherwise healthy. I'm here, and I plan to stay here for a long damn time." I stamp my foot and cross my arms, and feel the tension in the room dissolving as everyone laughs.

"Anyway, my goal today is to show you an example of how a person," I point to myself, "can look not at all infected even when they are. I want to open up your eyes, to help you see that HIV and AIDS exists in your community, and that it's a virus we can defend against when we're prepared and vigilant. My hope today is to educate you, and to provide up-to-date info to you about what HIV and AIDS are and aren't. How you can and can't catch it, as well as to work toward removing the stigma associated with the disease and put a human face to HIV/AIDS." I finish on a long breath, "Okay, I know that was a lot." I pause to take a sip of water and to let the information sink in.

"My biggest goal, though, is to teach you to protect yourself. To be safe if you're sexually active, and—most of all—to point out that HIV and AIDS do not discriminate. It doesn't care about your age, race, gender or sexual preferences. HIV and AIDS is an anywhere, anyone, any-one-time-without-protection-you-could-catch-it kind of disease." Taking the stool from behind the podium, I drag it to the edge of the stage and take a seat, mic in hand again.

"One of the misconceptions that drives me batty is that you can get HIV or AIDS from kissing or touching. Let's set the record straight. HIV is not passed through saliva, sweat, tears, touching, feces or urine. In order for HIV infection to occur, two things need to exist. First, a transmission fluid such as semen, breast milk, vaginal fluid or blood. Second, an entry point into the body. Say a mouth, vagina, anus or vein, or skin with micro-tears, abrasions or open wounds. There has never been a documented case of infection of HIV from saliva. So feel free to kiss away…unless you've got a significant open wound in your mouth, then you might want to wait as a precaution." I pause, uncap my bottle of water again and take another sip.

"I think for me personally, the other misconception I struggle with most is when I hear people commenting that HIV/AIDS is simply a disease affecting gay men. I'm proof that this is not the case." I wave my hand from my head to my toes. "Sure, it began showing up as an epidemic within gay communities back in the early-1980s, but we learned very quickly that HIV and AIDS was actually a worldwide epidemic, one that didn't discriminate based on age, sexual orientation, or gender. I'm a living example of a non-intravenous drug-injecting heterosexual female living with HIV, which was transmitted from a heterosexual relationship."

I stand, then pace from one end of the stage to the other. This part of my talk is a bit heavy with facts, but it's important that the students hear it.

"Does anyone know how many people in the world are currently infected with HIV or AIDS?" I ask.

"Seventeen million," someone shouts from the back.

"More," I answer.

"Twenty-two million."

"Higher."

"Thirty million."

"Close. Worldwide, unfortunately, there are 36.5 million people infected with HIV/AIDS. *36.5 million.* In the US alone, there are 1.2 million people infected, and it's projected that one out of every eight people living with HIV doesn't even know it. In 2014, it was estimated that around 16,000 people living with HIV in Canada were infected but remained undiagnosed. Imagine that number. Here in Canada, there were 75,500 reported cases of people living with HIV at the end of 2014. If you research that number, you'll see that just over 35,000 of those were, in fact, homosexual men. But let's look at the facts: that leaves about 40,000 spots left for heterosexual males, women, those infected via blood transfusions and birth—and let's not forget IV drug users, who number around 13,000. Therefore, to say that HIV is just a 'gay plague' only proves that you're uneducated, and could use an afternoon going online at Starbucks getting your facts straight with a latte."

I take a breath while the crowd applauds at the end of my little tirade.

"Here's a good spot for me to add an important note: hepatitis C is another disease communicable via sex and IV drug use facing many people worldwide, and it's also potentially fatal. It's a liver killer. Remember to always play safe, people. Condoms and clean needles don't just protect against HIV and AIDS, there are many other issues—like hep C and other STDs—to consider," I say, running my hand across my forehead and sweeping my pinkish bangs off my face.

"But there's good news. With proper treatment, people like myself can live a pretty normal life, with the same potential and possibilities as non-infected people, including sexual relationships, marriage and having healthy babies. The world is making extraordinary gains in the fight against this epidemic. And that's pretty incredible if you ask me." I raise my water bottle in a toast before taking a drink.

I spend the next fifteen minutes clarifying a few misconceptions, and telling them about the first part of Blake's Facebook message that I read, and my disastrous final date with Jared when I told him the news (with their names left out, of course).

9

Trinity

"THANK YOU FOR listening to me today. I hope my story pops into your minds in the future when it come time to choose to use protection, or decide whether or not to engage in high-risk activities. We've got..." I glance at my phone, "...about twenty minutes left. I know there are a lot of questions, so let's have a question and answer period. Please step up to the mic in the centre aisle and ask away. I'm an open book. Please feel comfortable asking me anything." I smile and nod at the clapping. I steal a glance at Uncle Dex, who is beaming at me from the darkness of the wings. "Thank you very much."

This part of the presentation is what makes me the most nervous. I never know quite what to expect. I love, though, that the students are free to ask about whatever makes them curious. It's unscripted and refreshing and changes every time.

I've been visiting schools and universities for eight months now, travelling and speaking on behalf of The AIDS Network, a program located about half an hour from where I now live in Stoney Creek. Lindsey Hosker is the youngest member of the board of directors, and went out of her way to take me under her wing when I first showed up there, panicked and terrified, looking for information and support. Soon after meeting her, I began volunteering and attending many of the group therapy sessions and social activities they have at the Network. I've met a lot of great people who, in a short time, have become my pseudo-family. I needed to build a new network of people to count on, especially after my parents' reaction to my news. The AIDS Network gave that to me and I am forever grateful, so I'm glad to help out in anyway I can. It was Lindsey who got me started speaking at the schools.

"Hey, my name is Vince. I was wondering, how did your family take the news when you were first diagnosed?" The voice cuts through my thoughts.

"Hi. Good question. Truthfully? It went badly. I don't speak to most of them anymore. It's crazy how some people can't understand and accept this disease as being something that's manageable. My mom and dad lost it. Full-on, wanting nothing to do with me, lost it. They can't get over thinking that I brought this onto myself and to them, that I was 'tainted by this disgusting gay men's disease'. That's me quoting my uneducated mother, by the way. Trust me, I tried to educate her. I even offered to take her to Starbucks with our laptops, so we could open up Google and research the stats together. I *even* said I'd buy her a latte…" I joke, and there are a few uncomfortable laughs at my dark humour. "Unfortunately, ignorance is bliss and she was happier just to cut me off. That can happen sometimes."

I pause, hearing some gasps and a few whispered 'Jesus's'. I move on before the pity can start creeping back in again.

"Don't feel too bad for me. Honestly, we weren't that close. Growing up, they were always sending me off to my Uncle Dex and my Aunt Tillie's house. I think my parents being older and me being a surprise was a huge factor in that. Over time, I came to see Dex and Tillie more like my parents and their kids—my cousins, Nadia and Joe—became my best friends. We'd always been the three musketeers, and after my diagnosis they accepted me with open arms and not an ounce of judgment. I've not spoken to my parents since they kicked me out of the family."

I give a long sigh. Thinking of my parents and their reaction pisses me off each and every time. "Wow, that was a doozy, Vince," I smile, looking around the room and seeing a mixture of surprise and shock on many faces. It's always like this. It's as if I have the only closed-minded parents on the block. Which, I guess, is a good thing. It shows that attitudes are starting to change as time goes on, but the shocked reactions always catch me a little off guard.

"Sorry to hear that, that sucks. Sounds like you're better off."

"I am. I'm very lucky. Don't get me wrong, though, it's definitely a hard thing to accept. I mean, before I was diagnosed, there was a family. For them to just drop me like that is taking a long time to process and heal from. I'm getting better at accepting that I might lose a few people along this journey of mine, but I've gained a few, too."

And it's true. It's taken quite a few therapy sessions to help me get over losing my parents the way I did. In the end, I've come to see it as their loss. A loss I hope they never live to regret, because from what I'm learning, regret is the last thing I ever want to feel, especially if or when my disease progresses. I want to leave this life feeling happy and accomplished. *Live life, love, and always get it off your chest.* That's been my mantra over the last year as I've worked my way through all my crazy emotions.

A clearing throat brings me back to the present.

"Sorry, I totally zoned out there for a second," I admit. "Yes, next question."

"Hi. I'm Alisha. First off, this is amazing. I've learned a lot and I think you're pretty great. It's totally your parents' loss."

"Thanks. That means a lot. What's your question?"

"I was wondering why it took so long for you to get diagnosed. I thought technology was more advanced, I guess. I assumed an HIV or

AIDS test would be standard."

"That's a really great question, and you're right, we are far more advanced than we've ever been. But if you don't have a reason to believe you've been infected, then it's not the first line of testing. And with some people, like me, it can take a long time for HIV symptoms to present themselves. Some people have symptoms within two weeks, but for others, it can take years. Like, in my case, it took awhile, and the symptoms weren't specific to only HIV or AIDS. I'd had the flu on and off more frequently the year before I was diagnosed, but it had been a long cold winter that year, too. I'd been tired, like bone-wearily so, but I'd also just started a new job in Toronto, which I'd moved away from my family for. My stress levels were elevated so I assumed it was all just part of that. And my doctor never suspected HIV based on my sexual history, therefore my symptoms at the time didn't really warrant that specific blood test. Then two years ago, I broke out in this weird rash, which finally led my doctor to do an HIV blood test, just to be safe. That led to my diagnosis."

"That's scary," she says, before thanking me.

"You're right. It is. I never, ever considered that it could be HIV."

"Hi, Trinity. I'm Cassie. I guess what I want to know is: did you ever confront the guy who gave you HIV?"

"Ohhhhh…that's another good one. In my mind, I have a million times, but in reality, no, I never have. I still haven't opened that message on my Facebook I told you about earlier. Don't think I ever will. I like to believe that he didn't know he was infected at the time, and that he's sorry. Knowing or thinking anything different might set me back emotionally, so I just kind of roll with my thinking, if that makes sense? Besides, my therapist told me that was okay," I laugh.

"Thank you for sharing all of this with us, Trinity. You're very brave. And I've learned a lot today," she says before returning to her seat, and her words make my heart swell.

This is why I do this.

Looking around the room, I realize how grateful I am that I have this opportunity. I've come a long way since I began giving these presentations, and I feel more confident than ever, like I might actually be doing some good. But catching the look on the next student's face, I can tell already this question might be a doozy.

"Hi, Trinity, I'm Sara. I might be in the minority here, but I agree with that guy you dated. I mean, you have a life-threatening disease. Sure, no-one's probably ever gotten it from just kissing, but what if you'd gotten all hot and heavy. Would you have stopped to have 'the talk'?" she air quotes. "Being honest, I don't think I could ever be with someone like you, or see it the way you do. People deserve to know as soon as they meet you. It's just mean, otherwise. You know: their body, their choice," she says, shrugging before walking away. I admit I'm a little stung by her accusatory tone, but then again, I can understand where she's coming from and decide to use this opportunity to educate them further.

"Thanks for sharing your opinion, Sara. I hear what you're saying. I get it, I do. It's been an experience that I replayed over and over in my mind a million times. I can definitely see both sides. I mean, I get that my partner needs to know, of course, but it's a struggle to decide when the 'right' time to disclose is. I feel I have the right to keep my medical information private, to a point, when I'm first getting to know someone." I pause. "In my mind, I think it's fair to maybe wait a few dates before I share my status. But I won't move around the 'bases' until I've had the appropriate conversations with my partner, and that includes heavy kissing. I don't ever want to experience a reaction like that again. It was awful. Does that make sense?"

"It does, actually. Thank you."

"You're welcome," I nod, glad she sees where I'm coming from. The Jared experience has truthfully left me terrified to try and date again. The feeling of being perceived as a deceitful and vile person never goes away.

"Hey, I'm Damir." The deep voice cuts through the tension that seems to have fallen over the room. "I was wondering if you plan on having kids? I know you said with early treatment the chances of mother-to-baby transmission are low, but I'm curious to know if you'd take the risk? And how would you even go about it without infecting your partner?"

"I've actually thought about that a lot. The right answer is 'yes', because I believe in the medical advances of today, which include home insemination with a syringe, while others choose assisted reproduction technology which may include in-vitro, intravaginal insemination or sperm injections. There are multiple ways for HIV-infected women to safely conceive these days. But despite knowing all this and all the precautions, the chicken in me would be too terrified to risk it, I think." I laugh. "I guess I don't have a proper answer on that one. I'm still not sure, I guess."

"Naw, that makes sense. It's a big decision," he agrees.

"Alright, I think we have time for, say…two more." I look up at a tall girl with beautiful long black hair waiting at the mic.

"Hi, I'm Saanvi. I was wondering, what's been the hardest thing you've had to do since you were diagnosed? Other than telling your family. That would have been really hard, obviously."

"I think having to call the two sexual partners I'd had after my first partner and telling them I was HIV-positive—even though we'd use condoms—and that they needed to get tested was the worst part of it all. It was pretty scary. I decided to do it over the phone to save face. And I'll tell you, I'm really glad I did it that way. The news wasn't exactly taken very well, which is fair, I guess. I get that. Luckily, they both tested negative, I found out later."

"Next. Hi, sir. Go ahead."

"Hey, Trinity. I'm Mr. Fowler. First off, I wanted to say it's been great having you here for the students today. I think we've all appreciated your presentation. I know I'll be working on a follow-up activity for my classes next week; I see a research project in their future," he jokes, looking around the room as a few students snicker at him.

"Thanks. I really appreciate the compliment." And I do. I always love it when the faculty participates, too.

"As for my question, I was wondering what you do for a living?"

"I work at my uncle's garage. He's a slave driver, let me tell you," I say, looking over at Dex, who's shaking his head at me. "But I wouldn't do anything else. I have my Bachelor of Commerce from Queen's and I had just started working for a major finance company in Toronto when I was first diagnosed, but with needing to take care of myself, I had to make some changes. So, I moved back to Stoney Creek and started working at his shop. I'm a multifaceted part of the place. I do all the finances, and I'm the world's most amazing receptionist."

"Sounds like you've managed to make a happy life for yourself, Trinity. I'm very happy to hear that. Keep at it," he nods before leaving the mic. I feel my eyes tearing at his kind words and observations. I really have come a long way from the person I was two years ago.

Looking up, I see a familiar face.

"Hi. It's me, Shane, again."

Amused, I welcome him back to the mic.

"I just wanted to tell you, you're super hot, even knowing you've got HIV. It shouldn't matter. I just wanted to tell you that." I feel myself blush, and the audience hoots and hollers. "I guess my question is: are you dating now? Have a boyfriend?"

"Oh, the dreaded question," I mock, tsk-ing. "I have dated. Well, I *tried* is a better answer. Not in the last year or so, though. Trust me, the last guy really let me have it once I told him my status. It really got me thinking about how to date in my world, what was proper etiquette. So, I've decided to hold off for now, despite my cousins and their attempts to find me a love connection," I joke. "Seriously, my friends and family are always trying to set me up, trying to find me my Mr. Right. But I kindly decline the set-ups. For now, I just can't seem to muster the courage to risk seeing the face of rejection staring back at me again when it's time to have 'the talk'. I guess the answer is: I'm working on it."

"Well, I'd give you a chance if I were older," Shane says, and there's a collective "aww" and hoots from the audience. I have to admit, it's a nice thing to hear.

"Thank you for being open-minded and accepting. Now, you'll just need to step into my time machine so we can age you a little," I wink, and the crowd laughs. "We're almost out of time," I say, looking down at my phone. "Again, I want to thank you for having me today, you've been a brilliant audience. I think we've got time for one last question…"

By the time I was done, the looks of pity were gone. And all they saw was *me*, waving goodbye, as I skipped off the stage.

10

Hendrix

"THANKS FOR THE help, man. Wanna beer before you go?" I ask Cannon, who's been helping me move my stuff into the shop. We're both sweating our bags off. These tool cabinets weigh a ton-and-a-half and are a real bitch. Thankfully, he was free to give me a hand tonight.

The plan is for me to start working at Ignition Inc. full-time on Monday. I wasn't expecting to start moving in until Saturday, but once I realized how much crap I actually had, I saw that it was gonna take me more than just the weekend so I popped in today to meet the guys in the shop and get a start on unpacking. Flynn gave me a set of keys last week, so I told my new employees they could head out a little early tonight, and that I'd lock up since I was pretty sure I'd be here awhile. Figured it was a nice gesture, considering it was Friday and starting Monday morning I'll be their boss.

"Sure," Cannon says, and I toss him a can of Canadian from the small cooler bag I brought with me. Normally, I wouldn't have beer at work but since it's after-hours and I'm not officially on the clock yet, I thought: why not?

"This is a pretty nice place, dude. I'm happy for you. I can see how cool it'll be when you take over and really make the place yours," he says, popping the tab and taking a long sip.

"Yeah, thanks. For now, I'm leaving it as-is out of courtesy to Flynn. There're a few things I plan to fix and update, but I don't want to make him feel like I'm changing everything before he's even out the door. Plus the place is half his—until the end of the year, anyway. But, yeah, it definitely feels good to be settling into my own place."

I glance proudly around the garage, taking in the four car bays, the door leading to the painting bay, the walls of tools, the diagnostic machine and the waiting room off to the left where Flynn's office and the reception area are located.

"Cool. I might have to leave Wheel Wizards, after all. I could definitely see setting up shop in this place."

"Anytime, man. You know I want you here," I say, raising my beer at him before taking a swig.

My phone vibrates. Pulling it out of my pocket, I see it's Greyson McAllister, a guy I've been in talks with about restoring his old Chevy. I'd been holding him off until I was set up here, 'cause it's a big job and I needed room to get it right. I'd called him this morning to let him know that I'll be able to start his job next week.

Raising a finger, I signal for Cannon to hang on for a minute. He nods and starts walking around the place while I take the call.

"Hey, Grey. What's up, man?" I pause. "I assume you got my message. Does Monday work for you?"

After firming up the details, I slip my phone back in my pocket.

"That was Greyson. We got the job. I'm gonna need your help with some of the paint details later on," I say, grabbing my iPad from my knapsack and pulling up the overhaul plan and estimate.

"Yeah, no problem. Just let me know when and I'll get it done," Cannon says, looking down at the plans. After twenty minutes of tweaking a few things, both Cannon and I are pleased with how the classic Chev will look when it's done.

"Alright, Brother, I'm gonna bounce. I told Devon I'd meet him at

The Dugout for the game. You staying here or coming? It's Game Two, you know. The Jays might just pull it off this year."

"Naw, I'm gonna stay. I gotta shit-ton of stuff to get sorted and set up."

"Hen, it's the playoffs. Fuck, this is *important*, man. The Jays need us."

"I'm sure between you, Devon and Jett, you'll have 'em covered. I can't tonight, but trust me, I'll be there for every Leafs game during the playoffs."

"Okay, well, text me when you're done. We'll probably head over to Voltage after. It's ladies' night, after all," he says, trying to lure me with the prospect of pussy as he's walking out the door.

I rub the back of my head looking at all the shit I still need to do before Monday. *Sure, I'd rather be getting my dick sucked tonight, but shit's gotta get done,* I tell myself, before getting back at it.

'Cause come Monday morning, I'm the motherfuckin' boss.

11

Trinity

"Here we are," Uncle Dexter says, pulling into the lot of the now-closed Ignition Inc., the garage he owns. It's also where I happen to live.

When I was initially diagnosed with HIV in Toronto, I thought nothing in my life needed to change. But as the days passed and the news sunk in, the "what-if's" began, and my overactive imagination started playing on high-speed. After a few weeks of deliberation, Uncle Dex made me an offer, and I decided that moving back to Stoney Creek was the best option. Bearing in mind the emotional state I was in, I needed my extended family more than anything. It's incredible how many things there are to take into consideration when you're faced with adversity, crazy how much you overanalyze and dissect every part of your life before you can decide to move forward.

For me personally, there was no way I was going to spend any more of the time I had left working as an under-appreciated staffer in an overstressed accounting office working twelve hour days in downtown Toronto when I had many other things I could be doing. I needed to have more fun; I wanted to live my life my way, no matter how long I got to live it. Another big factor for me was the scrutiny I'd feared I fall under at work. Once my coworkers found out—if they found out—would the way I was treated change? I mean, look how my own parents reacted, and they're supposed to love me unconditionally. Would I lose all my credibility and friendships? Would they all see me as the "sick girl" and offer me nothing more than pity? Don't get me wrong. I'm not saying all of that would have happened, but that was the scenario that would plague my mind as I was deciding what to do with my life going forward. Sometimes, the voice of self-perseverance deserves to be adhered to, and for me this was that situation.

When considering places to live once I'd given my two-week notice at Crowe Soberman LLP, I'd called Dex and asked if he'd be willing to rent me the apartment that had been sitting empty for years above his auto shop. Luckily, he thought it was a great idea, joking that he'd be able to save a few bucks having a live-in alarm system. After one hell of major clean-up and a couple coats of fresh bright paint—and Tillie, Nadia, Shannon and I adding a few feminine touches—it became the perfect living space. Then Uncle Dex offered me an accountant/receptionist job in his shop, as well, and I've been here ever since.

Moving above Dex's shop and starting work at Ignition turned out to be the right decision for me and I haven't regretted leaving the corporate world once. I love working here; the guys are great fun, and Dex pays me decently. Not that I need much money, considering the pest only charges me minimal rent.

"Thanks for coming with, and driving today." I lean over and kiss his hairy cheek.

"That's what I'm here for. I wouldn't miss one for nothin'." And it's true, he doesn't. He never has. He leaves Joe and Brody in charge of the shop to come with me, and never complains about the long drives or the fact that we sometimes don't get home until after dark.

"I know," I say, opening the door. "Send Til my love. Tell her I'll call her tomorr—"

Ding—my cell goes off.

"Shannon?" my uncle asks, because he knows as well as I do it's my best friend checking in to see how things went. I swear she has a tracking device on me. I get motion sickness when in the car, so I never respond to text messages until I get home. And after every speech, pretty much the minute I walk in the door, Shannon is checking in like she knows the exact second I made it back. I seriously love that girl. Even if she did steal my chocolate pudding cup in first grade and convinced me that it was a great idea to stuff my bra with Kleenex when she sprouted before me when we were twelve. To say that leaving a trail of tissues behind me during suicide drills in gym class wasn't mortifying would be a lie. She's just lucky that I've always been forgiving.

"She can wait. Anyway, tell Aunt Tillie I'll call her tomorrow."

"Will do, kiddo. Now go, I want to make sure you get in okay."

Pulling out my cell, I wave to Dex before sliding open the text message and reading it as I walk down the side of the grey brick building towards the back, where the stairs to my apartment are.

Meow. Meow.

Shannon: *Hey, how did it go? Going to bar tonight. Come? Jays game!*

Stopping at the bottom of the stairs, I decide to reply so she isn't waiting on me, and because I hear Beast. *What's he doing out here?*

"Beast. Come here, little kitty," I say, looking around the large fenced concrete lot as I text Shannon. Walking toward the garbage bins, I hear purring. *Gotcha!*

Me *Hey hey, it went really well. The kids were great! No thanks, next time. I'm beat, today was long.*

"Come here, Beast. Trinity has some food for you," I coo, seeing his little ginger head peeking around the corner of the garage.

Meow. Meow.

Shannon: *Boo, but okay. Dinner tomorrow? Drinks with the girls next Sat? Mark it down we need some catch up time. No excuses!*

Shaking my head, I pull up the calendar on my phone. Other than working and a doctor's appointment, the last two weeks of September are pretty open. In fact, my social calendar is always pretty open.

Shannon's right. Afraid to put myself out there, I admit I tend to avoid social gatherings. Despite Shannon's best efforts, I usually come up with an excuse not to join her and the girls when they head to the bars. And most of the time, she lets me. But it's been a few months since I last caved, and after replaying what Shane and a few of the other students said today, I decide to step out of my comfort zone.

Me: *You're on.*

Shannon: *Did you just say yes to both? Love ya*

Me: *I did!*

Shannon: *I might have just yelped! No take back!!!*

Me: *Whatever. See you tomorrow*

Shannon: *Look at my girl committing!*

Me: *You won. I gotta go. Have fun. Love ya*

Beast approaches, his orange-striped tail flying high in the air and curled into a question mark shape. I tuck my phone into my front pocket, ignoring one last ding, knowing it's Shannon saying good-night, and bend down to pick up the small stray I befriended a few weeks ago. The one Dex decided should be named "Beast". The one Dex also pretends doesn't live in the back storage room. The one I've caught him petting more than a handful of times now.

"There you are! Now, tell me…who let you out? It's too dangerous for you out here at night on your own, you're still too little. Remember the nice cozy garage with lots of food? That's your home now."

Unlocking the door and walking into the shop, the familiar smell of gasoline and oil floating in the air hits me. It smells like home. But I also hear Pink Floyd's unique sound blasting heavily in the open work area. As the lyrics to "Comfortably Numb" echo in my ears, I register that the overhead fluorescent lights are still on in the shop. We're supposed to be closed. *What the hell? The guys are never here late on Friday nights.*

Moving into the shop area of the garage, I stop in my tracks. My eyes land on a very tall, very built and very shirtless man who's standing with his back to me. Looking around, I'm not sure exactly what to do. I mean, I know I should take off and call Dex or the police like a normal person, but I'm like the cat I hold in my arms—curiosity has a hold on me. *Hopefully, it won't get me killed.*

"Shit," I mutter, holding Beast a little tighter as I stare at the stranger. I'm captivated by his stature and his very muscular back. Looking further, I note his short dark brown hair and the large tattoo of a sword on his back. I'm completely hypnotized when I see his muscles rippling under the colours, reacting with each move of his arms. I hear the sound of tools clanking.

He's standing in front of the cabinet where we keep the impact-, torque- and pipe wrenches. Not our most valuable tools, that's for sure, but a large tan Rubbermaid tote resting on the floor beside him has me curious as to what the hell he's doing. Therefore, using my mad detective skills, I deduce that he's either stealing our cheapest tools—which would mean he's the world's worst bandit—or he's moving in. I'm going to guess that it's probably the latter, because I've never heard of a criminal who played loud music and left the lights blazing while he robbed a place, although there's a first time for everything. Also, I notice that there are two very large red tool cabinets along the wall to his right which weren't there when I left this morning.

After watching him for a few beats, he does appear to be unpacking. Swallowing my initial fear, I toss aside my internal Panic-Mode

Barbie to make way for Heat-Seeking Missile Barbie. A hot pulse floods my veins as my eyes linger on his toned biceps, and his ass-hugging dark blue jeans, as well as on the array of colours making up that illustrated piece covering most of his back. My desire to make a closer inspection is daunting, a reaction I haven't had to any member of the opposite sex in a long time. And, hell, this is all before even seeing the front! *I am seriously hurting.*

The music's rhythm mirrors the beating of my heart. The lyrics Roger Waters is singing about his hands feeling "just like two balloons" pretty much sum up the way mine feel right now as my nerves take over—*numb.*

This stranger hasn't noticed me yet—which is a good thing—because I need a plan, and drooling isn't the best course of action when faced with a potential intruder, even if it might turn out that he belongs here. *Who the hell is this guy?* I don't remember anyone mentioning a new hire, but I guess it's a possibility. The shop has been getting busier lately, and I can't see any signs of a break-in, but wouldn't I have been told if there was going to be a new employee so I could add them to the payroll?

Deciding it's time to confront the stranger, I move in closer, grabbing a tire iron resting on top of the counter at Brody's station with my free hand as I pass—just in case.

Taking another step, my eyes are again riveted on the stranger's back, specifically to the tattoos gracing his tanned skin, which I can see almost perfectly from this distance. The main piece is a large Excalibur sword running down the middle of his toned back in the most shimmering silvers, greys, blues and blacks. It's an intricate piece that's incredibly masculine, and breathtaking, to be honest. The sword's tip is encased in a stone, and the handle is pronounced, as if ready to be pulled out by the one deemed worthy. A blue-grey shield is propped against the side of the rock, and the words "IN PERPETUUM ET UNUM

DIEM" are written in bold Olde English letters across his shoulders, the black ink spanning from blade to blade. Jesus, it's a beautiful tattoo, on a beautiful canvas.

Meow. Beast glances up at me, looking pleased with himself. He obviously missed Spy Training 101. *Never speak*; *the element of surprise is key.* Luckily, the music hid his meowing from everyone but me. Shaken from my tattoo-induced trance, I'm reminded that I still have no idea who this man is.

Shit. Shit. Shit.

I gently set Beast behind my feet, readying myself for battle.

"What the hell do you think you're doing in here?" I call out loudly right behind him, the tire iron gripped firmly in one hand and my cell poised to call 911 in the other. In case I'm wrong and he really is robbing us, I'm ready. "Better yet, who *are* you?"

He jumps, hitching up his broad shoulders, clearly startled. And then, just like in the movies, the intruder slowly turns, revealing himself. His eyes are a mix of brown and gold with flecks of yellow, reminding me of autumn, and lined with the darkest lashes I've ever seen. His strong jaw is tense, a scowl marking his otherwise ruggedly handsome face. He's extremely hot, in an "I'm trouble" kind of way.

"And why did you let my cat out?" I snap, my tone accusing as I gesture down at Beast with my phone.

The sexy-as-sin intruder's full lips unfurl as he takes in the tire iron and cell phone in my hands. I think I see the right side of his mouth pulling into a half-smile as his eyes roam down my body, taking his turn to check me out.

My own eyes can't seem to focus on his face; not when the smooth lines of his chest are drawing my attention and I see even more tattoos I'd like to explore, along with a whole bunch of muscles down the centre of his stomach.

Holy shit. Who the hell is this guy?

12

Hendrix

Meow.

What the fuck? I swear I put that furball out back.

"What the hell do you think you're doing in here? Better yet, who *are* you?" I hear a high sharp voice yell behind me, making me jump. I pause, giving it a second to see if someone's calling the cops or pulling an alarm, but I don't hear anything that tells me I should be worried.

Putting down the wrench in my hand, I grab a cloth and wipe my hands, deciding I'd better deal with this, and quick. I've got crap to do. Turning to face a mystery woman who's giving me a shit ton of attitude, she barks another question at me, this one making the lightbulb above my head go off. *I know exactly who she is.*

"And why did you let my cat out?" she demands, looking down at the feline hiding behind her orange runners. She doesn't have too far down to look; she's really short. She's jutting out her chin under her long pink bangs, and it's kind of cute. That's when I notice the tire iron in her hand, and a right-pissed-off look across her beautiful face.

Christ, what a sight she is. If this is my welcome present, then thank you, Mr. Flynn. She's a tiny little thing, but, fuck, is she ever pretty. And it seems she might appreciate the sight of a shirtless Hendrix from the way she's eye-fucking the shit out of me. Regardless of her angry tone, I see her hunger, and I can't deny that I can feel the heat licking over my body where her eyes trail.

"I might ask you the same thing, Short Stack."

"'Short Stack'?" she repeats, cocking her head, the move making her tits bounce a bit. I see that they're quite perky and a bit large for a chick her height. *This girl is hot.*

"Eyes up here, Ogre Man," she points to her face. She's got this crazy pixie-cut, all messy and dyed a fucked-up shade of pink, but it suits her perfectly.

"Huh. 'Ogre Man'. You're a witty one, I see," I grin, taking her in.

"Better than 'Short Stack'."

"Would you prefer Halfling? Pix, Little One, or maybe Little *Bug*? Cause right now you're kinda *bugging* me. I'm working here, got shit to do." I glance at the open boxes, at all the tools I have left to put away.

"None of those names are any good, asshole." She raises the iron bar. "Now tell me. Who. Are. You?" She punctuates each word, stepping in close, our chests almost brushing. The look on her face as she suddenly realizes how close we are, and how far up she's having to look, is one of the sexiest things I've seen in a long fucking time. Nothing is hotter than when a beautiful woman is riled up, and this one is pulling it off tenfold.

"You gonna hit me with that thing, Fruitloop?" I ask, bending my head down to take in more of the sweet smell I got a whiff of as soon as she crossed into my personal space. She smells like a bloody fruit roll-up, and I'll be damned if I don't want to eat every inch of this girl.

"You did not just call me 'Fruitloop'," she warns, stepping back and folding her arms over her chest. Of course, my eyes follow the move. *Yeah, she's definitely got a nice rack.*

"Sure did," I tell her honestly. "'Fruit' 'cause, damn, baby, you smell sweet, like one of those sticky strawberry fruit roll-up things, and, fuck, would I like to get all sticky with you." I bridge the gap she just created between us, and place my hand over hers, the intake of her breath letting me know she likes what I'm saying, even if she wants to pretend she doesn't. I grip the tire iron. "And 'Loop' because you're fucking loopy if you think you're gonna hit me with this thing." I pull it, forcing her to let it go.

Thankfully, she doesn't fight me, and I think it's because of our close proximity. I'm affecting her. Just as she's affecting me. Her intense grey eyes are a mix of anger and lust and I swear I can smell that she's turned on. *That's okay, Fruitloop. I am, too.*

"Please," she says, looking up at me and taking a deep breath. "Obviously you're not robbing my uncle, so can you just explain what you're doing here?" And with that I confirm my earlier lightbulb moment.

"I'm Hendrix, and you must be the stipulation." I extend my hand, loving the look of utter confusion on her face. Of course, she doesn't shake it.

"The—*what?* My name is Trinity. Trinity Adams. And Dexter Flynn is my uncle," she huffs, her lack of patience clear. "Now tell me who you are to Dex—and exactly what you're doing here—before I call him, or better yet, the cops. You've got to be trespassing or something."

"Trust me, I'm not doing anything wrong." I pull the keys out of my pocket. "Let's try this again, Trinity. I'm Hendrix. Hendrix Hills," I say, imitating the way she introduced herself, "and this," I gesture with the tire iron, "is my new shop. Well, fifty percent is, anyway. So, I guess that makes me your new half-boss," I chuckle, stepping back to lean against the workbench so I can see the show my Fruitloop is about to give me as she goes off.

Yeah, I like this little stipulation just fine.

13

Trinity

"You're lying. There's no way Dex would sell the place without telling me. I mean, I knew he was thinking about it, but he would've told me..." I say, more to myself than to Hendrix.

"Well, he did sell it, and here I am."

There's no way he'd sell it to this asshole, no matter how good-looking the ogre might be.

"Call Flynn. Ask him yourself," he challenges.

"I will. There's no way he'd sell it to a guy like you." I give him my best dirty look.

"Shit, you're cute. This is gonna be fun, and here I was worried about having stipulations."

"What stipulations? And why did you call me that?" I ask, totally ignoring him. *What the hell did "and you must be the stipulation" mean, anyway?*

"I called you a few things, Fruitloop. Which one are you most confused about?" he asks, his tone laced with "I'm-a-cocksucker" arrogance. "Let's review shal—"

I cut him off.

"Stipulation," I huff, getting pissed off all over again. "Why did you call me that?"

"I suggest you call Flynn and get him to explain, it's not really my place. All I know is you're part of the package deal. And after spending five minutes with you, I'm more than happy with my purchase," he winks, then turns around and starts putting shit away again. Clearly, I've been dismissed.

Furious, I scoop up Beast and decide it's time to get the hell out of Dodge before I hit him with more than just a tire iron. After making sure Beast is safely returned to his storage room, I head to the back door, stop, then look back over my shoulder and give him a final warning. "New boss or not, let my cat out again and you'll find your tools in the hazardous waste dumpster," I harrumph, satisfied I've gotten the last word.

As I reach the door, I chance a peek over in Hendrix's direction. *Sexy bastard has me all flustered, pissed off and—dare I admit—excited?* And, of course, the big jerk's standing with his arms crossed over his chest with a huge smirk on his face, watching me.

"I think we're gonna be great friends, Fruitloop. I like crazy." He waves, and I roll my eyes. In order to preserve some shred of dignity, I keep my trap shut as I slam the door and exit the garage.

Stomping up the stairway to my apartment, I make a mental note to overfeed Beast tomorrow morning, because there's no way in hell I'm going back down there again tonight.

Opening my door, I drop my keys on the counter and hang my purse on the coat rack. I pull out my cell and dial Dex and Tillie.

"You've reached the Flynns. You know what to do."

I hang up after the beep.

"Dex is getting a cell phone for Christmas," I tell myself, frustrated. I mean, who still has an *answering machine?* It's probably best I talk to him in person, anyway. I toss my phone beside my keys and beeline through the open-concept kitchen, stopping in front of the fridge. Pulling open the freezer drawer, I take out my emergency pint of Ben & Jerry's Chocolate Peanut Buttery Swirl. Grabbing a spoon, I settle into the overstuffed grey couch, which comforts me instantly. Popping the lid, I toss it on the wooden coffee table and kick my feet up, letting out a long exasperated sigh.

"What the hell just happened?" I ask aloud around a huge spoonful of sweet and salty ice cream, my mouth thanking me as I uncover a chunk of peanut butter.

It's been a while since I've allowed myself to look at a man and see him as anything other than a hurtmachine, I'll be damned if I let this Hendrix asshole get to me. He's got bad news written all over him, and that's the last thing I need in my life. Even if he *is* super-good looking and has a body I'd like to explore up close and personal. Maybe if I was someone else I'd be falling at his feet, but I'm not. I'm me, and things are different now. Plus, I bet he has enough chicks to fill his days of the week as it is. Guys like him don't get serious. And that whole "friends" thing? No, thank you. Like I'd ever be friends with a man who can make me go from zero-to-a-hundred that fast.

"I think we're gonna be great friends, Fruitloop. I like crazy." His parting comment runs rapidly through my mind. What's with the "Fruitloop"? And I'll *show* him crazy if he thinks he's going to be my boss or messes with my cat again, that's for sure. *Asshole.*

"Like we'd ever have a reason to be friends. He's the crazy one," I say out loud, rising from the couch to put the ice cream back in the freezer before I devour the whole container.

14

TRINITY

"YEAH, COME IN," Dex's gruff voice calls.

I'm outside his office door. It's taken me five minutes to find the nerve to knock. It was easier having the conversation I'm about to have with Dex with myself last night, but as I stand here now, I realize that Dex doesn't even really owe me an explanation. If anything, it's me who's in debt here.

It was Dex and Aunt Tillie who helped me pick up the pieces of my life when HIV shook my foundation. It was Dex who offered me an amazing job that I love, a supportive family and a place to live. The last thing I should be doing is acting like an ungrateful brat.

But him selling the garage behind my back hurts. And if living with HIV has taught me anything, it's taught me not to live a life with regrets and unhappiness, and this has been bugging me all night so I need to talk it through with Dex. It was this thought that gave me the courage to finally put on my big girl pants and knock.

Opening the door, I smile at the sight of Dex running his fingers through his beard, a telltale sign he's frustrated.

"What are you doing?" I ask. He's balancing his tablet in one hand, his eyes scrunching, staring at a small piece of paper he's holding in his other hand, as far away from his face as he can.

"Hey, darlin'." He looks up, his green eyes shining as he takes me in. "Trying to read our access code for this year's car show. I gotta confirm our spot online with this stupid number by the end of today, and I can't find my readers anywhere. Old man eyes're fuckin' with me this morning, and my arms are getting too short."

I reach for his tablet, laughing. "Here, I'll do it."

"Thanks, sweetie. You're the best helper I got," he says. "I don't know why they make the print so small." He shakes his head. Any anger I had been harbouring evaporates.

Whatever our talk reveals, I know if Dex has sold the place, the reason for his secrecy wouldn't have been malicious on his part. He'd never intentionally hurt me, and I feel like an ass for thinking otherwise. I'm an idiot for allowing myself to lose sleep about it.

But, okay, let's be honest. Dex wasn't the only reason I was losing sleep; a certain beefcake might have played a role. It was as if his scent had drifted up the stairs after me, an unrelenting hint of bergamot and grapefruit dancing in the air, an intoxicating mix that I couldn't seem to shake.

"You're here early for a Saturday," Dex says, rummaging in his desk for his glasses. "Shit, they have to be here. I thought I'd left them right on top last time I used 'em."

I clear my throat. "I wanted to feed Beast and change his litter box. I didn't get a chance last night and don't want him to starve. Funny thing, though. His dish was already full. Know anything about that?" I ask, knowing full-well my uncle's developed a sweet spot for the kitten he didn't originally want to move in.

"Nope. No clue. Must have been that damn gnome again," he muses.

"Those gnomes sure seem sweet on that kitten," I tease. The cat has been an awesome addition to the Ignition Inc. family. I found him alone—shaking and starving—in between two of our blue recycling dumpsters a few weeks back. I wanted to bring him upstairs, but Aunt

Tillie suggested the shop might be better, seeing as I'm down here most of the time anyway. She thought our back storage room would be a nice big space for him, and he could earn his kibble by keeping the mouse population under control. Dex and the others weren't too keen on having the cat as they worried he'd be underfoot, but Beast ended up staying out of the shop and now that he's here, the guys like having him around, and he's become the resident mascot. (Well, all of the guys except Hendrix, I guess).

I place Dex's tablet on the desktop. "All set. You're confirmed, and I sent the payment via PayPal, too, since I figured you probably don't remember the password." I pat his shoulder.

"Watch it, kid. I might be blind, but I ain't senile, yet," he grins.

"Um, so…yeah. I…uh…I met the Ogre Hendrix Hills last night. That was interesting and informative, to say the least." I plunk down in the leather chair in front of his desk.

"Shit. Trin. I didn't plan for you to meet Hendrix before I talked to you first, or for you to find out that way. I'd planned on telling you what was going on first thing this morning," he sighs.

"So it's true?"

"Let me explain, darlin'. It all happened so fast. I was gonna talk to you, but with your school tours and me unsure if I was ready to sell, I wanted to wait for the right time. I knew it would be an emotional conversation, with you no doubt offering to move out before I even decided what I was doin', and I didn't want to lay any unnecessary stresses on ya. And Hendrix wasn't supposed to move in until today, but he had a lot to do so I guess he ended up here last night. I had no idea, and for that I'm sorry. Must have given you a bit of a surprise."

"No kidding. I'm not too happy with you, Dex. I left the garage feeling pretty pissed last night. That guy's an ass. I wish I'd've known you sold the place to him."

"I know. I should have said something earlier. It was all just sinkin' in, you know, me about to be half-retired and only workin' part-time from now on, and all that. Heck, I didn't tell Joe and Brody either, until Hendrix called me yesterday before you and I left, sayin' he was popping by in the morning to drop off some paperwork for me. I know I could have told you in the car, but I figured it could wait one more day. Lesson learned." He rubs his beard. "I was planning to introduce you guys later today."

"I'm glad you're doing what makes you happy, Dex. I was just caught off guard," I whisper, not quite able to hide my emotions. "One more thing. He called me 'the stipulation'. What does that even mean?" I ask, getting annoyed as the asshole's self-satisfied grin comes to mind. *Sexy jerk.*

"As regards the stipulations, there were a few conditions that I wanted met before I'd sell. One, he had to keep all our current employees, and two, he'd have to let you keep living upstairs until you chose to move. Now, I know there's a chance you might be thinkin' about maybe getting back into some fancy finance gig one day, but truth is you're doin' a great job here, darlin', and I think the place still needs ya."

How can I stay mad at Uncle Dex? "I feel stupid. I threatened to hit him with a tire iron, Dex. I thought he was robbing the place," I groan, embarrassed.

He lets out a loud belly laugh. "Hell, I wish I coulda seen that...you in all your pissy glory, ready to lay the beats down. I bet you were a sight."

"Not the point, Dex." I can't keep a straight face, my own laughter breaking through. "I can hold my own, just so you know."

"I have no doubts, darlin', I have no doubts." He shakes his head and wipes a tear from the corner of his eye. "Listen. Til and I had been talking about selling the place for a while, as you know. I'd talked to Joe and Brody first, seeing if either of them was interested in takin' it over, but they're both happy just working as mechanics and aren't looking for more right now. I only listed it to see if I'd get any bites, and I wasn't expecting any so fast. Next thing I knew I was meeting Hendrix, saw the fire in his eyes, and he agreed to all my terms. It just became final a couple days ago. I accepted the offer, agreeing to have him partner up with me for a year before I relinquish the whole thing to him. He's okay, Trin. He'll keep the place the way we built it, he'll uphold the name. He's a good guy. Just give him a chance."

"He seems like an idiot, if you ask me," I snort, crossing my arms over my chest like a bit of a spoiled child, admittedly.

"Is that 'cause he's good looking?" He looks at me, his eyes twinkling.

"Dex! God, no. He's rude and big and has tattoos and smells like a player…" I look up to find Dex staring at me, a knowing grin splayed across his bearded face.

"Well, Tillie told me he was one attractive man and that I'm lucky I'm as irresistible as I am, otherwise he'd be giving me a run for my money. Then she mentioned maybe you two might hit it off," he chuckles.

"No, thank you! Remind me to call off the dogs. There's no way I need *that* in my life." *I'll need to have a word with my loving aunt.*

He raises his hands in defeat. "You're right. The last thing I want is a soap opera up in here. Glad we've got that sorted."

By the end of our conversation, any ill feelings or thoughts I had about the situation are gone. I can't believe Dex would go so far to make sure that the sale of his business wouldn't impact my life at all. What's more, I can't believe I doubted him in the first place.

It's also not lost on me that a man like Hendrix was so accommodating to a virtual stranger in agreeing to the deal. Maybe—just maybe—he's not a complete ogre after all. But I quickly tamp down those thoughts, because there's no way I'll allow myself to get close enough to find out. *Ever.*

15

Hendrix

IT'S ONLY MY second week working at Ignition Inc., and I gotta say I fucking love it here.

The place is a well-oiled machine. Joe and Brody are wicked mechanics, and we're really starting to mesh well together. Business is steady and with the clients that have followed me from my old job at Wheel Wizards, I'm guessing things will only get busier. Flynn has taken me under his wing, showing me all the aspects of the business side of things, and has allowed me to take over a few of the management tasks to break me in. We've decided that we may want to look into hiring another mechanic, too, something he's putting me in charge of.

The only downside to this place is Trinity. I can't get this chick out of my head nor can I get her to utter more than five sentences to me. My first week here, I barely saw her, seeing as I was so busy. A part of me thinks it was deliberate on her part, too. Seems she managed to work her schedule around mine. I've made a mental note to ensure I work the exact same shifts as her. You know, just to get to know her like I have all the other staff.

Earlier this week, I decided to offer Trinity an olive branch, a means to bury the hatchet, if you will, since she's refused to warm up to me. There's nothing hotter than a girl that's hard to get, and she has proven herself that. Part of me that thinks she's enjoying this one-sided game of Silence Wars she's got us playing, so I decided to up the ante and do something over the top to show her that I'm not actually the asshole she thinks I am, that working together could be a lot of fun if only she'd give me a chance and accept my apology. I thought it would be nice to send her some flowers at first, but since I'm not really a flowers kind of guy, I opted for something more unique, something she might get a kick out of. I found one of those fancy chocolate places that do custom orders.

Boy, was I wrong about her reaction...*dead wrong*. I did, however, find her response exciting as hell, especially when she came storming into my work bay fuming mad. I almost keeled over laughing...

"Hendrix!" she yells, stopping right in front of where I was working at my bench, a carburetor and its parts spread all over. "You really are an asshole, aren't you?" she asks, her face flushing with anger as she waves the plastic-wrapped chocolate tire irons around, giving me a piece of her mind. "You think this is funny?"

One of the little purple ribbons detaches from the cellophane and drops to the shop floor.

"I do," I smirk back, watching her tits bouncing under her white tank top as she flaps the chocolate tools at my face, continuing to tell me off.

"You are not *looking at my boobs right now!" she shouts, and believe me, it takes a lot of restraint not to shut her mouth with mine as she goes on and on about respectful working conditions, and how normal bosses don't do this immature shit.*

"Sorry, I don't mean to stare, but they're eye-catching. Kinda like you," I say, regretting the words as soon as they fall out of my mouth.

This is not going the way I had planned at all.

"Jesus, Hendrix, you're a harassment lawyer's wet dream," she says behind a small grin, one she tries to hide.

"I know, Fruitloop. It was supposed to be funny, and I'm sorry, but you're beautiful, can't help lookin'," I say, shrugging, trying to appease her.

"Stop. Just stop," Trinity calls out, raising her hand. Unfortunately, all I can do is start chuckling again at how fucking adorable she is, standing there giving me a piece of her mind, paying no attention to the guys watching from their bays or any customers who might be lurking around.

"Well, it's the truth. You're smok—"

She cuts me off.

"Stop right there. I'm about to shove these so far up your ass, Hendrix Hills. It isn't funny, and I don't accept. Keep your gifts, you big jerk," she says, whipping four of them at my head before stomping off.

"Well, this is gonna be fun to watch, Hen," Brody laughs. "Trinity just handed you your ass on a plate. She doesn't take anybody's shit. Man...good luck with that." He continues to chuckle as I stand there, stunned, watching every jiggle her retreating backside makes.

"Lunch is here!" Brody calls, shaking me from my thoughts and tossing me a white deli bag.

"Thanks, man."

"Don't thank me, it was Trin. She dropped them off before she left for the afternoon. She usually brings us lunch on Fridays," Brody shares before biting into his ham on rye, lounging on one of the stools he's pulled out from under the workbench.

Huh. And she got me lunch, too? Maybe there is *hope?* Maybe the Starbucks I left her this morning helped, but probably not.

"I'd try and thank her if I didn't think she'd try to bite me."

"At this point, she just might," Brody teases, wiping his mouth.

"That's all right. It's only temporary. I'm determined to win her over no matter how long it takes. I really am a great guy once you get to know me. Charming as fuck," I laugh, thinking about what a pain this girl is being, even though I've been going out of my way to apologize. *I swear she secretly loves watching me grovel.*

"Yeah, she's not a big fan of yours yet, eh?" Joe asks, walking over to join us. "Not sure you'll win that one over. She's pretty self-contained so good luck with that," Joe adds, giving Brody an odd glance and making me feel as if I'm missing something, before he bites into his pita.

"What's her deal, anyway? She always such a pain in the ass, or am I the lucky target?" I ask them. Despite Brody being married to her cousin, Nadia, and Joe being her cousin, I was hoping maybe they'd give me some insights. I want to know what makes her tick, what makes her happy. I wanna get to know the things that piss her off and the ones that make her smile, too. Besides, she's too fucking nice to look at, so it would be a win-win to at least wear her down a bit to the point where she doesn't want to rip my head off with a tire iron—chocolate or otherwise—every time I'm near her.

Looking between them, Joe nods, and Brody says, "She's been hurt in the past, has her guard up high around new people. And you pissed her off, so that puts you on her shit list, despite your valiant efforts." He chuckles. "I can't believe you sent her tire irons. You're such an idiot." Brody shakes his head, and Joe laughs right along with him at my expense.

"Whatever. I'll get her to like me. Just wait," I add before taking a bite of my roast beef sandwich.

Everyone had, of course, heard about our chance meeting and had been watching me trying to suckhole around this maddening woman all week. They all thought my gesture had been a nice touch at the time, a good way to show I was sorry, despite them throwing it in my face now. Unfortunately, everything I do seems to have the reverse effect with her. Trinity Adams is a little firecracker and I can't wait to set her off, over and over again. I just gotta get her to actually talk to me, because she hasn't said a word to me since the chocolate debacle, and that was four days ago. Since then, even though she's been avoiding me, I see her watching me, and fuck if I don't like it.

Now to figure out how to make her let me in, to see that I wasn't trying to be a dick the night we first met, that maybe we could be—I don't know, maybe...*friends?* Jesus, I'm not sure what to expect from her. It's not like I'm looking to become buddies with some chick, but for some reason I feel as though us being in each other's lives is in the greater plan. I'm drawn to her and, I'll admit, I'm curious about my Fruitloop, too.

"Whatever you do, you better not hurt her. She's been through enough. Trin doesn't need any more stress in her life," Joe says, and I know it's the protective cousin thing coming into play, so I let the implied threat slide. We finish up our lunch spending the next forty-five minutes shooting the shit about everything from the Jays to the next few jobs we have lined up.

"How long before the McAllister restoration's done?" Flynn calls from the glass door separating the offices from the work area, effectively ending our downtime. "Hendrix, come get me up to speed when you're done eatin'."

I've been working on that complete overhaul of Greyson McAllister's '54 Chevy Bel Air as my first big project, and it's been a real bitch. But with Brody's and Joe's help, we're killing it. After cleaning up, I make my way to Flynn's office, where I lean against the doorway and knock despite the door being open.

"Come on in, son. Have a seat." He juts his chin at the chair in front of his desk.

"Okay, tell me. Where are we with the McAllister job?"

"Not much longer. Maybe another week at most, Flynn. I've got my buddy Cannon working out some paint details over at his shop. We need to get that guy to leave Wheel Wizards and come work for us," I tell him, because it's true. Cannon would be a definite asset around here.

"Agreed," he says, "there's gotta be something we can offer to get him to make the move."

"I'll try to convi—" I'm cut off by the ringing of Flynn's desk phone.

"Shit, it's Trinity. I've got to get this," he says, picking up the receiver. "Hey, darlin', what's up? I'm in a meeting."

A strange desire to hear her voice washes over me, but I quickly dismiss it. I've got a date tonight and that's what I should be thinking about, not some chick that snubs me at every turn.

"You sure you're okay?" Flynn asks, and I want to ask him what's wrong with her, but I don't. I try to pretend I'm not listening in. "Look…okay, yeah. You sure? Alright, sit tight. I'll be there soon, sweetheart. I told you to let Joe look at it last week, so I'm not happy. It's getting a complete tune-up, I hope you know." Ending the call, he stands. "Got to be the most stubborn woman I know…" Flynn mutters, reaching for the tow truck keys. I couldn't agree more.

"Everything okay?"

"That shitbox car of hers broke down at the Walmart over on Centennial. She had an appointment in the plaza there. Thinks it's just the battery, but I'm guessing it's the alternator. I'm gonna head out and grab her."

"I'll go." I lean over and grab the keys before he can. "Might help get me into her better books."

"Not sure that's the best idea, kid. She was pretty pissed about those chocolates. Was in here checking on our harassment policy after she admitted all the things she wanted to say to you," he barks, laughing. "For some reason, you're high up on her shit list. Funny, never seen her react that way to anybody before."

"I can handle her," I say, heading out the door.

"Well, good luck, kid," he calls. "You're gonna need it."

16

Trinity

Every Friday for the last year-and-a-half, I've attended group therapy.

It was Lindsey—whom I met at The AIDS Network—who convinced me that it would be good for me to have a place where I could vent and share my feelings, and to listen to others who were walking in my shoes. She described it as a positive buffer to reduce stress, since people living with HIV can be impacted by different stressors than people with other chronic illnesses, because of the type of disease and the stigma. The group has been a blessing and I've built some great friendships with a few members in particular, but I feel respect for every person in the group. As Lindsey promised, it keeps me from feeling isolated. The best part is having a place to go where, no matter what someone discloses, seeks advice about or shares, it will be kept within our circle. Group therapy has also given me the opportunity to open up about my own fears and experiences, and to seek advice from others who share the same struggles, people who understand—who *get it*. It's funny how quickly we can bond with people when we know they're facing the same issues that we are, and most of all, when we know they won't judge us. It's not always easy, as we've lost a few members to the disease since I joined, but I couldn't imagine my life without these Friday sessions. They've definitely had a positive impact on helping me adjust to living with HIV.

"Alright, everyone. Thanks for another great session. See you all next Friday. Same time, same place," Lindsey says, ending our meeting.

"Cheers to next week," we recite back.

Months ago, Tim—one of our older members who'd contracted the disease through a blood transfusion following a car accident—had suggested that ending our sessions with a kind of "we'll meet again"-type mantra might lift our spirits. We agreed, and Helena, a cheeky woman with an Irish accent, voiced the phrase we all soon adopted.

"Hey, chick. You have time for a chat?" Andrew—or Andrea, as she prefers to be called now—asks, as I head to the back to put away my folding chair.

We met a year ago when she decided to see what our group had to offer. The first time Andrea attended, she was a handsome man named Andrew who was wearing a business suit, complete with a tie—and the stress of hiding who she really was. As she spoke, I could feel the pressures she faced every day and the hardships she endured living a double-life as Andrew, when all she craved was to be accepted as Andrea. By the third session, Andrew felt comfortable introducing us to Andrea, who has proven to be a fun-loving transgender woman with a penchant for the fashions and music of the 1980s. This woman who was tired of hiding behind a suit is now comfortable in an environment where she knows we accept her.

Diagnosed with HIV a little over a year ago, she has yet to open up to her family or workplace about her status or her lifestyle. I was in complete awe of Andrea after she spoke about her life, her struggles and how—if it weren't for her illness—she'd love to have sex reassignment surgery to become the woman she knows she is. I went right up to her after that session to give her a hug and the offer of friendship. We've been each other's saving graces ever since.

Andrea's disease has progressed a lot faster than many others' in the group. She says it's because she refused to start the medications right away, having lived in denial for more than six months after diagnosis. Some people in our group struggle with not judging Andrea (even though rule #2, after confidentiality, is not to judge) for keeping her HIV status from her loved ones, especially from Simon, the man she's been living with now for the last three months. This is despite the fact that she's shared and stressed about how she'd been taking every precaution to keep Simon from contracting the virus while she figures out how to tell him. It's not that the others ever say anything mean or derogatory; it's seen in the expressions on their faces or in the slight nods or shakes of their heads. Thankfully, Andrea doesn't pay it any mind. But as time goes on, we're both seeing the faces becoming more understanding, which is, of course, is all Andrea wants, to be understood.

"Sure, I'd love to talk. Let's grab a coffee and sit at that table over there." I gesture in the direction of the bistro tables set up on one side of the large meeting room right beside the windows.

After grabbing our coffees, we sit. Andrea fiddles with the silver ALEX AND ANI "Unexpected Miracles" charm bracelet I gave her for her birthday last month. Then her hazel eyes meet mine and she drops a bit of a bomb on me.

"I didn't want to tell the group until I spoke to you first, but I'm going to tell Simon tonight." She pauses.

"Oh, Andrea, I'm so happy you've decided it's time. I know you've been worried; I'm sure he'll take it well. He loves you, I've seen you two, you were adorable at your birthday dinner. He seriously couldn't take his eyes off you all night. I really think it'll be a good thing," I smile, covering her hand with mine in support, and hoping like hell I'm right.

"I'm scared. I mean, we both have friends who have the disease, and he's always saying if either of us were ever to test positive we'd get through it together, but I think sometimes it's easier said than done. I don't want to lose him," she admits, wiping a tear from her cheek. "There's more, though. I went to the doctor's last week and got some news on Tuesday morning. News that confirms why I need to tell Simon sooner rather than later." She sighs, and a seed of worry roots itself in my stomach. I don't like where the conversation is going, hearing a second unexpected bomb whistling before it crashes to the ground.

"I've got Kaposi's sarcoma. And my CD4 cell count has fallen under 200, which means I've progressed from HIV to AIDS. I'd noticed a little bruise on my calf awhile ago, then another under my armpit. Turns out, they weren't bruises, but KS lesions…"

I sit in stunned silence as her words trail off. I know in theory what having a low CD4—or T-cell—count means. It means her immune system is deteriorating, that it won't be strong enough to fight off even the most common illnesses, so she can't afford to get sick. *A cold could kill her.*

I know all of this, so hearing my friend tell me her disease has progressed, my brain just shuts off. I process nothing. I say nothing. All I can do is cry with her, and that's the last thing Andrea needs from me, but she's my friend and I could lose her. The reality of this disease and its course are once again a blatant reality that's hitting me right in the face. The virus is winning and my beautiful friend is starting to lose her battle.

After a few minutes of silence, I finally find my voice. I question her about her treatment plan, offer to accompany her to appointments and to be with her when she tells Simon, if she wants. And, like always, she thanks me and tells me just having someone to listen to her is all she needs. Andrea rises and hugs me tight again, thanking me for listening and for never judging; she says that is always enough.

After promising to text me later, she and I part ways in the parking lot. I feel nauseous as I unlock my car and take my seat behind the wheel.

I need Shannon.

And I need red wine.

Rrrrrrrr-rrrrrr-rrrrrrrr-rrr-rrr…

Rrrrrrrr-rrrrrr-rrrrrrrr-rrr-rrr…

*Rrrrrrrr-rrrrrr-rrrrrrrr-rrr-rrr…*what I don't need is for my car not to start.

Piece of shit!

Digging out my phone, I call Dex, who thankfully answers on the first ring. The last thing I would want is for some stranger to see me right now. I'm dripping snot.

"Hey, darlin'. What's up? I'm in a meeting…"

Thankfully, he'll be here in fifteen minutes. Until then, I sit in the car and wait, a slumping mascara-streaked mess crying for a friend, for those I've already lost, and for myself, because the reality is that I could one day lose my battle, too. Being healthy today doesn't mean I will stay this way. It's these types of thoughts which make me realize I don't really want to hide anymore. Maybe it's time I put myself back out there and lived a little? Maybe even dated? I need to stop hiding behind the incident with Jared, have to stop using that as an excuse. Most of all, I need to remind myself that not all men will be like him.

"Gotta live, Trin," I whisper to myself, almost confidently.

Before I know it, I hear the familiar chug of a diesel engine as our tow truck pulls up beside me, the purple and silver Ignition Inc. door logo flashing. I drag my forearm across my eyes to wipe away the tears and sit up with the best smile I can muster, feeling instant relief that my knight in shining armour has finally arrived.

The truck door slams. But instead of Uncle Dex walking around the front bumper to come to my rescue, I see Hendrix.

17

Hendrix

WALKING AROUND THE front of the tow truck towards Trinity's old silver Jetta, I smirk when I see her registering that it's not Flynn driving the truck, but me, instead.

"You've got to be kidding me," is what I read on her lips as she suddenly bolts up and lunges out of her car, the smile falling from her face.

"What are you doing here?" she grits out, and that's when I notice she's got black shit from her eyes smeared across her beautiful face as if she's been crying. Instantly, my back stiffens, wanting to know who or what the fuck made her cry.

Standing in front of her, I gently tuck my knuckle under her chin and tip her face up so she has to meet my eyes. "Why are you cryin', Fruitloop?" I ask gently.

Next thing I know, I've pulled her into my chest. Rather than pulling away like I expected she might, she gives in to my touch and allows herself to find comfort in me. We stand, hugging, her face buried in the middle of my chest, deep sobs wracking her tiny frame. It's like holding a live wire.

"Trin, I'm gonna need you to tell me you're okay. I'm about three seconds away from losing my shit." I rub her back softly; her hold on me is iron-clad. *Yeah, this girl is definitely gonna be letting me in.*

"I'm all right, I'm not injured. But I am really upset. I just need someone to hold me, even if it's you." she acquiesces, gifting me with a subtle smile along with her dig before pulling away. Looking up at me, her eyes beg me to let it rest, to simply comfort her—and that's exactly what I do. I'll question why the hell this feels so right later.

We stand in the same position for what feels like forever before she pulls away again, as awareness of our closeness dawns on her. Instantly, I miss her warmth.

"Thank you. I'm—I'm sorry. I didn't mean to maul you." She steps back, then points to my shirt. "I'll wash that for you. I'm sorry…" she begins again, and I pull her back into my chest.

"This is what friends do, Trin," I say, resting my head on top of hers. *Fuck, she really is short.*

"We're not 'friends', Hendrix," she mutters into my chest.

"The hell we aren't." I angle my head to look down at her face. "I have the snot marks to prove it. I think this is the beginning of a beautiful thing."

She pauses. "I'm not sure us being friends is such a good idea. Maybe I don't need any new friends," she says, looking up at me, the storm clouds from whatever has her upset lingering in her grey eyes.

"Maybe I need one, Fruitloop. Maybe I need a new friend. One who's familiar with how to handle tools, especially tire irons. You can never have too many of those friends," I tell her, giving her the sweetest smile from my repertoire.

I'm almost sure I see a little grin twitching at the corner of her mouth. I wrap my arm around her shoulder and help her up into the tow truck, settling her inside before rigging up her car. I don't even bother looking under the hood.

Hopping back in the truck, I take her cell phone from her hand, program my number into her contacts list, then shoot myself a text. To my surprise she doesn't protest.

"Call me next time this happens."

"Okay." It's a quiet reply.

Was I referring to her car breaking down, or when she *breaks down?* Something tells me I'd gladly help her with both. I have no idea who the hell Trinity Adams is, and I'm not sure I like the way she shakes my head up, but I'm going to find out.

"Let's get you home," I say, pulling out of the lot.

I'M SERIOUSLY FUCKING losing it.

Here I am on a date eating a nice dinner at Vecchio's Italian restaurant with Macy, a pretty brunette with curves for days, and a "come get me, big boy" attitude that would normally have me packing up our meal for take out.

Normally. But not tonight.

Fucking Macy is the last thing on my mind, let alone whatever she's been babbling about for the last hour or so. I should have cancelled. I don't do "dates" without sex, but sex is the last thing I want from her tonight.

"Have you ever been to Valentino's? We should go there..."

"Sorry, did you say something?"

"Yeah, I was wondering if you'd been to Valentino's before."

"Oh, okay."

"Are you all right?"

"Great," I smile, taking a swig of my beer.

Trinity.

My thoughts keep drifting back to Trinity. She's the only thing on my mind, how she felt in my arms, her fruity scent, and, most of all, wanting to know what made her so upset. She was tight-lipped the whole ride back to the garage.

"I'd love to cook for you..."

"Sure."

"I love your tattoos..."

"Great."

I tune Macy out, giving one-word answers and nods when I think it's appropriate. *Yeah, I'm suddenly the worst date ever.* I keep wondering how Trinity is doing, and what she's doing, and whether or not she'd maim me with that tire iron if I stopped by. *Fuck. I don't even know the girl and she's already under my skin.*

I hated seeing her like that. Sure, I don't like to see any woman cry, but the way she was hanging on to me, anchoring herself to me as though I were a life preserver, fucked with me more than usual. Each time I've excused myself from the table to piss, I've pulled out my cell, brought up Trin's contact info, and typed and deleted more text messages than I care to admit.

Me: *Hey Fruitloop, just wanted to see if you're alright?*

Delete.

Me: *Hey, Trin. I hated seeing you like that today, here if you wanna chat.*

Delete.

Me: *You okay?*

Delete.

Me: *God you're fucking me up. I need to know you're ok.*

Delete. Delete. Delete.

After managing some passably flirty conversation and enduring the longest meal of my life, Macy and I are both finally finished our pasta. I'm hoping she doesn't want dessert so we can get the hell out of here.

"I'm too stuffed. I'm gonna pass on dessert," I say, rubbing my gut, hoping she goes along and agrees.

"Oh, well, I've got a little room. I'm not completely stuffed yet," she winks, thinking she's clever.

Not interested. God. I'm such a dick. I've wanted in this girl's pants forever, and here I am, about to pass on this golden opportunity. *What the actual fuck is wrong with me?* I've never had this happen to me before where, rather than wanting to take a woman back to my place and bury myself balls deep, I simply want to drive her home.

"You wanna get out of here? Maybe grab some dessert at my place?" Macy's sultry voice breaks the silence that has fallen between us.

"Actually, I need to head back into work. I have an emergency," I spew and it's complete bullshit. Macy probably knows it, too, but I'm praying she lets it be. She knows full-well that I'm a mechanic; what "emergency" can't wait 'til morning? I should have said a friend was in trouble, something more believable.

"Oh, boo. I was hoping you'd cover my body in chocolate frosting like a yummy cake. And then gobble me all up," she giggles, and it sounds like nails on a chalkboard. I swear to Christ, I have to hide a laugh. *Do I really fall for this shit?*

Yes. Yes, I do. I'm an idiot.

"Maybe another time," I offer, before signalling the waiter. "Sorry, Macy. A part I've been waiting on was delivered and I really need to make sure it fits before tomorrow morning."

"Well, if you get done early maybe you can come by and we can play 'see if the part fits'," she purrs, and I swear to all that's holy, I, Hendrix Hills, in this moment, vow to raise my standards in regard to the women with whom I keep company.

Now, I have to convince a certain girl that she wants my *company.*

18

Trinity

"YOU SURE YOU'RE okay, Trin?" Shannon asks, filling my glass with more red wine in our booth at Stonewalls. A candle flickers on our table.

"Yeah, I'm just sad. I keep checking my phone hoping Andrea has texted, but she hasn't. I'm really worried." I didn't go into too many details with Shannon, but she's met Andrea a few times, having come to a couple of our group's family therapy nights, and she now knows things have progressed with Andrea's disease. Andrea had said earlier it was all right for me to let Shannon know, since they'd met. She knows I tell Shannon everything, and we both know Shannon would never say anything to anyone else. Besides, I need to vent. After Hendrix dropped me off, I called Shannon right away, telling her I needed drinks and a shoulder to cry on tonight.

Thinking of Hendrix just now makes my heart rate accelerate. The way he was with me today was unlike anything I would have expected. It took everything in me to not unleash all my worries onto his big, thick, and, might I say, solidly sexy shoulders. Being in his arms felt right; he felt right. *God, it felt good being close to him like that.* I should text him and thank him again, but I think better of it as Shannon distracts me and returns me to the present.

"I'm sure Andrea's fine. She'll text in the next day or so. I bet she and Simon are coming to terms with everything. I have a feeling that if things weren't going so well you'd have heard from her by now."

"I guess you're right, I would have. So, let's consider the silence a sign that things must be going well." I raise my glass bottoms up and take a huge sip, the smooth flavour of Inception Deep Layered Red dancing across my tongue.

"We need to get your mind on something else or you're going to be a sloppy drunk soon," Shannon laughs, taking a sip from her own glass. "What's the deal with that new ogre in the garage?"

I roll my eyes and change the subject.

After another bottle of wine and some much needed laughter, we share a cab to my house, then she carries on to hers.

Before crawling into bed a couple of hours later, my phone buzzes. I have a text.

Expecting it to be Andrea, I swipe it immediately, the anticipation killing me. When I see it's from Hendrix, a different kind of anticipation takes over.

Hendrix: *Hey, I wanted to check in. Hope you're holding up, friend.*

Me: *Hey, I'm holding. Thank you again for today. I hope your shirt survived.*

Hendrix: *What are friends for? Yeah it's all good. A bit of an ungodly stain in the middle now tho. Luckily I own a hundred more t-shirts.*

Me: *Hey! I offered to wash it.*

Hendrix: *If you want to check out my chest again, friend, just say the word. I kinda like when I catch you looking at me ;)*

Oh, my God. He did not just call me out. There's no way he's caught me. I'm a pro spy! I laugh aloud, and it feels good. I'm starting to think maybe we can be friends. *Maybe. At least he's entertaining.*

Me: *I'll have you know, I have no desire to see your chest without its* *shirt on, and I do not check you out! And stop calling me friend. We don't even know each other!*

Hendrix: *Wow, too many exclamation marks!!!!!!!!! Am I getting you excited?!!!!!!! LOL We ARE friends!!!!!!!!!!!!!!!!!! What do you want to know about me so you can just accept it?*

Rolling my eyes, I type furiously, having way too much fun with the innuendos with him. It's been so long since I felt even a little giddy over a man. Although I know we could never be more than friends, it's nice to have a guy to flirt with. You know, to keep me on my toes in case I ever really do decide to have at it again. After today, the idea doesn't seem quite as far away as it did yesterday. Pushing my thoughts from drifting back to Andrea, I read the next text instead.

Me: *What's your favourite colour?*

Hendrix: *Green. What are you wearing?*

Me: *Ignoring. Green is disgusting. Mine's orange. What's your favourite movie?*

Hendrix: *Die Hard. What's your favourite position?*

Me: *Friends don't tell friends that!*

Hendrix: *See I knew we were friends :)*

Me: *Urgh! Going to sleep now. See you at shop tomorrow*

Hendrix: *Does this new friendship mean I'm forgiven and we'll talk now?*

Me: *I guess. But don't push it. Keep the chocolates for your girlfriend.*

Hendrix: *I don't have a girlfriend, but I like when you fish like that. Makes me feel wanted.*

Me: *You're impossible. Goodnight.*

Hendrix: *Night, Fruitloop*

And for the first time in two years, I fall asleep with a smile on my face, and don't wake up thinking it's all just been a bad dream.

19

Trinity

"If I'm able to sneak out at a reasonable time, I'll make sure I stop by," I tell Andrea over my Bluetooth. She just invited me over for dinner tonight with her, Simon and a few of their friends, but with it being a holiday I already had plans with the Flynns. Now she's trying to get me to at least come for coffee and dessert.

"Try to escape if you can, but if you can't, I guess I'll understand. We'll just have to go for an extra long coffee on Friday. I have a lot to fill you in on."

"Yes, you certainly do. I still can't believe how long you left me hanging. But, yeah, that sounds good. Chances are I won't make it, but thank you for the invite. I hate to miss it, and I miss you. Besides, you keep bragging about that pumpkin pie of yours," I laugh, as I pull into a spot near Dex and Tillie's.

"Best pie ever, and you're missing out," she teases, knowing pumpkin is my all-time favourite.

"Now, that's just mean, you witch."

"You know it," Andrea chuckles.

"Whatever. I'll text you either way, but I'm here and I better go. Looks like I'm the last to arrive," I tell her, scanning the area and noticing familiar cars parked all over.

"Sounds good, sweetie. Tell the family 'hi' from me, and have fun."

"Will do. Talk soon."

"Bye." She hangs up and I turn the car off.

It's Thanksgiving weekend, admittedly my favourite holiday. Every year, Aunt Tillie cooks a huge-ass turkey and we all come together for dinner. The guys watch sports and we ladies chat and drink a lot of wine. It's been a couple of weeks since Andrea told Simon everything and, like I'd hoped, Simon took the news well and he's been amazingly supportive. He even came to the last family group therapy session, which didn't give Andrea and I much of a chance for our usual girl talk afterwards. I need to hear the full details of how it went down exactly, but I know she'll fill me in when she can. All I know is that it went well and that he's been taking good care of my friend, as I knew he would. He's a wonderful man and I'm relieved that Andrea was able to open up to Simon and for him to have been understanding.

Walking into Dex and Tillie's, my senses are immediately on overload. The smell of roasting turkey permeates the air, along with the subtle hints of sage and rosemary that are the key ingredients of Dex's secret stuffing recipe (the one he refuses to share).

"Happy Thanksgiving," I shout, stopping in the hall to remove my shoes and jacket, but I leave my sweater on. It's not too chilly out yet, but there's a definite bite in the autumn air, and I know from experience that we ladies will be taking our wine and sitting out back around the fire at some point.

"I thought I heard the door," Tillie calls, peeking around from the kitchen. "Come in, sweetie." I make my way to the kitchen to kiss Aunt Til, and am about to poke my head into the living room to say "hi" to the guys, when I suddenly hear Hendrix's deep timbre rumbling over the men's laughter. *I didn't know he'd be here. Shit. Why didn't he say anything when we were texting this morning? Sneaky bastard.*

Rather than popping in to greet the boys, I slide over to Tillie double-time to talk, because I'm not quite ready to face the feeling of excitement that's overtaken my body knowing Hendrix is here today. *God, I need to shake the feelings I'm having for him right the hell now.* The last thing I need is to get involved with my boss.

Yeah…that's it—he's my boss*—so he's off limits.* That's the perfect excuse for why I cannot afford to develop feelings other than friendship for him. It just wouldn't be a good idea career-wise. It's not because I'm a chickenshit, that I fear losing the way he looks at me, how that would immediately change once I told him I'm HIV-positive; no, certainly not.

Okay, I'll come clean. Seeing him looking at me any differently would destroy me. I would never want to do anything to jeopardise the way he sees me. For now, there's a hunger behind his eyes when we're together and it's a look that makes me feel wanted, almost special, like he only has eyes for me. Even if I know he's got eyes for a lot of women, from what I hear, I enjoy thinking this way more than I like to admit.

Over the last few weeks since he first texted me, Hendrix and I have definitely come a long way from our first meeting. We laugh, a lot. He drives me crazy with his flirty comments (which I secretly love, of course) and best of all we text for a few minutes before bed every night. The smug bastard is right. We are friends. And I haven't felt so light and settled in a long time. *Who knew having Hendrix in my life would fill a void I didn't even want to admit was there?*

"Aunt Tillie, what on earth is Hendrix doing here? How come no-one told me?" I ask, not meaning to sound accusatory, but it kind of comes out that way.

"What do you mean? We have the guys from Ignition over for Thanksgiving every year. He's part of the shop now, I'd say, being part-owner with Dex." She looks at me like I'm crazy.

"No, I know. I guess I just would have liked a little notice so I could be prepared," I let slip, and then cover my mouth. Tillie is way too perceptive to let that slide, and is about to call me out in: 5, 4, 3, 2, 1…

"All right. Spit it out. What's with the focus on Hendrix? Your uncle sees the way you look at that boy. Now, Trin. Tell me."

"*Nothing.* We've become friends, I guess, and he's pretty hot as I'm sure you know, and…I guess he makes me a little nervous. I haven't reacted—or allowed myself to react—to anyone in a really long time, so I'm freaking out. And I just like to know when he'll be around so I can make sure to have my game-face on," I blurt in one breath, which causes Til to burst out laughing.

"Oh, dear. You're quite smitten, my little kitten, aren't you? This calls for wine," she says, grabbing two glasses from the cupboard. Our attention is drawn to the living room where we hear a loud cheer and see the guys high-five-ing as the Blue Jays take the lead in Game 3 of the series.

I don't give Aunt Tillie an answer; I don't need to. Instead, I take in Hendrix. He's wearing distressed blue jeans and a long-sleeved Hurley shirt that hugs him in all the places I'd like to visit. *God, I wish he'd kiss me already.* I swear we've come close a few times and if I wasn't me, I'd lean up one of these times and give myself a taste of what I imagine would be like nothing else I've ever had. But thinking of kissing him, as innocent of an act as that normally is, makes Jared's words resurface as though it were yesterday: *"Before we kissed. You should have told me. I hate fucking surprises. I mean…fuck! We've kissed!"* and *"…you have* AIDS, *for Christ's sake!* I *could have it."*

As these memories darken my mind, I remember why kissing Hendrix can never be *my* reality. Why I'll never be the girl who's confident enough to make the first move, even if I wanted to.

"I think it's wine time, sweetheart. Everything's on track for now. Go sit out back," Tillie says, and I'm relieved to get out of my head.

Right on cue, my older cousin, Nadia, and Shannon come bustling through the swinging door which connects the kitchen and formal dining room.

"Trinny! You're here! Didn't hear you come in." Shannon comes to give me a big squeeze.

"I can't believe you beat me here. You're always late," I smile, taking in her cute grey sweater dress. "You look great. I'm borrowing this soon."

"Anytime," she smiles. "I think Tillie's onto me and my tardiness. She asked me to pick up a few bottles of wine, so I knew I had to get here early, being the one in charge of the most coveted goods in all of Thanksgivingland. Well, along with Dex's stuffing, of course." She peeks into the oven. "Are you sure this velociraptor will feed all of us? Jeez, Til. That's a big bird."

"Oh, shush. It's not that big, besides I make soup tomorrow with the leftovers, once I make sure you kids have had enough."

"Well, personally, I love turkey so I'm happy it's a big one." I pat my belly, moving to take a peek for myself.

"Will you two stop opening the oven door? You're letting all the heat out! Out with you, go have some wine. Everyone out of my kitchen," Tillie shrieks.

After giving me a hug, Nadia gets right down to business. "Let's go sit out back. I need some girl- and wine time. I'm beat." She sweeps her hand across her forehead. "The tables are all set, and I even added some of those cracker thingies that the kids and I found at Dollarama. They aren't only for Christmas anymore," she says proudly. "The kids are down watching Halloween movies, the big babies have their game on, and now Mama needs to unwind from all that work."

"Armed and ready," Shannon jokes, holding up two bottles of Inception, my favourite red wine.

I'm about to comment, but then I feel Hendrix entering the room before I see him.

"Hey, Fruitloop." He palms my exposed neck with his large warm hand, running a thumb along my skin, a move he's coined over the last week, one I secretly love. *Sexy bastard.* "When did you get here? I didn't hear you come in." He stands beside me, his calloused hand still in place.

"Oh, you guys were pretty involved in the game when I got in. I didn't want to interrupt," I say sheepishly. "I didn't want to risk getting a bad rep and being blamed if they missed the ball or something as I was saying hello. Some people are really serious about that stuff. You know, like believing if you don't keep your eyes on the game the team won't win or whatever? I didn't want to chance it..." *Holy shit, I'm loopy!* I'm just rambling on and on, and have no idea what the hell I'm even talking about. *See? Preparation is everything around this man!*

I look around the peach-coloured kitchen to see that Aunt Til, Shannon, Nadia and Hendrix are all staring at me. The women share a knowing grin, and Hendrix is simply watching me. And then he lets out a loud laugh, a deep rumble that I feel in my bones. It drifts over my body like a sweet heat, bringing my dormant senses to life. It's a reaction that he seems to elicit so easily. And it's one I haven't felt in a really long time, which only confirms what I already know: that Hendrix is dangerous for me. Despite knowing better, however, more and more I think I might want to take a risk with him anyway.

"I...I assume you've all met?" I manage to ask.

"Oh, yeah, we all met Hendrix. Trin, you neglected to tell us how hot your new boss was," Shannon blurts, like it's the most natural thing in the world to say. *Never have I wanted to throat-punch my bestie as much as I do right the hell now.*

"You think I'm hot?" Hendrix questions, and looks at me with a cocky smirk.

"No. I mean, you're alright looking, I guess." I shrug my shoulders and we all know it's total bullshit.

Running that goddamn thumb along my neck, he gloats, "You coming to join us, ladies? Game's getting good. Jays are batting next." He looks between us.

"Nah, we're heading out back for some wine time before Til puts us back to work," Shannon says, thumbing towards my auntie. "Trin, can you grab some glasses for us? Let's go, Nad. We can get the fire pit going." She leads Nadia out the back door.

"I see. Well, you all have fun," he nods, making his way to the fridge. I move to the cupboard that holds the glassware. Reaching up, I feel a cool breeze on my skin. I know my sweater has ridden up in the back. Trying to keep it pulled down, I'm stretching up to get the last two wineglasses when I feel his heat on my back. He's caged me in, and my heart begins to pound in my chest.

"Let me, Fruitloop." His words brush against my ear, the subtle smell of beer—and *him*—heightening my awareness of his proximity.

"Th—thanks," I say, coming off my tippytoes.

"No problem." He rests a hand on my hip. "That's what friends are for," he adds, while starting to rub a small circle on my exposed skin, igniting a fire so deep I feel it everywhere. He glides his thumb over my hip again, before pulling my sweater back down. "Have fun with the girls."

He kisses the back of my head, and walks out, several bottles of beer held by their necks between his fingers.

See? Really fucking dangerous.

I stand in the middle of the kitchen, stunned. Aunt Til bumps into me, trying to place a hot saucepan on the counter. She flaps a dishtowel at me. "You too! Out! Scat! Shoo!"

DINNER IS SERVED, and everything is perfect. Hendrix and I steal glances and tease each other with one-liners here and there, ones that have everyone laughing. He really does fit in with my family, and for the first time since our meeting, I'm happy Dex sold the shop to him. I know he'll do right by my uncle's life's work.

"You hot for him? You keep staring at him," my cousin, Mia, whispers, her brows raised with curiosity. I must admit, she's right. I can still feel his touch on my hip, and that kiss. My eyes keep finding him even when we're not teasing each other. It's like they're determined to seek him out, despite my willing them not to.

"No. We're just friends. I tried to dodge it, but the stupid ogre forced me into a friendship with him."

"I heard that, Fruitloop." He taps my shin under the table where he's sitting across from me. "You know you begged me to befriend you."

"Ha! Like I'd beg you for anythi—" I eat my own words before completing that sentence when I catch the sudden heat behind Hendrix's golden eyes, at the words 'beg' and 'you'. *Shit.* Apparently me begging has us both thinking about unfriend-like things. "*Friends*," I remind him.

"For now," he hisses over our plates. Luckily, everyone is looking at Gavin at this point, so they don't hear. Gavin is Nadia and Brody's eight-year-old son, who's currently doing some kind of magic trick at the end of the table with his dad's napkin, making it look like a live dove tucked in the crook of his elbow.

"Behave," I mouth at Hendrix before standing to help clear the table, taking all the empty plates and serving dishes into the kitchen before we serve coffee and dessert.

"Trin, I've got some bad news," Nadia says, grabbing my attention away from grinding the coffee beans.

"Yeesss?" I look over to her and smile. "What can I do for you, madam?" I ask, dumping the fragrant grounds into the coffee maker.

"Don't kill me, but you know how on Thanksgiving Monday we always take the kids to the pumpkin patch? Well, I have to cancel tomorrow. I have to work on a proposal. It's taking me a lot longer than I anticipated, and with having spent the time here today, I can't risk not finishing. I meant to mention it before, but I forgot. I'm sorry, but we'll have to reschedule," she says, a little deflated. I know her job has been stressful over the last few months since she was promoted to advertising coordinator at Metroland Media.

"What if I take them on my own?" I say. "I'm pretty sure I can be trusted with small humans. It'll be fun. Then the house will be quiet for you. I was looking forward to it, and I really need a candy apple in my life. Let me and the rugrats have a Trinny, Gavin and Bella day."

"Are you sure?" Nadia eyes me skeptically.

I laugh. "I know…it's odd, eh? Me actually volunteering to spend time with children? Crazy. But you forget, I get to give them back so spending the day with them is super for me," I grin.

"Okay. Well, thank you. They'll be very excited. I thought Bella was going to cry when I broke the news to her that we couldn't go."

"My pleasure. Now I'm going to go unbreak the news and become their favourite second cousin."

"I adore you, Trinity Adams. I owe you," she calls, as I turn on the coffee maker and run off to find the kids.

"Pay me in wine!" I holler back.

20

Hendrix

"CAN I HELP you, sir?" a voice calls from behind the wooden post I've been leaning against for the last fifteen minutes (looking like some creep, I'm sure).

"Uh, no," I'm about to say, but then change my mind. I figure I might as well grab what we need before they get here, that way it'll be my treat. Shoving off the post, I move to the ticket window. "Actually, yes. Four tickets, please."

"Okay, great. What about the hayride? That's extra. Will you want to go on the hayride?"

"Hmm. Yeah, sure. Toss those in, too, please."

"Alright. How's the ten-thirty ride?"

Looking down at my phone, I see it's already ten. I can't fucking believe I'm at a bloody pumpkin patch on a holiday when I could be sleeping in. *What the hell am I thinking?* Clearly, I'm not. But after seeing Trinity's face last night when Nadia and Brody kept teasing her about not knowing what she was in for today, I knew she was nervous about bringing the kids on her own. So, when Gavin and I were playing air hockey after dessert and he asked me to come along, there was no way I could say no. I mean, how could I possibly pass up an opportunity to make even better friends with Trin? I can't wait to see the look on her face when she sees me.

"That'll work. Thanks, Phyllis," I say, handing the grey-haired woman my credit card, having read her nametag. I return to the dusty parking lot to wait near my truck. With winter coming, I've put my Camaro in storage; there's no way my baby should be subjected to the harsh Canadian ice and snow. I'm halfway to my blue Ford F-150, when I hear Gavin's voice shouting my name.

"Hendrix! You're here! You came!" He rushes up to me.

"Hey, little man." I extend my fist so he can bump it. "I told you I'd come. And, here I am."

I look behind him for Trinity, my eyes finding her gorgeous smiling face as she makes her way over to us, Bella tiptoeing in tiny strides at her side. *Damn, she's a stunning woman with that pixie-cut, the long pink bangs sweeping across those beautiful grey eyes of hers.* Her eyes match the armour she wears, especially around me; armour that doesn't stand a fucking chance against me. "IN PERPETUUM ET UNUM DIEM". That's how long I'll wait for this girl. That's my plan.

Despite her smile, I see the underlying worry and stress she tries to hide, and I see whatever burden it is that she carries on her shoulders when she's not smiling. And the way her eyes go flat when no-one's looking. One day, when she's ready, I hope she'll let me in and I can be the reason they never go flat again. I want to be the one to always make her happy. *What the hell? Next, I'll be reciting Shakespeare and writing my own fucking sonnets.*

She's wearing tight blue jeans, those black UGG boots that all the chicks love, and a matching tight-fitting sweater that not only hugs her full chest, but highlights the white-pink tinge of her hair. She's actually pretty fucking sexy.

I try to hide the smile and the warm feeling that's taking root in my chest. There's something about this girl that calls to me.

"Hendrix. Hi! You're really here. Gavin said he invited you, but I figured you might have a billion better things to do than hanging out picking pumpkins," she beams, the smile so genuine it lights up her whole face, and it's like finding a pot of gold at the end of a rainbow. *A treasure.*

"Yeah, I…uh…hope you don't mind." I bump her shoulder. "Figured you might like the help. Some company and some man candy."

Again with the smile, the one I'm getting a serious crush on. Especially when it's aimed at me.

"Well, in that case, I would, and, yes, I'd love some. If you see any, be sure to point it out."

"Ouch. I'm wounded." I cover my heart.

"You're impossible."

"So I've been told." I put my arm around her, liking the feel of her under me way too much. I steer her towards the entrance.

"Awesome. Well, thank you. Let me just grab the tickets and we'll head in." She says, moving out of my hold.

"Already taken care of. We're on the ten-thirty hayride."

"Wow, you've thought of everything. Let me know how much I owe you," she says, reaching in her purse pulling out her wallet.

Stepping in closer, I lean down towards her. *God, she smells sweet, like sugary fruits and vanilla.* "Your money's no good here, Fruitloop. Friends are allowed to treat each other."

"Right…*'friends',*" she repeats, breathlessly meeting my stare, her eyes reflecting the same heat, and it takes everything—and I mean everything—for me not to pull her in and kiss the hell out of her.

"Thanks, Hendrix," says Gavin, staring up at us. "I'm glad we're friends."

"Yes, thank you again, Hendrix," Trin says. "I owe you a drink sometime."

"Are you asking me out on a date, friend? 'Cause I'm more than ready to take this to the next level."

"Hendrix," she whispers.

"It's the truth, Trin. I'm not gonna hide behind wanting to be friends any longer. I want more."

"I can't give you that right now," she hisses. She turns and starts walking away from me. "Come on, the kids are getting too far ahead." She nods to where Gavin and Bella are climbing the straw bales at the entrance.

"Hey! You two ready to go have some fun, my friends?" I call.

"Yes!" they both call out in unison, and run back to us.

I put my hand on the back of Trin's neck as we walk towards the woman collecting tickets for the Haunted Pumpkin Mansion.

"Sorry, Trin." I rub my favourite spot on the back of her neck.

"Don't be. I'm the one who's sorry. I wish things could be different," she says, but winds her arm around my lower back. We follow behind the kids as they tear into the haunted house. I decide to let her cryptic reply go. *For now.*

We spend the rest of the day having a blast (*at a pumpkin patch—who knew?*) and, yes, I crushed a whole lot harder on this crazy, spirited girl who continues to rock my world, especially the more she lets me see of the real her.

Now, if she'd only see me.

21

Trinity

Walking into the sterile, stark white, not-one-speck-of-colour-anywhere room to visit Andrea, I'm beyond nervous. I'm trying to control my emotions and failing miserably. She took a turn for the worse just after Thanksgiving. The last thing I want is to spend our time with me crying and unable to hold an actual conversation with one of my best friends, one of the strongest, most resilient women I've ever met.

Holding tight to the small bag of healing gemstones I brought as a gift, I adjust my face mask one last time to be sure it's covering my nose and mouth as I walk into the room. Taking a deep breath, I brace myself for what I'll find when I reach the bed closest to the window. I let out a little sigh. At least she's got a nice view, despite having to share the room with another patient.

"Hellooooo?" I call, before peering around the half-drawn white curtain. "Are you decent?"

"Even if I'm not, you better get that sweet ass of yours in here right now. It's been way too long since I've seen my chick."

Wiping my tears before she can see them, I breathe deep again and approach her bed. I pause, mid-step, as I take her in. Seeing her now-frail body lying on a bed that consumes her guts me. More lesions mar her once pale skin making her body look bruised and battered. My eyes dart around her bed, noticing all kinds of tubes and wires poking into and out of and around the woman who's become my saving grace—a friend whom—like Shannon—I've come to trust and share all my happiness and sorrows with.

I can't contain myself any longer. The dam breaks as realization that this is really happening settles in, and I start to sob. Reaching out a shaky hand out for me, Andrea coaxes me closer and I go willingly. She pulls me down onto her, tight. As I wrap my arms around her shoulders, I barely recognize the shape of this friend I've hugged so many times before. *She's disappearing.*

Crazy how things can change so quickly. For the last few months, she and I spent our after-therapy coffee talking about regular gossip and our daily lives. She'd pester me about my lack of a love life, and I lived vicariously through hers as I listened to her gush on and on about Simon. Next thing I knew, she was confiding in me about how her illness had progressed, how she now had AIDS, and how she was planning on finally telling Simon everything. Through it all, she stayed strong and confident, assuring me that she still had time even with the Kaposi's sarcoma she now had, saying that she just needed to be more careful.

And she apologized over and over again for taking so long to tell me all the details of Simon's reaction because they'd been too "busy", if I knew what she meant. I'd been so excited for her. Andrea admitted that, if anything, her telling Simon the truth had brought them even closer. They've been spending every spare moment together, making up for the time they know will one day be stolen from them. I was happy for her, despite knowing it could be short lived. I just didn't expect it to be this short.

The Friday following Thanksgiving was when everything changed. Simon texted me from Andrea's phone, telling me that Andrea had been admitted to hospital with pneumonia so she wouldn't be at therapy that evening. He said she most likely wouldn't be able to come for a while, either, not with her immune system so weakened. He also told me that she couldn't risk having visitors at that time. He swore, however, to keep me updated and he did. But even once they had the pneumonia under better control, her body just couldn't bounce back well enough for her to go home.

Andrea's been a patient at the Juravinski Hospital for almost a month now, and this is the first time she's agreed to let me come visit. Despite my protests, she asked me to respect her wishes and stay away and, reluctantly, I had. Thankfully, we'd at least texted nearly every day. But texts did not prepare me for the Andrea I now see before me.

"I thought I told you: none of this," she admonishes, pulling away and smiling. "You promised, no tears." Her voice is almost a croak.

"I'm a liar. I admit it," I say, doing my best to laugh, moving to sit in the chair beside her. The last thing I want to do is hurt her.

"I told Simon you couldn't be trusted," she wheezes, "and that together you and I'd probably set off the panic alarm with our tears and dramatics. Nurses will be running in here any second now." She also laughs, a bit of that familiar sparkle showing in her eyes.

"God, I've missed you," I blurt. "I hate Fridays without you. It's not the same." I wipe my eyes with the Kleenex Andrea's passed me.

"Yeah, I really did keep it interesting, didn't I? All my issues. Whatever do they talk about now?" she teases. "Trust me, I've missed you, too. Texting isn't the same as our post-meeting coffee-and-gossip sessions, that's for sure."

"Agreed. I pretty much just run out of there at the end, now. It doesn't feel the same," I shrug.

"Aww. I love you, too, chick."

I want to ask how she's feeling, but I don't, because it's obvious. She's dying. I can pretty much infer that she feels like crap. I don't need to make her think about it when I'm here to be a positive distraction.

"Spill," she says, cutting through my thoughts.

"Spill what?" I play dumb, or at least try.

"I wanna hear more about how much you're falling for this Hendrix person," she eyes me knowingly, "'cause if you ask me, he's totally got it bad for my girl."

"I told you, we're friends. Nothing more. You know I can't do more. Took me long enough to accept that we could even be friends."

"Bullshit. You're hiding. And trust me, Trin. It's not worth being a shadow when you deserve to be the light. And you, my beautiful girl, most definitely need to open your eyes here. I'm living proof. Did you know my boss came in yesterday?"

"No! What? He did?"

"Yeah, crazy, eh? You know what he told me? That he always thought I was a great guy, and that he regrets not being able to have met the incredible woman he now knows I am."

"Wow, how did he even know?"

"Well, I'd called HR, to see how to go about giving my notice. The next thing I knew, Simon was escorting him into my room, and I was dressed as me, hence it all became obvious." She gestures at her long auburn wig. "We'd always gotten along really well, so it was a nice surprise that it didn't change anything between us."

"Amazing. I'm really happy you got to have that closure. I know that was a huge struggle for you."

"Me too, Trin. Me too. So take my advice, please."

"Alright, lay it on me, old wise one. I might not take it, but I'll hear you out." I reach for the water jug, pouring some into the styrofoam cup sitting on the rolling hospital table, noticing Andreas's voice sounding scratchy.

"Shush you." She thanks me then takes a long sip before going on. "Think about it. You wanted Jared to see you, but he obviously had blinders on. Now, with Hendrix, I think you might be the blind one. Sounds to me like he's a good man who, so far, likes what he sees, Trin. He's been a good friend. He's trying. Not to mention, I have a good feeling about this one. Call it a dying woman's intuition."

"Oh my God, don't say that. That's terrible," I fuss.

"Relax, it's just a bit of bedside humour."

"Well, I'm the one at your bedside, and that isn't funny," I mock scold. "Now, go on already with this genius advice. I'm riveted."

"You're such a brat sometimes."

"It's what makes us click," I smirk.

"Anyway. Here's my thinking. Maybe you need to let him in a little." Andrea cocks her head, eyes pleading with me.

"I can't. I'm scared," I admit. "Petrified actually. He's too intertwined into my life now—the shop, with Dex and the boys, with me…he's a great friend, you're right. And my feelings do cross the line, believe me. It's hard for them not to, he's way too hot for his own good. But I tamp those feelings down because the thought of hurting him destroys me. He deserves so muc—"

She cuts me off. "Don't you think he deserves to decide what he deserves, or what he wants?" she challenges. "Maybe he'll surprise you, Trin. Some people do. I've met two men, no less, who have recently surprised the shit out of me. And you want to know the ridiculous thing? Sometimes we walk around playing victims, thinking we're the only ones subject to stigmatizing and assumptions, but you know what? I think sometimes we're our own worst enemies. In this case, Trin, I say you need to see where it goes and not be so closed-minded. Jared was a dick, but Hendrix doesn't deserve to be punished because of some asshole from years ago," she says, like she hasn't just given me the biggest platter of food for thought I've ever had.

I spend the next couple of hours with Andrea, laughing, crying, and soaking up every minute of time I can with this incredible human being. Before leaving, we make plans for me to visit again in a few days.

Now to go home and try not to choke on the piece of humble pie she just dished out to me.

22

Trinity

I PAY AND thank the Uber driver before slipping out of the woman's Honda Accord in front of Ignition Inc. Walking through the glass entry door, I feel lighter than I have in a long while. I had a really good visit with Andrea, and I'm confident that somehow I'll make peace with the inevitable.

I'm looking forward to seeing Hendrix right now. Maybe he'll give me one of those hugs of his I love so much. Nothing beats the way his strong arms envelop me, the way his smell sticks to my clothes when I reluctantly pull away from the cocoon his body makes around me. *Maybe I* will *start working on letting my guard down with him, somewhat? Andrea's probably right…*

Stepping into the lobby, my good mood immediately vanishes because of the ogre that lives inside Hendrix. He doesn't often come out, but when he does, it's a complete one-eighty from the man I've come to call friend.

"You're late," he scowls from behind the counter, as the door chime rings above my head. The door closes behind me, and my good mood and thoughts about moving on with my life are now apparently fleeing for the parking lot. I scowl back.

"Sorry. My car wouldn't start again, and the Uber was slow." I shrug my shoulders, making my way towards the sexy man-o'-anger.

After I left Andrea, my piece of shit car wouldn't start—again. I know I was supposed to ask Joe to tune it, but I never brought it up. Besides, it's been working great since Hendrix put a new alternator in it a few weeks ago. I knew the shop was booked solid with appointments today, and there was no way I was going set them back any further on account of me, so I left it in the hospital parking lot.

"Call next time," he grits, annoyed. *Is he freaking kidding me right now?* This is the last thing I need after the emotional morning I've had. He better prepare for battle if he thinks I'm going to take his crappy mood.

"Jesus, I was ten minutes late, boss. I didn't think I needed to call in for that. An hour late, sure, but not ten minutes. I mean let's be seri—" I cut myself off as he stomps around the counter to stand in front of me.

"For a ride, Fruitloop. I meant call for a ride. You know I'd come pick up your sweet ass in a heartbeat," he says innocently, like his comment was the most natural thing to say. "Can we work now?" he asks, and it's then I realize I've been standing there fish-mouthed, staring at him.

"You had me ready to take your head off, and then you say that? Jesus, you are impossible."

"So I hear. A lot. Can we work, then, now that you're here and I know you're safe and I don't gotta worry about you. It's a busy afternoon and I have back-to-back appointments. Got shit to do. And I know you're not about to tell me where you've been or anything, but I can tell you've been cryin' again and I hate that look in your eyes. It pisses me off. So let's get to work, so I can bang some shit." He moves to return to the shop but I reach for his arm, stopping him. Turning back, he steps forward and looks down at me.

"I'm sorry. I didn't mean to worry you. We can get back to work now. It's why I took the Uber. I knew you guys were swamped."

"No. You call. Always," he grunts, and I nod in agreement.

"And you're right, I'm not ready to talk about any of it yet. I don't know if I ever will be. But I'll try harder to be a better friend," I say honestly, because he deserved at least that.

Placing his palms on each side of my face, he stares at me and I see it: the worry he felt wondering where I was, even if it was only ten minutes. I'm never late, and I really should've called. Lesson learned. I can see that Hendrix only transforms into an ogre when he's worried. And also that Hendrix doesn't deserve to pay for the sins of the past.

"One day, you're gonna talk to me, Trinny. And I'll promise you, I'll fucking listen. You just gotta try me, baby."

"Sorry," I whisper, leaning into his touch and closing my eyes.

"Yeah, you said that. Don't. Do. It. Again. Call." He drops his hands and walks away, a satisfied look on his face. Clearly he enjoys the reaction he elicits from me.

Leaving the computer to start up QuickBooks, I make my way to the staffroom intent on making a fresh pot of coffee for the waiting room since we'll have many clients coming in and out, along with making my own afternoon tea. Walking into the tiny galley-style kitchenette, I see that not only is the coffee already percolating, but my favourite mug is also sitting on the counter, an Earl Grey teabag resting unwrapped inside along with a spoon, all ready to go. Smiling, I go to fill the electric kettle. Picking it up, I'm shocked to find it's already been boiled and is still fairly hot. Hitting the boil button again, I can't hide the giddy feeling I get knowing that Hendrix did this for me. That he was thinking about me. Trying not to melt on the spot, I set about refilling the courtesy tray with juices, doughnuts and a variety of K-Cups for the Keurig in the waiting room. I decide it's time I sit down and start being honest with myself about my feelings. I want Hendrix.

Now I just have to force the terrified part of me to let me have him...

23

Hendrix

"HENDRIX, I NEED to see you in my office!" Flynn bellows out the reception door.

"Ohhh, I think Junior Bossman's in trouble," Joe mutters from his bay, where he's replacing the starter in a shitbox Acura.

"Shut up, man. He probably just wants to make plans for the car show I volunteered for. Figured I'd help you fuckers get some more business with my awesomeness."

"You wish. Besides, I think only Trin and Flynn are going this year. She made some crazy computer presentation thing. It's more articulate and to the point than any of us would ever be. So consider yourself in shit, bud," Joe chuckles, before rolling under the car with the replacement part.

"You wanted to see me, Flynn?" I say, standing at his office door.

"Yeah, come on in and close the door behind ya, would ya?" he asks.

Stepping in, I close the door. *Fuck, maybe I am in shit.*

"Have a seat." He gestures to the vacant and worn leather armchair in front of his desk. "Been thinkin'," he starts, his hand stroking his beard as he pauses, contemplating his words.

"This thing with you and Trin. It's not gonna affect her working here if things go to shit, will it?" he asks, not beating around the bush.

It's a trait I admire, one my dad possessed, too. One I wish I had when it came to Trinity.

"Not sure what you mean, Flynn. We're…friends." I sit back, crossing my legs and resting my elbows on the arms of the chair.

"Bullshit. I see the way you two eyeball each other, like you can't wait to be alone. Trust me, I look at Tillie the same way. And I saw your hands all over her at Thanksgiving. So no bullshit. I need you to tell me that I don't have to worry about her. That if things don't work out, she'll have a place to live and a job here even after you take complete ownership."

"I'm kinda pissed you even have to ask me, Flynn. I think I've proven I'm not some asshole. Besides, I already agreed to everything you asked. I'd never fuck her over."

"You're right, but I ain't gonna apologize. She's my family, and Til, the kids and I are all she has, so damn straight I'm gonna ask. Gotta make sure she's okay before I give you my blessin' and help you out where I can. I like you, son. I really do. But I hear you boys talk, and I know you ain't got no shortage of girls to pick from. I just don't want my Trin to be something to pass the time. She's not that kind of girl."

"First off, she has me, too, Flynn," I say. "I've grown to really care about her and I'd never fuck her over like that. Ever. No matter what happens or doesn't happen between us. Second, I haven't been able to think about any girl other than Trin since we met and she threatened to clobber me. She's got me fucked up like I've never been over a girl before. I feel like a fucking excited teenager half of the time," I admit, a bit annoyed that we're even talking about this, despite the fact that I totally get where he's coming from. "But right now all she wants from me is friendship. I don't think you've got anything to worry about, unless I can convince her otherwise."

"Trust me, kid. My niece does not just see you as a friend. She may be putting out signals that that's all she wants but give her a little more time and keep doing whatever it is you're doing, 'cause let me tell ya, it's working. I haven't seen Trinity smile or laugh as much as she does when you're around in quite some time. It's a sight to see."

"That all?" I ask, standing.

"No. I want you to go with Trin to the car show in Toronto next month. Drive her, and help her out with her presentation. You okay to do that?" he asks, grinning up at me.

"Definitely."

Walking out, I can't hide the smile that's tugging at my lips. I feel like I just got the permission I needed to finally go after my girl.

24

TRINITY

AFTER I FINISHED helping Hendrix reorganize the storage room, I did an inventory of parts and supplies, made a list of items to order Monday morning, changed Beast's litter, took the used oil filters to the outdoor disposal bins, scheduled the waste pick-ups for next week, and—to top it all off—I took care of payroll, sent out invoices, paid bills and did the banking.

Now I'm exhausted. The last thing I feel like doing is going out on some stupid double date. I'd rather spend my Friday night riding the couch with Netflix and a bottle of red wine. *And maybe even Hendrix.*

I'm willing to admit that he's wearing me down. It's getting harder and harder to resist that man. All week, things have been escalating between us, the flirting has definitely amped up on both our parts. Like, today, he was just so…just so…*him*. So flirty, but also so witty about it. How did he turn the tables on me, making me admit shit? *The big jerk…*

"Hey, Fruitloop. Wanna come play with my compressor?" Hendrix asks, a wicked smile on his face, and I know I flush because I can feel the heat on my cheeks. This man and his dirty little digs drives me loopy.

"What? No! Hendrix! Friends do not play with other friends' air compressors." I put my tea down on the desk, knowing I'm likely to spit it out if

this conversation continues. "Besides, I'm busy. I'm making sure the minions get paid," I say, and finish inputting Joe's shift times.

"But it's pretty and it feels so good," he whines, coming closer. Like it's magnetically attracted, his hand leaps to the back of my neck.

"I imagine it does," I say without a thought, relaxing into his touch. Realizing my mistake, I inhale and pull away.

"Aww, you do *imagine me, Fruitloop. I bet you see me touching you in your dreams, pretending what it'll be like when I finally get my hands on you."*

"No," I lie. "God, you're impossible."

"But undeniably irresistible."

"I know! Believe me, I know," I yelp. "Shit. No. I mean, no, you aren't. You're annoying and repulsive."

"Seems like I might be more irresistible than not, eh, Trinny? The way your chest is moving right now, that pink flush coming up all over your skin, these goosebumps…" he runs a finger along my arm. "Yeah, I'm going with you finding me irresistible. And I can't wait until you give in and let me show you how irresistible you are, too," he whispers right against my ear before walking away.

Smug bastard.

"Oh, and Trin? One last thing," he says. "This compressor really is pretty fucking cool. I've already used it to change seven sets of winter tires. I really think you'd like my power tool if you gave it a chance." He winks and I toss my pen at his retreating head. Unfortunately, he makes it back into the garage unscathed while I sit there in my office a smitten, damp mess.

The creaking of the stairs leading up to my apartment shakes me from my Hendrix fog. Placing my glass of Inception on the counter, I brace for Hurricane Shannon dressed as Date-Night Barbie as she barges through my door.

"Hey, hey! I'm here to make you even prettier, if that's at all possible," she whoops. She gestures to the huge makeup case she's carrying as she passes, heading straight for my room.

"Oh, great," I feign, following behind, but not before scooping up my drink, the bottle and the empty wineglass I had set out for Shannon.

"Oh, don't be such a suck. You promised you'd be my wingwoman tonight. I think I really like McHot," Shannon says, rifling through my closet and tossing clothes all over.

Rolling my eyes, I remind her of some facts she's clearly missed. "You're right, but a key concept was that *'you and I'* would go out. When did that translate into a blind double-date? I don't date. We know this. So, no, I'm not excited or getting all dolled up to meet some guy I'll have zero interest in." I cross my arms over my chest in revolt, my mind flashing to the image of Hendrix flirting with me earlier, recalling the way his touch electrified my skin when he ran his finger along my arm.

"Listen, I'm in the mood for a little Bearded Burglar. It's been scandalously too long since I've been laid. Hell, you need to get robbed, too, sistah, but I'll tell you what. We'll go to Voltage and meet McHot and Co., but if you absolutely hate the guy you can bail. Fair?"

I swear the only thing I heard was "Bearded Burglar".

"Jesus, Shannon, tell me that you didn't just call the guy's dick that? What are we, fourteen and reading Cosmo for the first time? Yuck." I wiggle my shoulders, weirded out.

"Are you saying I'm too old to speak like that? Shit, I better stop listening to my young hires at the salon, they're corrupting me. Here I thought I was becoming cool again. They told me I could pull it off," she shrugs, laughing, and I follow suit because this woman is insane sometimes.

"If this is any indication of how our evening's going to go, then it looks like we're in for a bumpy night. Just promise me you won't use anymore weird dick names. I might stay a little longer," I joke, finishing the last drops of my wine.

I fail to mention that the only reason I agreed to go on this double-date is that I'm hoping it will lead to that asshole-of-an-ex of hers, Mario, officially getting booted from the picture. He keeps managing to weasel his way back into Shannon's good graces and it's time she left him behind for good.

Half an hour later, my outfit is Shannon-approved: an off-the-shoulder black knit shirt with a silver skull on the front, paired with dark-wash skinny jeans and black kitten-heeled ankle boots. We've gone with light make-up and made my hair all edgy with whips and a few spikes at the back.

"You look freakin' hot, Miss Trin. Mystery dude is gonna think it's his lucky night."

"You look beautiful, too, Shannon. I love that dress. The green looks great against your tan and that black hair. McHot is going to be all over you."

"That's the idea."

Seeing our taxi pull up, I lock my apartment door and vow to try to have a good time tonight. Despite my reluctance, I owe it to Shannon. She's been the bestest friend I could ever have asked for, and if this is what she asks of me in return, then it's the least I can do for her. And also for Andrea, because I know she'd want me to be out enjoying my life, to be out tonight kicking up my heels. *Now more than ever before.* Shaking my head, I don't allow thoughts of Andrea lying all skinny in her hospital bed to consume me. Instead, I silently vow to have a good night out in her honour.

"I'm having big drinks," I say, "and you'd better dance with me. I don't care how cute this guy of yours is. You can let him 'rob' you," I air quote, "or whatever you called it, later on when I leave."

"And this is why I love you." Shannon holds my hand as we scamper down to the waiting cab.

"Where to?" the cabbie asks once we're in.

"Voltage!"

...where I get a pretty big shock.

25

Hendrix

AGREEING TO BE Cannon's wingman was not how I planned on spending my Friday night. *Nope, not at all.*

I had every intention of asking Trinity if she wanted to come over to my place, maybe grab some takeout and watch a couple of movies. I'd been building up the nerve to ask her all day when the jackass I'm now waiting for at the bar sent me a text reminding me I'd agreed meet him at Voltage tonight for a dreaded double-date, therefore ruining my would-be plans with Trinity. *Fuck, I was pissed that I'd agreed to this.* I guess Cannon met this girl at The Dugout when he was watching the Jays try to win a spot in the World Series.

To say things have changed drastically since I agreed to this shit would be an understatement. I'm not in the market for random pussy anymore. That in itself tells me I'm all kinds of fucked up over this girl, and you know what? I couldn't care less. I'll gladly admit it, the only woman I wanna spend any time with these days is Trinny.

This week has been incredible. She's been giving it back to me just as good as I've been giving it. Like on Tuesday night when I finally fixed that damned car of hers once and for all…

"Fruitloop, do me a favour?" I call into the reception area where she sits doing her thing. Fuck, what a beautiful woman; a timeless beauty

with those big grey eyes and long lashes, and that smile that stops me dead in my tracks. *She's wearing this huge wool sweater wrapped around her tiny form. I don't blame her, it's pretty cold in there—the November weather's definitely upon us—but too bad that old sweater hides her sweet curves. Her pinkish bangs are swept across her face the way I love, and Beast is sitting on the counter beside her while she strokes his back.* Lucky little bastard.

"Sure, but I don't give out favours to just anyone who asks, you realize?" she says, then slaps her hand over her open fish-mouth, realizing how it came out.

"Nice, you're takin' a page from my book," I say. "But I'm assuming I'm one of those who qualifies for favours, though, right?" I ask, and her cheeks turn a shade of red I adore on her.

"Shut up, you know what I meant. So, what do you want me to do?" She looks at me, eyes widening again, realizing her mistake.

"Jesus, Fruitloop, you're killing me here. The fantasies are running on overdrive. Oh, the things I want you to do to me."

"Hendrix! Friends don't say shit like that!"

"Well, stop trying to be just friends and let me cross the line, then. Honestly, though, this was all on you." I raise my hands, as if innocent. "All I asked was if you could do me a favour."

"Grr. You're just twisting my words," she says, ignoring my bit about being more than friends.

"I'd rather twist something else, if you'd let me," I quip.

"You're impossible!"

"So you keep telling me. Now can you please grab your piece of shit car and drive it into my bay? I wanna give her a good tune up," I say, moving closer. She stares at me, her wide eyes running up and down the length of my body. I see them darken as if she might be fantasizing about me, the little minx.

"Eyes up here, friend," I say, using her line from months ago, having

caught her in the act of checking me out.

"Urgh. You drive me crazy!"

"Oh, I wanna drive you, Trinny. Trust me, I plan on it." I mutter the last part. "Meetcha in the bay," I call cheerily as I walk back into the shop.

"Hey, bud. What's with the stupid grin?" Cannon comes up behind me and slaps my back, yelling to be heard over the sound of Dave Grohl singing "The Best of You". Turning in my stool at the bar, I fist bump him.

"Nothing. Just sitting here, waiting on your ass. How's it going?" I ask, chuckling when I notice he looks a bit too giddy for this date shit. Naturally, being the awesome friend I am, I push. "Aww, and don't you look pretty this evening. That why you're late?" I laugh, eyeing him up and down, making a point to give him a slow, approving nod as I go with an appreciative whistle. He's wearing a black button-down with jeans and brown boots. His black hair is spiked in the front and shaved close at the sides. I can tell he likes this girl; he never wears anything other than t-shirts, even to the club. "Don't worry. You're worth the wait," I rib him again about my twenty minutes wait.

"Shut up, man. You're just jealous my girl actually wants to date me," he says, lobbing a low one, and it hits the nerve he intended. *Asshole's lucky I don't swat him upside the head for being such a perceptive prick.*

"Leave that shit alone, Can. You've got no clue what the fuck you're sayin'. I'll get the girl. I always do. You just focus on your date, okay, pancake?" I pat the side of his cheek before taking a long pull from my Heineken, and passing Cannon his.

"Thanks, asshole," he says, taking the beer. "I see you managed to get most of the grease off your hands for the occasion. And you look mid-way decent, considering you're an ugly fucker."

"I sure did." I hold my hands out on display. "But that's

ly 'cause your mum's expectin' me later and she's germaphobe," I jab back.

"Nice try, dick, but Mom's got standards. She'd never slum it with you," he snickers. "Cheers," he says, taking a swig. "Jesus, it's like warm piss. What the hell?" Cannon scrunches his face in disgust, his brown eyes barely visible.

"You're late. You told me eight. I gotcha a beer twenty minutes ago. Next time, don't take so long getting yourself dolled up." I salute my almost empty bottle in his direction, taking a final pull. "Cheers."

I almost drop that bottle when my eyes land on a certain pink-haired beauty who's making her way across the crowded dance floor.

"I'll be damned. There's no way..." I mutter to myself, trying to get a better look. But I lose her. I scan the place, leaning up taller in my seat, my brain willing my eyes to get her back. Crazy, in a place littered with people, my eyes seek then find her again immediately. Like Superman to danger—I'm drawn to her. I'm there.

"What?" Cannon asks, looking up from his phone. I ignore him, my eyes transfixed on Trinity.

"You've gotta be shitting me." Instinctively, I stand, wanting to go to her, but I don't move. I stand and watch her as her body moves fluidly through the crowd, weaving her way to the back where I lose sight of her again amongst the dimly-lit booths and the few leather couches nestled around a fireplace and sidebar.

"They're here," Cannon's voice interrupts, shouting over The Chainsmoker's "Don't Let Me Down", ending my perving. "She said they'd meet us at the back. They got us a booth, the second-to-last one. Grab your beer. Let's go."

Shit, my palms suddenly feel sweaty. Trin's over there. The last thing I want is for her to see me with Cannon's girl's friend and think it's more than it is.

Which is nothing. Especially after how good things have been going between us. Not only is Trin funny and beautiful, she's also got a huge heart, and drives me crazy with her sass and those fucking curves of hers. I can't wait for the day when I can finally get my hands on her. It's fucked up, but I haven't been with a chick since Katie. Every time I've gone out with the guys, the last thing on my mind was pussy. Well, other than Trinity's. I can't stand the thought of her seeing me out with another girl. Maybe I should tell Cannon I'll find him in a few minutes so I can go talk to Trin first? Just so she knows it's not a date, just a favour for a friend. *Wait. Who the hell am I? Didn't she friend-zone me? Hasn't it been her keeping me sidelined? Right. Fuck that. Let her see me.*

Grabbing the fresh cold beer the flirty male bartender delivered moments ago, I follow Cannon as he cuts across the overly-crowded floor, nodding to people I recognize but not stopping to talk as a few guys clap me on the back, trying to get me to stop and chat. My sole focus is all on finding Trinity. I see a few girls trying to get my attention, as well, some familiar, others not, but their laughter and the loud music are barely noticeable as I continue to move, ignoring it all. Finally, at a set of four stairs, I spot Cannon waving to whom I assume is his date. Looking back over my shoulder, there's still no sign of Trinity.

Reaching the last step, I stop mid-stride. I can't hide my smile when my eyes land on the booth where Cannon has stopped.

"Well, isn't this perfect," I grin. It must be my lucky night.

Cannon's date is Trin's friend, Shannon.

What a small fucking world.

And sitting in the booth across from Shannon is Trinity.

If this isn't some kind of sign then I don't know what is. *Man, she's gorgeous,* I think as I reach the table. Don't get me wrong she's always beautiful. But tonight she's wearing a bit of makeup. Her eyes are a smoky grey, highlighted by some shimmery stuff around them. She looks sexy and sultry and I'm having a hard time not pulling her out of the booth, intent on walking us right out the front door.

"Hey, Fruitloop." I slide in next to her. "Fancy meeting you here." I nudge her shoulder, her eyes widening, a sexy grin spreading across her honey-coated lips.

"Hendrix. Hi."

"Wait, you all know each other?" Cannon asks, surprised.

"Yeah, this is Trinity." I introduce them. "Shannon is Trin's best friend. And I'm Trin's date," I smile, like a fucking Cheshire cat.

"What are you doing here?" she asks, her voice breathy, while her eyes take me in like she's having a hard time processing that I'm here. I fucking love the hunger I see in her eyes while they linger on my mouth, then travel down to my chest before they drift lower to where I've got the sleeves of my white shirt rolled up to show the ink that covers most of my arms.

"I'm here with Cannon. He promised me a hot date. And for the first time in my life, I think I'm in love with him," I say, leaning in close to her, "'cause, damn, baby, you're fucking smoking tonight," I compliment. She blushes my favourite shade of Trinity. I stare at her, my gaze drifting to her bare shoulders, and I smile at the smattering of freckles that match the few I've noticed on her nose and cheeks. "What are *you* doing here?" I ask the same of her, a shit-eating grin on my face. The answer is just as obvious, but I let her go on. *Damn, she's adorable.*

"I came with Shannon," she says, gesturing across the table to her dark-haired friend whom I met at Thanksgiving, but Shannon and Cannon appear to be in their own little world, completely ignoring us, which suits me just fine.

I need to interrupt their breakout session, though, because the opportunity to bust Cannon's balls doesn't present itself very often. Once again, being the good guy that I am, I take advantage. Waving, I get their attention. “Wait, dude.” They both stop and look at me. “We need to go,” I deadpan, keeping my face serious.

“Why? What the hell? We just got here,” Cannon says, obviously pissed.

“Yeah, but I cannot allow you two to date,” I say, pointing between them.

“And why not?” my little Fruitloop pipes in.

Looking at her pretty face, I offer her a smile before I add, “’Cause, baby, we absolutely cannot have friends named ‘Shannon and Cannon’ that date. It’s too fucking ridiculous.”

“Oh my God!” Trin claps her hands. “It never even dawned on me. Oh, God, you rhyme. I agree with Hendrix, you can never get married or have babies,” she adds, full on belly-laughing, and I adore the sound. It brings me to life. I’d have no problem if my job until the day I died was to make this woman laugh like that. Seeing her in this light—young, carefree, and happy—is a special kind of wonderful. And fuck it if I haven’t fallen hard for her.

“Easy there, Life Coach, we haven’t even had a full date yet. You can tuck the Save the Date cards back into your breast pocket,” Shannon says, and I bust a gut laughing.

“Oh, I like you. I forgot how funny you think you are. I get why you two are friends.” I nod from Shannon to Trin before passing them the drinks the server just delivered.

26

Hendrix

THE DOWNSIDE OF going to Voltage for a date is that we know too many fucking people here. More specifically, I know way too many women here. And they most certainly know me and aren't shy about letting it be known, either.

First, it was Shelby. Fuck me. I was right in the middle of telling Trin a joke. I had managed to move in extremely close, had my arm wrapped around her. Hell, I'd even rubbed that soft bare shoulder a few times and she'd let me. I was on my game and it was going well. Leaning in, I'd asked her, "What does the sign on an out-of-business brothel say?"

"Oh, God. Do I even want to know?" she'd giggled, before giving me a dirty look. It was sexy as hell, and I was completely caught up in her. "Okay, I give up, tell me," she'd said, after taking a sip of her rye and coke and thinking about the answer.

"Beat it. We're closed." I'd slapped the tabletop with my hands in a *ba-da-ba* way.

"Ha! That's hilarious!" she said, tipping her head back in laughter. It had taken all of my restraint not to lean my face into the crook of her neck and run my tongue along her slender neck, taking in her wicked scent. *Christ, I'd never seen her looking so at ease and relaxed before,* I'd thought.

I dream of this woman, I dream of touching, tasting and entwining myself with her forever. I was about to tell her another joke…and that was when I saw her. *Shelby*. And she was headed straight for us. Or rather, straight for me.

I'd felt Trinity tense up when Shelby approached the table, her huge fake tits on display for all to see. I guess that's what happens when your little black dress is a few sizes too small, a dress I might have appreciated and found sexy a few months ago, but tonight it only looked trashy. I'd rested my hand on Trin's knee to reassure her, but I could tell it was too late. The spell we'd been under was broken. Trin's walls had been summoned and it was my fault.

"Henny, hiii! I've missed you, baby," a drunken Shelby had slurred, toying with my hair while she staggered beside me. "How about you let me sit down? I could give you one of those special massages you like when I sit on your lap." She'd even winked, and I swear to God Trin gasped.

Fuck me.

After denying Shelby's many futile attempts, I'd finally succeeded in getting it through to her that I wasn't the least bit interested. Luckily, I managed to get her friend Rita's attention, and she came over and took Shelby away before things got worse.

So, now I'm asking Trinity if she wants to hear another joke, hoping I can slide us back into our happy place.

Then I feel a tongue licking my ear, and hands snaking their way around my neck and down to my chest from behind me. Turning my head sideways, I want to shout, "Are you fucking kidding me?" when my eyes make contact with Katie's. *Seriously, I'm never coming back to Voltage again.* I really need to reevaluate the company I've been keeping. Never have I been so pissed about a woman's presumptuous touch until just now. It feels dirty, and it feels wrong with Trinity beside me, her so perfect, bearing witness to the person I suddenly no longer am or want to be reminded of. Sure, we all have a past, but it seems that mine is out to fuck with me tonight.

Watching Katie make her advances, Trinity finishes her drink, knocking her glass down on the table a little louder than normal. I know she's uncomfortable and I know she won't stay if I don't stop this train wreck.

"Hendrix, you never called me," Katie pouts. "I've been coming every week. You've been hiding," she says, sliding her face into the small space that exists between Trinity and me.

Looking over at Cannon for a lifeline, the prick doesn't say shit. He just sits back like he's enjoying a fucking movie.

"I was hoping I could get another dance," Katie giggles. "I mean you and that tongue of you—"

And that's when it happened.

"Well. *I'm* ready to dance, I think. Shannon? You ready? I'm ready, more than ready. This DJ is really good, and I love all these songs," Trinity blurts, and my adrenaline spikes, knowing I'm losing her. "Let's go. That way, Hendrix can visit with all his friends in privacy and we don't need to listen to the show," she adds, waiting for Shannon to agree, not casting a second glance my way.

"You're right, the music is awesome. I'm ready," Shannon agrees, nodding her head and whispering into Cannon's ear. The asshole smiled and agreed to whatever the hell she said before he shifted to let her out. "Come on, Trin, it smells like whore over here. We need to go. And I think we need a couple of shots before we shake our booties. We look too good to ride this booth all night, anyway. And it's not every day my girl comes out," she digs, and I feel it in the pit of my stomach. It's not lost on me that Trinity doesn't have much of a social life outside of the shop and hanging out with her family. We talk everyday. I know this, and it makes the situation even worse. Because we were having fun. She was having fun, fun with me.

Of course, Katie misses the whole fucking thing, and only moves in closer after hearing that the girls are going to be leaving.

"Please let me out," Trin says, not meeting my gaze, her voice small.

"No. I like you here just fine. I want you here. Stay."

"No. I don't want to interrupt. You catch up with your…*friend*," she says, over-pronouncing the word—*our* word—and I fucking hate it. "It seems she's really excited to see you. Besides, I've monopolized enough of your time already. It's not like this was a real match-up anyway, Hendrix. Don't feel you need to hang with me; I'm not a pity date. Be with your friends, you obviously have a few of them here you can choose from. I'm good. I'm going to dance for a bit, then head home. I'll see you at the shop." She shrugs, looking a mix of pissed off and disappointed. She looks exactly how I feel.

"Bullshit, this was a—"

"Just let me out, Hendrix. I'm done."

Relenting, I give her what she wants. I stand up so she can slide out, and as soon as she does, that bitch Katie slips in.

"Have at it," Trin smiles ominously, watching Katie take her place. Then Trin bolts. And the worst part? I can't blame her. I'm such an asshole. I've never regretted my past until tonight, when it came back to slap my Fruitloop in the face.

I didn't sit with Katie. I tell her where we stand, wish her a good night, and bail.

An hour later, Cannon and I are playing pool, keeping an eye on Trin and Shannon. It turns out this night isn't a total bust, for Cannon at least. He and Shannon are going out for dinner tomorrow night. Alone.

"Your shot, man." Cannon jerks his chin at the table.

"Right, sorry." I shake my head, planning my next move. I take the shot, sinking the yellow ball in the left corner pocket. I'm about to take my next shot when I see some dude standing with Trinity's phone in his hand, the same guy who's been rubbing up on her for the last few songs. The same one I've been allowing to dance with her because so far he hasn't been pushing his luck. I know, because I've been keeping my eye on him, and he knows it, he saw me watching them. Luckily, he's been respectful.

Until now. It looks like he's typing something into her phone and all I gotta say is, it better not be his number.

Un-fucking-acceptable.

Tossing the cue on the table, I motion for Cannon to follow.

27

Hendrix

"Beat it. You're done here, bud. I'll take over from here," I say, standing behind Trin's dance partner. Her eyes go wide when she sees us approaching.

"I'm not sure that I *am* done, guy. Seems to me I was gettin' her digits. I think I'll stay awhile longer," the punk has the nerve to reply.

Stepping sideways, I nudge myself between him and Trin so I can face this piece of shit. I glare at the motherfucker, my fists clenched of their own volition, my jaw tight, body rigid. I'm ready to toss his ass, but Trin's warm hand touches my shoulder, calming me immediately.

"Hendrix. Stop. Let him be."

"No," I grit, ignoring her request.

"Yeah, Hendrix. Stop," the douchebag repeats, grinning.

"Not a chance, asshole." I step closer.

"Hendrix, please. Let's go talk," she says. I bet she says it just because she knows I'll agree. Nodding, I take a step back. This fucking gnat is lucky I'm getting my way.

"Let's go then." I clasp her hand in mine, leading us off the dance floor into the dimly lit hall, where I test a few doors until I find one that leads to a staircase.

Pushing us inside, I lock the door and take a deep breath before turning to look at her. It's time I put myself out there. I can't keep denying what I want, pretending I'm happy with not getting to hold or touch her every time desire strikes.

"Hendrix, explain what that was?" She looks up at me, irritation lacing her tone and her body language.

Well, guess what? I'm fucking irritated, too. Tired of her keeping shit from me, hiding that she feels it, too. I know it's bullshit, and so does everyone around us. We all see what's been brewing between us.

Without hesitation, I move in closer, putting us chest to chest, the closeness forcing her to stare up at me. When we're standing like this, all we can see is each other.

"Why don't you want me?" I ask, a little more harshly than I intend, but I can't help it. I'm pissed and upset. "Why choose him?" I ask, my voice hoarse due to the emotions I'm feeling. The last thing I want to do is push her too hard, but I can't risk her not hearing how I feel and ending up in another man's arms. The thought alone guts me.

"I didn't choose him or anyone. It was just a dance."

"Bullshit. Choose me." I run my hand along her cheek. "Please, Fruitloop. Choose me."

"I did. We're friends, despite my better judgment. Not sure you really needed a new friend…" She rolls her eyes, and I want to smile at her jealousy, but she's hiding again behind this friendship façade.

"I wanna be more," I respond, looking her in the eye.

"I don't." She's quick to refuse me. She looks to the side.

"Lie."

"I'm not interested in you that way."

"Another lie. We both know it. It's time to get real, Trin."

"I can't." She pauses. "I can't have you, Hendrix. I can't be what you need or deserve. I need you to see that, to respect it." A tear cascades down her cheek.

"Bullshit, baby. You're all I see, and I know you see me, too. I fucking ache at the thought of you not being with me, of us not taking this chance. Shit, Trin," I huff, exasperated, "I wanted to kill that guy. Still do. The thought that he was good enough to get your number when all I want is a chance fucks with me." *Jesus, this girl riles me up like no other.* Never have I opened myself up like this—laid my shit bare. But regardless of what happens afterwards, she's worth the risk. At least I can walk away knowing I put myself out there for her, made my intentions clear, that I took my shot.

"Hendrix," she whispers, lifting her hand to my cheek and running her fingers along my jaw.

"It's true, Trin. I want you, and I know you want me, too. I see it. Better yet, I fucking feel it. Try to tell me it isn't true. Look into my eyes and tell me."

"I do want you," Trinity surrenders, her voice a whisper. "You're what I want, too, but I can't have you, Hendrix. Please understand and trust me. It's too selfish."

"What the hell does that mean? God, baby, take me. Be selfish all you want with me, 'cause where I'm concerned, I'm greedy as fuck when it comes to you. I want it all." I cup her face in both my hands. Leaning in, I brush my thumb along her lip, where I want my lips to be…"Say yes, Trinny."

"Hendrix, I can't. Please accept it. But we're still friends."

"I won't accept that. Not ever. Tell me what's holding you back," I press.

"Please. Leave it."

"Not gonna." I stare into her grey eyes, willing her to give in. I'm pressing her, pushing her, and I couldn't give any fucks. She belongs with me. I've waited long enough.

"Tell me why, Trin," I demand a little more harshly, no room for argument.

"Please, Hendrix, don't make me tell you. Things will change forever. And you'll hate me, and the thought of…" Her lower lip starts shaking. "…of you looking at me with anything other than with that fire and lust like you always do scares me. The thought of losing that makes me sick. I wouldn't be able to handle it if that flame was extinguished. I—I like it too much. I thrive on the way you see me right now. Too much to risk losing that. I love seeing the way you are with the Trinity you think you know, not the Trinity I really am. I can't…please…" she begs, her lips curling now as huge tears stream down her beautiful face.

"Trinity." I pull her in tight, taking her body into mine, wrapping her up in a hug. "Nothing you tell me could ever change the way I see you. Not in a million fucking years. Trust me, baby, you're all I can see." I lean down and kiss her forehead, causing her to let out another loud sob.

She hooks her arms around me, pulling my head in closer. And I feel instant relief. I'm finally winning, getting through.

Standing on her toes, she ghosts her mouth over my ear. "I'm sorry, Hendrix. I can't. I like the way you see me too much to taint it."

And with that, she unwraps her arms from my neck, steps out of my embrace, unlocks the door, and storms out of the stairwell—all before I have a chance to begin to process what the hell just happened.

28

Trinity

"ARGH."

I wake, my head throbbing as though the Seven Dwarves were mining on the surface of my brain. "I'm never drinking again," I tell myself, pulling back my purple duvet cover and rubbing the sleep from my eyes.

I need water. I need Tylenol. And I need them stat.

Padding into the kitchen, my housecoat wrapped tight to fend off the cool morning air, my eyes land on my cell phone, a glass of water, two Tylenols and a note. Picking up the piece of paper, my eyes read the lines a few times.

No. No. No.

Trin,

After your stairwell incident, you and I hit the vino pretty hard once we got back to your place. I tried to convince you not to wine and text, but you're stubborn.

Take the pills, drink the water, freak out a little, then call me.

P.S It's about time you do this. You better do it, Trin. I like him, and we can double!

Love you!
Shanners

Downing down the pills, my mind flashes back to last night. To Hendrix angry on the dance floor, to the sadness in his eyes as I rejected him and denied us what we both want. The way I ran, ruining Shannon's date with McHot even more when she refused to let me leave alone. Taking my cell phone, I swipe my finger to open my text messages. The first one I send is to Shannon.

Me: *I'm sorry I'm drama. I hope you and Cannon don't hate me! Thank you for giving up getting burglarized for me. Thank you for drinking with me and being my best friend. I haven't looked at the texts I sent yet, am petrified.*

Her response comes immediately.

Shannon: *Shut up. It's what we do. Now go see your truth. Read the messages you sent, wine=truths! Xox*

The second text I read and reply to is from Andrea.

Andrea: *Can't wait to hear how the blind date went. Can you see if Starbucks will make me a gingerbread latte? I know it's early in the season, but see what you can do. Time's a tickin'...*

Me: *Say that shit again, and I'll break all the clocks. I'll see what I can do, it's barely November!*

Andrea: *Use all that charm of yours!*

Me: *Whatever, I'll see Tuesday.*

Then I move to the ones I'm trying my best to avoid, but I need to see what the hell I've done.

And there they are: to Hendrix, to Hendrix, to Hendrix. All putting myself right out there, all of my drunken confessions.

And not one reply.

I begin to shake, fearing maybe this time I've completely lost him.

Me: *I'm sorry.*

Me: *I do like you, muches.*

Me: *I madde a mistakes.*

Clearly I've had wine by this point.

Me: *I havent done this in yearz.*

Me: *I want to do it with you. Both things! Hehe?*

I'm mortified! I slap my hand over my mouth, shaking my head. *Never. Drinking. Again.*

Me: *I'm scared. I has secret. Biggest one. I scared you'll not look at my the same. I luv you looks. No. The way you look to NO me at me.*

Me: *I likes McDavid's we should have it 2morrow mrnin here. I like the McEggmuff.*

Me: *And you.*

Shoot me right now. I am not allowed to ever, ever touch a drink ever again.

Just as I'm about to put my phone down and go bury myself back in my bed in complete humiliation, my phone goes off, alerting me to an incoming text.

It's from Hendrix.

Hendrix: *I hope it's McDonald's you wanted cuz that's what I brought. I wasn't sure what a McEggmuff was so I got you a few choices. BTW, I like muffs too. How about you come open up and let me in, my Fruitloop?*

My Fruitloop.

Yeah, I like the sounds of that.

I make my way to the door and let *my* Hendrix in.

29

Trinity

"I COME IN peace, Oh, Little Powerful One," Hendrix grins, offering me the brown McDonald's bag he's holding in one hand along with a tray of coffees from the other. Instantly sagging, I feel a tremendous amount of relief to hear Hendrix's usual easygoing humour toward me. It makes me feel a twinge of hope. Even if I keep trying to push him away, I wish for him to be the man who might want me enough to see past my disease.

I wish for it with all my might.

"Thanks for bringing breakfast. Come in." I step aside, allowing him to pass. His unique scent flows by in his wake, awakening all my senses; he really is his own brand of yumminess.

Then I notice him removing Beast from the inside of his jacket, placing him on the floor of my apartment. Beast instantly comes to me, rubbing his face against my ankles. "Hi, baby," I say. I place the steamy bag and tray on the butcher block countertop, then pick the kitty up and give him a snuggle.

"I stopped in and fed him. Thought you might not be up to it. Decided the furball looked lonely, so I brought him along." Hendrix shrugs like it's nothing, when in reality it means so much. Hendrix Hills is one thoughtful man.

"Thanks. You're right. It definitely would have taken me awhile to get down to him this morning," I admit.

"I bet. Rough night?" he asks, bemused, and that's when I notice how good he looks, not hungover at all. Taking him in, I stop—panicking—realizing I probably look like complete shit by comparison.

"Um, why don't you help yourself?" I tell him, putting Beast down and flapping my hand in the direction of the food, intent on diving quickly into the washroom to fix my hair before he really has a chance to see me. "I'll be right back," I call, my back to him, while I walk a few steps down the hall. "Start eating. I—just—I'll be right back." My plan is to quickly check myself, maybe even brush my teeth and comb my bird's nest hair. Too bad for me, my attempt to flee is thwarted by an ogre.

"Stop. Come here, Trinity." His voice booms through my kitchen. I stop. Hating the awkwardness I'm responsible for creating in the first place, and seeing him in my space being all forgiving and not being an asshole like he should be after last night, I move to him without hesitation. *How could I not?* "You okay?" he asks, sincerity reflected in both his tone and the way he's looking down at me. His eyes take me in softly and he sweeps my bangs gently off my face with his hand. "That's better. Now I can see those pretty eyes of yours. Are you alright, Trin?" he repeats.

"I'm better now." I meet his gaze with my own. "I hated last night," I admit. There's no point in holding anything back. Today will be a day of truths.

"Me too, baby. I barely fucking slept. It took everything I had not to come over here last night," he admits, running his hands through the front of his short hair, leaving it disheveled in a sexy bedhead look only certain guys can pull off.

"I thought you were mad at me. You never responded to my texts. I thought I blew it," I say, taking in his face, handsome despite the dark circles and more-than-five o' clock-shadow gracing his jaw this morning. He's the most gorgeous man I've ever seen, and I want him so damn much.

"Trust me. It killed me. But you were being so honest and open. I didn't want to risk you stopping. It seemed you just needed to get it all out. Well…some of it, anyway," he says, reaching for my hands and taking them into his much larger ones. "I thought about you all night. The things I want to say to you, things I want to do to you…" he says, that sexy smirk of his pulling at the side of his lips as his eyes rake over my short pink robe. "You look beautiful right now. I want nothing more than to kiss you and claim you as mine, but I know we have to talk first. You gotta talk to me, Trinity. After last night at the club and your texts, we have to admit out loud that there's more than friendship between us, Fruitloop. I know it for a fact now. I even have proof," he says, waving his cell phone around, and I know he's referring to my drunken "I like you" texts.

I shake my head, unable to hide how happy I feel that he's not giving up on me, even if I know that what I'm going to admit next will likely turn everything good between us into bitterness. But he's fighting for us, the least I can do is fight alongside him, even if I'm almost guaranteed to lose the battle. At least I'll be able to walk away knowing I was finally brave enough to take a risk and put myself out there for someone special again.

"You're right. Let's talk," I say, placing my hand on his muscular chest. "It's time I let you in. Even as my friend, Hendrix, you deserve to know everything. Can we please eat first, though? I need time to sort my thoughts, and, honestly, the smell alone is curing my hangover. I can just imagine how good I'll feel once it *gets in my belly…*" I rub my stomach, giving him my best Fat Bastard impersonation.

"You're crazy. Let's get you fed." He pulls me in to give me a hug, and I pray it's not the last one. I'd miss the feeling I get from being close to him a whole hell of a lot. Hendrix makes me feel so safe, so protected—and most of all, wanted.

After a few beats, he breaks away and leads us to sit side-by-side at the breakfast bar where I left the McDonald's.

"HOLY SHIT, THAT was something to see," Hendrix says, leaning into my shoulder and giving it a teasing bump. "I've never seen anyone mow food down like that before. I thought you were gonna choke for a second, Fruitloop. Did you even breathe? Maybe 'Hoover' would be a more accurate nickname for you…" he laughs.

"What? Sausage McMuffs are my remedy. I feel great right now," I beam, before taking a delicate sip of coffee.

"Well, muffs do seem to have a magical quality, I would agree with that," he says, that mischievous glint sparkling in his eyes like it always does when he's being a shit. *God, I really, really, really like this man.*

"Yes. They're like unicorns. And, by the way…you're impossible."

"So I keep hearing, Fruitloop, so I keep hearing." He shifts our stools so we're facing each other, then encases my knees between his large muscular thighs. "You ready to talk to me now, sweetheart?" he asks, his voice growing serious, his beautiful warm eyes meeting mine.

Avoiding his gaze, I look anywhere else I can, anywhere but at him. Letting out a deep breath, I admit, "I don't know if I can do it. I can't look you in the eye and tell you; I can't bear to watch the reaction on your face. I think it might destroy me. I care about you too much, Hendrix. I care about what you see and think of me. The thought of seeing the way your eyes reflect light and happiness when you look at me changing to a shadow that will no doubt come and obstruct that light, it's—it's too much for me. I'm sorry." I heave a big sob, not even realizing that I had started crying.

"Trin. Jesus, baby. What the hell happened to you? Nothing you could tell me would ever make me see you as any less than you are.

Trust me, you're all I fucking see. I couldn't give a shit. There's no secret that will make me see anything other than the Trinity I've come to know, the one I admire, respect, and—fuck it—the one I've fallen for."

"Hendrix."

"It's the truth. It's my truth. Here, I have an idea. Stand up," he says, jumping to his feet, tucking his stool back under the counter before reaching for my hand and guiding us to the middle of my kitchen.

"What are you doing?" I ask, as he wipes away a few of my lingering tears.

"We're gonna play a game. Turn around."

"I think you might be the crazy one," I huff, but do as I'm told and turn, giving him my back.

30

HENDRIX

I TURN AROUND so my back is pressing against Trinity's, and take her hands in mine.

"I think you might be the crazy one," she says. "I might need to start calling *you* 'Fruitloop'," she giggles, and that right there tells me she's starting to return to her usual cheeky self. My Trinny is fun, confident and sassy with me; I hated hearing and seeing that cloud of doubt hovering over us. It's time to clear this shit up for good.

"Maybe, but give me a chance, Trin. Have I steered you wrong yet?"

"No, but there's a first time for everything," she retorts.

Fuck. She's right, though. I must be out of my mind to do this with her, but seeing her looking unsure and hearing her worry over my potential reaction to something she needs to tell me is both upsetting me and pissing me off. There really isn't anything that will change the way I feel for this girl, I just hope this stupid game of mine will help her feel safe enough to confide in me. And I pray that the shit I share doesn't make me look like a chump who can't get over things, or make her reject me.

"Okay, we're going to play a game. I call it 'Truths'. All we do is tell each other things that are true—"

"Pssht…no big deal, eh?" she mocks, sounding nervous.

"Trust me, alright? We'll start off easy and work our way to the hard stuff. We'll stand back-to-back and stay that way throughout the game."

"Why?" Trin cuts in again.

"If we stay facing away from each other, we can't see each other react to what we're disclosing. It's a safety net for both of us. My mum and I used to do this when I was young, when I had something I needed to get off my chest but was afraid to tell her, and it always worked. I'd feel better after, like a weight had been lifted off my shoulders. Please trust me and play along, and let's take whatever weight it is you're carrying off you. Plus, I have skeletons, too, that I'm not proud of. I'm sure last night didn't leave me looking very angelic or worthy in your eyes."

"Hendrix," she says.

"Yeah, baby?" I say, stealing a quick glance at the back of her head before facing away from her again.

"You're pretty incredible. I just wanted to tell you that, before we start. Friends or more, past entourage of women or not, I'm crushing pretty freaking hard on you right about now. I want you to know that I'm going to do this because I think you deserve all of my truths, even if you decide you want nothing to do with me afterwards..." Her voice falters, and I rub my thumbs along her soft hands before entwining them even more tightly with mine. Inching back, I lean against her a little harder, putting us as close together as we can be, needing to feel the warmth of her.

Squeezing where our fingers are connected, I ask "Ready?"

"As I'll ever be." She exhales deeply.

"I'll start, you know, just to show you how it's done."

"Sounds good," Trin says, voice still unsure.

"Truth: I hate mushrooms," I tell her, the thought making me cringe. "They are the devil's food. I can't stand the look of them." She lets out a small laugh. "Honestly, so don't ever try to make me eat them. I refuse."

"Got it, no mushrooms. Can people around you eat them?" she asks.

"Yes, as long as they don't come near me," I chuckle. I decide to give her another easy one, as it seems to be helping her relax. "I'll go a few more times, to make sure you see how slowly we can ease into the tougher stuff."

"Okay, but I have to say, this stuff is deep already. I mean, like, take to my grave deep," she jokes.

"Well, I gotta start somewhere. I figured you needed to know that critical piece of information. How could I be with a girl who might see my not liking mushrooms as a deal breaker? You could be mushroom-obsessed," I say.

"You're insane."

"Maybe. Alright, next truth: I'm obsessed with the Toronto Maple Leafs. They're my team and I can't miss a game. Now, I'll give you a bigger, more in-depth truth. You ready?" I give her hands a squeeze.

"Go for it. Those were thrilling, but I'll need to know juicier ones if I'm going to share mine," Trin says honestly, and I hear the uncertainty creeping back in her tone. It's time to move on to more serious admissions, especially if I want her to build up enough confidence to tell me what's stopping her from giving us a chance.

"And now I'll share the big ones." I let out a sigh, knowing what I plan to share with her will be hard. I don't do well with not holding grudges and I've held a grudge towards relationships for a very long time. I'm only hoping this game of mine serves its purpose. "Truth: I lost my virginity when I was sixteen. She was nineteen, and my friend's sister. We were home alone at his house and she seduced me," I laugh, knowing she won't buy the last bit at all.

"Oh, I just bet she did. Always been the ladies' man, eh?" she laughs.

"Yeah, yeah, yeah. See? It's easy, even if you judged me. I can't see your face so it's easier to take," I joke. "Now, you can share something of your own. Got it?" I ask.

"Got it. And I didn't mean to sound like I was judging you."

"No worries, I get it. I do have a hell of a track record. But I plan on fixing that. Okay, your turn."

"Okay, I'm ready. Truth: I didn't lose my virginity until I was in university. I guess I was a late-bloomer."

"Wow, that's incredible. Have you seen yourself?" I ask, unable to keep it in. Because, let's be honest, between her looks and her personality—once she warms up—she's an amazing woman. One I assumed would have been asked out and chased a lot.

"I guess I never liked anyone enough. Before I knew it, I was going off to Queen's a virgin." I feel her shrug. "God. That was embarrassing."

"It's not. I think it's pretty awesome, Trin. Shows a lot. Okay, here goes. Truth: you're quickly becoming one of my favourite people. I've never been like this with a girl before. Never," I admit, then wait, letting it sink in.

"Truth," she repeats, her voice a bit shaky. "I feel the same, Hendrix. I look for you, look forward to our nightly texts…I even like how impossible you are."

"I knew it." I squeeze our hands. "Truth: my mum lives in England, and I miss her everyday 'cause I'm a total mama's boy," I share.

"I love that!" Trin says, and I can hear the smile in her voice. "Truth: I don't speak to my parents. Their choice, not mine. And it used to hurt, but now I'm better for it. I have the Flynns," Trinity shares, and I want to pry and ask more, but I know this was a big truth for her to share with me. I let it go and decide to flirt a bit more to try and lighten the mood before we get serious again.

"Truth: I get very fucking hard when I catch you peeking at me at work, and see the way your hips sway when you walk through the bays, and how your tits bounce when you laugh. I fucking love it all."

"Jesus," she mutters, a bit breathless. I love when she does that shit.

"Truth: I wanted to kiss you last night," I add.

"Hey, it's my turn," she quips.

"Sorry. Go."

"Truth: I like you. A lot. But you terrify me. You clearly have way more experience than me, I've only ever been with three men," she admits, and I swear the thought of her with even one guy pisses me off. Knowing there are three men out there that have been with my Fruitloop makes me feral. Given my own history, that's completely insane, but I can't help it. Something about her makes me selfish, protective, and possessive.

Deciding it's time to share my biggest truth with her, I take a deep breath before starting what I hope will lead to our last round. "Truth: I haven't had a girlfriend or trusted a woman since I was eighteen. Callie, my girlfriend at the time, went a little off her rocker when I decided to end things. She showed up at my parents' house one night saying she was pregnant. Then a few weeks later, when I'd finally processed everything and actually gotten excited at the idea of being a dad, I lost it all. Just when I'd decided I could happily be the man my parents raised me to be. My mum had suggested we go over and talk to Callie's parents, to sort things out, to make sure they knew that I was planning on being a hands-on father, and that my family was going to help us however they could. That's when everything went for shit. I'll never forget it. We showed up at Callie's place, then she took one look at my mum and me and began to cry. Turns out it was all bullshit. That she'd been lying. Callie broke down and admitted in front of everyone that she'd made the whole thing up. She thought if I thought we were having a baby then she wouldn't lose me. We'd had unprotected sex one time, 'cause we'd run out of condoms and I was too horny to wait—learned my lesson there, eh? And because of that one time, I'd believed her without question. I haven't trusted a woman other than my mother since. The whole thing sucked hard, and after that mess I vowed I'd never be a fool again," I spew, pretty much all in one breath. Anger I thought I'd repressed is surfacing again as I dredge up the memory. I knew if I didn't get it all out in one go, I might not have been able to go through with it. But I wanted Trinity to know. I want her to get me and to understand that for some unknown reason, she's different, and I trust her. For the first time in years, I want someone to know all of me. We're silent for a beat before I feel her try to turn around, but I don't budge. I work to keep us back to back.

"Hendrix, please. Let me turn around."

"No, Trin, we're still playing. I can't let you see me yet."

"But I want you to see my face, to see, to know that I'd never do that to you. Ever."

"Trust me, Trin. I know. In the short time we've known each other, it's one thing I know for certain. It was a long time ago. It's my hang up, and I'm working on it. Being with you makes that seem like more of a possibility than ever. You've already helped me so much. I've never been friends with a woman like I am with you. Nor have I ever wanted a woman as badly as I want you. I see a future with you in it," I admit before I can stop myself. *It's true, though, so fuck it, might as well own it. She can have all my truths today.* "I want you, Trinity. And I know you want me, too. Show me you're on the same page, that you feel the same way. It's time you share your biggest truth with me. Can you do that, baby? Can you give me your trust back?"

She lets out a loud whimper that has me fighting not to turn and take her into my arms. I wait, giving her the time she needs.

"Okay," she says. "Truth: I haven't dated in over a year. Last year, I shared this same truth with a guy who ended up destroying my confidence in men and in myself. After that, any hope I had of finding someone who could see past everything that's happened to me just vanished. Jared broke me, and, Hendrix, I tried to deny you, tried to friendzone us, but, honestly, I want so much more. I'm just scared you're going to hate me and be repulsed by me, like Jared was. God, I—this is hard," she sobs.

"Everything's going to be okay, Trin. Trust me. I can be an asshole, sure, but I'd never hurt you."

"I believe you. I just need a sec."

"I've got all day, sweetheart. I'm not going anywhere," I promise, hoping she hears the conviction behind my words.

"Hendrix?" Trin asks, after a few moments.

"I'm here, Fruitloop. I'll always be right here." I feel her tighten her grip, while trying to step back into me some more, as if she needs me closer.

"Truth: two years ago, when I was twenty-five, I…I tested positive for HIV. I'm HIV-positive, Hendrix. I'm not a sure thing, or a happily ever after."

She stops. I feel her shoulders slump.

I feel my stomach drop, my heart following right behind it.

There's a lump in my throat.

I feel dizzy, and anger pulses within me.

What the fuck?

What the actual fuck?

I'm going to fucking lose it.

I let go of her hands; I can barely contain the powerful emotions, which are rushing through me. I spin, and see her back go rigid as she freezes, waiting for me to say or do something.

Finally finding my voice, I say hoarsely: "Turn around and look at me, Trinity. Now."

31

TRINITY

"TURN AROUND AND look at me, Trinity. Now."

I feel like I can't breathe. I can't catch my breath…

He didn't say anything the whole time I let loose, and now he sounds pissed.

I can't look at him. I won't. I can't bear to see that look in his eyes, that familiar look that leaves me feeling nothing but shame. I have to get out of here. A loud sob wracks through my body, and my fight-or-flight instinct kicks in. I move forward, ready to bolt out the door. Tears blur my vision as I estimate it will only take me six or seven steps before I can make my escape. *If I can just make it outside, I'll be able to breathe.*

I need Til and I need Dex. I can't go through this again, not with Hendrix.

As if sensing my plan, his muscular arms wrap around my waist from behind, stopping me from making tracks.

"Easy, Trinny," he growls, his deep voice against my ear as he pulls me flush to his chest. "I'm not letting you go. Turn around, baby, and face me. Please, my brave girl, don't you dare give up on me now. 'Cause there's no way in hell I'm giving up on you. Look at me, Fruitloop. *See me.*"

His words fall on me like a soothing blanket on a chilly night. I want to turn and savour the warmth of his words and trust the comfort they're giving me, but I'm so fucking scared. But I also know I'm going to cave, I'm going to turn, I just need a second. Swallowing my fears and doubts, I decide I am going to give him my trust. To let Hendrix see all of me, and to really see him.

"I—I—I—"

"Take, a deep breath, Trin. I'm here; I'm not letting you go. I'm right here with you."

Shaking my head, I wipe my tears before slowly turning around and stepping a few paces away. I need space.

God, he's magnificent. We're both so bare, so open right now. His eyes meet mine, and he's still here. Waiting. Speaking about Callie couldn't have been easy, and hearing about me having HIV couldn't have been easy. Yet, here we stand, supporting each other, standing face-to-face—no judgment, no harsh comments, nothing but understanding. He's gazing down at me kindly, not scowling, and I feel both happy and relieved.

Is this real? For the first time since Jared, I feel hope that maybe I can do this—maybe I can be in a relationship with a man. With a man like Hendrix. He's the unexpected force that didn't give up. He's my friend, the person I want to tell all of my truths to, about how terrified of this disease I am, how I am scared to lose Andrea, how I miss my mom so damn much, how I secretly long for a family, and most of all, long to be loved and to give love. I want everything, and I'm starting to believe I want it all with him.

"There she is. There's my girl."

"My girl". I definitely like that.

He sees me.

"Can you do me a favour, Trin? Can you tell me again? Not about that cocksucker, we can revisit that later, but the rest."

I try to speak, but I can't. I'm too overwhelmed with emotions.

Just when I think things are going to be good, I panic and start thinking the worst. *Maybe was I wrong? Maybe this is some sick joke. Does he want me to watch him while I say it again so I'll see the look of disgust on his face? No, he wouldn't do that—he's not Jared. Hendrix is nothing like that man.* Too verklempt with emotion and conflicting thoughts to speak, I shake my head over and over, silently telling him no.

"Tell me again." He cups my cheeks in his hands, to stop my head from moving. "Relax, Trinity. I'm not asking to be mean, trust me. Just do this for me," he begs, before leaning in and putting his lips to my ear, his voice laced with the same emotions I'm feeling. I know this is a lot for him, too, but he's being incredibly patient. I think, deep-down, I knew he would be.

Whispering, he tries again. "Tell me, Trin. And watch me when you do. Pay attention to my reaction. Look in my eyes, at my facial expression, because, yeah, it's a life-altering fact, but it's one that doesn't change the fact that I care about *you*—and not about you having HIV. I care for you so much. The HIV, that's not what got me pissed. What has me shaking with rage is the fucking asshole who made you feel you needed to hide, who convinced you that I might be the same as that coward. And I'm pissed off at anyone else who has been stupid enough to let you go because of something that is a part of you—might even change you—but in no way defines you." He kisses my forehead.

"That's what Shannon says," I whisper, "that people who can't see past my status—ones who see it as my definition—don't deserve any piece of me."

"See? I knew I liked that girl," I hear him grin, and I can't avoid him any longer. I look up, his intense acorn-coloured eyes meeting with mine.

"I've lost a lot of people along the way already," I say. "I couldn't stand thinking I might lose you, too. You've kind of become a fixture in my life. One that makes me feel special, unique."

"I fucking adore you, Trinity Adams, and I want nothing more than for you to give us a chance. Now, tell me again to my face, and pay close attention to how much I see you. I see you, just as much as you see me, probably more. I see today, tomorrow and a whole shitload of days from now. I see us together." He runs his thumb along my cheek, gifting me with a smile that is just totally, him. "We both know nothing's changed here today. You having HIV doesn't change the way I feel about you. Sure, it's a shock and we'll need to talk it through, but right now, I only want you to look at me and see how I see you. You're perfect."

Breathing heavily while I take in his words, I can't stand the distance I've put between us any longer. "You're the perfect one," I say, wrapping my arms around his neck and jumping up into his arms, wrapping my legs around his strong waist, craving his proximity. I want him to hold me as desperately as I want to hold onto him, to comfort him as he is comforting me. Pulling back a little, I look deep into his eyes and repeat, "I am HIV-positive. I have been for two years. It doesn't change who I am," I add, with the renewed confidence he's given me in this moment. "And I see you, too, Hendrix. So much, and I want this—you—so much."

"That's the best news I've heard all day, baby," he says, his gaze meeting mine again, and what I see reflecting back at me is beautiful. It's my Hendrix, with his confident shit-eating grin in place, and his soft eyes looking down upon me, silently telling me how much he still wants me even with the knowledge of my illness. Best of all, I still see that spark with which he looks at me still shining in his eyes. There aren't any shadows lingering or making their way to the forefront. His view of me isn't one of a tainted woman; it's a view filled with clarity and the promise of wonderful things to come. He looks at me simply like I'm a woman he likes and desires, and that feels incredible. He sees my light.

Hendrix sees me. He sees all of me: the person I am today, the girl I've always been, and the woman I might become. I just hope he also sees the Trinity that is looking right back at him, the one who already loves him so much.

I sigh contentedly, finally relaxing.

Knowing my biggest truth, Hendrix Hills still wants me.

32

Hendrix

HIV.

H…I…fucking…V!

What the fuck?

What the actual fuck?

What do I say?

Do?

This shit is deep.

HIV…

Three fucking letters. A whole list of red flags.

What the fuck?

I want to leave, so I can wrap my head around this shit.

But then I look at her, feel her clinging to me, and I start to come back.

It's Trinity. I just got her, there's no way I can leave her. And, truth: I don't want to. If it was any other chick, there's no way, but it's *her*. And since the second my eyes landed on her gripping that fucking tire iron, looking sexy as hell, showing how feisty she can be, there's been that voice in my head telling me that she's special, different.

I need to wig the hell out for a second, but for now, I also need to keep my cool and listen. The ringing in my ears is starting to fade. Holding Trinity in my arms is helping, but I can't stop my mind from reeling at the information she just laid out for me. But, unlike she expected, it doesn't change a damn thing. *Nothing has changed.*

Sure, I'll need to educate myself, and I'll probably fuck up here and there, but that's what a relationship is. *I can deal with this.* I want to take this on with her, to help her. Nothing will change, well, other than my fierce need to protect her which is suddenly more present than ever before. Shaking, I hold her as tight—if not tighter—than she is holding me. When I saw her looking to bolt, I thought I'd lost her, but this thing between us is stronger than that. I'll never forget the look on her stunning face when it dawned on her that her being HIV-positive didn't change a damn thing between us, the way her breathing calmed and her eyes lit up as she started to believe me. Sure, we've got a shit ton to talk about, but that can wait. Right now, all I want is to reassure her that she and I are on the same page.

HIV-positive. How the fuck did such an innocent woman with such limited experience get HIV? Transfusion? Needles? Sex? I formulate question upon question that I want to ask, but I don't want to seem on the offensive. The last thing Trin needs is to feel attacked when she's at her most vulnerable.

Nuzzling into her neck, I inhale her sweet fruity scent. The feel of her ass in my hands isn't lost on me, either. She's the sexiest woman I've ever met, so strong and brave. And I want to take this woman like none before her—but not now, not like this.

"Does this mean I can finally kiss you, Trinity?" I ask into her neck while I walk her over and lift her onto the countertop. The need to taste her lips is one thing that can't wait. I've imagined this woman's taste for way too long, and I'm going to kiss her, to show her how badly I want her in spite of what she's just revealed. Nudging her legs apart, I step in close, craving nearness.

Standing to my full height, I meet her watery eyes, and my heart sinks at the lingering uncertainty I glimpse behind those piercing greys.

It's in this moment that I vow to be the best thing in her life, because in the short months I've known her, that's exactly what she's become in mine.

"I'm so sorry I didn't tell you sooner," she hiccups, looking up at me.

Honestly, I don't know what to say. I'm in shock here. All I know is that it doesn't matter to me. All that matters is us moving forward together. *Her and me.*

"I understand, Trin. Don't apologize. From what I gather, you've got a really good reason why you didn't. I want to hear and know everything but I'll be honest, I'm so fucked up right now that I think if you tell me everything that asshole did wrong to you, I might lose my shit." I'm fighting for composure here. She tries to pull away. *Like hell there will be any of that.*

"No," I say a little more harshly than I meant. "No, it has nothing to do with you. It's me, and this need to protect you, to make you happy. I want to hunt down every fucker who's ever done you wrong or looked at you with anything other than respect and I want to bring them a world of pain for making you doubt how amazing you are."

"Hendrix." She says my name like it's a prayer. "You can't be like that. You need to focus on the good. I'm starting to see that, finally. *Today.*" She gives me one of those fucking smiles that lights up her face. My favourite kind.

"I mean it, Trinity. You're mine and I protect what's mine, so fuckheads beware."

"Oh, Lord, don't tell me I'm going to have to keep you on a leash now?" she giggles, and it's the best sound I've ever heard. *Yeah, my girl is incredible.*

Feeling needy, I ask again, "You gonna let me kiss you now, or what? 'Cause, *truth:* I'm dying to, and I think I've been a very patient man." I tilt her chin up and she nods, giving me the silent permission I want like my next breath. “Is this why you didn’t kiss me last night? Did you think I’d freak out or some shit?”

“Yes,” she admits, barely audible. “I didn’t want to kiss you. Not without you knowing first. I didn’t want to take away your right to decide or change your mind about me. I’ve made that mistake before.”

“The fuck I would.” I rub my thumb along her bottom lip. “I’ve been dreaming of these lips, of kissing you, for months, Trin. I might not know everything yet, but I do know you can’t transmit HIV from kissing. Now give me those sweet lips of yours. I’m dying over here.” I move my face closer to hers, waiting and willing her to make the next move.

“You’re an incredible man, Hendrix. If we do this, I might never let you go,” she whispers.

“That’s exactly what I’m hoping, Fruitloop. Now shut up and kiss me.”

And she does. Wrapping her hands in my hair, she pulls me in and takes my lips against hers. She’s hesitant at first, but when my tongue seeks entrance, she obliges, and I swear my knees go weak. Letting out a moan, I pull her closer, and our tongues mingle in a perfect duet, a symphony of electricity that has my body humming in perfect harmony. My hands move, finding their way into her hair, while my tongue continues to explore her sweet mouth. Moaning, Trin picks up the pace, her tongue caressing mine as we explore one another for the first time. It feels like no kiss I’ve ever felt before.

Her lithe body begins to shudder as my hands grip her ass, pulling her towards me to feel my excitement. Pushing forward, she grinds down on my cock and it’s intense and hot as fuck. I know we need to slow down, but she feels too fucking good. Breaking the kiss, I move down, kissing from her jaw to her neck, opening her robe, loving the way she feels. Tilting her head back, she grants me the access I crave. I’m trying desperately to imprint myself on her. Moving my hand, I cup her heavy breast over her tank top, under her plush bathrobe. "Shit, baby, you feel so good. I want nothing more than to sink myself into you," I kiss her mouth again, "but I know we need to stop. We'll need to talk more first."

"God, I know. I want you so bad. It's been so hard not jumping you," she laughs, and again, it's like music to my ears.

Christ, this woman's amazing. "How about you give me a few more kisses and let me grope you for a bit longer, then I'll be a good boy and listen?"

"You're impossible," she says, giving me her favourite line.

"Yeah, and you love it." I kiss her lips, swallowing her cheeky reply. Rather than giving me more grief, she pulls me back in and kisses the shit out of me.

Fuck me, this girl is perfect.

No matter if she—or any anyone else—thinks otherwise.

33

Trinity

AFTER OUR GAME and those amazing kisses, I made us a pot of tea (another cup of coffee was the last thing my nerves needed). We spent some time on my couch, me sitting between Hendrix's legs resting my head on his chest, while he rubbed my neck and shoulders and encouraged me with his attentive words, soft prompting and kindness.

Despite coming off as gruff and intimidating sometimes, Hendrix is actually a very sweet ogre, and a lot more sensitive than I would have ever imagined. I told him about when I was first diagnosed, about Blake and how he was my first—and the only person I'd ever had unprotected sex with. I shared about the Facebook message I'd sent to Blake, and the reply I'd never been able to bring myself to look at beyond the first sentence. He offered to read it with me if I ever I wanted to, which made me cry again.

He told me about his father passing away, and I told him about my parents kicking me out of the house, about Andrea, The AIDS Network and how Dex and Til stepped in as my family. Hendrix was incredible, to say the least, so much so that I couldn't help ask how he could be all right with everything I'd dumped on him?

"How are you taking this so well?" I ask now, rubbing small circles on the hand of his that I'd been holding. "I—I guess I expected some kind of freak out, some kind of fallout, Hendrix. You've taken this almost *too* well."

"Trust me, I'm reeling. I'm processing it. But I guess I get it, I do. I can kind of relate," he sighs, placing his palm on my neck the way I like. "I had a friend with a similar situation. Mind you, he should have known better, but at the time he was in a bad way. And he ended up paying the consequences," he says, and I lean up, dropping his hand so I can face him, curious to hear more.

"Did he have HIV?" I ask.

"No. My buddy, Ren, we were real close after my dad died. I was in a dark place, drinking too much, smoking weed, hanging out with the wrong crowd. I was always at house parties getting into trouble. I met Ren at one of 'em and we hit it off, even though he was into some heavier shit than I was. Then, a year or so into our friendship, he got real sick. Eventually, he found out he'd contracted Hep C from sharing needles. He was like a brother to me. I learned quickly that him being sick, it didn't change who he was, despite the label some people put on him. So many of the guys turned their backs on him. And it pissed me off. He was one of my closest friends when I'd needed him, and at this point he needed me, so there was no way I'd walk away. I lost a few friends because of my decision to stick around and support him, you know, because they judged him. But I decided fuck them, it was Ren. He was always making me laugh, helping out with my car…shit, he even let me crash at his place when I wasn't seeing eye-to-eye with my mum. Him having Hep C didn't change any of that. It didn't stop him from living and, other than being a bit more cautious in certain situations, it wasn't a big concern. It definitely forced his ass to wake up. Mine, too. Crazy as it seems now, that could have been me. Do you know how many times after my dad died that I thought about trying heroin, about just taking a little hit off a buddy's needle to see if it would numb me? Way too many times. Luckily, for some reason I didn't. Something always seemed to keep me away from those particular parties, or I'd get interrupted at those times when the temptation was at my fingertips. Maybe my dad was watchin' me, who knows? Anyway, after all this stuff with Ren, I stopped doing drugs, drank a lot less, and decided to get my shit together. And Ren, he finally got himself clean, after admitting he had a heroin addiction. Eventually, he moved back home, Down East where his family was. We lost touch after he went, but while he was here getting himself sorted we were still good friends. Yeah, he was kind of a victim of the circumstances he created, but, hell, it could have just as easily been me, and the last thing he needed was me judging him. I like to think he's doing okay. I've been tempted to try and find out, but then I chicken out, afraid of what I might hear. Maybe he didn't get the liver transplant he was hoping for, ya know? Or maybe he relapsed? I don't know. But I wanted nothing but good for him after he was good to me," he huffs, rubbing his hands over his face, his emotions obviously going a little haywire. Our conversation hasn't been easy.

"Thanks for sharing that with me. God, you've been through a lot. How have you managed to stay so sweet and not just be some jaded asshole?" I ask, moving to sit in his lap, wrapping my arms around his neck and pulling him in close to me.

"I *am* a jaded asshole. Remember? I'm the ogre. Maybe it's you taming me? You seem to have an effect on me, makin' me want to open up and trust my instincts about you," he shrugs. "I'm happy when we're together." I squeeze him tighter.

"Me too," I smile, then say, "Maybe I can help you look him up one day, when you're ready? You have a huge heart, Mr. Hills, and I'm blessed to call you mine." I kiss his forehead.

"I'm going to make you love me. I'm determined. It'll happen, Fruitloop."

"I'm pretty sure it's unavoidable, Mr. Hills," I tell him honestly, and he rewards me with another one of those amazing kisses I'm coming to crave.

We spend the rest of the morning kissing, crying, holding each other, and talking about everything from my daily medication cocktail to how my life has changed since my diagnosis. It felt cathartic, almost surreal.

And the best part? By the end, this big sexy man was still here with me. And my hangover was gone. Being on antiretroviral (ARV) medication, I don't usually allow myself to have more than two or three drinks when out. Last night was obviously an exception, one I make every now and then. But alcohol and drugs can weaken my already shaky immune system, so the last thing I want to do is something in excess that may affect my kidneys or liver, or cause me to skip doses of my ARV because I'm feeling too hungover.

Hendrix left a few hours later, both of us agreeing that we could use some alone time to process everything. Of course, it took him another forty minutes to actually leave, since he felt the need to ensure I was okay and that I knew that things between us were better than ever.

Three hours later, he texted saying he was hungry, that he missed me, and that I should get ready because he was coming to pick me up, that we were about to go on our first official date.

Things have only gotten better since then.

34

Hendrix

"Hey, Flynn. Trinity and I are going to cut out now," I say, standing at the threshold of his office.

"Okay," he says, looking down at his watch. "I'll cover the front. We aren't too busy today, we'll be fine here without you." Flynn shuffles through the piles of paper on his desk. "Now, where are my goddamn glasses? I swear you boys hide 'em just to fuck with me."

"Maybe it's time we get you one of those lanyard things to hold your glasses around your neck. Something with rhinestones? Seems this is a reoccurring issue, old man. Can't keep blaming us." I cross my arms and laugh as he flips me the bird.

"Some days I wish I could fire your ass," he mutters.

"Naw, you like me too much."

"Haven't you left yet?" He shakes his head, continuing to mutter, while searching his desk. I don't tell him that his reading glasses are perched on top of his head. I'm sure he'll find them eventually.

Trinity and I are leaving early today to attend a meeting I've arranged for us. After our dinner Saturday night, we spent a long time discussing everything, including sex. Trin opened up about her reservations and fears, and I blame that son of a bitch she dated for making her feel that sex is now something to view as stressful, versus an act of passion or love. I'm determined to show her it's abso-fuckin'-

lutely nothing to stress about, particularly with me. My goal will always be to make her feel nothing but sexy, wanted, cherished and loved.

I was stunned when she admitted that she hadn't been intimate with anyone in two years, and that she'd stopped dating altogether over a year ago. Honestly, though, hearing that she hasn't had sex in over two years sends a bit of a thrill straight to my cock, knowing that I'll be the one to reacquaint her, the one to help release her pent-up inner vixen, the one that's been laying dormant for way too long. I know she's in there; I've seen glimpses and cannot wait for more.

First things first, though. We need to get her mind to stop interfering with her body. Trin and I have been together every night since Saturday, and it's getting harder to resist sinking into her sweet pussy. We literally make out like teenagers—tops off, bottoms on. And it's fucking killing me. But I get it. She's apprehensive despite my words and the many Google searches we've done together researching safe sex and HIV. Trinity is hesitant to move to the next level, although we both know we're more than ready. There have been a few nights this week where dry humping to the point of orgasm wasn't enough for either of us.

With that in mind, I made an executive decision, and today I'm taking Trin directly to the horse's mouth, as they say. To an appointment that I hope helps her realize that we can have sex. Lots and lots of sex. *Safely.* That I will not get HIV from touching her the way we both crave desperately, as long as we take appropriate precautions.

I swear, you'd think she was the one uneducated about this stuff, stuff she knows probably better than most. I guess it's not always easy to practice what you preach, which I do understand to some extent. It's a huge burden to shoulder when you've been called awful names and lost relationships along the way. This is my way to ease the pressure, to hopefully allow her to confirm what she already knows deep down. I get that there are risks that we need to be aware of, but I want Trinity to realize it isn't the big deal she's made it in her head. At the end of the day, we're both consenting adults who can make educated decisions that are best for each of us. I will do my best to get her to see that she's my choice. It's her, all the way, every way I can get her, and that includes getting her beneath me—and fucking soon. My Fruitloop has me sporting a huge case of the "blues", if you know what I mean.

"Got 'em," Flynn shouts, pulling his glasses off his head in triumph, bringing me back to the here and now. "Hendrix, you son of a bitch!"

"Christmas is next month. I'm totally adding that lanyard to your list, old man. I may even toss in a magnifying glass, 'cause we both know that even with them tied to your neck with a string, you'll still lose 'em," I jibe letting out a loud laugh.

"Alright, Chuckles. I've had enough of you. You two kids get outta here before I change my mind about you dating my girl." He gives me his best cut eye. "Remember, son, you best be good to my niece."

Rolling my eyes, I nod. "Trust me, I'm very good to her, and I promise to be even better," I add at the perfect moment, feeling her slender arms snake around my waist from behind.

"Hendrix!" she scolds, reaching up and twisting my nipples through my shirt, which causes me to bark out a pained laugh.

"*What?*" I shrug. "It's true. I have plans to take very good care of you for a very long time, woman. You need to get your mind out of the gutter. Such a pervy, pervy girl," I laugh, looking behind me to where she's resting her head on my back, her cheeks now rosy.

"Thought you two were leavin'? I'm suddenly feeling extremely nauseous with all this mushy shit," Flynn bellows, before adding, "Shit, Til's right. Maybe I am a matchmaker." He shakes his head. "First Nadia fell for Brody when she worked here, now these two. I run a damn garage, not a fucking dating service. Young people just can't seem to keep it in their pants…" he trails off.

"Ready, baby?" I turn and face Trinity.

"I guess. You haven't told me where we're going," she pretends to pout, looking up at me as I kiss her nose. *Too fucking cute.* Flynn sticks his finger down his throat and pretends to gag.

"Let's go and all will be revealed."

I take her hand.

35

Hendrix

"Good afternoon, Hendrix. How are you?" Dr. Troy Millman greets us, a friendly smile on his goateed face as he enters the small exam room, my file clutched in his left hand.

"Hey, Doc. I'm good. How are you?" We shake hands, his blue eyes moving from me to Trin.

"I'm great," he says, taking a seat on the rolling chair in front of us.

"This is Trinity, my girlfriend," I introduce them, and love the way Trin's eyes widen, acknowledging my claim in having said "girlfriend".

"Nice to meet you. You know to watch out for this one, right? He's a real pain. He's been my patient for far too long," he says, gesturing toward me and laughing. "In fact, I'm thinking of trying to find a new patient to replace him. Are you interested?" he asks her.

"Ha! Don't I know it," she agrees, rolling her eyes. "Thanks for your kind offer, but I haven't completely worn out my current doctor."

He chuckles, then gets down to business. "Grace said you wanted an appointment to discuss some pain you've been having in your side?" he asks, looking up from my folder before rolling over to his workstation.

Looking over at Trinity, I smile. "Well, not entirely. I lied."

"See what I mean?" The doc looks at Trin and they share another laugh at my expense.

When I'd first pulled into the medical building's lot, I cut the ignition and told Trinity that we had an appointment with my doctor. I'd admitted wanting us both to feel at ease moving forward in our relationship, and wanting to get us both some first-hand information. I also didn't hold back with my intentions, either. I had a lot to say and I wanted to make sure she understood where I was coming from.

Leaning across the console so we were facing, I'd taken her face in my hands and whispered, "I want everything you are, Trinny. I'm serious. I've never been more sure. Not about my mum moving back to England, not about the garage—*nothing*. And from the way you are when we're together and the things you tell me, I know you want it with me, too. I feel it."

"Hendrix," she'd said, her voice going small. "I can't believe you've done this for me."

"It's for *us*, Trin. I think hearing a doctor confirm what we already know will put your mind at ease," I said, taking her lips against mine. "I see the light in your eyes when I talk about us in the same sentence, about all the things we want to do. It's time we figure out how to be the us we both want," I'd added, before kissing her deeply.

Pulling away, she'd drifted her soft hand across my jaw. "Let's do this. It's crazy," she muttered, looking me straight in the eye, a huge grin lighting up her beautiful face.

"What's crazy?" I asked, a little confused.

"We're going to be an 'us'. It's been so long since I've considered being a part of anyone else, or having a relationship. I'm excited to have it be with you," she said, before she'd leaned over and rested her head on my chest. "You're amazing," she'd whispered. "I'm sorry, I was wrong. I feel guilty for seeing you as someone who wouldn't accept me, and I'm going to make it up to you, I promise."

"Oh I know you will, baby," I added, rubbing her back.

"You want to know the best part, though?" she had asked, having perked up a bit.

"What?"

"I love knowing you get me. And you're right, I am a bit loopy, but know beyond any shadow of doubt I want an *us*. I want it so badly that I'm done hiding and I'll fight every day for it. Going forward, there will always be truth between us."

"Thank Christ, baby. You had me at 'us' and 'fight for it'; that's all I care about."

She'd laughed, and it was sexy as fuck, her hand resting on my heart.

She leaned over and kissed my cheek. "Now, let's go talk to your doc. I need in these pants, and soon…" she'd smirked, reached down and rubbed her hand across my jeans, back and forth over my hard length.

"Jesus. You're killing me, Fruitloop," I'd said, "but you're going to make us late."

"Hendrix?" Dr. Millman's voice brings me back to the conversation.

"Sorry, I was lost in thought. Anyway, I really wanted to talk to you about something else, but I didn't want to tell Grace what it was for before I'd cleared it with Trinity." I look at Trin, and see her warm eyes.

"Alright, then. It must be important to you. What can I help you guys with?" he asks, and I don't know quite how to start. Suddenly, I'm all emotional at having to say the words out loud, as if saying it to someone else will make it real. I can't seem to get past the lump that's lodged itself in my throat. *Luckily, I don't have to.*

"I'm HIV-positive and I'msoscaredtohavesexwithHendrixbutI'm-dyingto," Trin blurts, then covers her hand over her mouth like I've seen her do when she shocks herself with her own words.

The doctor and I burst out laughing.

"Thanks for the save, baby. I couldn't get it out."

She grabs my hand.

"I know, it's hard to say sometimes, when you start thinking of everything you're admitting. I get it." she says, offering a small smile.

Fuck, I adore this girl. She's honest and true, and best of all, she gets me, she accepts that this is hard. No matter how well I initially took the news, it will always be hard to accept. Things might not always be simple where her health is concerned, and it's as if that idea finally took root in my mind when he asked me why we were here. Trinity might not always be the healthy woman I see sitting beside me. Her disease could still win. Shaking my head, I tamp those thoughts down, deciding to lock them away. There's no room for that shit, not today, not when she's healthy and we're both happy.

"That's perfectly normal. You're not the first couple I've had come see me about this same issue. It's a lot more common today than people realize," he says, looking between the two of us. "First off, I want to commend you for being proactive. I'm glad to help in any way I can." Dr. Millman smiles warmly, reaching for his tablet. "What questions do you have?"

"I worry mainly about Hendrix having all the facts, and being sure that we take everything into consideration before having sex or being intimate, I guess. I'm stressing that I might make Hendrix sick. It's the last thing I'd ever want; so when I think about my desire for intimacy with him, it's making me feel selfish. I'll feel better when he hears it all from his own doctor, versus simply believing everything I've been saying and what we've been reading on the Internet together. I'll feel better knowing he has all the information, you know?"

"Informed consent, as it were," says Dr. Millman.

"Yes. I know if we're careful, the chances of transmission are very low, but I'm happy to have you confirm that. It's crazy. I know all this, I teach and preach all this, but it's completely different to tell another human being—one you care about and want to be intimate with—that the risks are low. I wouldn't ever want to appear as if I was being deceitful to get what I want sexually," Trinity tells us, blushing, sweeping her long bangs from her eyes and letting out a deep breath. I place my hand on her knee and squeeze, letting her know I'm here with her.

"Thank you for being so conscientious about keeping me healthy. This is exactly why we're here. To make sure we're both aware and ready, and to put us both at ease. 'Cause I think you're ready, Trin, and I was months ago." I raise my brows up and down, making her laugh.

Clearing his throat, Dr. Millman interrupts, bringing us back into focus. "Okay, lovebirds. Let's start with your first concern, then move through as much as we can in the time we have."

We both nod, and Trin speaks first. "Condoms. Are they really enough protection?"

"Yes. When worn properly and consistently, they are sufficient protection when having intercourse or for oral sex. Now, of course, they can break, abstinence is best, but that's not a realistic option for people who want to be sexually active."

"Oh, and we do," I chime in.

"How about this: why don't I review the lower-, medium- and higher-risk activities, and then if you have specific questions we can answer those?" Dr. Millman offers, and we both agree. "Alright. Touching, holding hands, sharing drinks or food, kissing—and French-kissing—are all safe, lower-risk act—"

I cut him off.

"First, I need to know about oral sex? Then we can move backwards. That's my biggest question, sorry. I didn't mean to cut you off, but I really want to know," I say. I couldn't help it. He was telling me stuff I already knew, and I've been thinking about tasting Trin for far too long. I want Dr. Millman to tell me it's all right.

"Oh, God, Hendrix. This is embarrassing!" Trinity slaps my arm.

"What?" I ask innocently. "I'm curious. It's a good question."

"I guess I'll start with oral sex, then, so we can put Hendrix out of his misery." Dr. Millman shakes his head at me, and I mentally give him a high-five for getting to the good stuff.

"Thanks, Doc."

"Oral sex does present some risk of transmission because it can lead to an exchange of bodily fluids, but it's rare and unlikely. There have been minimal cases of transmission via oral sex reported, all in which sex had occurred afterwards, so we don't know for certain. But it is considered a lower-risk activity. There are a few 'look fors' to consider, before engaging in oral sex, but not too many."

"Okay, what are they?" I blurt.

"I'm getting there," Dr. Millman says.

"Sorry, go on."

"The things to look out for are pretty straightforward and common sense, such as making sure there are no open cuts, sores or bleeding at the time of contact. Don't perform cunnilingus on Trinity when she's close to menstruating. At that time, the HIV levels in her fluids are higher. I assume you're on medication, Trinity?"

"Yes. I take Atripla once a day as my ART therapy, and I began it as soon as I was diagnosed two years ago. My last CD4 count was 1200 cubic millilitres, when I was checked last month," Trinity says, lowering her head as if embarrassed to be sharing this information.

"Don't." I move off my chair and crouch before her. "Look at me."

"I'm sorry, it's hard to talk about, especially with you here. I feel dirty…unworthy of you."

"Fruitloop," I whisper into her ear and she finally looks at me, unshed tears making her eyes look glassy. "None of this matters to me. We're a team now, Trinity, and you talking about this makes me proud; ecstatic that you'd put yourself out there for me. You're fighting every day, remember? You're brave."

"Yes. And I'll always fight."

"Good." I kiss her forehead. "Dr. Millman will give it to us straight, don't worry. You're mine now, Trin. And it's our decision."

"You're right. I'm sorry," she says, giving me a smile, then looks past me. "Sorry, Dr. Millman, this is hard for me."

"No need to apologize, Trinity. Here, let me help make you feel better," he says warmly, handing Trin a chart. "See here? Your count is very good. Anything between 500 and 1200 is healthy, as I'm sure you remember from first being diagnosed. It means your viral load is actually quite low, so there isn't much reason to worry about oral transmission. The fact that you take your meds daily also helps immensely. My only suggestion where oral sex is concerned is to avoid it a few days before and after your cycle, just to be sure. Other than that, you and Hendrix can have a healthy and active sexual relationship." He takes a few things from a cabinet and holds up a small square package. "And if you're still worried, you can always try using this. It's a dental dam, a small piece of latex you position over the vaginal area as a barrier when performing oral sex. Some people like to use them and others don't, it's your decision as a couple. Condoms when performing fellatio are also an option," he says, handing me a few packages of the dental dams along with some condoms. He also hands me a prescription for a pre-exposure prophylaxis (PrEP) medication called Truvada. It's a preventative therapy that was approved by Health Canada in February 2016. Despite its high cost, seeing as it's not covered by insurance, I think it will still be worth it if it'll give Trin and I some piece of mind and further reduce our risk level.

We spend another few minutes asking questions and, best of all, my girl even laughed once or twice. By the time we left, I could see the tension in Trinity's eyes dissolving. My spunky girl who loved to give as good as she got was coming back to me.

On the way home, she opened up about a few last truths. She shared all of the dirty things she wanted to do to me, which had me pulling over at the side of the road needing a taste of her sweet mouth.

Taking her to see Dr. Millman was the best decision I've made in a long time, and I cannot wait to reap the benefits.

36

Trinity

"Man, he's perfect for you, Trin. I'm very happy for you; I can't believe he took you to his doctor! I mean, how many guys would do that? Gah, I love him a little bit more right now," Shannon says, gushing through the phone.

I decided to give her a call once we got back; I wanted her feedback on my decision to have sex with Hendrix tonight. I seriously don't think I can wait much longer, and he's been incredible with me.

Except once we got back to the garage, when Hendrix suggested that I head up and relax, maybe have a nap. He said he imagined that I might be a bit drained after our appointment. And, of course, I got pissy…

"A nap?" I cross my arms over my chest as we stand at the bottom of the stairs leading up to my place.

"Yeah, I got a few things to finish up. Flynn told us to take the rest of the day, but I figured I'd work a bit while you go up and have a nap." He shrugs like he doesn't see what he's doing.

"I'm not sick. I feel great, and I don't need a fucking nap. I have to feed Beast and change his litter. Don't you dare suggest I need a nap!" I spew, and I'm pissed right off. How dare he treat me like this, like I'm fragile and need a nap after being a bit stressed? *Before I can speak, he's*

right up in my face, pulling at my crossed arms before moving us so our chests are touching. We're both clearly worked up, chests heaving, our eyes dilated with a mix of lust and anger.

"Listen to me, Fruitloop. Calm yourself down, and hear me good," he grits out, pulling me even closer to him. "I don't think you need a nap 'cause you're sick. I was only suggesting you get some rest before I come up and slip my raging hard cock between your legs, over and over again for the rest of the night. I thought after I took care of the cat and a few things, I'd come up and show you just how fucking good you can feel," he says, his tone cocky.

"Oh."

"Yeah, 'oh'," the smug bastard repeats. I know. I'm an asshole. *"That sound good?" He leans down and pulls on my bottom lip, while taking my hand and placing it on his thickness.*

"So good." I squeeze him.

"Good. Now go rest up for me. I'll be up soon," he says, before kissing me.

"Yeah," I sigh dreamily, "he really is something. I think there's definitely going to be a *burglary* tonight," I squeal, before laughing so hard I almost pee.

"Oh, my fuck! It's about time. Yay, Trin, I'm excited for you!" she says. "Now, tell me all the juicy details. Does Hendrix know tonight's the night? What did the doctor say? Eep!"

After I respond to Shannon's Spanish Inquisition, I draw a bath, shave and trim all necessary parts, and gather the dental dam and condoms from my purse, placing them on my white night table.

"TRIN?" I HEAR Hendrix call from the kitchen.

I'd unlocked the door for him a few minutes ago, once I got his text saying he was on his way up.

I'm a mess. My heart's going to jump out of my chest, and butterflies fill my stomach as I stand in the middle of my bedroom waiting for him. After my bath, I put on my sexiest lingerie, then quickly covered it with flannel pants and a loose Depeche Mode concert shirt, not wanting to appear too presumptuous. *And because my nerves got the best of me.*

"In here," I call, my voice wavering, my nervousness clear.

"Were you slee—" He stops once he opens the door. "Hey, baby. You're up. I thought you might be napping." His eyes rake over my body, a small grin tugging on his lip.

"Nope. I had a bath and, since then, I've been waiting for you," I admit, as he takes a step in and closes the door behind him.

"I like hearing that. I've been thinking of you, too." His eyes flare as he steps closer to me. "But I was definitely not thinking of *that*," he smiles, pointing at my docking station, and I roll my eyes at his comment.

Justin Bieber's "Let Me Love You" plays from where my iPod is docked on the dresser. Despite Hard Rock Hendrix's disdain, to me the lyrics couldn't be any more perfect for this moment.

The song ends as we both stare at my iPod. I switch it to another playlist. "Better?" I ask.

"Marginally, but it'll do. But I'm not here to listen to music tonight. What have you been thinking about me, Trinny?" he asks. His voice is gruff and his eyes are hazy with lust, reflecting my own desire.

Any lingering doubts I may have had crumble into a heap of ruins as we stand face-to-face. I'm going to give in to him, to this, to everything that's between us. I'm going to always be open and honest with him, willing to put myself out there one hundred percent where this man is concerned. I'm overcome with the emotions I'm feeling towards Hendrix now that he's in my bedroom standing right in front of me.

"I was thinking how much I love you. About how you're an incredibly kind, honest and caring man. One I'm so deeply in love with it scares the shit out of me, but at the same time, makes me feel like I could do anything, like I could fly." I step closer, resting my fingers on a button of his plaid work shirt. "This will change everything," I say, looking up into his dilating eyes as I start undoing the buttons, revealing a white muscle shirt underneath. "You'll really be mine now, Hendrix."

"I already was, since the second I set my eyes on you."

"You've changed me. You've helped me heal so much. Thank you for being you, Hendrix." I kiss his exposed chest and arms, running my lips over the ink that graces his strong collarbone. I kiss the colourful four-point star on his biceps, and run my tongue over the Latin quote, "Timendi causa est nescire" (*Ignorance is the cause of fear),* that's peeking out beneath the strap of his undershirt.

He responds by gripping the hem of my t-shirt. "Change is good, Trin. You've helped me, too. You've let me see you, and I've learned to open up. And I'm completely in love with you. It's immeasurable…the way you make me feel. I'll never take it for granted, ever. It's you and me, Trinny, for as long as we get. We're a team, and you're my forever. And this change, this right here—seeing you like this, giving yourself to me—is fucking perfect." He gently slips my shirt off over my head, and his eyes widen when he reveals my lemon yellow satin bra.

"I love you. You're my happy," is all I can muster as his eyes rake over my full chest and his face starts nuzzling my neck, a hint of tongue running across my neck, jaw and chest.

"Jesus, you're spectacular. Tell me, Fruitloop, do the panties match?" he asks, before taking my mouth, ravishing it with his. Our tongues begin their familiar dance. Inhaling one another, we become lost in the sensations, overcome with need for one another. As our tongues duel, he groans, and it's the sexiest sound I have ever heard. Reaching up, I lock my hands behind his neck, fusing our bodies even closer. He's driving me insane with desire and excitement. Lowering my hands, I pull on the hem of his undershirt, silently letting him know I want it off. One of his hands rests on the back of my neck, pulling me impossibly closer, while the other grips my hip.

"I can't remember what colour they are. Maybe you should check," I finally gasp, breaking the spell his kisses have on me. I smile against his lips before pulling his shirt off to join mine. He's a sight, all toned and tanned, his tattoos running everywhere. I want to take the time to explore him, to run my tongue over each vibrant piece: the dragon, the script, the koi fish and the sword piece on his back. But…another time. I'm too far-gone to slow this down.

"See? Best change of my life. Getting to really touch you." He slides his hands down my bare ribs, resting his fingers on my waist. "*You ready for me?*" he asks intently, his eyes boring into mine. I look up to meet them once I'm done perusing his beautiful chest all the way down to that sexy "V" sculpted into his torso, with those muscle cut lines I ache to lick.

"Fuck, yes," I admit, while running my hands appreciatively over his taut pecs and arms.

"Damn, you make me hard. That sexy little mouth of yours…I love hearing you talk dirty, Trin." He goes down on his knees in front of me, giving me an upside-down glimpse of his amazing back tattoo as I look over his shoulders. I run my hands along the bit I can see. "IN PERPETUUM ET UNUM DIEM."

"What does it mean?" I whisper.

Pausing, he looks up at me, eyes intense but warm, a boyish smile breaking out over his face. "What, my back tatt? It's Latin for 'forever and a day'. It's always resonated with me, so I got it inked." He shrugs like it's nothing, like there isn't some deeper meaning, and I let it go.

"It's beautiful. I can't wait to explore it up close."

"You're what's beautiful, Trin," Hendrix says, kissing down my stomach and taking my flannel pants along for the ride. "Ah, matching panties. Very fucking sexy," he mutters, placing his mouth against my pussy, his hands on my ass cheeks. Pulling me forward, he inhales me deeply while running his tongue over the scrap of satin that's covering me. "Spread 'em, Trinny. Let me in."

I do it instinctively, my hands tangled in his hair for stability, and I keep them there for balance as he moves his tongue over the inside of my thighs. He licks along the path where my thigh meets my hip, his subtle scruff tickling, making my legs wobble. The sensations cause me to move closer to him, my pussy clenching with desire, my hips starting to buck, hinting at my need for more.

"Oh, shit, that feels so good…" I blurt, because it really fucking does.

"These need to come off now. I can't wait any longer. Finally, I get to taste my sweet Fruitloop," he says, inhaling me again, acknowledging my not-so-subtle hint. "I can't wait to get sticky with you, Trin. I fucking ache for you. I need to be inside you," Hendrix murmurs against my pussy, before slipping my panties off and tossing them behind him. "Look at you, baby. I knew you'd be perfect," he mutters, sliding his calloused fingers along my lips, no doubt feeling how ready I am.

37

Hendrix

FUCK FOREPLAY.

I need inside Trinity right now.

But it's been two years for her and my girl deserves to be worshipped. And worship her is exactly what I plan on doing, even if I come out looking like a teenage boy for blowing it in my briefs.

"I want to go slow and explore every inch of you," I say, taking in her aroused scent while running my finger along her wet lips, "but I don't know how long I can wait. I'm gonna blow my load just from smelling your sweet pussy." I add another finger into the mix and run them both along her slit. Looking up, I see her eyes heavy with desire, so dilated they're almost black. "How about you get on the bed and let me make you feel good, baby? Let me touch you properly," I beg, looking up at her and seeing her nod in agreement.

Standing up, I take her mouth with mine as I guide her backwards onto her bed. She really is a work of art, her body toned and lush in all the right places. She's got killer legs that I can't wait to feel around my neck, as I fuck her deep. Frozen at the foot of the bed, I take her in. She's sexy as hell in only her bra, her bare pussy teasing me to come play. I watch her move to the centre of the bed. "Spread your legs for me, Trin. Let me see that wet pussy. And let's take your bra off. I wanna see those fucking gorgeous tits of yours, too." I lick my lips in anticipation. My dick is rock hard and throbbing, straining against the fly of my jeans. Unable to take the pressure, I remove my pants, leaving me in my blue boxers.

"Christ, you're perfection," I say, moving to the bed. Resting one knee on the mattress, I move my hand along her thighs before pulling her down closer to me, where she belongs. Moving back to rest on my haunches, I start to lick up from her left foot, trailing my tongue ever-so-softly over her velvet skin. Nibbling at her calf, I run my hand up her other leg, while my tongue continues its slow languid movements toward the final destination. The teasing causes her to squirm and to try to move up the bed.

Hearing her admit she was thinking about me this afternoon has made me horny as fuck. Then hearing that she loved me nearly knocked me on my ass. My heart and soul have never felt so completely connected to another being as they do with this girl. I'll be thankful everyday for the time I have with her, no matter how long it turns out to be. Trinity Adams was made for me. I will make sure she never feels anything but love between us. And right now, I'm going to show her just how much I crave, love and adore her.

"Come back down here, baby. I'm gonna taste you." I lean over the foot of the bed, positioning myself above her pussy.

"God, Hendrix, yes," she says, voice trembling.

"Are you nervous, sweetheart?" I ask, giving her legs one last tug, getting her right where I want her—with her ass off the bed's edge. Running my hands up her smooth legs, I say, "You're so fucking soft, too fucking sexy." She is, and touching her is driving me wild. Trinity deserves to hear how incredible she is, and just how much she affects me. Looking at her, her skin flushed, her breaths shallow, I ask, "Want my mouth on you, Trin? You ready?" I lick my lips, driving home the fact that I'm beyond ready.

"So much. Excited, too," she replies, licking her lips. "It's been too long. You're sure?"

"Yes. That's my girl. I want you to be excited. I'm gonna fix that right now. Just enjoy my mouth while I consume you. No thinking about stupid shit, though, Trin. Focus on feeling me, okay, baby? You're with me, now."

"I—I'll try," she nods.

"That's my good girl," I say, running my index finger along her wetness. *Shit, she's more than ready for me.* "You're fucking wet, baby. You like my touch, eh?" I ask with a grin, smothering her clit with the pad of my calloused thumb. She bucks off the bed and I swear I'm gonna blow from how responsive she is, like a Ferrari. "Pull your nipples for me, sweetheart. Pull 'em while I suck on your clit and take this pussy with my mouth."

"Hendrix! I—caan't," she cries, as I put my head down and swirl my tongue over the sensitive nub. I slide two fingers inside. She's fucking tight, and so fucking warm. Her pussy spasms, clamping down on my fingers, gripping me, and it's taking everything for me not to completely lose it.

"My God, you're tight. Feeling you grip my dick like this is gonna fucking destroy me, baby," I tell her, before taking her clit in my mouth and pulling it just enough that it sends her body reeling. She's panting as I continue to lick and swirl my tongue down the length of her pussy, my face practically gliding between her lips. She's so wet, and her taste is like nothing I've ever experienced. She's tangy with that perfect blend of sweet, her pussy soft and velvety against my tongue. "Too fucking sweet," I say, keeping the momentum, steadying my pace and rocking my tongue and fingers at the same time. I feel her clenching and I know she's close.

"Do it, Trin. Grab those luscious tits, and make those nipples hard for me. Get them ready for my mouth." I look up from between her legs and smile, seeing her give in, wrapping her hands around her beautiful breasts, pulling her rose coloured nipples like I asked. "That's it, my sexy girl. Fuck, you taste so goddamned good. You should see how fucking hot you look right now, your face pink, your tits bouncing, those big beautiful eyes watching me as I devour you. Yeah, you like my mouth between your legs as much as I do. Shiiiiit, I could stay here all night."

"Oh, oh, yes, please! It feels so good, so, so, so good," Trin moans, her body shaking from the pleasure. Unable to stop myself, the thought of having this woman's excitement all over my face becomes all too consuming. Her scent and taste drive me to the brink, fuelling my desire to give her everything and have her explode on my tongue. My hands move up her legs. Sliding them under her ass, I grab both cheeks and lift her up, pulling her closer to my mouth. I start relentlessly lapping, licking and sucking her pussy with a wild determination I've never known before.

"O—ohhh, yes, there, there, yeah, yeah," she calls out, her body heaving and wiggling beneath me as her orgasm rocks through her. She's left panting and breathless and looking like a fucking goddess.

"Fuck it, I need inside of you. I need to feel you come on my cock now, Trin. Are you ready?" I ask, moving up her body and lavishing each pert nipple with swirls of my tongue. She tastes like perfection everywhere.

"God, yes. So ready. I want you inside me, I'm more than ready," Trin says, but then starts to sit up, a look of panic crossing her face. "Oh, no. Shit. I'm sorry," she pauses, her hand flying to her face.

"What's wrong, baby?" I move her away.

"We didn't use the dental dam," she says, leaning up on her elbows, her facial expression one of worry.

Rolling off her and to the side, I move up the short distance to join her, and lean my back against the headboard. "Trin," I pull her around and up towards me. Good thing she's tiny; I easily manage to position her so she straddles me. Running my thumb down her cheek, I ask: "Truth?"

"Always."

"There was no way I was using that thing. Condoms are enough of a barrier between us when we make love. There was no way I wasn't tasting you. Screw the dam." I rest my forehead against hers. "That all right with you?"

"Yes," she nods.

"Now...do you want me?"

"Yes, I want you inside me, badly. Hendrix, now. No more waiting."

With that, she arches her back, reaching over to the nightstand for a condom. I lick up her breastbone to lap at her tits.

"You gonna ride me, Fruitloop?" I ask, moving us down to the centre of the bed, positioning us so she's wrapped around me, her legs on either side of my thighs hugging me tightly. Her tits rub against me and it feels sensational, the hardness of her nipples bumping along my chest, turning me on more and more with each shift and movement. Her gorgeous ass rests in my hands, which are ready to help glide her tightness up, down, and all around, over and over, when she rides my rock-hard cock.

"Yeah, I want to. I'm well-past ready for this," she replies, as she rips open the condom package, then reaches down between us and sheaths me. *Tingles*. That's what her hands on my cock for the first time feel like. It's a feeling of rightness that's being perfectly defined before my eyes; Trinity Adams is going to be my undoing.

Raising herself back into cowgirl position, she slowly lowers herself onto me. Feeling her slip me inside her body is surreal. Her hot walls grip my shaft as if they're welcoming me home. The warmth of her pussy hugs me, pulling me right into the place we both want my cock to be—deep inside of her. "Fuck you're beautiful," I moan, thrusting up, moving so she can take every inch of me. It's a euphoric feeling, instantly addictive. She leans forward and our chests rub together, and her nipples harden immediately from the contact, making my dick even harder. I will need to have this every day for the rest of my life.

"Fuck, Trin," I gasp up at her. "Is this what love feels like? 'Cause, I've never felt anything like it before."

I hold her tight while she moves her hips, rocking them ever so slowly. *God, I love her.* When I'm with her I'm overwhelmed, and captivated. I've never felt this way before. It's perfection, the way her body just melts with mine, her tits bouncing on my chest, her pussy sucking me into her, and her tiny moans—all for me. "Fuck, baby, this feels too goddamn good."

"Yes," she says, and reaches up to run her hands through the back of my hair, her breathing low and hitched as I push up into her, moving in and out and grinding myself against her clit. It's a languid motion, perfection as our bodies connect for the first time. "I've never felt anything this right in my life. Nothing compares to the way I feel being with you."

Our eyes and lips find each other once again as she picks up the pace; after a few beats however, she sits back up, leaving my lips feeling neglected and longing for more. Trin leans way back, her hands behind her on the mattress to bear her weight, and the movement gives me a perfect view of her magnificent body. I stare down to where we're connected, and can see my cock as it slips and slides in and out of her slippery pussy. Her tits bounce while she thrusts and swivels her hips around my cock, breathing heavily, moans of pleasure escaping with each push, taking me into her lithe body all the way to the hilt. The room is filled with the sounds of our desire, our bodies moving and breathing in sync, and the whispers of how good this all feels. Lana Del Rey's "Young and Beautiful" plays and Trin moans, suddenly picking up the pace as tempo changes. She rocks sexily on top of me, her hips taking me hard and fast, bringing us both to the precipice. Her pink bangs flap against her sweaty forehead in time to the rhythm. Our eyes lock and then, with a few swift and frenzied moves of our hips, the intensity of the feeling builds until it can't go any higher and we tip over the edge, both shouting out and exploding at the same time.

Our hearts beat erratically. Our breaths are uneven as we come back down. I pull her down to me and kiss her forehead, wrap my arms around her and hold her tight, enjoying the moment.

"Jesus, you're incredible. That was incredible. Thank you for giving that part of yourself to me, Trin. It means everything. I love you."

"I love you, Hendrix. Thanks for being patient with me. Thank you for making love to me, for making it special. For today. For being you," she says, gazing at me, her beautiful face serious. A lone tear escapes down her cheek. She smooths it away before adding, "I can't wait to do that again. You ready?"

She gives me one of those smiles, the ones that not only lighten her whole face, but my whole goddamn world. I laugh and stretch out on the mattress, dragging her down to lay beside me, her head resting on my chest. *Perfect.*

In Perpetuum Et Unum Diem. Forever and a day, that's how long I'll love this girl. I was being honest before; I never knew why that phrase struck me so intensely when I first saw it, but now it's never been clearer.

It was meant for *her.*

38

Trinity

It's been too many days since Andrea's allowed me to visit but rather than bitch about it, I let it go. I need to make the most of whatever time I get to spend with her. We text daily, but she's been bypassing my attempts to visit her in the Palliative Care Unit at the hospital.

Then when a text arrived this morning asking if I could come see her, I literally dropped everything—including my date with Hendrix—so I could be here. To say I was happy was an understatement.

"Thanks for coming, Trin. She's been asking for you all day," Simon tells me as we enter Andrea's room. I notice he looks pale, tired, and his usually twinkling blue eyes are dull, telling me he's hurting, worried. He gives me his best attempt at a smile before rubbing his hand along his jaw, his ginger-coloured stubble now a full beard. We both pull our face masks over our noses and mouths.

Making my way over to Andrea's bed, I smile down at her before giving her a gentle kiss on her forehead. I arrange her usual order of a tall gingerbread latte—along with the black coffee I brought for Simon—on the small table.

"I have," she says. "It's true. But only because I missed the smell of gingerbread and needed some Hendrix gossip. Quit your fussing and sit," she says. I take off my pea green winter coat and hang it on the back of the chair.

"Patience, woman, I just got here. Behave or I'll tell you nothing," I quip, taking a seat.

"I just want to know about the sex. The rest of the gushy shit you can keep to yourself," she laughs, and I internally cringe, noticing how laboured her laughter is, more of a series of wheezes. And her breathing is more erratic and shallow-sounding than the last time I was here.

It was Simon who'd texted this morning and asked if I'd stop by, saying Andrea needed to talk to me. Hendrix offered to come up, but I figured I'd best come alone until I knew what she needed to tell me. I really want Andrea and Simon to meet Hendrix, but I want to make sure she'll be all right with it. Even though she texts me everyday telling me to bring her my eye candy, I want to be sure she'd actually be up to it. Hendrix, being Hendrix, was fine about not being invited along for the visit, but was adamant that he be the one to drive me to and from the hospital. He knows how hard these visits are and he didn't want me driving upset. Plus, it's been snowing off and on for the last few days. I thought he was being over-protective, but caved anyway because it's an awesome feeling having someone care so much about your wellbeing…I mean, someone other than your aunt and uncle.

"And you'd better tell me everything, or you won't be allowed to visit me anymore," she laughs again, and it causes her to cough.

"Funny. Seems to me certain people have been limiting my visits. Not sure they deserve my gossip." I cross my arms over my chest in mock protest.

"Oh, zip it and spill it. You know you want to," she says, taking the proffered sip from the Starbucks cup Simon is holding near her mouth, helping her to drink.

I fight back tears at seeing my friend so helpless. Andrea doesn't look good at all, and I'm worried the news she has to share with me today isn't going to be anything I want to hear.

It's been two weeks since I last saw her. Between work, Hendrix, and Andrea being either too tired or having had a bad day, it's been way too long.

"You're lucky I missed you," I say as I lean forward, shifting my chair closer so I can rub her arm. "How come you're keeping me away?" I ask, barely audible. I'm upset that she's kept me at arm's length. I don't mean to be selfish, but I'm just not ready to lose her so fast, and from my conversation with Simon a few days earlier, Andrea doesn't have much time left. And I can see that now just by looking at her.

"I didn't want you to remember me this way. And I've been making decisions and plans and I wanted to see you when I was ready to tell you. And now I'm ready. You're not going to like it, and I don't wan—" She cuts herself off with another coughing fit, reaching out for a blue crescent-shaped tray on the side table. Simon places it under her mouth, and I feel tears pricking my eyes as blood dribbles from Andrea's mouth into the waiting receptacle. I adjust my face mask.

"Andrea." I squeeze her hand, tears falling now that her coughing spell has stopped. Seeing her like this, I'm unable to keep them in anymore.

"I know, Trin. I know." She gives my hand a weak squeeze back as Simon fusses about, wiping her mouth with a gloved-covered hand.

"All better, beautiful," Simon murmurs, kissing her cheek before heading to the adjacent bathroom to rinse the tray and dispose of the soiled tissues. And my heart literally breaks, at seeing how strong these two people are. I feel suddenly hot and a bit dizzy, as if I might be sick. Thankfully, Simon comes back in time to hand me a bottle of water, as if he can see it on my face.

"Thank you." I twist off the cap, pull up the bottom of my mask and take a long sip.

"Sorry you had to see that. This is why I don't want visitors," Andrea says, her voice weaker than before.

"You know I could care less. I want to be here for you. I love you."

"Oh, sweet girl, but you are and you have been. You've made the last year bearable," she hiccups, and I see that she's crying. "You've helped me so much, Trinity, given me courage I'd never had. I love you, too, my dear. So much."

"I can't lose you." I take a tissue from the box Simon has passed me, and try to wipe away my tears, but there are too many.

"I'm going to go for a walk. Let you two talk." Simon gives me a sad smile before kissing my cheek and leaving us alone.

"Simon's taking me home tomorrow, Trin," Andrea says, then pauses, to give it time to sink in.

"What? How can they let you leave, you're sic—Oh. Oh, no…" I say, covering my mouth with my hand to lock down the sob that wants to escape so badly.

"I'm going home to die. There isn't anything left that they can do for me here. I'm exhausted all the time. The cancers are spreading. They can't find where the blood is coming from and I won't survive a surgery. And my lungs are shot. My doctor has agreed to let me go home, to spend my final days with Simon in comfort and in peace. In *love*," she says, and gives me a warm—but sad—smile.

"Oh, Andrea," I sob. "I'm so sorry. Please let me come over and help you be comfortable. I can cook and clean, I can help with anything you need," I offer, but even as I say it, I know it's too risky for me. Although my immune system is strong at the moment, things could easily change if the right virus or bacteria happens upon me. I know she and Simon wouldn't be willing to put me at risk me by being in such close and intimate contact. Regardless, I offer, because if she said she needed me, I'd be there.

"And, what, let you risk getting sick? I can't do that. And don't ask me to. It's bad enough I've let you come today. Soooo…you won't be able to come see me again until I've passed," she says, as huge tears drip from her once vibrant eyes. "I needed to be the one to tell you. To say goodbye now, before I can't."

I can't speak. I can't find any words, they've escaped me. All I can do is sit and stare at Andrea, my beautiful friend, and commit her to memory as I listen to her tell me one last time how proud she is of me for moving forward with Hendrix, to never take a day for granted, and how I was one of the best people she'd ever had the pleasure to know.

By the time Simon is back, I'm too overcome with emotion to speak or move. At some point, he must have taken my phone because the next thing I know, Hendrix is rushing to me and lifting me into his strong arms, whispering sweet words in my ear as he rubs my back and tries to calm me. I wrap my arms around his neck and cry big splashy tears as sobs and whimpers tear through my body. I kiss Andrea on the forehead, and Hendrix and I wave both soundless goodbyes to her and Simon as Hendrix and I leave the room for a nearby waiting area. He gives me some time to calm down, then walks me out of the hospital and drives me home.

Hendrix is always what I need, in the best of times and in the worst of times.

Later that night, Andrea called, sounding a little stronger, and we talked. I apologized for my breakdown, and she told me to shove it. But not before telling me how hot my boyfriend was (even with his paper mask on) and that she could die a happy woman having seen the man who loves me coming to my rescue the way he did, after seeing the man who finally saw *me.* Then there's a silence, and Simon comes on to tell me that Andrea's fallen asleep.

I'm going to miss these calls…and her.

39

Trinity

PACING THE LENGTH of the hotel room, I'm livid. The feeling of the soft carpet under my toes does nothing to calm my anger as I pace and pace, waiting, waiting.

Clutching my cell phone to my ear, I silently will Shannon to pick up her damn phone already. Even if she is out with Cannon, it's Code. We always pick up for each other. I need to vent before he gets back. *Boy, is this man in the doghouse right now. He's gone too far with his bossy-assed shit this time, let me tell you.* A girl can only take so much before she loses it.

Tonight was supposed to be a romantic getaway. Hendrix and I had a great time at the car show today. We made an amazing team, and we managed to drum up a lot of potential business for Ignition Inc. Hendrix booked a complete overhaul on a '66 Mustang that completely made his day, and I got lots of great comments on my Powerpoint presentation.

One of the best parts about today was that it was a perfect distraction, one I badly needed. I only looked at my phone about half a million times for updates on Andrea. Thankfully, the only message all day was from her. She wished us luck and pretty much demanded that I send her pictures of Hendrix and me throughout the day, before adding that even solo pictures of Hendrix leaning against some muscle cars would be okay, too. At first I was going to be a shit and write something cheeky back, but then she texted that she was only kidding, she really did want pictures of us both, that she was missing me. Which of course made me weepy. Hendrix had hugged me tight to his chest the way I love, which made me feel a lot better.

It's been a few days since Andrea was moved back home. She hasn't changed her mind about me visiting, and I'm really trying hard to respect her wishes. I do, however, talk to Simon a lot, and I might have even popped in to see him and quietly help out the other day, too, doing some cooking for him while she was sleeping. *What Andrea doesn't know won't hurt her.*

By the end of the car show today, I managed to send her twenty pictures of Hendrix and me in all sorts of crazy poses and with some pretty cool old cars, too. She loved them, told me I'd made her day, and that made me happy. I even sent a few of just Hendrix in front of a hot rod, 'cause I'm nice like that, and he was thrilled to make muscles and pose for her. It honestly was such a great day for both of us; we should be out celebrating. Instead, I'm angry, and he's out.

"Come on, come on. Pick up..." I'm about to disconnect when Shannon finally answers.

"Hey, you! How was the auto show? I bet everyone loved your presentation. Did Hendrix have to fight to keep all the hottie mechanics away from his woman? I bet he went all caveman, eh?" she drones, then hesitates. "Wait. Why are you calling me? You're supposed to be living it up in Toronto with your man. Didn't you have dinner reservations?" She stops, allowing me to get a word in.

"I know, we did, but we're sort of fighting right now," I say, walking over to the black bar fridge and grabbing the Sigg water bottle I'd tossed in there earlier.

"What? How is that possible? That man is a dream and you're...well, *you?*" she asks, surprised.

"He's being ridiculous. Overbearing. And way too bossy for my liking, the stupid ogre-head," I scowl.

"Wow, you really are pissed off if you're breaking out the big names," she chuckles, and I smile a little, but then scoff, realizing I might need to reevaluate my friendships. This one might have run its course.

"Shut up. I'm angry. Don't make me laugh. I'm mad. Whose side are you on, anyway?"

"Yours, usually, but it's Hendrix we're talking about here. That man is crazy about you."

"Well, he's completely in the wrong today, so you're on Team Trin, okay?"

"Alright, tell me what he did. Wait…he better not have left you alone in downtown Toronto. Tell me that's not the case, before I hop in my car and come kick his ass." *And there she is. Friendship saved.*

"No, of course not. He went to grab us some takeout from that Persian place that's supposed to be amazing, the restaurant we should actually be sitting in right now," I sigh.

"Oh, God. That jerk! The nerve!" she exclaims sarcastically. "Imagine, him bringing you some awesome takeout to eat in bed, followed by, I presume, a dessert of hot sex? You're right. What a dick," she harrumphs.

"Well, that shouldn't matter. It's what he did before that counts."

"I'm listening."

"We were supposed to go out to eat, but I had a headache after the show so he cancelled. Told me I needed to *rest*. And I lost it on him. Told him that I don't need another doctor, that I felt fine, that I was a competent adult who can handle going out with a headache. Sheesh, it was probably just from being under those goddamn fluorescent lights all day."

"What? You got mad at him? Why? Because he worries about you,

Trinny? Do you hear yourself? Besides, if every time he suggests you might need some rest you freak out and have a temper tantrum, doesn't that kind of prove his point?"

I don't answer her. I keep talking, my frustration overtaking my rational side.

"But this isn't the only time! It's been more and more lately. Heaven forbid that I drive myself to my doctor appointments, or to group therapy on Fridays. He insists it's because it's snowing, but he's treating me like I'm made of glass all of a sudden. Not that he'd admit to it, but I know that's why. And when I went to see Simon, Hendrix insisted on driving me and picking me up. I'm not his goddamn child, or his burden; he has a garage to run and I can drive for Pete's sake. Who *does* that? Or get thi—"

"Trin, listen—" she says, trying to interrupt my tirade, but I'm nowhere near done yet.

"Then, ha! Listen to this! This—this one, you'll see he's nuts. This morning we needed to leave to come to Toronto. I was going to feed Beast and change his litter before we left. And Hendrix lost it, forbade me from ever changing the litter again!" I start to talk louder, my hands flying around as I tell her what happened, almost shouting into the phone.

"Fruitloop, come on. I don't want to hit traffic on the 401, and we gotta set up. Doors open at ten," Hendrix says from the kitchen, where he's entered my apartment.

"Okay, I'm almost ready. My bags are there," I say, pointing to the couch. As I make my way into the kitchen, my steps falter as I take him in. He's wearing a light-brown button-up which hugs a little across his broad chest, and his distressed blue jeans look great wrapped around his legs. I'm a little jealous of the denim getting to hug those muscular thighs and that gorgeous ass all day. His warm brown eyes meet mine, and I can tell by the

sexy smirk that I've just been busted checking him out.

"Like what you see?"

"Hell, yes. Let's just go straight to the hotel."

"Keep staring at me with those fuck-me eyes and we just might," Hendrix says, eliminating the distance between us. "You look beautiful, baby. And I want nothing more than to slip inside you, but we really gotta go." He kisses my forehead, "But I'll definitely make it up to you tonight."

"Deal. How about you take my bags, and I'll meet you at the truck in, say, seven minutes?"

Chuckling, he walks towards my couch and picks up my laptop and overnight bags. "What's gonna take exactly seven minutes?" he asks.

"I have to run down to feed Beast and change his box, and give him a little love. I know he already misses me," I beam.

"The hell you are," Hendrix all but barks in my direction, completely taking me off guard. I haven't heard him speak to me in that tone since the first time we met.

"Pardon me?" I ask, not hiding the shock in my voice at all.

"I said 'the hell you are'. You're not to change the cat litter anymore. Joe, Brody or I will do it. I already told them and they agreed. No way you're gonna touch that again, ever."

"You've got to be kidding me? Why the hell not, exactly?" I tap my foot to keep myself from throat-punching him. "I'm seriously getting tired of this alpha bossy shit you've got going on lately."

"Too bad. I'm not compromising on this. Not gonna risk your health over some goddamn cat litter…"

"Stop talking, Trinity!" Shannon's voice cuts through my rapid thoughts and ramblings.

"What? I'm not done yet," I reply, annoyed.

"Jeez, let me talk. You're going on and on…"

"Sorry. I'm just crazy mad."

"I get that, but, man, did you call for my opinion or to simply make me suffer while you vented down the line at me?"

"No, I need advice. Sorry," I say awkwardly, taking a long sip of water, my throat dry from being long-winded.

"Did he tell you *why*? Knowing Hendrix, there must be a reason for it."

"Yeah, he mentioned some parasite that cats carry in their feces. I guess pregnant women and people with inadequate immune systems can catch it and get really sick. Apparently he's been Googling all kinds of stuff about HIV and AIDS. Anyway, it's called toxoplasmosis—or something or other. I got pissed because you catch it from touching cat shit, Shannon. I'm not touching the shit, I always wear disposable gloves. He's being a tad too dramatic and way too overprotective," I sigh, angry all over again as it accumulates in my mind. Not just about the catbox incident, per se, but when all the other incidents are grouped together with it, the whole picture seems like overkill. I'd already more or less gotten over the cat litter thing this morning. *How could I not, with an apology like this…*

I'm about to tell Hendrix to leave, when he scoops me up and places me gently on the countertop despite my protests. Nudging his way between my legs, he takes my face in his hands and begins rubbing his thumbs gently along my jaw. "You can't be mad at me. You can't fault me for loving you so much, and wanting to do everything I possibly can to keep you healthy and safe." He rests his forehead on mine. "I intend to make you be my forever, Trinny. Don't want any stupid shit that I can prevent taking you away from me." His sincere words completely obliterate my anger.

"Exactly," I hear Shannon mutter, breaking me away from my thoughts about the first time he pissed me off today yet managed to convince me to forgive him. *Not this time, though. He's gone too far telling me that I need to stay home and rest. This is supposed to be a romantic getaway!*

"What does that mean? You're seriously not taking his side?" I shout.

"Trinny, he's not being *too* dramatic. Hendrix is being protective of what's his. Sure, he's a bit over-the-top and could probably improve in the communications department, but give him a pass once in a while. He's also a man who's so deeply in love with you he can't see past it. Hendrix may be a little overbearing but that's okay with me, since it's only because he wants to keep you healthy for as long as he can. He's scared to lose you. It's got to be in the back of his mind, especially after seeing Andrea in that hospital bed. I love him all the more for that. I get it, because even though I ignore it most days, sometimes the thought of not having you in my life creeps to the forefront, too, and I think the worst. Only for a second, but it guts me. So, yeah, Trin, I get him. And I'm on his side this round," she says, and I hear her sniff. Then I hear Cannon in the background asking if she's okay.

"Shit," I groan, sitting on the edge of the bed. "You're right. Oh my God, you're right. He's just trying to keep me safe. To protect me as best as he can. Jesus, I've been a complete bitch, haven't I?"

I hear the keycard door lock beeping, signalling that Hendrix is back. Even if he is a little too much to take sometimes, I realize he does have the best intentions, wanting to keep us together for as long as possible. *How did I ever question that logic?*

With my heart beating out of my chest, I stand in the small foyer, ready to grovel and make up with the man I adore and love. *And to think that I almost ruined our whole night…*

"I gotta go, Shan."

I hang up, tossing my phone who knows where.

40

Hendrix

Slipping my keycard into the lock, I'm a bit nervous about what I'll find on the other side of the door. Trin was mightily pissed at me. Sure, I see her point and all, but she's completely misreading my intentions.

I'm not trying to control her, like she's convinced herself I am. I'm merely struggling to keep my fucking cool every time I think of her getting hurt or reading some article about the triggers for HIV to AIDS. The other day I read an article about a woman who'd gotten seriously ill from her pet cat. I had no idea cats carried a potentially fatal parasite that could be transferred via their shit. Of course, I flipped the fuck out thinking of Trin with Beast.

But, needless to say, I could have handled that situation differently this morning. Communication has never been my strong suit; clearly, I'll need to work at that going forward. I also need to ease up on my Internet searches. If I keep it up, I'll be putting her in a bubble. A guy could seriously go nuts from worry. *And this guy is.* I've never felt or been this way before and I'm not about to start apologizing for my newfound characteristics, but I will work on my delivery. I'll do everything in my power to keep my girl safe and with me, where she belongs. She can tap her foot, cross her arms, and sass me all she likes. I'm not budging.

Opening the door, my senses are on high alert because it's quiet. Too quiet. That is, until a barrelling Trinity rushes at me, jumps into my arms and wraps her arms around me. Pulling me in close, she starts kissing all over my face.

"I'm…*kiss*…so…*peck*…*peck*…sorry…*kiss*…I…was…*kiss*…*kiss*…w rong… I…*peck*…*love you*…*kiss*…*kiss*… I'm an ass." She stops, much to my dismay, and pulls away from my grasp. Taking me by the hand, she leads me inside our suite, drops the takeout bags on the desk, and pushes me to sit down in the leather swivel chair.

Once she has me where she wants me, Trin leans in, resting her hands on the chair's armrests, caging me in on both sides. Her gorgeous body's covered in a flimsy purple t-shirt and a pair of flannel bottoms. She looks fucking sexy, with her nipples all pert, her full tits giving me a silent nod and a goad at the same time. I deny my tongue permission to go in and try to lick each peak, because I'm not sure if I'm fully out of the doghouse yet. Things are looking good, but I don't want to push my luck, not just yet.

Trinity moves further into my space and leans down, her beautiful face meeting mine. Our eyes crash as she stares deep into mine. She grins stunningly before asking: "Wanna make nice with me, now? Now that I get it?" She places her knee up on the tiny bit of space that exists between the edge of the chair and my now steel-hard cock. The shift is perfect, it brings her fruity scent washing over me. I hate that we've wasted this time arguing.

She cocks her head, lifts her index finger and softly runs it along my bottom lip as she continues. "And because you love me so much, we're just going to move right past this. I'll be better at not being too offended at your sometimes controlling ways, knowing your intentions are good, and you'll try to not be as bossy and barky."

I wrap my arms around her waist and rest my cheek on her chest. I look up, waiting to speak, but she keeps talking without letting me get a word in edgewise.

"Trin—" I try to cut her off, but she ignores me and keeps talking.

"So from here on out, there will be no more arguments and I'll stop being a pest about you driving me around like Miss Daisy." She tugs my hair, and I can't help giving her tits a little motorboat action in response. *How can I not, with my head right there?* The move makes her squeal and she grips me closer. I'll never tire of having her tight against me.

"Trinny." I stop my assault, our eyes meeting once again.

"What?" she asks, laughter lacing her tone, those grey eyes of hers so intense, so clear.

"Think we could move on to the make-up sex? You had me the second you met me at the door, and your lush tits are keeping my face comfy and warm, but I need to be inside you, Trin. I'm rock hard." I bite her bottom lip. "We were supposed to be making up for our missed opportunity this morning. You owe me, woman."

Moving her knee off the chair, she straightens herself in front of me, her pink lips taking on a slight curve, which tells me my Trinny is up to no good. I'm about to stand and demand she get on the bed so I can taste her, but she beats me to the punch.

"Take your pants off," she commands, leaving no room for argument. Naturally, when a gorgeous woman commands you to take off your pants, you listen. Too bad for me, I'm a bit stunned at Trinny's boldness. I've yet to experience this side of her and in this moment I'm a bit shocked, which leaves me frozen. Smiling, Trin slips down between my legs. "I *said* 'pants off'. My version of make-up sex involves a little of me grovelling, with my mouth…" she pauses, looking so fucking naughty and too damn sexy, "…around your big cock," she adds. She inches closer, her hands running up and down the outsides of my still jean-clad legs. My muscles contract at her touch. *Fuck, she affects me.* "I can't wait to have you on my tongue, and down my throat."

Holy Christ, this girl is a fucking minx. I swear I almost come from her words alone. Cocking her head in that sexy way she does, she continues to torment me. "Think you might like that?" Trin asks, stifling a laugh when it finally clicks and I need my goddamn pants off yesterday. I lift my hips from the chair, not wanting to make her leave her spot in front of me.

"Hell, yes," I reply, as I struggle to undo my belt and pull my jeans down. Thankfully, Trin takes over, removing my pants and boxers then tossing them aside without any fucks.

"I think we should fight at least once a day," I tell her, giving her my best shit-eating grin.

"I'll bet you do. Condom?" she asks, as always. *See how sweet and caring and considerate my girl is?* Every time we engage in anything sexual, she stops and asks if I want to use a dental dam when I go down on her, or a condom when she gives me head. And every time I tell her, "No, baby. I just want to feel you."

And it's true. The only time we use a condom without fail is for sex. Anything else I feel is low-risk as long as we're cautious and know when we shouldn't, like Dr. Millman advised us. I can't fault her, though. If anything, it's this that makes me love her that much more. Trinity has always explained that she wants me to have the choice and to be safe, always. That she will do everything she can to make sure she keeps me safe. Ironically, the same impulses I have toward her have branded *me* as an over protective asshole.

"Not a fucking chance," I tell her, pinching her chin with my thumb and index finger, pulling her in for a deep kiss. "I want to feel your wet mouth around my cock. I wanna watch you suck me." I kiss her again before releasing her face and slouching back into the chair.

"My pleasure." She pulls off her t-shirt, giving me a full-frontal view of her sensational rack. Her perfect tits sway and jiggle as she moves into position. I watch them, mesmerized, with rapt fascination.

"Yeah. We're definitely gonna be fighting more," I say, before leaning forward and taking each pink-dusted nipple into my mouth. No way I can deny myself any longer, not when they're this close.

"It's my turn," Trin says, pulling her tits away from my mouth. "Let me make you feel good, Hendrix."

"Yeah, baby? You going to suck me?" I ask, while she watches me stroke my engorged cock a few times, her eyes widening.

"Yes," she replies breathlessly, swatting my hand away and covering my cock with her hot mouth. The contact has me lifting my ass off the chair again, her mouth feels so perfect.

"Fuck, yes," I grit, as I feel her swirling around the head of my dick, her tongue darting as she laps up a bit of pre-cum that's surfaced from the contact.

"You taste so good," she says, looking up at me, her tongue now running along the underside of my cock. She slides her fist up and down my now-glistening shaft while she continues to tease the head of my cock with her tongue, over and over, before taking me all in. Between her hands, her tongue and how she keeps running her lips along the edges of my tip, I'm in fucking heaven.

"Shit, that's it, baby. Take it." With her eyes glued to mine she moves to take me all the way in again. The hand that was wrapped around my shaft has moved and she's cradling my balls now. She looks sexy as hell with my dick in her mouth and my balls in her grip.

"I'm not gonna last…" I say, after a few minutes of this exquisite torture. I arch my back and push my head back against the chair, but then Trin pops me out of her mouth, takes her hands off me, and licks her lips. My control snaps. Shifting out of the chair, I reach down, lift her up by her ass cheeks and walk us over to the bed.

"I want to come inside you. I want to feel you milking my cock with that sweet, sweet pussy, Trin. I can't wait another minute," I whisper hoarsely, hovering over her, taking her lips in a demanding kiss.

"God, yes." Thankfully, my girl's just as desire-filled as I am. Grabbing a condom, I tear it open with my teeth and quickly roll it over my cock. Trin pulls my hips in close and I slide perfectly into my girl, and fuck her 'til we're both screaming. *Damn the neighbours.*

We spend the rest of the night eating our cold takeout in bed, making plans for the shop and talking about how we need Cannon to make a move to work at Ignition Inc. full-time. Trin comes up with a few ideas to make that happen and, once again, I'm caught up in how wicked smart my beautiful girlfriend is. Wrapping her in my arms, we fall asleep.

In the end, I think, as I drift off to dreamland, the car show turned out even better than I hoped it was going to be.

Everything is perfect until the next morning.

AS WE HEAD for home in Stoney Creek, taking the Fruitland Road exit off the highway, I hear "Superman" by the Kinks begin to play loudly from the depths of Trin's purse. She looks at me, startled, then dives for her cellphone.

"It's Simon," she says. Before she even answers, I know. Simon rarely calls, he always texts.

Looking at me with unshed tears already forming, I can see that Trinity knows, too. She thumbs her phone, sending the call to voicemail rather than picking it up.

"I know, baby. You going to talk to him, or do you want me to?" I ask, my voice tender. I reach my hand over, taking hers in mine, then navigate the truck to a safe spot on the side of the road, putting the transmission in park. We're about ten minutes away from the shop, and I know this is going to be hard for her. I can't be driving when all I want to do is hold her.

"No. I can't do it, I don't think." She gives me a small shrug, while staring at the phone as it keeps ringing, over and over. Simon must be trying multiple times to get through. *What choice does he have? This isn't something you can leave on voicemail.*

"Simon needs you now, babe," I say.

Taking a deep breath, Trin removes her seatbelt, and shifts out of her seat, climbing over to sit in my lap. It's cramped, but I welcome her immediately, pulling her into my chest. The rings come a few more times before there's a lull.

"You gotta do this, Trin."

"I know," she sniffles, "but I don't want to. It will only make it true." She plucks at my t-shirt, and it pains me to think that the hurt is just beginning.

I'm about to speak when her phone goes off again. This time, she answers.

"Hello." It's barely a whisper. She looks up into my eyes. I offer a small smile, before I start wiping away the tears pouring down her beautiful face. I can barely make out Simon's words, but I hear the pain and sadness behind each word he forces out.

"I'm sorry, Trin…"

"…she loved you…"

"…peacefully…"

"…miss her so much…"

I stroke Trin's shoulder while she utters monosyllabic words here and there, hearing the news that Andrea—one of her dearest and bravest friends—passed away last night in her sleep, losing her battle with AIDS.

A battle that my girl could someday lose.

Suddenly, my reality is way too fucking realistic.

41

Trinity

Sitting on a stool at my kitchen island, I swirl red wine in my glass and think about Andrea. It's been a little more than a week since she died, and today we laid her to rest.

Simon and Andrea had decided she would be cremated—with only Simon and I in attendance as her final escorts—and that a celebration of her life would be held at their home afterwards for family and friends. It was such an 'Andrea' thing to do, and it made me miss her even more.

I think she would have been happy to see the turnout of people who came to joyfully celebrate her life. She would have loved seeing the outpouring of folks bringing Simon food and offering to help him out in any way they could. Friends from our therapy group at The AIDS Network arrived, bringing an offer for Simon to come and join our Friday sessions, an offer I thought showed how much we all cared for her. A few of her work colleagues came and ended up sharing a ton of wonderful stories that made us both cry and laugh. Andrea was definitely loved, both as Andrea and from when she was still Andrew. It seems that other coworkers, not just her boss, had also been aware of her alternative lifestyle, but no-one had wanted her to feel judged therefore they never spoke to her about it. This piece of information was hard for me because, for so long, all Andrea had wanted was to be accepted. Their silence, although well-intended, meant she never knew she was. This shook me up more than I expected, and it took me a few minutes in the washroom to compose myself once they had all left.

All in all, it was a peaceful afternoon, a wonderful event filled with laughter and love as we paid our last respects to our amazing friend. Inside Simon's and Andrea's home, it was a lovely bit of brightness on a rather stormy, snowy day, ending one of the hardest weeks I've experienced in a long time. *Why is that anyway? Why doesn't the weather ever cooperate? It seems that every time we say goodbye to our loved ones, the weather is always shit. Why can't we say goodbye and send our friends off into the light with light?* It's a strange juxtaposition that's always made me wonder, especially now as I sit feeling contemplative and shitty, staring out the kitchen window at the snow whipping around in the wind.

It's been a few hours since Hendrix and I returned to my house after helping Simon clean up and making sure he was all right. Thinking of him rattling around by himself in that deafeningly silent house now that everyone has gone home is breaking my heart. And hours later, I still can't stop thinking about how much I'm going to miss Andrea, about how it will take me a long time to even admit that she's actually gone. All week, I've been checking my phone for texts from her, as if my brain hasn't registered what my heart knows deep-down.

So, here I sit, drinking a glass of Inception, re-reading our old text messages, smiling, laughing and crying. She really was one of the most wonderful people I've ever had the pleasure of knowing, always encouraging me to live my life without regrets, to be brave and to take risks with my heart. Through photos, a video chat and texts, Andrea came to love Hendrix in her last days, and he, too, quickly came to see what an incredible person she was. I promised her in our last text that Hendrix and I would always take care of Simon, and she—being her, of course—simply ignored my trying to be serious and again asked for pictures of my eye candy standing beside one of the hot rods he was working on. I laugh out loud at the memory…she was crazy. *Good crazy…*

I take a long sip of my wine and boot up my laptop. There's something I've been needing to do for a while now, and, after Andrea's passing, I want to fully take charge of all parts of my life, as she did. And this is the first thing on my list that I need to get out of the way to give me a completely clean slate. I'm doing this for closure. I have nothing but peace and love in my life now, so it's time.

It may have been a journey to get myself here, but I am still here, and I want Blake to know I'm all right.

In my heart, I know he never planned for this to happen, that he didn't intend to infect me with HIV. I like to believe that he loved me. I need this, we both need this; he deserves to hear back from me. It's been more than long enough. I feel a weight lifting from my shoulders, and I know it's because I'm about to do something that I should have done long ago. I'm going to finally close the door on a part of the past that's been weighing me down. *No more. It's time to leave it in the past for good.*

"Shit, it's really coming down out there," Hendrix says, stamping his feet as he comes in from outside, a blistering wind and a few flakes of snow following him in through the door. He's been outside for the last forty-five minutes or so, shovelling the steps and the path to my apartment before going into the shop to feed the cat.

Hendrix carefully unzips his parka, and Beast jumps out from where he was nestled inside. As usual, he runs straight for me with his tail high in the air, blinking at me and rubbing his face against my ankles. Hendrix and I have been letting Beast hang out up here more often since that first morning Hendrix smuggled him up in his jacket. Today, I need the extra support that only a warm and furry Beast can provide. He purrs and lets me pick him up to cuddle him, and I whisper into his velvet ear. He's a very understanding kitty.

"Here," I say, jumping off the stool to greet Hendrix as he removes his heavy jacket and snow boots. I take his coat, black knit toque and scarf, and hang them in the closet. "Thank you, Hendrix."

"Brrr. It's bloody cold." Hendrix blows on his hands, trying to warm them, and then takes Beast from my arms so he can thaw out his hands in the cat's fur. Stepping into the kitchen, I grab the glass of brandy I'd poured for him a few minutes ago.

"This'll warm you up." I give him the glass before stepping in and wrapping myself around his midsection, giving us both comfort in the moment—for him, it's the warmth of my body; for me, it's simply having him back inside to be with me.

"Thanks, Fruitloop." He takes a sip before dropping a kiss on my forehead. "You okay, baby?" he asks, walking us into the kitchen. He places the glass down on the butcher block counter, then moves to look me in the eye.

"I'm all right. Just sad. I worry about Simon, and I miss her so much," I shrug. "I really hope he takes us up on our invitation to dinner this week. I can't imagine how lonely he'll be. Maybe even a little bored," I say, with a soft chuckle. "He's been taking care of Andrea everyday. How do you suddenly just...*stop?*"

The more time I've spent getting to know Simon, the more I've come to adore him. He's turned out to be one of the most resilient and completely-in-love men I've ever seen. Once Andrea finally let Simon in and told him everything, nothing changed. Simon didn't bat an eye. If anything, it was like the truth made him love her more. *Kind of how I see Hendrix...pure acceptance.*

Backing me up until I'm parked on my stool again, Hendrix moves in behind me. He wraps his big warm arms around me and kisses my neck, silently telling me he's here when I'm ready.

"I love you," he whispers, looking over my shoulder at my phone, open to my old text chats with Andrea, and also seeing my computer open to Facebook. Open to the Messenger window. I feel him stiffen slightly. Letting out a breath, I ask the question that's been gnawing at me for the past week.

"Will you read Blake's message with me?" I ask, turning to see his reaction, despite already knowing he'll say yes. He's told me over and over again that he would be there whenever I was ready.

"You know I will." He kisses my cheek then stands tall, his palm automatically resting on its spot at the base of my neck, his thumb rubbing as he asks: "Where do you want to do this. Here? Or in bed? We could get all snuggled in the way you like. It's starting to snow heavy again. Don't think we'll be going out anytime soon. It's supposed to go all night…might as well get comfortable and relax?"

"Let's get in bed." I finish off my second glass of wine, and grab the wine bottle and my laptop, leaving Hendrix to bring the glasses. "We're going to need more alcohol for this," I admit, and I hear a low chuckle. It isn't lost on me that once again it's storming outside, as it was the day I last messaged Blake. Thankfully, this time I'm not alone—and I'm happy.

"Alright, baby. But we're not going to let you get too sloppy. I know you're upset, but we can't mask the hurt. It's better we talk."

"I know. I'll just have one more glass, I promise. I'm gonna need it. You probably will, too."

"You're right. I might need a couple after we do this," he says honestly.

"Thank you for doing this with me," I say over my shoulder, stopping in the middle of the hall.

"I'd do anything for you, Trin."

I know he would. Without a shred of doubt, I know to the marrow of my bones that this handsome, strong and somewhat bossy man absolutely would. That thought has tears starting. It seems like it took so long to get here, but I finally feel I'm getting my happily ever after.

"God, I'm a mess—*again*," I sniffle. "Maybe we should watch a little Netflix and fool around first?" I joke, trying to pick up the mood.

"Whatever you need me to do, sweetheart, just say the word," he says, walking close behind me with one hand on my hip as we move into my room.

Once we're settled in my king-size bed, I rest the laptop on a pillow on my lap as we cuddle side by side, blankets and quilts half-burying us.

"I love you," I say, reaching for Hendrix's hand and intertwining mine with his.

"Nowhere near as much as I love you, baby. C'mon, let's get this over with. I want to snuggle with my girl the rest of the night."

"Sounds good." I let out a deep breath and tap the trackpad, bringing the laptop back to life.

"You sure you want to do this tonight?" he asks.

And I want to say, "Hell, no, I don't want to do this, today or any other day. But I need to make some changes to move forward, so I'm going to do it anyway."

However, I say nothing. I just sit quietly, my lips becoming grim.

As long as Hendrix *doesn't change, I know everything will be okay.*

42

HENDRIX

"YOU SURE YOU want to do this tonight?" I ask, some reluctance in my voice, when she props open the laptop resting on the pillow. Grabbing the remote, I aim it at the docking station and fiddle with it until I find a good station. Soon the room fills with the sound of X-Ambassadors singing "Unsteady", and I laugh a little, thinking how the lyrics reflect how we're probably both feeling right now.

Today was rough; more to the point, it was fucking *hard* for my girl, but she was nothing but the strong and resilient woman I've come to love. She puts on one hell of a brave front, that's for damn sure. But privately, she'd pulled me into Simon's kitchen at one point and took my arms and wrapped them around herself wordlessly, taking what comfort she needed from my touch. Honestly, though, I have to admit there were a few times when I felt sickened myself throughout the day. I couldn't stop putting myself in Simon's shoes. It was bloody awful; I can't even begin to imagine how difficult it must be—and is going to be—for him. There were a few times when I needed to leave to compose myself, unable to rid my thoughts of what it would be like losing Trinity this way. Before we left, I made sure Simon knew that he wasn't alone, that both Trin and I were here for him and to call anytime, even if he only needed an ear.

"It's the closure I need. Andrea was right, I have to do this," Trin assures me, inching in closer to me under the covers.

"Alright, baby." I put my arm around her. "You want me to read it, or are you okay to?" I ask, and a part of me hopes she'll want me to read it to her. Like maybe if it came from me, in my voice, hearing what this asswipe had to say might not be as hard for her.

"You'd do that?" she asks, sitting up, gripping the computer's screen.

"Of course I would," I tell her, and see her nod before passing me her laptop.

I open the Messenger section and see that there are only two chats, one with Shannon and the other with Blake.

Opening Blake's and Trinity's chat, I take a deep breath as I scroll up to read the first message sent by Trinity over two years ago, in February. "I'm going to read what you wrote first, okay?"

"Yeah, that's fine," she says. "I was really upset when I wrote it, I'm not even sure how I managed to type. I needed to know if it was Blake that gave it to me, if he even knew he had it, you know? Like, once I found out I was HIV-positive, I couldn't get past the fact that Blake had never contacted me. I kept thinking, 'maybe he didn't know'? One of the first things I did was message the other men I'd dated, knowing I would need to contact everyone I'd had sex with after Blake. Luckily, it was only two."

"It's 'cause he's a coward, and you're my brave girl." I squeeze her close while she takes another big sip of her wine. Joining her, I take a gulp from my glass before putting both of our drinks down on the nightstand.

"Ready?"

"As I'll ever be, I guess," she huffs, sticking out her lower lip and blowing her bangs up in the air.

"Before we do this, I want you to know, you're pretty fucking incredible, Trin. Today's been hard, and you've been a champ. I'm proud of you, baby."

"Thanks, I have the best support system around to keep me from crumbling. He's pretty incredible, too," she says, elbowing me, before slouching down to rest her head on my chest. Beast jumps on the bed and curls up between her knees, purring. "And you're pretty incredible, too," she tells him. He beams at her.

I squeeze her shoulder, clear my throat and start to read aloud:

"Blake,

Tell me you didn't know.
Tell me you didn't know and that's why you never contacted me.
Tell me you didn't cheat on me and risk my life without thought.
Tell me you didn't know you gave me HIV.
Please.
Tell me something.

Trinity."

"That's a lot nicer message than I would have sent, trust me," I say honestly.

"It took me hours to figure out what to say. I think I typed and deleted fifty messages. Part of me was hoping maybe I didn't get it from him, but once the doctor's words actually processed, I realized it had to be him. I'd never used drugs, had a transfusion, or had unprotected sex with anyone but him. Like idiots, we never used protection because he was my first..."

I try to block out the last comments. The idea of another guy feeling what's mine makes me go apeshit. I know it's crazy, but I don't give a shit. Trinity is mine and, regardless of her past, the thought of any other man with her makes me physically ache.

Scanning down, I see the next message is dated the same day—but a few hours later—as Trinity's message.

"So, you never opened the reply?" I ask, wanting to clarify.

"No, I didn't. Look," she says. Using the track pad, she hovers the cursor over the Messenger icon and a text box pops up to display the first line of any incoming messages. *Huh, I never knew you could do that. Not that I Facebook much, anyway.* I read:

"I'm so sorry, Sunshine. I didn't know…"

"Wow. So, his reply's really been sitting here all this time? You sure you want me to keep going? Ready for me to read it?" I ask, my eyes starting to scan the page, my heart rate accelerating as I see certain words jump out. I need to rein in my temper here, because I'm about to go ballistic and that's the last thing Trinity needs.

"Yes, go ahead," she whispers, and I hate that she's doing this to herself, although I understand why. All I know is that this guy better stay in Hong Kong because I just might kill him otherwise.

"I'm so sorry, Sunshine. I didn't know…I didn't know how to tell you. First, I did cheat, but it was only a couple of times. I'm not even sure if it counts as cheating, we weren't really exclusive. Please know I never thought this could happen. I just wasn't thinking about consequences. I mean, who thinks about that stuff? It was when we were first dating. I was drunk. They didn't mean anything. I barely knew most of them. I've just always hated condoms, so I never used them unless I was forced to. I thought I was clean. I never would have willingly hurt you. It's not an excuse; I'm ashamed of my behaviour now that I look back on things. I was young and stupid; I was trying to find out who I was. I experimented with a lot back then: drugs, sex and whatever else I could find that would help me. I wanted to tell you many times, wanted to open up and share who I thought I was, and who I wanted to be for you. When I found out I was HIV-positive, I couldn't bring myself to admit everything to you out loud, it would have been too complicated. I'm a coward. I fucked up everything, and for that I'm sorry. I never knew what to say to you then…to any of you, for that matter. I don't know how or when I transmitted the disease, and for me that's the scariest part. I'm not sure how long I've

had it. There was a lot going on that I didn't know how to tell you. And for that I'll always be sorry. There will never be the right words, Sunshine.

B.

"Oh my God! Hendrix, I—I—I feel like I can't catch my breath." She sits up straight, her fingers clutching the duvet cover, her chest and shoulders heaving in time with her erratic breaths. Immediately, I toss the laptop aside and begin rubbing her back, whispering low, soothing sounds of comfort. She takes a deep breath and continues. "He—he *knew*. He knew and he didn't tell me. I could have known sooner, could have been on medication sooner. How could he not have told me?" she yells, reaching for any available pillows and throwing them furiously across the room.

Worried that it's too much, I put myself in front of her so we're face to face. I hate the hurt and confusion I see shining in her eyes.

"You have every right to be mad. Let it all out, sweetheart," I say, keeping my voice low and calm.

"He 'hated condoms'?" she screams, her fists clenched. She pounds both hands against the mattress. "He says it like it's no big deal! It's a huge fucking deal. Why did I think I was the first person he never used one with?" She shakes her head, tears pouring down her beautiful face. "Why was I so stupid? Oh, fuck, who's to say that when he cheated he didn't already have it? Oh my God!" She shakes off my hand, one that I was using to try and cover her fists, and slaps her hand over her mouth. Her breath hitches as she tries to inhale, and a tiny moan escapes. She begins to tremble. "Jesus, Hendrix, how many people has he slept with without protection since he got HIV? How many of us are there? I—I'm going to be *sick*..." she cries, sliding off the bed and rushing to the washroom. From the bed, I can see her lurching over the toilet as she empties the contents of her stomach.

The need to break shit is all consuming, but instead of losing my mind, I head to the washroom right behind her and wait until she's finished. Seeing her in pain, I slip in behind her on the floor. As soon as she feels me, she turns and wraps her arms and legs around me, anchoring herself to me, and she cries and cries. I just hold her, giving her the time she needs to let it all out, the pain from losing Andrea coupled with the hurt from reading Blake's note.

We sit in silence for what feels like hours. Suddenly, she looks up and says, "We'll write him back. I have to. I need to give him a piece of my mind. He needs to hear from me, needs to know he's not forgiven. Blake needs to know that it's not alright, even if he's sorry now. I needed him to have had a conscience years ago." She sniffs into my neck.

"Whatever you want, Trin."

With that, she nods, stands, moves to the sink and brushes her teeth, then washes her hands and face. She takes me by the hand and leads us back to the bed.

Once positioned side by side in bed again, she sighs and says, "I feel better. Sorry. I guess I needed to let it all out; it suddenly hit me like a Mac truck. It's been so long that I've wondered…to finally have it confirmed and it not being the answer I wanted…well, it was a shock," she shares. We settle back into our little cocoon under the blankets after a few minutes of silence.

"Don't apologize, Trin. I can't pretend to imagine what that was like. I know how I feel; I think you have every right to feel the way you do. I think a few meltdowns are allowed, and more than understandable." I lean over and kiss her before opening the laptop again. "Do you want me to type?" I ask, but then realize there's another message below. One sent a little more than a year after Blake's first one. *Shit.*

"What's wrong?" she asks, looking over at me, then at the computer's screen. "Why did you stop talking?"

Not sure I really want to tell her, I take my own set of shallow breaths before telling her.

"There's another message here. From just over a year ago."

"There is? What's it say?" she asks, then moves in closer to look at the screen at the same time as me. We read the first line together.

"Dearest Trinity, I hope you're keeping well. It breaks my heart..."

"...Oh, no. Oh, God. Hendrix..."

I open the entire message and begin to read it aloud. Once I start, I don't stop. It's like ripping off a Band-Aid, better done quickly.

"Dearest Trinity,

I hope you're keeping well. It breaks my heart to have to send you this message, especially through social media, and after Blake sent you that awful last message. First, I want to tell you that I'm truly sorry my son's past mistakes affected your life so significantly. Our family always thought very highly of you and it pains me to know the hurt and heartbreak that Blake's choices have caused you. Please know we're always here for you if you ever need a thing.

This past winter, Blake passed away. He was living in Hong Kong, with a friend he said he loved by his side. Kris informed us via email that Blake died from complications of the AIDS virus. From my understanding, Blake refused to seek medication or treatment. He felt he got what he deserved and essentially allowed himself to die. Another way to look at it is that my son committed suicide. This is the way I've been seeing it, and I'm beyond saddened that Blake chose that for himself, but I guess he never did make the best decisions or choices, did he?

We didn't even know he was sick until he died. It was a complete and utter shock to all of us. It was something we pieced together afterwards through Kris and our subsequent correspondence over email. I guess he decided to keep his illness private. Kris only contacted me via e-mail after I began leaving daily messages on Blake's answering machine, asking where he was, after no-one had heard from him for months. Kris finally replied, but only to explain that Blake had fallen ill with some mysterious disease and wouldn't be in contact for a while. Eventually, Kris messaged us again and asked if we wanted to come to Hong Kong to say our final goodbyes.

Unfortunately, we never made it; Blake passed away before we could get there. He'd waited too long to ask Kris to let us know, and a part of me wonders if this was intentional. I know I wasn't always the best mother to my son, but I did love him. I'm heartbroken to think that my own son felt he couldn't talk to me. I would have tried, or at least I like to think I would have. Blake's always been a bit wild and reckless, even as a child and early-teen, and I knew he'd been battling with some inner demons, but once he started dating you, we hoped maybe he'd figured himself out, that he was finally cured.

I'm not sure if he figured things out in the end or not, but in my mind, at least, I imagine he might have, and that he passed away with a woman who loved him—and whom he loved—by his side. With this, I feel a peace I haven't felt since he was dating you. I can finally allow myself to go back to church without the burden of wondering any longer. I've made it right in my heart.

When Kris emailed and told us that you'd also been affected, I needed to write. I just never knew what to say. When Blake passed, Kris gave me access to Blake's Facebook account so I could reach out. Everything on it had been deleted, but Kris left your messages on Messenger for me so I could respond.

Not sure if this information will help, but knowing how big a heart you have, Trinity, I wanted you to know that Kris and Blake made a list of women—and men—whom he'd slept with. From my understanding, Blake had been trying to contact as many of them as he could after getting your message telling him that you'd tested positive. It doesn't fix anything, but I sure am hoping it might have helped some others who might have gotten infected and were wondering who gave it to them. I pray every night that no-one else has been impacted by my son's terrible mistakes and that the Lord can find it in His heart to forgive Blake. It hurts my soul deeply to consider that he might very well be burning in Hell.

Know he cared deeply for you, Trinity.

Sincerely,
Miranda Pritchard

"...How? How is this possible? How can all of these people I know be dead? Andrea, and Blake...I thought we were advancing on this disease? I thought we were closer to curing it? My doctors tell me I can live a long and happy life...but how can I believe that when there's so much sadness and death, so many people losing their battles?" she sobs, gripping her pillow in her hands, seeking some sort of comfort from the gesture. "And Blake, oh my God, he...he...was he having sex with men, and other women...and *me*? At the same time? Is that—that's it, right? I mean, he...he was finding himself, he was lost, but, oh God, Hendrix, how long did he have it? He didn't make it, Andrea didn't make it, many others from my group haven't made it..." Trinity says, baffled, before going on. "What if I don't make it, either? I might lose..." she barely gets out, her voice dry and scratchy from crying so hard.

Seeing and hearing her sound this way destroys a piece of the naïve hope that I've been using as a shield, one that fully believed there was no way Trinity could lose this fight.

"And his mother, those 'burden' and 'burning in Hell' comments? And the going-to-church-again bit. I mean, who cares if Blake was gay, bisexual, or straight? He's no sinner. She's his mother, for Christ's sake! I knew she was always hard on him, but I never suspected... She never saw the great person he was. Poor Blake. What a terrible thing for a mother to say. He couldn't help it," she expels, shaking her head, and I notice she's trembling again. "I take back what I said earlier, about not forgiving him. I do. I do forgive him."

"You need to take a break, Trin. You're shaking. Have a sip, please," I say, handing her a glass of water. Thankfully, she complies. After taking a few sips, she passes it back and quickly starts talking again, and all I can do is sit with her and listen because that's what my girl needs. She just has to get it all out.

"Do you think Kris is a man or woman? Sounds like his mother wasn't sure, or is just in denial? I wouldn't have told her, either, if I were Blake and Kris. What kind of mother cares? I should hook Miranda Pritchard up with my mom and dad. God. I don't even know how to feel right now. I'm confused, I'm mad and a part of me feels sad for Blake, even when all part of me wants is to be mad at him. He deserves my anger, right? Or does he, even?"

"I think you have justification to feel all of these things, Fruitloop. It's definitely a lot to take in, to process. And you're right. His mum's letter didn't help."

"Truth?" she asks, looking me straight in the eye. Her grey eyes are the colour of storm clouds, mirroring what I'm sure is a storm of emotions raging inside.

"Always truth," I nod, shifting the laptop so we can be closer.

"I'm so fucking scared," she huffs, her breath coming out all rushed. Tears streak like bullets down her flushed face before she dives headfirst into my chest, her arms wrapped around my stomach. Holding her tight, I give her a minute to cry, massaging her neck, and offering a few soothing words before deciding I need her to listen to me now.

"Trin, listen." I pause, waiting for her to calm down. Then I lift her gently so she's looking at me. "They're not wrong, the doctors. You will live. You're healthy. Blake lived an irresponsible lifestyle, drugs and no condoms, sex with strangers—unprotected sex with men and women, a life of confusion and denial and avoidance of reality, from what it sounds like. That's not you, Trin. I bet he wasn't even thinking about the what-ifs, but just trying to find himself, to figure out who he was. As for Andrea, you're the one who told me that she'd also been in denial, that she didn't seek treatment right away like you did. Those are mitigating factors that have to be added into the equation here. You can't compare yourself to those two and their choices, or their outcomes." I pause, handing her some tissues.

"Unfortunately, within your circle and with your work with The AIDS Network and your therapy groups, you're going to have friends and know people who will die, have died, or are dying. Unfortunately, it's the hardest part of the disease, all the suffering and death. The loss, it's overwhelming, but it doesn't apply to everyone and you know this. And it will not apply to you. You are a strong healthy woman who fights. You take your meds, you seek regular medical attention, and you will benefit from today's advances in science. You have taken on this battle headfirst, and you're winning. Don't you dare give up on me, Trinny. Not now, not ever." I let the words fly out of my mouth, doing my damnedest to make her see, needing her to hear and to realize what I'm telling her.

After a few beats of radio silence, the tension lingering, Trin's soft voice interrupts our staring at one another. She rests her head on my chest again and says, "Close the laptop, please, Hendrix." Her voice is low and throaty, her eyes reflecting a hurt and pain so deep it stabs at my heart. Without hesitation, I slam it closed, tossing it not-so-gently onto the bedside table.

Laying with her in the silence of her room as the snow continues to fall in thick blankets outside the window, anger like I've never experienced begins to pulse through my veins. It's a slow simmer, and the more I sit here contemplating everything, it begins to heat and boil. The need to lash out is becoming all consuming. Jumbled thoughts stream through my head as the quiet in the room fuels my rampant thoughts.

How could Blake have been that irresponsible, so inconsiderate? How could he not see the consequences of his actions? Why didn't he talk to Trinity? She could have helped. Fuck, I can appreciate that he was confused, maybe even ashamed of who he really was because of his family, but he should have been smarter, should have trusted someone. But who am I to judge? I've never walked a day in his shoes. Blake's not much different from Ren, in a way, and I still love Ren in spite of his poor choices. Deciding I need to calm down, I keep my trap shut rather than letting all my own shit out, and work to tamp down my emotions. Thankfully, all it takes is one request from Trinity and the anger slips away.

"Hendrix?" Trinity says, breaking through my fucked-up thoughts. "I need you to hold me," she admits, her voice shaky.

"Nothing else I'd rather do," I tell her, then roll onto my side, pulling her in tight, her back flush to my front. I want to ask her all kinds of questions. I want to poke and prod until I know she's all right, but I know that isn't what she needs right now. I have to let her take the lead on this.

Right now, instead of talking, we are lying together in silence. But this time we're wrapped up in each other rather than alone in our thoughts. For a long while, no words are spoken and the only sound filling the otherwise quiet space is the snow gently tapping against the window, at the mercy of the wind's control. It's kind of like how Trinity has taken control of my world. I'd do anything for her, do anything she ever asked of me, go anywhere she needed me to go.

Right now, she just needs me to hold her, and to love her. And so, I do.

43

Trinity

"HENDRIX," I SAY, after what feels like hours of silence.

"I'm still here," he replies, rubbing small circles on my stomach where my shirt's ridden up.

I'm exhausted from everything I learned tonight, but my mind is full and I have to get this off my chest before we move on.

"I need to say something else and I want you to listen, and actually let me finish before you argue with me or cut me off." I've spent the last while mulling everything over, and decided that Hendrix was right. There's no way I can give up. Blake and Andrea did have very different situations than mine. I guess I just needed to be reminded of that.

"Not gonna guarantee I can do that, Fruitloop," he replies honestly, and I smile because it's totally a *him* answer.

"You're impossible," I huff, and I feel his chest move against my back as he chuckles into my hair. *God, this man can take it all away. He makes things better so easily.*

"So you keep telling me," he puts his lips to my ear and whispers. The warmth of his breath sends a wave of awareness through me, but first things first.

"I'm serious. Let me get this out."

"Then can I get in?" he asks, moving his hand to cup my breast. *I'm in so much trouble with this man.*

"If you're a good little listener, I'll definitely let you in."

"That's good, Trin, 'cause I really feel the need to be as close to you as I can get after today," he says, pulling in closer to me.

"Okay. I want you to promise me something." I let out a deep breath. "There's a chance I won't be here forever, despite all your protective caveman antics. My body might give up on me."

"Trinity," Hendrix growls, but I ignore him.

"Shhh, I'm not done," I scold, turning to face him. It takes a bit of effort but eventually Hendrix loosens his grip enough so I can face him. Placing my hand on his cheek, I rub the stubble along his jaw and continue. "In Perpetuum Et Unum Diem—forever and a day," I sigh, leaning in and placing a soft kiss on his lips. "That's how long I'll love you, even if I'm not here," I mutter against his lips before closing my eyes and taking in the comfort of him. "I might not always be here for you to see my love, but you'll always feel it. I'll make sure you feel me with you. Always."

"Stop, talking about this shit, Trin. Right fucking now," he grits, but I place my index finger over his lips.

"I'm almost done. No need to get all angerball-ish."

"Hurry it up, then. Get it out, 'cause after this, no more of this talk. I won't listen to it. I can't, Fruitloop, it guts me," Hendrix says into my neck now, gripping me tightly. "I hate thinking of this stuff, Trin." His muscular chest convulses, and I realize how upset he is.

"Me too, honey. I just need to say this once. I want you to hear me, to understand."

"I'll listen, Trinny."

"If anything happens to me, I don't want you to be sad for too long. I would want you to live your life, not to dwell, and not to get caught up in the past. I'd need you to move on and live, for both of us. If Andrea taught me anything, it's that it's so much better when you take risks and actually live. And you've taught me how to again,

Hendrix. You brought a part of me back to life, a part I thought I'd lost. You've given me a version of happiness that I never ever imagined I could feel again. I need you to promise me that you'd move on, if it ever came to that. That you'd let love in again, because you're really fucking good at it. Your love is so, so precious. Promise me you'd be brave and keep taking risks, even if it's not with me. You're too special not to."

"Fuck, Trin. I'm kinda mad at you right now," he huffs, and I see the moisture in his eyes.

God, I love him with everything I am.

"I know, baby," I say. "I'm sorry. Lying here, it's all I could think about. I'll never bring it up again. I promise."

"Thank, Christ. But if you make me promise that to you, then I ask the same. You never know what can happen, sick or healthy, anything can happen. But know I'll haunt the fuck out of any man who comes sniffin' around you," he laughs, breaking the tension the conversation created.

"Think it's time to seal the deal, then? Do you still want in?" I ask, entwining my leg with his and rubbing it up and down while lifting my eyebrows suggestively, trying to bring some light into the darkness.

"You're impossible, Trin."

"Hey, that's my li—" I'm cut off as his big body rolls over on top of me and he takes my lips in an unforgettable kiss.

"I need inside you. Now, Fruitloop. Gotta have you wrapped around me."

"Yes," I say, shifting my foot up to hook his pants and pull them down as my hands push them from above. "Take me slow, Hendrix. Make me forget the rest. Make me remember only this, with you," I rasp out, lifting my shoulders up off the bed so he can remove my shirt before his own.

"You'll only feel me, baby. I promise," he says, rolling a condom on before hovering over me, lifting my arms high above my head and entwining his fingers with mine. "I love you too damn much, Fruitloop. Never talk about that shit again. It's not happening, ever. You are the only forever and a day that I want."

"Hendrix," I call, as I feel him slide inside me.

"You're my heaven, Trin," he says while moving into me, his thrusts soft and gentle, his cock slipping in and almost-out of me, over and over, our breathing increasing as I wrap my legs around his ass and force him in deeper. "Always feels like perfection." He kisses my neck, before moving down to my nipples, our hands joined.

"Let me touch you," I plead, wiggling my arms and he sets them free. Immediately, I tangle my fingers in his hair, loving the softness.

"Thank you for loving me, Hendrix. For opening my eyes and helping me to see me the way you saw me from the start."

"In Perpetuum Et Unum Diem, baby," he mutters over my lips, and he continues to make slow sweet love to me on one of the hardest days of my life.

44

Trinity

It's Christmas Eve day, and for the first time since Andrea's death, I'm feeling giddy and excited about something. I'm actually almost cheerful.

I can't wait to see Hendrix's face when he sees one of his presents later today. He's been incredible the last three weeks. I took Andrea's death hard. With that and then reading Blake's message—and his mom's—I was so overwhelmed that it left me off kilter, even though Hendrix was there for me one hundred percent. It's taken several days of moping and feeling every emotion under the sun to finally be feeling a little more like myself again, and I'm glad.

Today, though, I'm completely over the moon. My plan to bring Hendrix's mum here from the UK for the holidays is working out perfectly. The fact that he has no idea what I've managed to pull off makes it that much more special. Kara Hills reached out to me by email a few weeks ago, mentioning something about needing to be introduced to the woman who's been making her son extremely happy. We've been chatting and planning ever since. Kara was thrilled when I asked if she and Arran would like to join us at Christmas as a surprise for Hendrix.

Looking at the office clock and walking out of the reception area towards his bay in the garage, I start to tense up. "Hendrix, are you ready to go? I don't want to hit traffic on the 401 or we'll be late. Tillie said my Aunt B.'s plane will be arriving at 1:50 p.m. at Pearson," I lie. For the sake of my surprise. "It'll take us at least an hour to get there. Let's go! Besides, it's Christmas Eve, Mr. Scrooge, and everyone else has gone home. Everyone else went home an hour-and-a-half ago."

"I'll be right there. I'm almost done. I need, like, five minutes. I just have to adjust this rear door, the fucker won't align properly. It's driving me mad. I can't leave it like this for the next few days or it will haunt me and wreck my Christmas. Fucker's off a bit at the top," he says, grunting against what I assume is said door.

"Okay, but hurry. I'm going to go feed the cat. You've got until I get back," I say, crossing my arms and pushing my tits together. Of course, his eyes flare with interest now that my chest is all fluffed up. I twirl the pompom on my Santa hat for added effect. "Then we need to go, regardless, unless you want me driving myself," I add, knowing full-well that will never happen. *Caveman issues and everything, right?*

"The hell you'll drive in this weather. There's black ice on the highway. And don't even think about changing furball's litter. I'll do it once we're back."

"Yes, bossy," I salute.

"Takes one to know one," he grins back, and I stick out my tongue.

"Now, now, Fruitloop, we do need to go. You stick that tongue out again, and we won't be going anywhere, except maybe Flynn's office. He's got a pretty nice new swivel chair in there."

"Five minutes," I say, ignoring him, rolling my eyes and walking away.

"TILLIE SAID TERMINAL 3, Flight TS723," I say, looking at my phone to make sure we're in the right spot.

"We're good. Aunt B. should come right out those doors." Hendrix points to the large set of sliding double-doors in front of us. The huge sign that reads "Arrivals" might also be a clue that we are indeed in the right spot. He's standing beside me, his hand resting on my neck, rubbing his thumb as usual, giving me goosebumps. I lean into his side and wrap one arm around his waist.

"Is this is Tillie's sister or Dex's?" Hendrix asks, looking down at me, swiping my bangs off my face.

"Tillie's. This will be her first visit to Canada in years, all the way from England," I say, diverting my eyes from his, not wanting to give myself away. I'm a horrible liar, always have been.

"Passengers, please collect all of your belongings before exiting. You will not be permitted re-entry once you pass through the final exit," we hear over the PA system, and I reach for my phone, making sure it's set up for video.

"I'm so excited!" I lean up and kiss his cheek. "Let's see if we can move in a little closer, I can't see too well from here." I step up on my tippytoes to further prove my point.

"That's cause you're a short stack, Short Stack," he teases, his brown eyes tender while maneuvering us closer through the crowd.

"Hey." I swat his chest. "Good things come in small packages."

"The best things," he muses, kissing the top of my head. "What does she look like anyw—"

He doesn't get to finish, his eyes having landed on something—or rather, *someone*—familiar. Suddenly, he steps away from me, then stops and turns back, then whips his head to and fro, completely perplexed. He continues to glance toward the double doors, then back at me, then once more towards the doors at a dark-haired, pink-faced lady in a red coat and the older, dignified-looking man walking beside her who've just stepped out of the Arrivals gate and are looking around hopefully. A cautious smile begins to break across Hendrix's handsome face.

Reaching for my phone, I press "record" as the scene begins to unfold.

"Mum?" he calls, waving to the brunette. She's beautiful, with tasteful streaks of grey in her lush hair, vibrant hazel eyes and a huge smile on her face when she finally zeroes in on Hendrix and me. She waves back, then covers her mouth with one hand. My heart melts seeing how happy they both are, at how surprised Hendrix is. He quickly turns to stare at me again, a silent admission of how craftily I've tricked him, then he and his mother lock eyes and rush towards one another.

Kara beelines her way through the crowd, followed by the man I'm assuming is Arran, who is staggering a little under the weight of a bunch of carry-on bags. Kara takes Hendrix in a huge embrace then pulls back from him and cups his face, smiling at him with tear-filled eyes. They chatter at each other for a few seconds, until Kara's eyes alight on me in my Santa hat. She waves me over with a radiant smile, bouncing up and down in excitement and clasping her hands.

Hendrix gives her one more hug and claps Arran on the shoulder, then returns to me, grabbing my hand and pulling me forward. He stops just before we reach his mum and Arran and pushes up on me, poking me playfully with his index finger.

"You. You did this?"

I smile brightly. "I did. With a little help from my partner-in-crime." I nod in his mother's direction.

"You did this. For me."

"Well, yeah. You miss each other. I thought it would be the perfect surprise to thank you for being there for me over the last few weeks."

"I don't know what to say, Trin." He places his forehead against mine. "I fucking love you so much right now."

"Hendrix! Stop mauling that young lady and bring her over to introduce us properly," I hear Kara call in her Birmingham accent. We turn. "You must be Trinity."

I am soon embraced in her warm hug.

45

Hendrix

"HENDRIX!" MY MUM shouts. "Oh, Hendrix. I've missed you terribly, my little Painini," she says, using the horrible nickname she started calling me back when I was in middle school. She claims it came about because that's when I became such a pain in the ass. According to her, I'd always been shy and quiet right up until I hit Grade 6—then it was like a switch flipped and I gave her and my dad a run for their money ever since.

"Ha! Did you just call him '*Pain*-ini?'" I hear Trin ask, giggling beside me, her steel-coloured eyes dancing with glee at the revelation.

"Nooooo," I chide, shaking my head in my mum's direction.

"Yes." Mum laughs. "Right? I've missed you very much, my son." She kisses my cheek. "And this lovely petite darling is of course our Trinity." Hearing my mum acknowledging Trinity as "ours" gives me a sense of peace I didn't know I'd been craving. Not having my mum here to know my girl has been weighing on me. With everything that's been going on recently, I realize just how much I've wanted them to meet. I knew they'd hit it off and get along, and it looks like I was right.

My mum took the news of Trinity's being HIV-positive exactly how I expected—she was worried for me, of course, but supportive, the way she always has been of me and my decisions. If anything, it just gave her something new to worry about. I know for a fact that Trin's been added to my mother's nightly prayer list. But these two already seem quite familiar with one another, I see, putting the pieces together.

"It's nice to finally meet you in person. Facetime and email are not the same," Trinity says, giving me a cheeky wink before moving into my mum's outstretched arms and receiving a warm hug. Meanwhile, I wrap my arm around Arran's shoulders and welcome him.

"Very excited you're both here. *Surprised* and excited. Let's say we get outta here?" I ask, squeezing his shoulder and nodding toward the exit leading to the parking garage as I commandeer their heavy luggage cart.

"Sounds good to me, son. I could use a pint and a wee nibble. Bloody airline food is rubbish; don't they know it's Christmas? They could have at least made it a non-plasticized meal in honour of the season," he jokes in his thick accent, and we all laugh as we make our way out to my truck.

"What hotel are you at?" I ask as we walk.

"Umm, about that..." Trin rushes up and locks my arm in hers, stopping us, allowing my mum and Arran to walk ahead.

"We'll catch up. My truck's the blue one, up on the left there," I point. "The Ford," I shout out to my mum, who's grinning like a loon.

"I told your mom and Arran they could stay at your place. I figured you could spend the time staying with me at mine? I assumed it would be alright, since we're at my apartment almost every night, anyway. Maybe we could bring a few of your things over and...maybe leave them there?" she says nervously, shifting her gaze everywhere but at me.

"Are you asking me to move in with you, Fruitloop?" I say, leaning in and placing my face in the crook of her neck, making her laugh when I dart my tongue out to tickle her.

Smacking my chest, she giggles and says, "Yeah, I think I am. I really like having you around. Figured I had room for one more supercool fixture. I mean, you would finish the place off nicely. The addition of a you would give my place that extra homey vibe it's been missing," she says, wrapping her arms around my neck. "What do you say, Hendrix, you want to be my home?"

Fuck, this girl never ceases to amaze me. It's almost if she can read my mind sometimes. We are so on the same page, it's scary. I can't wait to see her face tomorrow. Now more than ever.

Picking her up, I kiss her cheek. "I love my mum and Arran, but we need to hurry up and drop them off. We're heading home. I gotta get you in *our* bed…now." I set her down on the concrete then rush her by the hand all the way to where they're standing by my truck, watching us and chuckling, having managed to find their way without us.

"Easy, big boy. We need to visit with Kara and Arran, and then we have a mission to tackle before you can reap the rewards of becoming my concubine." She kisses my cheek as I open the tonneau cover, ready to start tossing the luggage into the bed of the truck, and then I see how full of shopping bags and shit it is already.

"What the hell are all these boxes and bags?" I call out to Trin, but she's already in the back seat of the truck with Arran. *Why do I have a feeling this is some kind of a setup?*

"HOLY SHIT, MUM. How much stuff did you get Trin to buy?" I ask, looking around my now-unidentifiable living room as Trinity, my mum, Arran and I sit on the floor about to start the exciting "wrapping party" Trin and my mum suckered Arran and I into attending. We were rather bluntly told that if we wanted to receive any Christmas gifts, we would have to wrap some. *See? I knew something was up when I saw all that loot in my truck. Damn straight, men have that intuition shit, too.*

"Oh, shush. It's not everyday I get to meet my son's extended family. I need to thank them for taking such good care of my Painini, and I could only fit so much in our bags," she says and Trin belly laughs, almost spilling her hot toddy on herself.

"I think these are making me a wee bit tipsy," Trin laughs, trying out a horrendous Cockney accent, before taking another sip of her toddy. This is Arran's special concoction of whiskey, hot water, honey, cloves, lemon and a cinnamon stick. Apparently he was in on this Christmas Eve wrapping session, because conveniently all of the ingredients happen to have been in one of the many bags hidden in my truck. *Traitor.*

"I think we need to introduce this yummy little guy to the girls tomorrow," Trin says with that breathtaking grin of hers that lights up…well…my whole fucking life.

"Ah, yes, there's plenty more. I'd be happy to whip some up tomorrow," he winks, raising his glass.

"Perfect. I definitely see this becoming my fall bonfire drink from now on. Wine, who?"

"Ah, Trinny, I knew you were a girl after my own heart," my mum says, and pats Trin's cheek softly as she hands her a roll of Scotch tape.

Seeing my mum and Trinity getting along is the best gift. I can't take my eyes off my girl tonight as she gets to know my family.

And she went all out to make them feel welcome and at home. I have no idea how she pulled it all off, but she did, and so far this has been a holiday to remember. We devoured the dinner of prime rib, mashed potatoes and glazed carrots that Trinity had sneakily prepared while I worked this morning, giving her Aunt Til my key and having her come make my house guest-friendly and do all the finishing touches on the meal while we were at the airport. Trin also put up some holiday decorations and one of those tiny trees, insisting they needed something "Christmassy" to make them feel festive over the holidays. I simply laughed and kissed her forehead.

I'm excited for tomorrow, and looking forward to Trinity, her family and my family coming together as one.

I have a feeling that this will be the start of many good things to come.

46

HENDRIX

"I STILL CAN'T believe you and my mum pulled that off. I had no clue, seriously." I shake my head, pouring hot water into two mugs while making Trin and I cups of Earl Grey tea. We're back at "our" place, and I'm thankful the wrapping duties are finally over.

We left my mum and Arran to sleep. They were exhausted from their flight and our visit. I have a feeling the hot toddies mixed with jet lag were just what the doctor ordered to help them get a good night's rest before another busy day tomorrow, despite them denying they were tired and trying to coerce us to stay longer. We promised to pick them up bright and early tomorrow as we made our way out the door.

And we nearly escaped unscathed, too, but at the last minute, Mum rushed off to grab us both our Christmas Eve gifts from her suitcase. They were matching "Christmas Eve pyjamas", a tradition she's kept for as long as I can remember. Seeing Trinity's face light up at the notion of getting special Christmas p.j.'s made me feel like an ass for giving my mum such a hard time about continuing the tradition well beyond the age I deemed it acceptable. *Hell, she can buy them until we're old and grey if it makes my Fruitloop happy.*

Speaking of getting old and grey with this girl, I was elated when my mum pulled me aside and whispered how happy she was that she'd be here to witness the surprise I have planned for Trinity tomorrow, that she could sense that Trin was definitely "my one". Her happy tears almost busted us, but, thankfully, Mum was quick to say she was simply being emotional about being here with us for the holidays. Trin's not the only sneaky one. *God, my Fruitloop better say "yes".*

"I can't believe your mum didn't tell you they were coming the other day, when you were on her about coming to visit you soon. She told me it was unbelievably hard to keep our secret and not spill the beans," Trin says, cutting through my thoughts.

Handing over her tea, I sigh and ask the dreaded question. "Please tell me we don't have any more gifts to wrap tonight?" I cringe, waiting for the answer.

"Nope. I've wrapped them all, including the ones I got for you. Which means we can snuggle and watch a movie. Maybe I'll even let you jingle my bells," she jokes, making her way to the living room. I follow her to the couch, placing my mug beside hers. "I'm so punny." She slaps her knee and giggles, sitting down close to me.

"You're something, alright. I think that's more of a euphemism than a pun, but you can jingle my balls later, if you want." Putting my arm over and around her neck, I tuck her in real close, whispering in her ear, "I have no doubt that mistletoe won't be the only thing you're under tonight, baby." I plant a big wet kiss on her cheek.

"Well, then," she says, then stands and yanks me up off the couch, a mischievous glint taking over her eyes. "I think we should move this party into the bedroom. We can get comfy, watch *National Lampoon's Christmas Vacation* in bed and see where things go." She scans me from head to toe in a slow, appreciative perusal.

"Promise you'll wear that sexy-as-fuck onesie my mum gave you?" I ask, walking her to our room. "I really think I'm going to enjoy that easy-access flap. I can open it from behind and slip right in, maybe in the middle of the night, or to say Merry Christmas nice and early tomorrow." I nip her earlobe, her breath quickening at my words. I start to undress us, leaving a trail behind us on our way to the bedroom. *Her sweater, my t-shirt, her tank top, her bra…*

"Only if you wear yours?" she pants, voice unsteady. She's already worked up from my fingers nimbly playing with her hard nipples, the heat from my bare chest hitting her back, causing goosebumps to surface.

"If it gets you as turned on as I think seeing you in yours will get me, then you can guarantee I'll be putting that shit on. Fuck, I'll wear it everyday if you want," I groan, pushing my hardness into her ass and she laughs.

"Can't wait to find out."

"I can't believe my mum bought us matching onesies, though. Tell me, what grown-assed man in his right mind would wear that shit?"

"One who is about to get tangled up in some wild onesie sex with his girlfriend," Trinity says, stepping away from me, picking up her new pyjamas and heading to the washroom. "I suggest you get ready, Mistletoe. I'm almost ready to *come* beneath you," she winks before closing the door, and I swear to old St. Nick I feel every single one of her words jingle all the way to my balls.

47

Trinity

Closing the door to the washroom, I can't help giggle a little. Here I am half-naked, about to cover myself up again. However, the idea of seeing Hendrix wearing a matching red-and-green plaid onesie will be worth it. The fact that he's even playing along makes me giddy. My big hard man continues to surprise and impress me. Hendrix and I both know he could have very easily had me beneath him by now, yet is allowing us to have this little game of dress-up.

"You better be changing," I call, tossing my white lace thong on top of my skinny jeans in a small heap on the white-tiled floor, "because I'm about ready to blow your mind with all my sexiness in this racy-assed fuzzy get up."

"That's not all you're gonna blow, baby," he chuckles, and I roll my eyes. *I walked right into that one, didn't I?*

"Impossible," I mutter.

"You love me," I hear him reply.

"Are you standing right outside the door?" I ask, not surprised really. The man is the definition of impatient.

"Hell, yeah. I'm ready and I look fucking hot. You're going to want to ravage me as soon as you open the door. I figured I'd save you the long trip to the bed. I'm waiting for you, too, Fruitloop. Get out here," he says, his voice dripping with promise, and it makes my skin tingle while my core hums with excitement.

My heart starts to pound in my chest as I zip myself up. He's right. Me wanting to ravage him is usually the case. Checking myself over in the mirror, I sweep my now-brown bangs over my face and fluff up the back up a little bit, not that it will matter. Good thing Shannon and I decided to go brunette at my last appointment; I don't think the pink would have looked so hot with this red-and-green outfit. Turning, I check out my ass. There's no doubt Hendrix will take full advantage of the button-down butt flap. *If only Kara knew just how thoughtful her gift really was.*

Opening the door, I inhale sharply when I see Hendrix, who's bracing himself against the door's frame.

"Damn, you're gorgeous," he says, standing tall and strong in all his fleece-covered glory. His arms stretch the plaid material; it's a tight fit over his bulging muscles. Gone is the laugh I thought would escape when I finally saw him. It's the opposite—I practically drool, instead. Although he does look a bit on the silly side in his fleece get-up, it comes off as charming. The look in his eyes coupled with his sexy lopsided grin and amazing physique do nothing but remind me and my lady bits just how handsomely sexy Mr. Hendrix Hills is, even in a fuzzy Christmas-themed onesie.

"You're not so bad yourself," I say, my cheeks heating under his scrutiny.

"Come here, baby. Keep looking at me like that and I'm gonna come in my new outfit," he smirks. "Let me look at you." He pulls me through the threshold. "Turn." He twirls his finger and makes a hissing sound as I spin, and I smile, knowing he likes what he sees. The onesie fits me a little too perfectly, showcasing my curves and highlighting all of his favourite places, places I can't wait to feel his lips, hands and mouth.

"I'm beyond ready to get tangled up with you, Trinny," he says, pulling me flush to him, roaming his hands across my body. "This might be the best present my mum's ever given me. I'm sure as hell gonna enjoy unwrapping you," he says, down on his knees at my backside, his hands resting on the buttons. "Ah, I wonder what's behind panel number one? Is your pussy wet and ready for me?" Hendrix asks, his smooth deep voice causing an ache between my legs. Instinctively, I clench, his words making my body to react in the most delicious way. *If I wasn't wet before, I sure as hell am now.*

"Maybe you should check?" I respond over my shoulder, meeting his smouldering gaze. My own voice sounds a little forced, as he's got my ass on full display in front of his face now, his mouth inches from my skin.

"I say we should find out, baby." He rubs the globes of my ass before running his tongue along my skin, then teasingly begins gliding a few fingers underneath me. They run along my slit, his fingers eliciting a slick sound as they slide, giving him proof of what he has no doubt already guessed. I'm drenched.

"Beyond fucking ready. Yeah, I love these p.j.'s. Go lay on the bed, Trin. I need a little taste. I wanna watch you fall apart. I fucking love the way you melt on my tongue, the way your body arches off the bed and how you tug at my hair while I eat that sweet pussy of yours. It drives me insane in the best possible way."

I climb onto the middle of the bed, desire humming through my entire body. Knowing how good Hendrix makes me feel—is *going* to make me feel—my body is shaking, ready for his touch.

"That's it. Now, lie down, gorgeous."

Falling onto my back, I squeeze my legs tightly in anticipation. His smooth tongue slides across my neck, igniting a fire I feel all over my body, awareness pooling between my legs as he rubs my clit through the fabric. "Such a good girl. You want me to make you feel good, Trinny?"

"Yes."

"Good, that's what I want, too." He kisses me while hovering over top of me. Taking my zipper's slider between his teeth and giving it a little tug, the zip moves down the smallest of fractions. "You're perfection, Trin, always so eager." Dropping the tab from his mouth, he kneels up, palming his hard length. My eyes immediately dart to the fleecy material covering his huge cock. "Do you see what you do to me? How bloody hard you make me?"

Watching, I'm fascinated as his big hands start rubbing over the fabric. The hard ridges of his cock stand out from under the material and I can make out his entire length, enjoying memories of what he feels like inside me. Licking my lips, I try to lean up on my elbows. I want him in my mouth.

"No way. Not yet, greedy. I want you first." He leans back down, taking the zipper in his teeth again. This time, he slides it down agonizingly slowly, inch by inch. I feel cool air on my stomach as Hendrix exposes my skin. "You smell like fruit roll-ups, Trin. Did I tell you they've become my new favourite snack over the last few months? Not as yummy as you, but I like 'em a lot. One day, I'm gonna stick 'em all over you and eat them right off this delicious-smelling body."

"Yeah…" is the only thing that comes to mind as his warm tongue tugs at my left nipple, the one he's just exposed. Running his tongue along my breastbone, he inhales my scent over and over while flickering his tongue along the sensitive skin, his stubble adding to the friction, making me whimper and arch my back up into his touch. His fingers work in tandem to tweak at my nipples, before he moves to cover each with his mouth in turn. The feeling of his tongue as he slides it along each pebbled tip is driving me crazy. Reaching for his head, I entwine my fingers in his hair and force his mouth against my breasts, in fear he'll pull away.

"I'm not going anywhere, baby. I know this feels good, I love sucking your tits and making you feel good, but I need your pussy on my tongue, Trin. I'm fucking aching for it," he growls, then moves back to the zipper and finally tugs it the rest of the way down, exposing my throbbing pussy.

"O—okay. Oh, fuck, I'm…I need you, yes…" I can't find the words as his tongue trails down my stomach to my hipbones. He runs his tongue along each one, eliciting multiple moans.

"Ready for this, Trinny? I'm going to devour you, then I'm gonna flip you over and fuck you from behind."

I'm incapable of speech. Bucking off the bed at his words is the best I can do to silently tell him: *Fuck, yes.*

48

Hendrix

TRAILING HOT KISSES down her stomach, I inhale her sweet scent. She always smells good, it's forever imprinted in my mind.

"Ready, for this, Trinny? I'm going to devour you, then I'm gonna flip you over and fuck you from behind."

She doesn't answer, but by the way she bucks her hips off the bed, I know she's more than ready. Kissing her stomach one last time, I move to her pussy. She's soaked, and I love knowing I'm the one who gets her going, who gets her hot and desperate for my touch. Dipping my hand down the front of her onesie, I circle her clit, causing her to moan and writhe beneath me.

"Tight. Jesus, you're fucking tight." I slip a finger inside her heat, her walls immediately clamping around it as I start to slide it in and out, finger fucking her. My tongue now rests on her clit, swirling at the tiny nub as it swells the more excited my girl gets. "Yeah, that's it, baby, give me the good stuff," I demand, the sounds of her arousal becoming increasingly noticeable with the insertion of a second finger, now working in sync with my tongue and driving her wild. Repositioning myself, I reach behind her, grabbing her soft ass cheeks and lifting her toward my mouth, slipping my face inside the opening of the onesie, my face consuming her completely the way she loves. I give her one, two, three swipes of my tongue from the bottom of her slit to the top, and it ignites a fire within her. She's panting, moaning, and calling out for me to fuck her.

"Please, Hendrix. Oh, Hendrix, p—please, I want you inside. I'm going to, I'm g—going to come, I'm going to come," she continues, while I lose myself in how beautiful and goddamn responsive she is. It's never been like this—never have I felt like this—with anyone else. My goal is to make her get off, make her feel good. I couldn't give a shit about me. Trinity owns me.

"Fuck, Hendrix. *Now.* I'm not kidding," Trin orders, and I cave. Unzipping myself, I release my cock and flip her over. "On all fours, baby," I demand, and she complies. Within seconds, I've sheathed myself in a condom and am sliding home. I'll never tire of this feeling, so warm, wet and smooth.

"It's about time. Fuck, that's good…" Trin purrs, pounding her ass back rhythmically to meet my cock.

"It's my fucking heaven. Do you know how sexy this is, Trinity? How amazing you look in this position?"

"No, can't say I do." She looks back, a cheeky grin sliding across her adorable flushed face, and she moves forward, almost slipping me out entirely, but doesn't let me go. She clings on and bounces right back, taking me in to the hilt. I hiss at the motion because it feels insanely good. I feel the tingles starting at my spine already. If she keeps it up, I'll be a goner in no time.

"Little tease," I say, slapping her ass, which is nicely exposed in the open flap of her onesie. "This. It feels like heaven, you sliding back and forth on my cock, seeing how fucking wet you are, your juices coating me, making my cock glisten and slide in easily over and over, …oh, fuck, it's too damn good. The way your pussy squeezes my cock, it's a fucking warm blanket. Each time you welcome me back in, you heat me back up. You drive me insane, Trin," I tell her, leaning into her ear, my hands reaching around her front to where her tits are hanging out.

Grabbing both in my hands, I pick up the pace, riding her hard as she meets me thrust for thrust. "That's it, Fruitloop, milk that cock. Take everything you need. Fuck, yes. You feel like perfection, the sweetest fucking perfection."

I kiss the nape of her neck before leaning back, letting her tits go. I grab her head, gripping my hands in her hair, and start fucking her even harder. We both move in tandem until my brain is suddenly shutting off. My spine is tingling and I'm panting heavily as I thrust harder and harder, then my orgasm starts coming on in rhythmic waves until it fully takes me under. "Fuck," I call out at the final thrust, pushing us both over the edge into oblivion. We collapse in a heap of panting, completely sated, unzipped piles of fleece on the bed, both catching our breath, donning the biggest exhausted grins.

"Best Christmas present ever," I say, nuzzling my face into Trin's neck.

"I definitely want in on this pajama tradition every year. We must be sure to thank your mother," she giggles.

49

TRINITY

IT'S CHRISTMAS DAY. And, just as he promised, Hendrix took complete advantage of the button-flap on my onesie. Not one—but two—times. I had to threaten to tell his mum if he didn't let us out of bed to get ready. He finally relented after one last make-out session and a blowjob. After long showers and picking up Kara and Arran, we finally made it to Dex and Tillie's.

It's been an amazing day so far. Of course, my family loved both Kara and Arran. It feels like they've been here with us forever, rather than just one day. Tillie offered to take Kara around Boxing Day Sale shopping and to see Niagara Falls this week, and Dex and Arran have made plans to tour Ignition Inc., then the local pub my uncle frequents. I'm lucky to have such a welcoming extended family, but it does make me sad that my mom and dad couldn't be more like Dex and Tillie. But with things as they are, I know I'm better off with my parents out of the picture, even though it makes me sad that my own mother and father are missing out on seeing how happy I am and meeting the wonderful people I've come to have in my life. *I wonder if they ever think of me?*

"You alright, Fruitloop?" I feel Hendrix's arms snake around my waist where I'm standing by the counter in Til's kitchen, and I'm glad for the distraction. I'm having too much of a perfect holiday to let thoughts like that get to me.

"Yeah, I'm good, thanks. I was just grabbing the cranberry sauce. Everyone is seated, why aren't you?" I ask, turning to face him.

"I was, but then I realized you weren't beside me. I didn't like that, so here I am." He takes the bowl from my hands. "You sure you're alright?" he asks, unsure, his head cocked to one side as he eyes me warily.

"More than. Promise. I was just wondering what my mom and dad were doing today, and whether they ever think of me. That's all. Sometimes I forget about them completely but then there are days I still miss them."

"Aww, baby. I'm sorry." Hendrix puts the bowl down and pulls me into him, giving me one of his hugs, the ones that make everything better. "It's absolutely their loss, you know that, right?" he says softly, kissing my head.

"I know. I just don't understand them, and it seems like Christmas is when it gets to me the most. It's silly. It's not like I could forgive them, exactly," I shrug, "but maybe…I just want to know that they do think of me once in a while, is all."

"I'll tell you what."

"What?" I ask, looking up at him.

"If you want to call them later, we'll call. If you want to drive by their house, we'll drive by. If you want to have a cry, you have a cry and I'll do whatever you need. But I'll tell you, it doesn't matter if they think about you, or what they think about you, because I think about you constantly and love you enough that I'll always put you first and do whatever you need me to. And I know for a fact that this crazy family of Flynns loves you almost as much as I do. So, I think you're covered, even if your parents were stupid enough to let you go."

"Hendrix," I whisper, and he wipes my cheeks where a tear has leaked out.

"It's true, baby," he says, swiping his thumb along my temple and sweeping my bangs off my face. "Now, let's go eat. Everyone is probably wondering what I'm doing with you and the cranberry sauce," he says, scooping up the dish once again.

"Speaking of which," I ask, "what did the can of jellied cranberry sauce say?"

"Oh, Jesus…what?" Hendrix replies, opening the door to the dining room where everyone is gathered around the large table ready to eat.

"You know you want a slice of this," I say, then jiggle and giggle my way past him as he barks out a laugh, in spite of himself.

"EVERYTHING LOOKS AND smells divine," Kara says. "Thank you all for welcoming Arran and I into your home and your holiday. We've very much enjoyed spending today with you, and if I may, I'd like to take a moment to thank you all for taking care of my boy. It's hard being away and I take comfort in knowing he's surrounded himself with wonderful people." Kara raises her glass. "Happy Christmas, everyone."

"Cheers! Happy Christmas! Merry Christmas!" We all raise our glasses and shout at the same time.

Hendrix laughs beside me as he passes me the cranberry sauce. "You're really corny sometimes, Fruitloop." He shakes his head and I smile like an idiot. I love knowing I make him laugh. I think that's been the thing that made it easy to fall in love with him, that easy banter and wit we share when we're together.

"So, you're hot for him, eh?" my cousin Mia blurts from where she's sitting across from us at the dinner table, having watched our little exchange. The same place she sat and asked the exact same question all those months ago. *Crazy, how so many things in my life have changed.* I went from being a self-inflicted-spinster and potential-cat-hoarder to becoming a girl in a loving committed relationship. I've handed in my copy of the *Ultimate Guide to Being Single* and I'm moving on to *Chicken Soup for the Couple's Soul* because of the beautiful man beside me. The one who laughs at my jokes, makes my toes curl and loves me unconditionally.

"Yeah, he's all right," I shrug, then wrap a hand over Hendrix's strong biceps before resting my chin on his shoulder, which is covered by a deep green Henley shirt, one that fits him perfectly in all the right places.

"I knew you liked him. It was obvious at Thanksgiving." Mia claps her hands together, gaining the attention of a few people around us. "I'm glad you finally fessed up. You two are cute together, one super hot-looking couple, eh? *Le sigh…*" she says, and puts her elbow on the table to hold her chin as she stares at us dreamingly, ignoring Nadia who is trying to pass her a casserole dish full of peas.

"I'm definitely a lucky man," Hendrix says.

"Hurt her and I beat you, though," Mia smiles, before raising her wine glass. "Merry Christmas, Hendrix." She smiles a toothy grin and I laugh while continuing to pass the hot and fragrant plates of food along, loading my plate with turkey, Dex's stuffing and all the fixings for a delicious meal.

"Pull my cracker," Hendrix commands, leaning over.

"Oh, honey, it's at least as big as a *cookie,*" I tease, bumping his shoulder.

"Funny," he deadpans. "Now pull my Christmas cracker, Fruit-loop. The king needs his paper crown before he can start eating," he winks, and I roll my eyes.

"Oh, Lord. I hate these things. The jokes inside are always awful, and the prizes are lame. Why can't they ever be good stuff?" I question, but take the end of the sparkly green cracker anyway. Looking up, I catch Hendrix's eyes and issue a challenge. "Breakfast in bed if I win the pull, Hills."

"You're on, Adams. After all, it is Boxing Day tomorrow. And this year," he whispers, "I plan on packing myself inside your box." He gives me a lopsided smile raising his brows, knowing he's lame, but charming enough that his words will still affect me. "Either way," he finishes, "it's a win-win for me. I'll get breakfast, and then I'll get you." He gives me a shit-eating grin, and I swear I feel it zap me between my legs. This man will surely be the death of me. Everyday he does something impossible that makes me fall even more in love with him.

"Who's punny now?" I shout, beginning a countdown for our cracker pull, and realize everyone at the table has stopped what they're doing to enjoy our show of witty banter, terrible puns, and silly jokes.

"1, 2, 3…" We both yank on our ends of the cracker until there's a loud bang. I look down, suddenly realizing that I won. "Yes!" I shout, seeing I have the biggest portion of the cracker—the part that has all the prizes tucked inside. *Well, except for one. The one that's fallen out and landed on the red Santa-themed napkin that's sitting on my lap.* "What the—?"

Immediately, my hand flies to my mouth. It's beautiful. I'm not sure it's real at first, but then I feel Hendrix moving beside me and I know this is happening. Like a switch, it clicks. I pick it up, watching it twinkle and sparkle as the light from the candles hits the diamond.

"Oh my God!" I yell, shoving away from the table, my chair scraping loudly across the hardwood. I stand, turning toward Hendrix, my prize held out gingerly in front of me between my thumb and index finger, like it might suddenly bite me.

"Trinny," he breathes, his brown eyes full of love as they focus on mine.

"Hen—? Oh…this. Oh!" I plop back down in my chair, unsure of what to do or say.

"Baby." He takes the ring from my hand and gets down on one knee in front of my chair. The boisterous room has gone absolutely silent, with all eyes now on us. "I need a queen. Someone to make me less impossible, and way punnier. Someone who sees all of me and loves me just the same. I need someone like you, to build a home—a life—with me. One where there's love, compromise, passion and, above all, laughter. Will you marry me, Fruitloop?" he asks.

"Yes. A billion times, yes!" I squeal, and throw my arms around his neck, hugging him so tightly it hurts. "But do I still get breakfast in bed tomorrow? Because I want that, too." I give a broad and glowing smile before leaning in close and whispering in his ear, "And you packing up my box, too, of course."

"Anything you want, baby." He shakes his head, and smiles. Taking my hand, Hendrix slides my sparkling new engagement ring onto my left ring finger, then kisses my hand. It's a beautiful square diamond halo setting surrounded by pavé diamonds. It's unique and perfect, and best of all, it's all mine. *And he's all mine.*

"I love you, Hendrix Hills. So much it hurts."

"You too, baby. For as long as you'll have me," he whispers, his voice gruff with emotion as he buries his face into my neck.

"So, you *love* him then, I'd say, eh?" Mia cries, and the table erupts with applause, laughter, cheers and toasts as Hendrix and I kiss.

We spend the rest of the night celebrating not only Christmas with our family, but also our engagement. It's a night I'll never forget, and once again, it's Hendrix who's responsible for the crazy amount of happiness I'm feeling.

The best thing I ever did was give in to his relentless demands and allow us to be friends—and more. *Not that I'd never admit that to him, of course.*

50

Trinity

It's been a month since Hendrix and I got engaged, a month since he officially moved in, and two weeks since Kara and Arran returned to England. They were reluctant to leave, and are actually in discussions to possibly move back. I know that both Hendrix and I would love that. With the wedding, I think Kara would enjoy being back in Canada where she can be a part of all the planning and fussing along with Tillie and Dex, but she's eagerly awaiting their next visit and will be here with Arran on the big day.

It was such a great holiday season. I had been worried for a bit that I'd never be able to move on, never get past my feelings of loss over Andrea and the feeling of betrayal I'd felt from Blake. Thankfully, with my family, friends and Hendrix, I've persevered and am the happiest I've been in a really long time. *Who would have thought my life could have turned into this?* Certainly not the girl who sat alone in her apartment in Toronto two-and-a-half years ago, that's for sure. It's crazy how, just when you think life has thrown you the biggest—and I mean the most humongous—lemons, you somehow manage to turn them into the sweetest and most amazing-tasting lemonade. I thought that with HIV I'd never feel true happiness again, that I'd never be anyone's happily ever after. But I do, and I am. I've never been so thankful to be proven wrong. And the best part? It's only the beginning.

"You need a hand with the chopping?" Hendrix asks behind me, his warm hands gripping my waist. His fresh scent envelops me while the heat from his body entices me to beg him to take me back to bed instead of cooking supper for company. Shannon and Cannon are coming over tonight. They're our first official dinner guests since Hendrix moved in.

"Thanks, but I'm almost done," I tell him, looking down at the last red pepper, the one I'm adding to the veggie appetizer tray I just made.

Today is Hendrix's thirtieth birthday, and he wanted a low-key dinner, just the four of us. I really wanted to throw him a big party but with the holidays, entertaining his family while they were here and working extra hours at the shop, I've been a bit more tired than normal. Hendrix keeps insisting I need to go to the doctor and I keep telling him to relax. Besides, I have an appointment booked for the twenty-eighth, anyway.

"Alright," he says, kissing the back of my neck before resting his hand there. Standing at my side, he starts placing the peppers in the veggie tray. "How are you feeling tonight, Trin?" he says, eyeing me skeptically.

"I'm fine. Please stop fussing. I'd tell you if anything were wrong other than just being tired. It'll pass, now that things have settled. If I was worried, I'd go in. I swear." I place the knife on the chopping block. "Now, can you make sure the fridge is stocked with beer and pour that bottle of red in the decanter, please? They'll be here soon." I nod to the counter, where the twelve-pack of Stella and the bottle of red I bought are sitting.

"Yes, Fruitloop. Whatever you need me to do." He taps my ass, making his way over to the fridge with the beer. Watching him move easily around the kitchen makes me smile. Of course, he catches me lurking, and in return blesses me with that breath-hitching smirk of his. "Not my fault I love you too much, you know," he says, scowling when he's done.

I can't help but laugh at how sweet my ogre really is. "I know. I feel the same way."

"Then you get me. You feel like shit, you tell me, Fruitloop. No bullshit."

"No bullshit, I promise. I'm just tired and my tummy's been a little queasy, but that's it. I'm feeling great, now."

"Okay. But when they get here, you're to relax. I got dinner covered. You prepped, I'll serve and clean up."

"Like I'd say no to an offer like that. *Pshaw*...know me much?" I laugh.

"It's okay. I know how you can pay me back. And the good thing about my payback methods? You can be as tired as you want, all I need is your mouth," he chuckles, tweaking my hip as he passes by to grab the wine.

"You wish, sick boy. It's my mouth that's the most tired," I tease, reaching over and smacking his ass in turn.

"I got the cure right here," he says, gripping his junk. "A shot of this and you'll be feeling like a million bucks."

"God, you're impossible," I giggle. *How ridiculous he is sometimes, the shit that comes out of his mouth...*

"It's 'Hendrix', but yeah...I kinda am godlike, aren't I?" He stands in front of me, posing. "At least in stature and the goods," he chuckles, running his hand down his body, ending at his groin.

"Can't you ever keep your hands off your compressor? See? *Impossible.* How do I even deal with you?" I joke, and he moves back over to his side of the kitchen.

"You're already too far-gone. It's too late for the likes of you; you already love me." He winks from where he's just finished decanting the wine.

"I sure do. And what's my reward for tolerating you, exactly?" I say, opening the fridge for some ginger ale.

"The best friendship we've both ever had?" he says, handing me a glass.

"Debatable." I cock my head and smile before taking a sip.

We spend the next half hour bantering and getting ready for Shannon and Cannon.

I will secretly admit it. He's not only my best friendship; he's my best decision…even if he is utterly impossible.

51

Hendrix

"PASS THE SALAD, please, Hendrix?"

We should have cancelled. I should have cancelled this stupid dinner. I know it's my birthday and it's a big deal to Trin, but I could give a shit. I see Cannon at work almost everyday now that he's working for me, so it's really not critical to have to celebrate it tonight. I know she's not feeling well; I can see it in her eyes. There's a cloud lurking amidst the warmth I've come to expect. She says she's okay but she's just drinking ginger ale, and that alone tells me she's still feeling queasy. My girl always drinks wine with Shannon.

"Hendrix?" Shannon's impatient voice cuts through my thoughts.

"Oh, shit. Sorry?"

"Salad. Can you please pass it?"

"Yeah, sure. Here you go," I say, picking up the bowl of Caesar salad and passing it to her. "I was just thinking about a carburetor I have to remember to order on Monday," I lie.

"Always thinking about work, eh? Things never change," Cannon jokes. "Even when he's got a girl, the man can't relax." I want to kick him, but he's too far away. In reality, now all that I think about is her. Work can wait for working hours. When I'm off, Trin is where my focus is.

"Shut up. I just don't wanna forget about it, dickless. I'm a responsible business owner now, and the story you were just boring us with about the paint job you're doing on that '74 Cobra II reminded me."

"Whatever," he says, taking a pull from his beer. "Pass the spaghetti, fuckface? By the way, it's really good, Trin," Cannon says, smiling graciously at Trinity, who's been somewhat quiet the last few minutes. I want to ask Shannon and Cannon to leave, but I know Trin would disown me.

"By the way, guys, did you see that the office space beside my salon is empty? They're looking to lease it. I'm considering expanding Moxie," Shannon tells us, pride colouring her tone, a feeling I can relate to being a business owner myself.

Cannon reaches over and grabs her hand. "I think it's an awesome idea," he says. I've never seen Cannon this far-gone over a chick before—especially one he met at a bar—but, then again, Shannon isn't like most of the girls he's dated before. She's independent, smart, and pretty. She's definitely girlfriend-material, and I'm glad he's finally taking a swim in the relationship pool like I am. He's a good guy and deserves to find with Shannon what I've found in Trin.

"Wow, that'll be amazing," Trinity says excitedly, her face seemingly a little less pale than a few minutes ago. "Let me know if I can help."

"Thanks, I will. The sign just went up last night. Who knows? I might be getting ahead of myself. My biggest obstacle will be to see if I can get the loan," Shannon sighs.

"I should give you my guy's name, he was great. He's over at the Scotiabank on Green Road," I offer.

"That would be amazing," Shannon beams, "thank you."

"Of course. Any way I can help, call me. I'm there," I tell her, before taking a bite of my pasta.

"Damn it." Trin stands. "I forgot the garlic bread. Save room. I'll be right back."

“I’ll get it.” I stand, but she shushes me.

“I’m already up, don’t be silly,” she says, walking away before I can argue.

“What kind of overhead do you have with a salon, anyway?” I ask Shannon, curious.

“It’s not too bad, really. The fact that I rent chairs to stylists really helps. They pay rent for their spaces and have their own client—” She’s interrupted by Trin.

“Here we go! Hot and fresh garrrr—” She doesn’t finish her sentence. Instead, the colour leaves her face. Her eyes suddenly roll back and she falls like a felled tree, banging her head off the laminate with a loud clunk as she lands, the pan and the garlic bread spinning greasily across the floor.

“Trinity!” I bolt out of my seat, my heart racing with adrenaline as I crouch beside her.

“Trin!” Shannon calls, moving over to where Trin’s lying. “What can I do?” she asks, starting to cry.

“I’m on with 911,” Cannon says hollowly.

I check her vitals as best I can. I make sure her airway is open, check for breathing and a pulse. Thankfully, Frank, our old boss at Wheel Wizards, had insisted that we all take First Aid and CPR training. After checking her over, I prop her feet on a cushion above her head level to prevent shock, while hoping she’ll soon come to. I keep calling her name and talking to her to see if she’ll come around. “Trinity! Trinity. Trinity…”

I’m not sure how much time passes, but it seems like mere seconds before the paramedics are knocking and rolling a stretcher through the door, carrying all their bags and knapsacks. Just as they are entering along with a draught of winter air, Trinity flutters her eyelids and regains consciousness. She’s disorientated and confused, but at least she’s awake. I step back to give them room, and bite back tears as I see the EMS guy strap a blood pressure cuff around her upper arm and start squeezing its bulb. He places his stethoscope on the inside of her elbow. The other is hooking up electrodes to her chest, her shirt now mostly unbuttoned and her pretty bra exposed. All I hear at first is the one medic talking into his radio saying something about "syncope".

"Anything we need to be aware of before we examine her? Medications, illnesses or recent injuries? That sort of stuff?" the shorter dark-haired paramedic asks, kneeling on the floor beside Trin. Blue vinyl covers his hands; he holds a pen ready to write my answers on his glove.

"She takes…Atripla, once a day. Trin is…she's, she has…" I can't finish. My tongue feels like sandpaper at having to say it out loud. As if telling another person is breaking some kind of secret code between Trin and I. As if saying it to this stranger will somehow make her HIV stronger. I refuse to let that happen.

"She's HIV-positive," Shannon says, resting her hand on my shoulder. Silently, I look up at her and nod a thank you.

"She's what?" I hear Cannon say in the background, but I could give a fuck. He can be pissed if he wants; it's none of his business. I know we're best friends and maybe I should have told him, but I didn't, because it doesn't matter to me. I love her regardless, and him knowing wouldn't have changed anything. Trinity was actually going to bring it up tonight, since she's gotten to know Cannon a lot better over the last few months and is feeling much more comfortable with him. She was surprised I hadn't told him already, but thanked me for keeping it private.

"Thank you. Let's check her vitals, blood sugar, and heart rate. Then we'll know more," the tall blonde medic says.

"Hi, Trinity," says the other one. "I'm Steve. It seems you had a little fall. My buddy Patrick and I are going to make sure you're okay, and then we're going for a ride to the hospital," he says, offering her a friendly reassuring smile.

Her eyes dart all around until they land on me, then relief crosses her face. "I'm here, baby. Right here with you."

"Hendrix," she says, almost inaudibly, her voice sounding tired and weak. I know what she's thinking, and I need to push the thoughts out of both our minds.

"Everything's going to be fine. I'll be with you every second. The doctors and these guys will figure it all out. Let's not get ahead of ourselves, okay? Just relax," I say, more convincingly than I'm feeling. I watch with bated breath as the paramedics finish their work and lift Trin onto the gurney. My heart lurches in my chest. I feel it pounding full-blast, and there's a ringing in my ears. My knees feel weak, and I feel like I might pass out myself.

"Cannon and I will meet you guys at the hospital, Hendrix. I'm going to call Dex and Tillie."

I hear Shannon, but don't give her an answer; I'm too numb. I only want confirmation that Trinity is all right. Thoughts of losing her plague my mind as I stumble behind the stretcher as the paramedics carry her out. I climb into the ambulance and all I can think of is that I'm going to lose her when I haven't had her nearly long enough. *Not even close.*

52

HENDRIX

"HENDRIX, PLEASE. I'M fine. I feel much better," Trinity calls softly from her stretcher in the Emergency Room. I'm patrolling up and down the white-tiled linoleum, waiting for the doctor. Despite my best efforts, my hands are shaking and my mind is reeling. I'm about to lose it.

"Come, sit down. You need to calm down. Everything will be good. I feel good," Trinity says, using a soothing voice. Unfortunately, it does shit to stop this sinking feeling from taking over my gut, even though she does look a bit better.

"I can't, Fruitloop." I stop and look at her. She scared the ever-living fuck out of me tonight. When I saw her go down, I literally felt my heart stop, drop and crumble at my feet.

"Baby, please…"

"Why aren't they back with the results yet?" I ask, shaking my head and ignoring her plea. I resume my watch in the small space where they have Trinity resting while waiting for her blood test results. Results I'm trying to prepare myself for.

A million thoughts and a billion worst-case scenarios run rampant through my mind despite Trin's attempts at calming me down. I can't seem to shake the doubts that are taking root. *What if her viral count is high? What if she's caught tuberculosis or some other virus that's making her immune system react? Fuck. Fuck. Fuck.* I run my hands down my face while glancing out the window and up at the stars. I'm wishing on something, praying to someone I'm not even sure I even believe in to fix this, to make it right, to make sure she's healthy.

"Hendrix. Stop. You're not helping me right now. You're kind of making me freak out, to be honest. I need my rock." I hear Trin's voice waver and it stops me in my tracks.

"Shit. You're right. I'm sorry. I'm—" I pause. "I'm scared, baby." I move closer to the bed, where I should have been the whole time.

"Me too, but there's no sense worrying until we know, right?"

"Right." I grip the bed rails, begging for the strength to compose myself. I'm being a selfish prick right now. *I gotta be strong for my girl, keep her from worrying. I can freak out later.* "You're right. Okay, no more negative thoughts. Everything's gonna be fine," I smile, and give her what I hope is a reassuring nod.

"That's my ogre. Now come lay with me. It's been a long night, and I could use a cuddle," Trinity says, giving me a sweet smile as she shifts over on the narrow bed, her hand gently tapping the space beside her. Suddenly, there's a motion at the curtain.

"Hello. Can I come in?"

"Y—yes," Trinity replies, reaching for my hand. I squeeze it, letting her know we're going to be all right before taking a seat in the chair beside her.

"It's going to be fine, baby. I have a good feeling." I kiss her hand, while silently pleading on the inside. *Please, don't pull the rug out from under our happiness. I'm not ready...*

53

Trinity

"Hi, Trinity. I'm Dr. Carmen Gallegan," the tall grey-haired woman says with a quick smile, taking a seat on the black stool.

"Hello," I say back, then motion to Hendrix. "This is my fiancé, Hendrix Hills." Hendrix nods before standing to shake the doctor's outstretched hand.

"Good to meet you, Doctor Gallegan. Please tell us you have some test results?" Hendrix says, letting out a long breath, and it pains me to see him like this. I know he's worried and I loathe knowing he's feeling this way because of me. This situation is a blatant reminder of what our future could hold for him, and sooner rather than later if we get bad news today.

"I'll get to that. I have a few questions first," she says, looking down at her iPad. "From what I understand, you had a bit of a scare tonight. Can you tell me what happened?"

"Yes, we did. I guess I…*fainted?* I've never passed out before. It was weird. All of a sudden I heard a ringing sound, saw a few black specks, and the next thing I knew I was talking to a paramedic on the ground," I tell the doctor.

"Yes, it can be a very strange and scary feeling. I'm glad to see you aren't too banged up. Sometimes when a person faints they can get quite hurt from falling," she says, looking at my chart. "I see they checked you for concussion, but it was ruled out, that's excellent. And can you tell me whe—"

"Sorry to interrupt, Doc," Hendrix says, sounding annoyed, "but it's been a long night and I'm gonna need you to rip the Band-Aid off. Is Trin alright, or not? I mean…the HIV. Is her virus load higher? Is that why she fainted?"

"Hendrix!" I scold. "She's getting there. Wait."

"Sorry. She's right," he says, looking a little embarrassed but not at all sorry. "It's hard. I'm losing my mind here. I wanna know."

"I understand," Dr. Gallegan says, barely hiding a chuckle. "My apologies, Hendrix," she says, "I don't mean to laugh. I know you're worried. Trust me. If it was serious, I wouldn't have spent time with idle chit-chat."

Letting out a relieved sigh, Hendrix frowns. "Then why'd she faint? There has to be something. I mean, she just told you it's never happened before."

"Hendrix," I grab his arm, trying to calm him.

"It's alright, Trinity. Hendrix is right. There is a reason, but rest assured it's not the HIV," Dr. Gallegan says gently. "And I'm hoping you'll be happy with what I have to tell you…"

"Thank Christ," I hear Hendrix huff beside me, and I immediately feel the weight of worry lift from around us.

"I'm okay, then? My levels are within range?" I ask, sounding as nervous as Hendrix has been feeling, I'm sure. Because—for a brief second—I worry. *If it's not the HIV, then what could it be? But…wait a minute. She said it wasn't anything serious…*

"It's good news, then?" I ask hesitantly.

"Well, that depends on if you've ever wanted children." She smiles kindly as Hendrix and I gasp at the same time.

"I'm *pregnant*? What? *How*?"

"I'm going to venture a guess and say condom failure. With your HIV status, I assume you and Hendrix use condoms as protection?"

"Yes, ma'am. Every time," Hendrix answers before I can form words.

Pregnant?

"Do you want kids, Trinity?" Dr. Gallegan asks.

"Yes. I mean, I've always wanted kids, I just didn't think I should, with the HIV and all." I let out an unsure and awkward laugh.

I'm going to be a mom. I feel the beginnings of a smile start to take shape on my lips. I blurt out again, "I'm pregnant?"

"Yes, Trinity. You're pregnant. You and Hendrix are going to be parents."

"Oh my God," I squeak, then cover my mouth. Looking over at Hendrix, I can't even guess what he must be feeling right now.

"I'm sorry, Hendrix," I say, causing him to move immediately from his seat onto the bed, right beside me.

"Are you kidding me? 'Sorry'? No need to apologize, Fruitloop. I'm fucking thrilled. This is the best news ever," he says, with a grin.

"You mean you're okay with this? What about that whole thing that happened before with Calli—" I start to ask, but he cuts me off with a gentle kiss.

"Don't bring that up. It's nowhere near the same situation. Never compare now to then, that was the past. You're my future. And you having my baby? What the hell isn't there to be okay with?"

"Hendrix, we're going to have a *baby*. You and me—us. Can you believe it?" I ask him, unable to hide my excitement the more I repeat it.

"We're having a baby," he repeats. A huge grin graces his handsome face, a thrilled look I'm happy to see replacing the look of worry and stress that had been etched over his features for the last few hours, the one he'd been doing such a shitty job of hiding.

54

HENDRIX

"WE'RE HAVING A baby," Trin laughs, repeating the words again. Then she lunges at me. Wrapping her arms around my neck, she whispers in my ear, "I'm going to be a mom after all." And fuck me if that isn't the most beautiful thing she's ever said to me.

"Yeah, you are, Fruitloop. And you'll be incredible. But, remember, it's actually pronounced 'mum'…" I chuckle.

"But, wait…" Trinity pulls back, worry lining her face as she glances at Dr. Gallegan. "If I'm pregnant, that means fluids must have been exchanged. That means…*Hendrix!* I could have given you…"

"Relax, Trinity." I try to calm her.

"This is what I was afraid of. Oh, God, Hendrix. What if I infected you?"

"Trinity, Hendrix. If I could, I'd like to talk a bit about next steps and what Hendrix will need to do in order to be tested."

Wiping her face with the tissue the doctor hands her, Trin nods, and we spend the next while discussing how, despite using condoms regularly and carefully, they aren't always foolproof; even when used properly they can fail. According to Dr. Gallegan, ten to fifteen women out of a hundred will become pregnant from condom failure. A number we both found shocking. The doctor also discussed the risks of mother-to-baby HIV transmission with us, and how the delivery would have to be a planned C-section at thirty-eight weeks in order to avoid transmission via the placenta during a vaginal birth. Dr. Gallegan felt with Trin's CD4 count being in the twelve hundreds, the chances of the baby not contracting HIV were promising, as it means that her HIV viral load is low.

It was a lot to take in, and I already know we will spend a lot of time researching mother-to-child transmission on our own, as well, plus ways to ensure the safest possible pregnancy. After speaking with the doctor, I feel confident beginning this part of our journey together. We've done everything we could, now it's a matter of hoping for the best.

We did, however, leave the hospital that day with another seed of worry. Since the condom failed, Dr. Gallegan suggested I see my own doctor. She said with my PrEP medication, Truvada, I would likely test negative, but as a precaution suggested I get an HIV test anyway, ASAP.

Needless to say, Trinity was a mess with worry. She thought that her biggest fear was coming true just as she had received her happiest news. I spent a long time willing her to understand that I'm a grown man who was educated on the risks we were taking and had made my own decisions. I also assured her it wouldn't matter either way at this point, I loved her regardless (although I admit I was feeling somewhat jarred by the possibility I might have become infected inadvertently. That's not news that anyone wants to hear).

In the end, we decided to skip the rapid-testing option (which can be done within a doctor's office, giving results in twenty- to thirty minutes). With the rapid test, there's a possibility of testing "reactive", which means it's uncertain. If this were to happen, I'd have to be tested again using the traditional lab method anyway. With that information, Trinity and I opt for the traditional blood test, which we feel is the best and most accurate method for our situation.

No doubt it was going to be the longest couple of weeks in our lives while we waited for the results, but I insisted Trin follow her own advice, that we try not to spend the time stressing about the things we can't control.

55

Trinity

"I REALLY CAN'T believe you picked these for your bouquet," Shannon says, laughing and handing me the arrangement.

"I know. Hendrix will love it," I giggle, looking down at the bouquet of chocolate tire irons I bought from the same place Hendrix used all those months ago. I decided they were a must-have for today. *Our Wedding Day.*

After finding out about the baby four months ago, and surviving the stress of the longest week of our lives while we waited for Hendrix's HIV test results—which thankfully came back negative, and sooner than the two weeks it could have taken—we decided two things. One, preventative medicines are definitely worth the money, and two, we couldn't wait to be married. Therefore, after a few phone calls and errands, everything came together quite nicely and here we are today.

Kara and Arran were over the moon to hear about both the baby and our wedding when we shared the news during one of our Facetime chats, and they booked their flights right then while live with us online. They were, however, not too happy that we told them about the wedding, the baby and Hendrix's HIV scare only once his negative results were back. It was a decision that Kara understood in the end, but she made us both promise to not keep things like that from her in future. We agreed.

"There. You look stunning," Shannon says, her eyes glassy with emotion as she finishes manipulating my just-above-shoulder-length brown hair into a mass of sexy curls, pinning one last jewelled hairpin into place.

"Absolutely no crying. I'm already hyperemotional as it is," I say, rubbing my small baby bump. I'm officially five months along today, and the thrill of the idea of becoming a mum never gets old. We found out we're having a girl, and to say I was excited is an understatement. Not that I'd be any less excited if I were having a boy, but knowing she's a girl gives me a little confidence boost. Since I'm a strong woman (so I like to think), it makes me believe that I have lots of quality girl skills to pass on to and teach my daughter. Hendrix, of course, claims he knew she was a girl and is already plotting how to handle the teen years with Dex and Cannon. All I know is I cannot wait to meet and hold our baby.

"I know, I know. I'm just beyond happy for you, Mama, and I love you." She pats her hand gently over my stomach. "Now, let's go get you hitched." She thumbs towards the door of Dex's office, where we've been putting on our finishing touches.

"I love you, too. Thank you for helping us pull this off so quickly. I know you think we're crazy for doing it here."

"Are you kidding me? Garage weddings are all the rage this year," she winks, as we make our way out the door. Call us unconventional, call us crazy, but both Hendrix and I decided we wanted to get married in the place we began, Ignition Inc.

Dex loved the idea—while Tillie and Kara thought we'd both gone mad—but once we'd shared the story of the night Hendrix and I first met, they both gushed and agreed it was the perfect spot for us to become husband and wife.

"You ready, kid?" Dex's gruff voice asks as he loops his arm with mine, soothing my last-minute nerves.

I nod. "I'm more than ready."

"You look exquisite, Trinity. I'm honoured to be the one walking you down the aisle today. I'm happy for you, sweetheart," Dex says, leaning in and giving my cheek a swift kiss, the hairs of his beard tickling me like always.

"Dexter! You're going to ruin my face!" I joke, wiping a few tears. Like I'd ever care about that. "I love you. Thanks to you and Aunt Tillie for always being here for me," I smile, pulling him a little closer to my side.

"Alright, kiddo, alright. Enough of the mushy stuff. Let's go find your future," he says, as "By Your Side" by Sade starts playing, giving us our cue, letting us know they're ready for us to move into the shop where Hendrix and our closest friends and family will be waiting.

"Let's do this," Shannon grins, as she takes the lead, making her way through the door leading into the garage, her pretty off-the-shoulder wine-coloured dress swishing with each step.

Taking a deep breath, I smile, feeling the most contented I've ever felt in my life. I'm not only going to be a mum, but also the wife of an incredible man who has given me so much love and happiness that I could die tomorrow and feel my life was complete. I have no regrets, and, best of all, the love of a man who sees and loves all of me.

"Now it's our turn. Let's go get your daddy and our happily ever after," I grin, patting my stomach gently as Dex and I step forward.

56

Hendrix

I STAND SILENTLY at the top of the makeshift aisle, waiting for Trin and Flynn to appear through the office door. We'd decided on a low-key ceremony with Shannon and Cannon serving as our maid of honour and best man, and just close family members and a few friends in attendance. I see my mum and Arran and Aunt Tillie beaming at me from the front row, and have to look away.

Suddenly, Trinity appears on Flynn's arm, and I swear I almost swallow my tongue when my eyes land on her. Trinity looks so incredibly gorgeous in a long, strapless, champagne-coloured dress that highlights her best assets. Her eyes are done up in this smoky look which makes them even more insanely beautiful, and her lush lips are their usual glossy colour, which reminds me how sweet they taste.

"You ready for this, big guy?" Cannon whispers beside me. "Gotta say, I never thought I'd see the day."

"I couldn't be more ready to make Trinity my wife," I whisper back, barely letting my lips move.

"She's gorgeous, man. Congrats." He claps my back before moving aside when Flynn and Trin are finally standing in front of me.

"Take care of my girl, Hendrix," Flynn says, shaking my hand before giving Trin a kiss, then returning to his seat with Til, my mum and Arran.

"Love the bouquet," I say quietly, as Shannon reaches over to take the chocolates from Trin. "Are they metric or imperial?"

"Knew you'd like it," she whispers back, giving me a knowing glance. "They're metric, of course."

"You're stunning," I tell her, taking her hands in mine and feeling the slight tremble in them, matching my own. I take comfort in knowing we're in sync with one another. Both nervous, but also more than ready to begin our lives together.

"I'm nervous, but excited," she whispers, her eyes getting a little glassy as emotions start to run high. "I can't wait to be yours," she beams, her grey eyes meeting mine.

"You've been mine all along, Trin. You just took a little time to catch on," I smile, running my thumb along her cheek, before giving her belly a little rub, letting our baby girl in on the moment.

"I think this is going to be an emotional wedding," Trin says. "Even the cake had *tiers*, I noticed," she adds, almost straight-faced.

"You're such a punny girl. You ready to become my wife now, baby, or do you need to get a few more out?" I ask.

"God, yes. No more puns…for now," Trinity answers, and I nod at Judge Coleman to begin when she's ready. We'd met the judge when she brought in her '67 Corvette for a brake job last month, and we both thought she'd make a perfect officiant.

"Family and friends of Trinity and Hendrix, I welcome you today, in this garage, to witness the joining…"

Judge Coleman's words blur as I focus solely on my future standing before me. I never expected to end up with this life, but no matter what the future holds, I know Trinity, the baby and I will fight tooth and nail to hold onto what we have. Regardless of what happens with her HIV, I vow to make Trinity the happiest woman, to remind her everyday she's loved, supported and that she's the part that makes me whole.

"Trinity, please take Hendrix's hands in yours and recite your vows..." I hear the judge say, gaining my attention again. I've been waiting for this part. Trin and I decided to write our own vows, and we've had a bit of a competition going to see whose vows will be the best. We've gone as far as warning everyone that we'll be taking a poll to declare an official winner after the ceremony. Unbeknownst to our guests, the winner not only gets street cred, but also gets to have the other act out a sexual fantasy of their choice. Hello, Boss/Employee fantasy—I can picture Trinity stretched out on the hood of my Camaro in my work bay. *Yes, please.*

Giving me a knowing grin, Trinity begins her vows.

"I, Trinity Paige Adams, take you, Hendrix William Hills, to be my lawfully hot, kind and beautiful husband. One I promise to let under my hood when needed..." she says, giving me a shit-eating grin that about brings me to my knees, "...especially when I start making that weird clanking sound." She smiles, knowing she got me good there. "I vow to hand you every tool you may ever need, and buy you the new ones you 'gotta have' as soon as they hit the market," she air quotes, and I chuckle, because she's right, I'm always asking her to order the latest tools and machinery for my collection. "I will support your choices and decisions in both vehicles and in our life together. I, Trinity, love you, Hendrix, with all the tire irons and onesies the world has to offer, and that will never change. You're my best friend, my very own ogre-turned-prince. I was incomplete until the night I walked in here," she says, gesturing around the garage, tears falling freely down her beautiful face, "and thought you might be the world's dumbest criminal stealing our wrenches. Turns out I was wrong; you were just stealing my heart. You saw the real me, the me I thought I'd lost. I love you, Hendrix. Very much. And that is my biggest truth."

"I love you too, Trin."

"Thank you, Trinity," the judge says, turning to face me.

"Beat that," Trinity mouths so only I can see, which causes me to almost laugh out loud. *This girl…*

"Hendrix, it's time to share your vows," Judge Coleman says.

I clear my throat and begin. "I, Hendrix William Hills, take you, Trinity Paige Adams, my Short Stack-turned-Fruitloop, keeper of all my truths, to be my wife, my life partner and my best friend. You are the person who makes my heart beat, and I will strive each day to make you smile and belly laugh, and to encourage you to continue on your mission to be punny. You'll get there one day." I stop and hide my smile as she mock-scowls. "I will be the rock of strength on which you can always depend. Whether it's in sickness or in health, I will always be there for you. I will shower you with onesies, tire irons and McEggMuffs from McDavid's, but most of all, I'll forever shower you with love. Love so strong you'll feel me for all of eternity. Remember, you're my *butter* half and *olive* you, Trin," I say, finishing off with a lame pun I'd found online. *One I knew she'd love.*

"Hendrix," Trinity says smiling, "I love you. Thank you." She squeezes my hands.

Looking at Judge Coleman, I ask, "Please tell me I can kiss her now?"

"Almost. I promise," she replies. "These wedding rings you are about to exchange are a visible sign of an invisible sign and commitment which will unite you in love, a love so deep it should be upheld and cherished. Let's get you a little further along the road to that kiss, Hendrix."

"Yes, ma'am. Please do," I reply.

"Place the ring on Trinity's finger and repeat after me…"

"Trinity," I begin, repeating the words, "I give you this ring. Wear it with love and happiness. This ring is a symbol of my lasting love, it has no beginning and no end."

"Now, Trinity, place the ring on Hendrix's finger and repeat after me…"

"Hendrix," Trinity says, "I give you this ring. Wear it with love and happiness. This ring is a symbol of my lasting love, it has no beginning and no end."

"I can now officially invite you to kiss the bride, Hendrix."

And I do.

And I will. Forever and a day…

57

HENDRIX

3 months later

SITTING HERE IN the crowded auditorium, I'm in awe. Watching Trinity do her thing is incredible. My girl's an inspiring advocate for those living with HIV and AIDS, a survivor unafraid of putting herself out there. She told me once that if she inspires even one person use condoms, she will have done her job. These kids are lucky to have her to talk to, educate and help them. She gets a lot of emails from students who have heard her speak and, Trinity being Trinity, she replies to each and every one. Today's speech is extra special because it will likely be her last school visit for a while. I know it'll be an adjustment for her not to have this type of therapeutic release in her life, but I think the trade off is definitely worth it for her.

Trinity up on stage now with her enormous tummy has me completely enamoured. I'm in the audience in the front row with Flynn beside me, both of us listening to her speak about her experiences. The smile lighting up her face is infectious as she talks about how happy she is, and how excited she is to become a mother. I shift in my seat, trying not to let my wife's beauty, coupled with her intelligence and charm, allow my attraction to get too carried away.

But let me tell you, it's hard. That whole thing people say about how a pregnant woman's libido increases is no myth, and it doesn't only apply to the female half of the equation. I've been more and more insatiable with every noticeable change to Trin's body. I can't explain it, but I've never wanted my wife more. I just need to remind myself that this is definitely not the time or place to get a hard on.

Shaking my head, I watch, smiling, as she waddles across the stage. Trin speaks passionately about the preventative measures she is taking for the baby's protection right now, about how she'll have a planned C-section, how she and the baby will both be carefully monitored, but that she won't be able to breastfeed, while I sit here trying to calm myself down. *I really am impossible sometimes.*

She glances down as she touches her belly, and I catch the glint of the diamonds resting on her ring finger. I'll never forget the day Trin officially became my wife—and our crazy vow competition, which ended as a tie according to our guests.

We both still need to collect on our wins…maybe after we leave here I'll take her back to the shop and lean her sexy ass over the '77 Celica I've almost finished rebuilding. Yeah, I bet she'd look fuckin' hot with her legs spread wide, her elbows on the hood, me taking her from behind with my hands wrapped around that cute belly…

"And now, I'd like to move on to my favourite part: the question and answer period…" Trin's voice breaks through my fantasy, and I smile up at her as she catches my eye from the stage, standing right in front of us. *Yeah, we're definitely going down to the shop later. I wonder what she'll make me do when she claims her half of the bet?*

Leaning in, Flynn whispers, "I've never seen Trin so happy. Thank you, Hendrix, for giving her that glow." He clasps my wrist. "Make sure you keep that shit up."

"Oh, I plan on it, sir."

"You better." He chuckles quietly, and we sit together and watch our girl wrap up her speech.

58

Trinity

"And now, I'd like to move on to my favourite part: the question and answer period. We have about twenty minutes for you to ask me anything and everything. I'm an open book."

I scan the large crowd at Centennial High. My eyes land on Hendrix who's sitting up front with Dex, grinning at me like a fool. *It's sort of the way I feel when I look at him, too.* Patting my baby bump, I head to the stool; my feet could use a break. Moving it to centre stage, I take a seat as the first young woman makes her way to the mic.

"Hi, Trinity. I'm Ashley."

"Hey, what's your question?" I say with a warm smile. After all this time, I still look forward to this part. For the most part, the students ask really well-thought-out questions and are usually less judgemental than adults. A part of me thinks it's because this generation is better educated about HIV and AIDS than we were when I was younger.

"I guess I wanted to know if you were scared when you found out you were pregnant?" she asks.

"Yes. Petrified, at first." I look to Hendrix and smile. "But my husband and doctors are amazing and together we've been doing everything we can to ensure our baby isn't affected. We've got a solid plan in place which involves a planned C-section and medication, both for me before delivery and for the baby afterwards. For six weeks after birth, our daughter will take a medication called Retrovir (Zidovudine), which is an anti-HIV drug safe for newborns, which essentially stops the virus's enzymes from creating the HIV virus. But the biggest thing we have going for us is that I'm one of the lucky ones, I have a low viral load and my T-cell count is in a healthy range, so there is a near-99% chance that I won't pass it along. Regardless, I'm worried—like any new parent-to-be—but not as terrified as I was at first now that I have more information. Now, I'm just more excited. I need her to hurry up and get here so I can meet her," I laugh.

"I wish you all the best."

"Thank you." Taking a sip of water, I look up and see a tall girl with bright red hair standing at the mic. "Hi! What's your question?"

"I'm Elise. I wanted to know if you'll breastfeed? I'm not sure if you already said or not, but I'm curious. I'm sitting up in the nosebleeds and couldn't really hear…" She points up to the last row in the back.

"Hi, nice to meet you. Great question. I did mention that it's a risk. Unfortunately, breastfeeding involves the transmission of fluids from me to the baby, so, no, I can't risk infecting her. Besides formula today is just as good, I'm told."

"Awesome, thank you," she nods, making her way back up to the top.

"Hi, I'm Veronica. I've been sitting here listening and I can't stay quiet anymore. I think you're making a mistake. I think you're playing Russian roulette with an innocent life. How do you sleep at night knowing you could be giving your daughter a death sentence…" I tune her out, but what she's saying are the same things I thought for months and months. It took Hendrix, my doctors and my family a long time to get me over thinking that way. Looking to Hendrix for a bit of a reprieve, I end up giving him a scowl as I notice he and Dex are both gripping their armrests as if they're struggling to not jump up and defend me. *If I know my husband, he's about to try to shut this down.*

"…and what type of mother is okay with that?"

I mouth "relax" over to Dex and Hendrix, who are glowering and shaking their heads, not happy with the comment. Seeing them sit back, I continue, giving them a nod.

"You have a point, Veronica. I felt the way you did for a while, too, before I got all the facts. I briefly contemplated termination. My husband and I spent many nights wondering if what we were doing was wrong. Heaps of Kleenexes were used, a lot of Googling was done and many doctor's appointments were made. But, thankfully, we did take the time to educate ourselves. And you know what? Our little girl has more of a chance of being born with a birth defect than she does of having HIV. Therefore, my answer is 'no'. I don't feel like a bad mom. I feel the same nerves all new moms feel, but I know our little girl will be loved and supported regardless of what happens. Hendrix and I decided that we already loved her too much not to live with the small risk of HIV transmission," I say honestly, but then notice she's already stomping away from the microphone. However, once I finish, I hear a bunch of whistles and hands clapping at my answer. I let out a huge breath.

"Thanks, guys, that one was probably the hardest question ever. I need an easy one next. I guess it's all baby questions today, eh?" I tease, but get exactly that.

"Hey, I'm Jay. I just wanted to say good for you, nice to see someone with some balls. Technology and modern medicine is in your favour. I say, congratulations."

"Thank you, Jay. And that's very true. The advances in medicine around HIV have been incredible."

"Hey, there. I'm Aamira. I wanted to know when they'll test the baby?"

"They'll be testing her around twelve days after birth, then again at six weeks, and again after twelve weeks. These tests are looking to see if the virus has presented itself in her blood. If all those tests come back clear, then it's safe to say that she's HIV-negative. As an extra precaution, we've decided to give her an infant post-exposure prophylaxis, also called a PEP. It's an extra medication that will fight the virus, too. We figure we need to do all we can, and we've seen firsthand how effective the preventative medicine was with my husband when we had the contraceptive failure."

"I think that it is very good that you have received all of the information you need to raise a healthy baby. I bet you will be an excellent mother to your child. I will keep your family in my prayers."

"I appreciate that, Aamira. Thank you."

After a few more questions about the baby, and Hendrix's and my future plans, I thank everyone and start packing up as the students file out. Hendrix comes on stage, wrapping his strong arms around my stomach, pulling me back into his chest.

"I'm proud of you, baby. You did an amazing job up there today." He kisses my cheek. "I can see you're tired. What say you let me finish the packing, then we can get outta here faster. I see a foot rub in your future."

"Sounds amazing," I agree, and move aside to sit with Dex. *I mean, who wouldn't, with an offer like that?*

59

Trinity

Walking into Burger Barn, my inner carnivore is in full-on "get in my belly" mode. It's either that, or the baby.

Burgers.

All the time...all the way.

Morning, noon and night.

They are my weakness.

Burgers are the food of champions...or of pregnant women named Trinity, anyway.

"God, think they'd let me move in for the next few weeks? You smell that?" I inhale the yummy charbroiled-goodness burger smell.

"Jesus, you're beginning to scare me a bit. I think you're starting to grow fangs," Shannon says, as Hendrix and I slip into the booth across from she and Cannon. They've been going strong now for months, despite a minor hiccup from Shannon's past popping in and trying to get her back. Good thing Cannon put up a fight, because the last person I want to see Shannon with again is Mario. Unfortunately, he's always been my BFF's weakness, but simply put, he's an abusive prick with "bad news" tattooed on his forehead.

"That's my T-Rex. All she wants is meat. Mostly burgers, but she'll take a sausage now and then," Hendrix adds, without missing a beat.

"You're impossible." I elbow him in the ribs.

"And you've got a dirty mind. I was simply talking about all that homemade sausage Flynn and Tillie made for us last week."

I roll my eyes in disbelief. "Oh, I bet you were."

We all laugh, knowing exactly what my husband meant.

"Hey, there. Welcome to Burger Barn. I'm Jenna. What can I get you to drink?" she asks, and we all place our orders, beer for them and pop for me.

"I can't wait to have some wine," I admit. "I think you guys should sneak me some when I'm in the hospital."

"We can totally do that," Cannon smiles, his eyes sincere.

Following the night I fainted, Cannon had come up to me at work a few days later to make sure I was okay. We spent a little time talking about everything, and he apologized for the way he'd reacted that night. He said he would never have suspected that I had HIV. He had a lot of misconceptions about HIV and AIDS, and I was really glad to get the opportunity to clear things up for him. He's been an awesome friend ever since and a lot of fun to work with, too. I told him that I had no idea what his reaction had been, and that it didn't matter anyway. As long as he was okay with being around me, we'd be all right. We've since become close; we even have our own little friendship now and I love it. I know it's a shock when you first find out a friend has HIV, especially when the person in question has just collapsed in front of you. Kind of a scary way to find out some pretty significant news.

"I'm glad we could do this," Shannon says, scanning the menu. "It's been way too long since the four of us were all free at the same time, plus soon it will have to be all G-rated conversations and outings as the mini will be here." She looks up and gives me a huge toothy grin. "I can't believe that in a few weeks we're going to have a baby!" she squeals, squeezing my hand, and I giggle.

"I'm glad you're so excited," I tell her, as the server brings our drinks and interrupts to take our dinner order. I, of course, order my all-time favourite: the mushroom, brie and bacon burger, and was already salivating as I handed Jenna my menu. I hope she didn't notice my drool before she returned to the kitchen. Hendrix looked green at the mention of mushrooms, but I can't help it, I've been absolutely craving them.

"Anyway, Hendrix and I want to ask you guys something," I say, looking back and forth between the two of them, a big smile on my face. I love these two people like family. Shannon is like a sister, and I can't think of a better person for this job. She's always been here for me, and I know she'd be the same way with my daughter.

A few weeks ago, I decided to contact my mom. Hendrix offered to do it with me, but I felt it was Shannon whom I wanted with me while I initiated the call. But as I half expected anyway, nothing had changed on their end. My parents prefer to keep things the way they are. My mom did, however, congratulate me on my marriage and pregnancy before she then chastised me and reminded me of my mistakes. She went on to tell me that I ought to be grateful I had found a man who was so open-minded and would risk getting sick to be with the likes of me. By the end of the call, I was a blubbering mess despite my resolve to not let my mother hear me cry, but with the emotions that go along with pregnancy, it was impossible. We signed off with her hoping that my child would live to be HIV-free, because it "wasn't the baby's fault that I was reckless". Once the call was done, I cried a whole lot more and Shannon, of course, snuggled us up on my couch and fed us ice cream as we binge-watched old episodes of *Friends*, while she cursed my mother over and over again, telling me how I'm much better off. And for the first time, I actually believed it.

"Yeah, we don't want to put either of you on the spot," Hendrix says beside me, snapping me out of my head, reminding me that this is a happy night. I decide to push thoughts of my parents aside, hopefully for good. "Cannon, you're my best friend, and Shannon, you're Trin's, so it seemed natural that it be you guys, if you're willing to do what we're gonna ask."

They both look at us with knowing smiles on their faces, coupled with a bit of surprise, as I'm sure they know where we're headed with this conversation. *How could they not know we'd ask them?*

"Whether you're together or not, and I'm just saying that to say it. You better be, but you know, we still want you both, because we love you and trust you and know how amazing you both are," I say, adding nothing to the conversation. I laugh out loud, because Hendrix is giving me a gentle nudge and shaking his head, smirking. "What? Sorry, I'm nervous. I ramble. They can't say no."

"I swear if you get down on one knee, I'm outta here," Shannon says, and we all laugh.

"You know I suck at this stuff, and now add this pregnancy-brain thing," I say, pointing to my head. "Trust me, dudes, it's a real thing," I tell them, widening my eyes and spinning my finger beside my head like I'm loco.

"What my not-so-articulate-at-the-moment—and yet beautiful—wife is not-so-eloquently trying to say, is that we would love for you guys to be the baby's guide parents. You know, positive role models in her life who will teach her things and love her like we do. Adults she can trust and rely on outside of our immediate families, ones who would also serve as primary guardians if anything were to happen to the both of us. We want to know that she would be in good hands, and Trin and I can't think of better people for our baby," Hendrix explains perfectly.

"Yes, I'd be honoured," Shannon says, wiping her eyes before she practically leaps across the table to hug Hendrix and me.

"Me too. Totally," Cannon interjects, reaching over to shake Hendrix's hand and giving my hands a tight squeeze. "This calls for another round!" Cannon motions for the waitress just as she is coming out of the kitchen to drop off our food.

"I'll bring you extra treats for the hospital, so we can all celebrate," Cannon winks as we toast, they with their beers, and me with my Pepsi.

"Deal," I smile, and take a sip, happy with our decision.

60

Trinity

"THAT SHOULD BE the last of it," gasps an out-of-breath Uncle Dex, who's perched on the small ottoman in the nursery. It's a fancy ottoman, one that matches the super-plush and super-comfy rocking chair that Nadia and Brody bought us for the nursery, the one Dex just carried up the stairs. The one all new parents must have, according to Nadia, anyway. "Looks good in here. Sure all this shit will fit?"

Looking around, I smile and shrug. "I hope so. It might take me a few days, but I'll make it work." Hendrix and Dex have been making trip after trip, bringing up all of the baby stuff that I've been storing at Dex and Til's while we moved into our new house and painted the nursery. "There is too much stuff in here. I didn't realize back at the shower just how much there was. Are you sure you and Tillie haven't been adding things?" I ask, looking around at the piles of stuff I need to find homes for, including a bunch of items I don't remember seeing before.

"Sorry, can't say. Must be those gnomes" he laughs, standing, his knees cracking. "I'm off. I better get home before Tillie misses me too much."

"You wish, old man," says a sexy Hendrix, coming in with the last few bags. He's wearing an olive coloured t-shirt that brings out his eyes; the fact that it fits snugly doesn't hurt, either. I want in this man's pants all the time. I have to bite my lip to stifle a moan from where I'm sitting on the carpet, sorting things in the lovely lilac-and-white nursery, the very one Hendrix and I finally finished the other night. It was worth it, though. It's become my favourite room in our new house. We painted alternating white and lilac walls, and added a crystal chandelier light that Hendrix picked out for his princess one day while he was at Home Depot, along with the matching white crib, dresser, and change table Til and Dex bought for us. We are officially ready for our baby. Or will be, once we get everything else put away. *If I can leave Hendrix alone for long enough, that is.*

"Bye, Dex," I say, as he kisses the top of my head and shakes hands with Hendrix before leaving.

The deep voice coming from Hendrix, who's now sitting behind me in the rocking chair, surprises me: "What the hell is that?"

Looking around the room, I'm confused.

"What's what? Are you talking to me?" I ask.

"Yeah," he says, and nods at the piece of clothing in my hand, and I giggle.

"Oh. It's a onesie!"

"The hell she'll be wearing any kind of onesie," he says, giving me a knowing look. My cheeks heat as my mind pulls up that particular movie reel. *Did I mention how hot Hendrix is looking today? Mmmm.*

"You're kidding, Hendrix. Babies live in these things for the first, like, three months, if not longer." I hold up the purple onesie sleeper that says, "How I roll" beside an embroidered bottle of milk.

"My daughter cannot wear that!"

"What? Why?" I ask seriously confused.

"You know why, and I cannot make those kinds of connections to baby clothes! It will totally destroy my lust for onesies," says my horny-assed husband.

"You're an idiot," I laugh, shaking my head. "They're totally not the same thing, so don't worry." Ignoring his crazy talk and mumblings, I continue to fold and pack away diapers, receiving blankets, and a larger pile of even more onesies which, sad but true, aren't even close to being as fun as the grown-up versions.

"All done."

"Need a hand getting up?" a smug Hendrix asks, his voice teasing, because he always asks and I always say no…at first.

A few moments pass with me struggling unsuccessfully to lift myself from the ground—like a ladybug who's been rolled over onto its back—and I finally cave. "Can you help me get up, please?" I ask a cocky Hendrix, who, of course, reminds me that he did offer in the first place but with me being the stubborn person I am, I needed to try myself.

"When did I get so big?" I huff, finally relenting when Hendrix's muscular arms come to my rescue and he props me upright.

"You're not big. You're beautiful, glowing and the sexiest woman I've ever seen," he says.

"Sweet talker."

"No, honestly. Want me to show you just how sexy you are?" He raises his eyebrows in invitation. I lean up and kiss him hard, wanting badly to say yes.

"I love you, Mr. Hills."

"You too, Fruitloop," he says, kissing my forehead and grabbing my ass, pulling me in close against him.

I'm about to suggest that he runs out and picks us up Big Macs so we can eat before we get it on, but that's when I feel it.

"Holy shit, are you ever wet for me…" Hendrix says in a sexy voice, and pulls back. But the sly grin on his face turns to a look of alarm as he looks down at the giant wet spot I've left on his bulge. I burst out laughing; I'm appalled, but there's no way I can't.

"Hendrix…I think my water just broke," I say, looking down and seeing a wet patch all over the crotches and down the legs of his and my pants. "I think my water broke!" I repeat, as reality hits.

"What?" He looks down again. "Eeyagh! Holy fuck. It did. Okay, let's go change our pants and then we gotta go. It's baby time, Fruitloop. It's baby time." Hendrix grabs my face between both his hands. "I fucking love you. Let's go meet our daughter." He kisses my lips then leaves me without a word.

I stand there for a minute, processing. *We're going to have a baby. I'm going to meet my little girl. I'm about to be a mum.* I thought I felt complete with just Hendrix, but having Hendrix and our daughter will make me whole. The ending I never thought I'd have a chance at…it's here, it's becoming my actual reality.

"Come on, Trin. I got the bags, and here's a towel and a pair of sweats for you to change into. Let's go…" I quickly clean myself off and pull the new pants on, then follow a mumbling Hendrix—who's already talking on his cell to who knows who—as we walk out the door as a couple for the last time.

Soon, we'll be a threesome.

61

TRINITY

"DEPECHE MODE OR Pink Floyd?" Hendrix asks, his eyebrows moving up and down as if he doesn't already know the answer, as he sets up our iPod in the delivery suite.

"As if," I huff.

"Fine." He shakes his head. "*Violator*, or *Music for the Masses*?"

"*Violator*."

"Excellent choice," a voice booms from the doorway, where I see someone whom I'm guessing is the anesthesiologist entering, wheeling a cart. "Trinity? I'm Dr. Ambrose. I'll be giving you your epidural this evening."

"Will it hurt?" I ask, my voice starting to shake, because I've heard horror stories about these things. Also, I'm having a contraction, which hurts like hell.

"I cannot tell a lie. Yes, it will, a bit. Try to focus on the music and a conversation with your husband, and I'll be as quick as I can," he says, setting up behind me. I'm sitting up on the bed as he directed, with my legs over one side. He unties my gown at the back. I do my best to focus on the thumping bass as "Policy of Truth" plays, and Hendrix holds my hands.

Once Dr. Ambrose finishes and leaves, I start to relax as the pain from the contractions lessens considerably and I feel myself going numb from the ribs down. Hendrix and I don't have to wait long before someone comes to check on us.

"Trinity, Hendrix! Hello, and congratulations," a familiar voice calls as the doctor I remember from the time I fainted enters the room.

"Doctor Gallegan, hi. It's nice to see you again," I say to the woman who first told us I was pregnant.

"Hey, doc," says Hendrix. She and Hendrix shake hands. "You the one performing the C-section?"

"No, OB/GYN isn't my specialty, but, depending how the evening progresses, it'll be one of two of my colleagues, Dr. Hussein or Dr. Cho. They're both on-call tonight in obstetrics. Believe it or not, there are about eight of you moms-to-be in here right now, it's a little crazy. So, our delivery ward is in party mode tonight. I'm only here passing through while it's quiet down in the ER. I saw your name on the board and wanted to pop in to say hello, and also to let you know Dr. Cho thinks, if everything stays on schedule, that they'll begin your procedure in the next hour or so."

"Thank you, doctor."

"Good luck, you two. I'll make sure I stop by later on," she says, before leaving. Suddenly, I'm exhausted. The excitement is hitting me all at once, and maybe the epidural is affecting me, too, but I'm not sure if it's that or not.

"Why don't you go out, make some calls, and update the family? I'm tired and I just wanna close my eyes for a few minutes before we start," I say to Hendrix, knowing he won't like the idea of leaving me, but will do it anyway, because I asked.

"You know I don't want to leave, right?"

"I do." I smile because I know him so well. "But they'll be worrying, and it's been a few hours now already."

"The things I do for you…" He kisses my forehead. "Lucky I love you, Mrs. Hills."

"The luckiest," I call, before he reaches the door.

"Be right back."

"M'kay," I say, closing my eyes and rubbing my numb belly. I still can't believe I'm going to be a mum, that I'm going to have a baby. I'm still in denial, to be honest. I wake up sometimes in the middle of the night panicked that it was all just a dream. Then I feel her kicking as if sensing my agitation and trying to soothe me, letting me know she is very real indeed. It's insane how you can love someone so profoundly when you haven't even met them; already, I know that this little girl is going to be my whole world. *Well, she and her amazing daddy.*

I know our lives won't always be easy, especially if she does test positive for HIV, and I'm not quite sure how I'll handle it if she does. I remember all too well how I felt when I thought I might have infected Hendrix; imagine doing that to a little baby? I'm not really a religious person, however, I have been talking out loud to whomever or whatever may be listening. I've been asking for my baby to be healthy, and for me to live long enough to see her grow, marry, and maybe even have kids of her own. I know, though, that whatever happens to me as I continue my fight with my HIV, that she'll be in good hands no matter what. I truly have the happiest life, something I never expected would ever be mine after finding out I was infected. Our little girl has no idea about the tribe that awaits her arrival outside this room. She may not have my parents, but she's got more than enough family and friends to love her and take care of her.

"Fruitloop." I feel Hendrix's warm breath on my neck. "It's time to meet our baby. Dr. Hussein is here, and we're ready to move you to the delivery room."

"Okay. I'm ready. More than ready, actually. Let's go get our girl."

"We're gonna finally meet our daughter, Fruitloop. I can't wait." He takes a deep breath. "Thank you for this, Trinity."

I nod, overcome with emotion. Hendrix runs his hand down my cheek and I smile before he covers my lips with his.

62

Hendrix

"Hendrix. She's perfect."

A groggy—yet still beautiful as ever—Trinity beams as she takes in our little miracle, while I lean in. I'm reluctantly taking our baby off her mummy's chest where she's spent the last few minutes bonding with Trin. Skin-to-skin contact was something Trin and I both wanted to be part of our birth plan. We loved the idea of our daughter getting to lay on her mum right after delivery not only to bond, but for the other positive effects it has, too, such as helping the baby to regulate her temperature and breathing. Enhancing bonding also helps the baby feel less stressed and she may even cry less, even having just been delivered by Caesarean. Here at West Lincoln Memorial, they support skin-to-skin contact even with C-sections, so we lucked out. I have to admit the whole event was pretty overwhelming and incredible to witness.

As soon as the baby had been removed from Trin's belly, the obstetrician put her directly on Trin's upper abdomen, and the medical team pushed our daughter gently up and underneath the concealing blue drape over her stomach which separated the doctor and nurses from Trinny and I. Our baby was then settled directly onto her mum's bare chest. A nurse came up and quickly wiped the baby off a little before covering her head and draping a blanket over both her and Trin to keep them warm.

I gaze down at them. "Now I have two perfect girls in my life. How the hell did I get so lucky? We went from tire irons, to friends, to you falling madly in love with me, and now there's a whole new person. Who let that happen?" I smile at my wife.

"I don't want to give her up to you yet," she jokes hoarsely, looking at our daughter who's now snuggling in my arms. I'm about to try and feed her as the nurse has just suggested.

"I can't believe she's finally here, that we're parents. It's surreal," I say, in awe. I'm officially a dad. *Me, the broody asshole.* Crazy how the right girl can make you see the light, and make you want to get so completely absorbed in it and in her that you change without hesitation or realization.

Trinity is my light. And, now, so is this little baby.

"Here's a bottle, Dad. Give it to her nice and easy. She might resist at first but rest the nipple on her lips a few times, and I bet she takes it soon. I've only put a few ounces in. We'll see how she does." The nurse pats my arm, then pulls a chair over on our side of the blue drapery so I can sit close, so Trin can watch. I know not getting to breastfeed was harder for her to accept then she let on. I could see the sadness in her eyes when we were at our last Lamaze class and they were talking about the benefits.

"You gonna be a carnivore like your mummy?" I ask, doing exactly what the nurse suggested with the bottle as I feed my daughter for the first time. She quickly clamps her lips against the bottle's nipple and starts to guzzle, and the bottle is empty before I know it. She's fierce, a little fighter, just like her mother. "She is totally your kid. She pounded it back. You'd think it was a hamburger, or a bottle of red wine," I laugh, and Trin gives me a dirty look, but then smiles.

"I can't wait to hold her and feed her. I can't wait to get us all home," Trin says, softly. I know she's tired. I can only imagine how tough having a baby is on the body.

"Hopefully soon, baby."

Thankfully, the Caesarean section went well, and the doctors are confident the baby didn't come into undue contact with any of Trin's fluids during the delivery. Time will certainly tell. I'm really hoping that we can go home in two or three days at the most. It all depends on the baby and Trin's recovery.

For now, we've been transferred out of the surgical suite and back to Trin's hospital room. I see Dr. Hussein entering the room across from ours with a big smile, a gurney, and a nurse, saying, "Neeeeeext! Are you ready, my dear?"

After feeding little Zara again, I stand and move close to Trin's hospital bed. "I love you, baby. I'm so proud of you." I lean in carefully to kiss Trin's lips; it's a chaste kiss, despite my wanting to devour her like I usually do. I know she's tired, and the grumpy nurse is sure to give me shit again. I've already gotten in trouble twice today for being *me,* as Trinity put it. *Whatever that means.*

Trin runs her hand over Zara's soft cheek as I sit next to the bed. "She's lovely. Just…lovely."

"You take after your mummy, my lucky girl," I whisper, leaning over Trin and laying a gentle kiss on the top of Zara's fuzzy little head where it pokes out from the pink blanket.

We decided to name our daughter Zara, which means "seed" in Hebrew, "star" or "flower" in Arabic, and "princess" in Russian. She is our little princess, and we've been there to watch her grow from the very start, and will see her blossom over the years into the amazing person she's destined to be. A woman, I predict, who will be strong and feisty like her mother.

"Does the family know she's arrived?" Trinity asks, but her voice is a little off, a croak in her voice making me alert. She sounds almost breathless, like she's out of breath and struggling. I notice her chest is rising and falling more rapidly. Standing back up, I take the baby and move away from the bed, hoping Trinity's just too warm and that it will help. I shift my eyes from Zara back over to Trin. Taking in her face, I notice she looks suddenly pale, and that her teeth…her teeth, they're chattering. *It's really warm in here, though.*

"Trin? Are you cold, baby?" I scan the room for another blanket, before looking down at Trin for an answer.

I get no response.

"Trin?" I say louder, stepping in right beside her bed again. I'm holding Zara closely, but I've placed her bottle on the bedside table.

"Trinity?" I shout now, my voice a deeper rumble. I try not to scare Zara, while trying to wake Trin. There's suddenly a flurry of activity happening, a whole bunch of people rushing in as an alarm buzzer sounds…and then another.

"Doctor? Doctor, I think something's wrong with my wife…" I state the now-obvious at the same time the medical team is surrounding her bed. I give Zara to a nurse I recognize, who had said earlier she was going to come to take Zara for a bath. I hand her off gently, despite not being able to take my eyes off Trinity, whose body has now started convulsing on the bed.

"Trinity!" I yell, moving in closer.

"She's seizing," I hear a nurse call, as a third alarm goes off.

"It's cardiac arrhythmia; we need to stabilize her," a voice booms to the team, and I look up and see Dr. Hussein. "We can't let her arrest." The doctor nods toward the heart monitor that's going haywire.

"Get him out of here," I hear someone order, and it takes me a minute to realize they mean me. I didn't hear it at first, not over the pounding in my ears or the blood as it rushes to my heart, making it beat unrelentingly as I stand paralysed. Over to the side, I see another nurse who's just rushed into the room prep the defibrillator while a third nurse jabs a needle full of something into Trinity's IV.

"No. She's my wife. I'm not leaving." I rush in, placing my hand on Trinity's face, trying to brace her neck. "She's going to hurt herself. Help her, please. Make her stop moving like that." I spit out the demand as a mix of anger and fear simultaneously sprint through my veins. Tears stream down my face as I am forcefully pushed to one side and stand helplessly watching, willing her body to stop doing whatever it's doing wrong. Willing her to open her eyes.

"I said get him out of here, Marie. I mean it," Dr. Hussein, the obstetrician shouts again.

"Sir, please," the nurse starts, but I ignore her, too focused on Trinity.

"Please, baby." My hands begin to shake and I step back in disbelief.

"Her pressure's dropped, it's too low. I need the husband out now. I need space. Get him the hell out of here. I need the paddles," the doctor yells at a nurse, who's suddenly being extremely kind to me.

"Please, sir, let them work," she says in a way-too-soothing voice. "The baby is having her bath, let's go see her. Your wife is in good hands, give the team room to work. You don't want to watch this. Please don't make me call secu—" I don't register the threat, all I hear is the doctor speaking to my wife.

"Damn it. You stay with me, Trinity." I back up, sidestepping the nurse so I can focus.

I stand there, giving my head a hard shake, hoping it will wake me up from what has to be a dream—a nightmare.

As he's doing chest compressions on her, I hear the doctor shouting: "Don't you stop fighting. You hear me? You've got a baby girl who needs you. Come on, Trinity. Fight. Fight. Fight, goddamn it. Clear!"

There's a loud bang and I see Trinity's body arch and jerk hard on the bed as the doctor takes the paddles off her chest. Stunned by the violence of the procedure, I watch, frozen again, in stunned silence as they work on my wife, and feel a hand take my own. It's that nurse.

It's like I'm here, but I'm not. *This isn't real.* I squeeze my eyes closed then open them, over and over again, but nothing changes.

"Let's give them space to help your wife. And your family needs to know what's going on. Let's go tell them," I hear the nurse say, who now has a tall security guard standing beside her. This time, I listen, and I reluctantly start to shuffle my feet toward the exit door. *Trinity doesn't need me making a scene. She needs me to be strong.*

"Okay," I whisper, still not taking my eyes off the bed where my wife lays fighting for her life, a nurse squeezing a bag attached to a mask on Trinity's face to make her breathe while a sweating Dr. Hussein pushes up and down harshly on her chest, his arms locked and a grim look on his face. I hear a cracking sound.

"The ribs are going…" a nurse says to the doctor.

"She's in the best hands, Hendrix. Trinity has the best team working on her…"

I barely register the nurse's murmurings as we walk to the waiting room where everyone's sitting, waiting for the good news.

News I just can't give them right now.

63

Hendrix

PACING THE LINOLEUM in the family waiting room, I'm about to march off to the nurses' station again to find out what's happening when I see Dr. Hussein walking down the hall towards us. A swooshing sound takes over my senses and a tingling sensation pulses through my body when I hear the doctor's tone as he asks, "Trinity Hill's family? Are they all here?" He glances around, taking us all in as we look up from where we feel we've been sitting and waiting for days.

"Yes. Here," Dexter Flynn calls, gesturing to the group of us before making his way closer to the doctor, soon joined by Tillie, then by me. A feeling of dread washes over me.

I know what he's about to say before the words even leave his mouth…

"Mr. Hills, I'm sorry. We tried…"

I think I'm going to pass out.

"No. It can't be…" Flynn spits out, shaking his head in disbelief. "No." He turns on his heel with his hand over his mouth and stalks over to the window, away from the rest of us, waving off Tillie as she tries to touch his shoulder.

"It happened so quickly…" I hear Doctor Hussein begin to explain, but I can't make out the words over the sound of my heart exploding in my chest.

"Not possible," I hear my mum whisper as she comes up to stand beside me.

I want to say something, but I can't find my voice. I feel as if my own body's shutting down.

"And the baby? Is the baby…" sobs my mother.

"The baby is fine, ma'am. The baby is just fine, she's sleeping in the nursery," says Dr. Hussein softly.

"Oh, Trinity," I hear Tillie cry. "Nooo. It can't be, it can't. Tell me there's a mistake! Not my sweet girl…" She moves across the room, now throwing herself at Flynn. "She can't be gone, Dexter. Not now. Pleeeaaase," Tillie howls, full of anguish and hurt.

No. No. This isn't real. I think to myself, unable to make a sound, because in this moment, I honestly believe that if I don't say it out loud, it won't be true. *That's the last fucking thing I want.* I feel as if I'm floating, dreaming. I'm here, but I'm not. I can hear, I can see, but I cannot move. I can barely breathe, or speak past the huge lump that has formed in my throat. *Even if I wanted to.*

"Mr. Hills?" The doctor says, putting his hand on my shoulder.

"Hendrix?" Flynn calls, holding Tillie tighter. I can hear Shannon, Nadia, and the others all crying and trying to seek some kind of solace, each in their own way.

"No," I shout, pushing past the doctor, running out of the waiting room straight to where I last left Trinity.

"Fruitloop?" I burst through the door, startling the nurse who's still inside, my eyes immediately looking at the bed, where I'm expecting to see her lying awake and holding our baby girl, to see her cooing and smiling down at her. *That's the way it needs to be.*

Instead, rushing in closer, I don't see Zara, and Trinity's eyes are closed as if she's sleeping soundly. Taking her hand in mine, I kiss the back of it. "Baby? Trinity? Can you open your eyes? Can you do that for me?" I ask, crouching down on the floor beside her bed, keeping her hand in mine and squeezing it a little. But she gives me nothing in return.

I sit, holding her dangling hand, splaying soft kisses on top of it, then stand again to look at her. "Fruitloop, please open those big beautiful eyes for me…please," I beg, my voice gruff, tears blinding me from seeing if my words are working, changing anything. "Trinity, you come back to me right fucking now!" I choke out.

Again she gives me nothing. I wipe my eyes. And now I see how pale her face is, how blue her lips are. And how one eyelid is ever-so-slightly open, just barely. And how still she is. *How perfectly, perfectly still.*

"Goddamn it, Trinity Hills, you hear me? Open your eyes and come back to me, to us. Zara and I need you so fucking much, you can't do this! You can't leave us. I love and need you too much, Fruitloop. You're my light…and I can't do this without you. We're supposed to grow old together. You were winning the fight. Goddamn it!" I cry, anchoring myself to her arm as I again drop back down to my spot on the floor.

She's my light…and she's gone…

The soft sound of footsteps registers as they make their way in behind me. "Mr. Hills, I'm so sorry for your loss. Is there anything I can get for you?" a voice asks. I don't bother to look; instead I stand in a state of continued disbelief, staring again at Trin's lifeless body.

After a few moments, the nurse speaks again. This time, a gentle hand is placed on my back. "I'm just outside if you need anything. You take all the time you need." She squeezes my shoulder before retreating.

"A blanket," I call out. "She was cold, earlier. I can't let her be cold."

"Sure. I'll go get you one right away." I hear her footfalls as she moves toward the door.

"A warm one, not just a sheet. She's going to get cold, I can't let her get cold," I argue, running my hand down her beautiful cheek, her skin so soft. *There's no way this is real.*

"I'll get the biggest and warmest one I can find," she replies kindly. "Did you want me to get the rest of your family?" she asks.

"She is my family." I shake my head, holding on to the bedrails. "Please, she's my light. I need her, and our daughter needs her. I can't let her go, we need her. Just her. Bring her back."

"I'm sorry for your loss, Hendrix. I wish I could. I'll go get the blanket and be right back, then you can let me know if I should get the others to come say their goodbyes."

"Thank you," I barely manage, past my emotions. "She's my home, you know… my happy…" I utter, letting out a huge body-rattling sob as she walks out to find me a blanket and to check in with the family.

The family who were all waiting to celebrate with us. Only now there isn't an *us.*

We aren't the right version of the *us* we're supposed to be today. Trinity is gone; now, it's just our little miracle and me.

Oh, God. My poor princess. She has just lost her mother.

How will we go on without her?

My light is gone.

"Here you are," the nurse says, beside me again, handing me a large baby blue blanket.

"This will be perfect, thank you," I sniffle, taking the blanket from her arms. I gently begin covering my wife.

Leaning down, I sweep her brown bangs off her face with my hand and kiss her cheek, whispering in her ear one last time. "I'll always love you, Fruitloop."

Suddenly, an overwhelming ache to hold my daughter consumes me. Turning to face the nurse, whose mouth is a thin line, I demand: "Take me to my daughter."

64

Hendrix

"It's okay, Zara. Daddy's here. I'll always be here." I cradle my two-week-old daughter as we sit in her nursery. The lyrics to "You Said You'd Grow Old with Me" by Michael Schulte coming from my phone ring true. This is the last place Trinity was alive when she was inside our home. I feel her here the most. I swear I can smell her fruity scent lingering in the air.

This is where I come to feel close to her. Not our bedroom, or the kitchen, but here, where she was last. *How did I go from joking about onesies and kissing my wife to coming home a single dad? A widower? I'm a fucking* widower.

Zara and I sit in here to listen to music and rock back and forth. It's become a part of our routine—she cries until I rock her to sleep, then I sit savouring the closeness I feel with Trinity when we're here. We do this, the same way, on and off all day, ever since we've been home. It's a bittersweet feeling, holding this precious little girl, feeling a love so strong it's inexplicable, while at the same time feeling as if I've been sucker punched by the loss of my Trin. Unable to catch my breath, I'm drowning, and my life preserver is missing. She's gone, and I'm not sure I'll ever be the same.

An amniotic fluid embolism is what killed my wife. A rare condition affecting only a small percentage of women—I think Dr. Hussein said between 1 to 12 woman out of a 100,000 will experience the condition. It can happen when amniotic fluid or something as simple as hair, fetal cells or some other kind of debris from the baby passes through the placenta into the bloodstream causing an inflammatory reaction, which caused her to die of cardiac arrest. Her HIV had nothing to do with it at all.

I mean, what the fuck? I'm in utter disbelief. *As if my girl didn't have enough shit thrown at her in her lifetime? How cruel can the world be to one person?* Anyway, my incredible girl never let it beat her down. She never let the shitty hand she'd been dealt get the best of her.

As quick as that train of thought enters my mind, though, I push it aside. Because if Trin could, she'd tell you she died happy. She'd tell you that together we lived a life she never expected to have…that of a very much loved wife and mother. Trinity may have started off a little broken on the inside after being diagnosed with HIV, but she portrayed nothing but beauty and happiness on the outside to everyone and in every situation. Trinity Adams Hills' strength and determination was not to be rivalled by even the strongest men and women. It wasn't the weight of her troubles I saw on her shoulders; it was a pair of angel wings. *I'll miss you everyday, angel.*

And even if it was only for a very short time, my Fruitloop was the best mum to our daughter, and it's my goal to make sure Zara grows up knowing her mother as if she were right here with us. Trin would tell you that she lived and loved and wouldn't change a thing. She'd tell you to get a move on, and not to dwell on the past. I have no doubt she'd be pissed seeing me like this. Too bad. I can't seem to accept it, even though I know that's exactly what my incredibly strong wife would tell me to do, if she could. *And, fuck, do I wish I could hear her voice, more than anything.*

Closing my eyes, I sit while Zara sleeps in my arms and reflect back on all the wonderful times Trinity's words rocked my world.

"You're impossible..." I grin at the way she always sounded exasperated.

"I like you. A lot. But you terrify me..."

I smile, remembering our game of "Truths".

"And I see you, too, Hendrix. So much. And I want this, so much."

I remember the admission as if it were yesterday.

"You're an incredible man, Hendrix. If we do this, I might never let you go."

You leaving me wasn't part of the deal.

"Thank you for loving me, Hendrix. For opening my eyes and helping me to see me, the way you saw me from the start."

You saw me, too, sweetheart, and for that, I'll always be grateful. Thank you for giving an ogre a chance. I just needed to find the light.

"Fuck, I miss you, Fruitloop." I move Zara up to rest on my chest a little more snugly, needing the comfort only she can bring in these moments. Sure, the others try and have been here daily, but it's Zara and me now...we're a team.

And I know, eventually, we'll make it through this.

Because Trinity would want us to, and all I ever wanted to do was make her happy.

EPILOGUE

"HERE YOU GO, boys," our server Amy says, placing the pitcher of Bud we ordered in front of Flynn and I. Amy's the newest addition to the Dugout staff, and she's been getting friendlier and more flirty with me over the past few weeks. "Anything else I can get you before your food's up?" She looks at me, a sincere smile gracing her glossy lips. Unfortunately for her, she's wasting her time and energy by putting her sights on me. Amy's cute, sure, but I have zero interest in reciprocating.

"Nope, we're great, thanks," I nod, sliding my empty glass towards Flynn so he can pour.

"Sounds good, holler if you need me." Amy pats my arm before leaving.

"I think you have a fan, son," Flynn says, watching her walk away. "She's a pretty one, too," he notes.

"I didn't notice," I tell him, truthfully. "Besides, I'm not looking for a replacement. Why would I want what can't be replaced?" I say, tapping my knuckles on the distressed wooden table top while I try to stop the memories of Trin from taking over.

"You can never replace the ones you love. And you shouldn't ever feel that's what you're doing by moving on," Flynn says, pouring our beer.

We're sitting in our usual booth at The Dugout. It's Thursday night, the one social night I agreed to start having after Zara's first birthday. It took me a year of listening to my mum, Arran, Flynn and Tillie, all trying to get me to leave Zara for one night and get back to living some sort of life outside my daughter and the garage. I finally conceded, and agreed that it was time for me to start being quasi-social again. That was three years ago. Thursdays have since become my pool- and beer night at The Dugout with Flynn, Arran, Cannon, Joe, Brody, and sometimes Simon.

Simon and I have remained close over the years after Trin's and Andrea's deaths, and he's become one of my dearest friends. He's a really great guy, very sensible; I guess you could say we bonded over our losses and Simon was an ear when I needed one most. Not to mention, he and Zara are thick as thieves, so much so that Zara calls him "Uncle Simon" and very much looks forward to his visits.

Speaking of Zara, Thursdays have also become a big night out for my girl. It's Zara's, Tillie's and my mum's girls' night in, one complete with a sleepover, pizza, Barbies and a movie. It's Zar's favourite day of the week, I swear, a fact I try to pretend doesn't bother me, especially when Tillie tries to get me to let her keep Zara on Friday nights, too. I keep telling her maybe one day if I have a date or something I'll ease up and allow a weekend sleepover, but, for now, when I'm home I want Zara with me. Otherwise, I might drive myself crazy with memories and allow myself to be consumed by the grief I feel every single day. The one night is hard enough; I couldn't imagine two nights away from my princess. It's bad enough having her in daycare when I'm at work.

"You know I'm right. It's okay to start getting out there. It doesn't have to be Amy," Flynn says, breaking through my thoughts.

"I know, you're right. I'm just not sure I'm ready to try," I admit. Brody, Simon, Cannon and Joe couldn't make it tonight, so it's just Flynn and me. We decided to forgo pool for wings and beer.

"Trinity would be losin' her shit if she saw you sitting here thinking this way. Worried you ain't ready, worried you'd be replacing her. I know you don't come right out and admit it, but I know you. Trust me. Thinking that you could replace Trinity is stupid, 'cause it would be different. You can't replace her, but you can restore your heart a little." He raps his glass on the table as if that will make it so. "Ain't no one gonna fault you for moving on. Trin would want that for you. And for Zara," he says cockily, raising his glass and taking a long sip.

"I know. She's probably shaking her head at me. I can imagine the shit she'd give me if she could. It's easier said than done, though. I compare everyone to her—her looks, her scent, her courage, her…everything *her*. She's irreplaceable," I say, chewing on a chicken wing.

"Listen, you gave Trinity her happily ever after ending. Don't for one second think she left this earth feeling unfulfilled, unloved, or with any regrets. You gave her that, Hendrix. Now it's time for you to move on. I know for a fact, both Shannon and Nadia have a list of women they think might be a good fit," Flynn says, his voice firm. He's right; it's been three years since Trinity's death, and there have been countless offers and attempts to get me to date—with many set ups and too many instances of me bailing at the last minute. *It just never feels right.*

"Easier said than done. I miss her so fucking much, every second of every day. How would that be fair to anyone else? I'm all baggage right now."

"Well, you never know until you try. Your own 'happily ever after' is what we all want to see for you," he air quotes. "That's what I'm sayin', if you wanna get all girly about it."

"You don't get it. None of you do. Fuck." I take a swig of my beer before running my hand down my face and continuing. "I already had my fucking happy ending, and now she's fucking gone, Dex." I grit out, calling him by his first name for probably the first time. "Want to know my happy ending? I need my wife, not some replacement. I can't just move on. She was my goddamn life. Zara and Trinity, they were my happy, and Zara testing negative gave me my ever after. I'm not looking for another woman to try and be what she can't ever be. You need to listen, old man," I say with a bit more bite than I intend, but Flynn isn't buying it.

"You're not listening, goddammit. You live for her memory. You survive and thrive day after day for your beautiful daughter. You're an incredible father. That girl longs for nothing, and knows she's loved. You keep on sharing stories about her mother like you and the rest of us do. You keep the pictures around the house like you have. But, fuck, Hendrix…" Flynn's voice cracks with the seriousness he obviously feels about this. He lets out a loud breath and offers me a warm smile. "Son, Trinity is still here. Maybe not the version you or the rest of us want. But in Zara, she's there. If ever I've seen her, she's a part of that little girl. You've got a daughter who will forever bind you to your wife. A special girl, one who is healthy—one who needs you now more than ever. You're her everything, Hendrix. Don't you think for one second that Trinity isn't pissed at you for waiting for so long to find someone who will love the two of you as much as she did. Zara needs a mother."

"She has a mother," I interject, getting pissed off. "No-one can replace Trinity," I hiss, giving him as solid case of cut-eye. A part of me is shocked he'd say such a stupid thing.

"Calm down. I'm not saying someone to replace Trinity. I know Zara has Tillie, Kara, Nadia, and Shannon, sure. Alls I'm sayin' is that the little girl needs a real flesh-and-blood mother, someone who's there at night, someone who will help her to fill that void she will surely feel as she grows up without Trinity. Zara needs and deserves that special bond. You both do. Enough is enough. Put yourself out there, man. Be the daddy who continues to shape and mold his daughter to grow up to be strong and loving like her mama, but also give yourself the opportunity to let someone else in. This is the first time in years you've let me talk like this without immediately crushing me in my tracks, that's gotta count for something," he implores. Reaching across the table, he pats my hand. "We're all behind you, son. It's time to rewrite your ending."

Overcome with feelings from his emotional ass-kicking, all I can do is nod.

"Right," Flynn nods back, raising his beer to mine. "Love ya, kid."

"You too, old man," I say, raising my glass.

"Now…think these fuckin' Leafs can take it this year, or what?" Flynn says, as if we didn't spend the last twenty minutes talking like two old hens, him helping me see that maybe he's right. Maybe it is time to open myself up to the idea of letting someone in. At this point, I've got nothing to lose but everything to gain for me and my little princess.

"SLOW DOWN, PRINCESS. Daddy needs to read his list," I say, following a determined Zara down the cereal aisle. Of course, she ignores me and keeps bee-lining it down the aisle anyway.

"Found it, Daddy!" Zara says, jumping up and down, before reaching for a box. The same box another arm is grabbing for at the same time. Suddenly, there are cereal boxes of all kinds and flavours scattered across the floor.

"Ooopps. Sorrwy, Daddy," Zara says, giggling, and that's when I see that the second perpetrator is a woman.

"You must like Froot Loops, too?" the woman asks Zara, smiling at her face to face amidst the mess of boxes all over the aisle.

"I wove them. Here, you have this box," Zar says, picking up two boxes from the floor and handing one to the lady. "I was runnin'. I'm sorrwy."

"Actually, the way I see it, we were both running for the Froot Loops, 'cause they are the best! I think our Princess Powers must be too strong today or something," the blonde woman says, crouching down to Zara's height. Looking all around the aisle as if she has a secret to share but only with Zara, her eyes briefly meet mine and she offers me a sweet smile before leaning in to my daughter and whispering, "I knew you must be a princess! All princesses love Froot Loops."

This causes Zara to clap and giggle while agreeing. "Yes, I'm Princess Zara, and I wove them so much."

As for me, I get a flutter in my heart that I haven't felt in a really long time. This woman is really quite pretty, I notice, the way her hazel eyes shine as she speaks with my girl. Inching in closer to get a better look at this mystery woman as she and Zara continue to engage in this crazy cereal-and-princess talk, I have to admit this whole situation has me both intrigued and a little spellbound. Grinning at the ongoing exchange, I see my princess is hugging her box of cereal close to her, squeezing it against her chest to the point of crushing it. I chuckle.

"I eat Froot Loops every morning," Zara adds proudly, and the woman looks up at me for confirmation.

"She really does, even if it's just for a snack," I offer, my voice hoarse. The fact that Zara asked if we could buy some Froot Loops the minute after I told her the story of her mum's nickname a few months ago makes my chest ache. Pushing the feeling aside, I persevere and try to finish my conversation. "It's quite the pandemic when we run out, like today." I gesture at the boxes of cereal that lay scattered on the floor from my little hurricane's pursuits. "Hence the excitement, because the store often runs out, you know," I wink, joking with her, and it feels good. *Really good, actually.*

"Hi, I'm Hendrix." I step forward, offering my hand.

"Hey. I'm Princess Karina," she says, taking both Zara and I in. "It's nice to meet you both. Zara, *every* day you eat them?" Karina asks, a shocked expression on her face.

"Uh huh," she nods, giving the box a little pat, as if it were Beast.

"Wow, you really do love them. Maybe even more than me. I didn't think that was possible," Karina says, straightening herself back up, eliciting another giggle from Zara at her surprise.

"I eat them, because my daddy used to call my mummy his Fruit-loop. I eat them everyday and fink of her, that way we still can eat together, Nanny Tillie says."

I place my arm on Zara's shoulder, pulling her back to stand closer to me. Not sure if it's to comfort her or to protect myself.

Cocking her head to the side, Karina looks unsure as she processes what Zara's just disclosed. Then it clicks.

"Oh, my. I'm so sorry," she whispers at me, and then looks up, embarrassed. Her gorgeous hazel eyes are turning a stunning green as tears seem to be forming. She glances at Zara, clearly concerned that she may have upset my daughter.

"Thank you. It's been hard." I offer a small smile, but I feel completely vulnerable right now. I'm not sure why, but I want to open up, to tell her more. "Zara's mum passed away after giving birth, they only had a little bit of time," I finish, and see this stranger's face radiating only comfort. Flynn's words from last week pop into my mind, words about taking a chance and moving on…about letting someone in.

"Do you have a liddle girl or boy who you share your cereal with?" Zara asks, breaking the tension and my thoughts.

"No, sweetheart. It's only me," Karina says, a shyness now falling over her demeanour.

"Wow," Zara says, echoing Karina's earlier amazement. "Your Froot Loops must last a longtime, no sharin'. You're lucky. Daddy says I have to share mine, and he eats them a lot, too…" Zara says, looking up at me with her little nose all scrunched up like her mother's. It's one of my favourite faces that she makes. Karina and I both burst out laughing at Zara's accusing tone.

"Well, I'd rather share them with someone, too, if I'm being honest. It's important to share the things we love with the people we love. I just haven't found someone who loves them as much as me yet, but I will one day," Karina shares, smiling, her cheeks taking on a pinkish hue, and I feel a wave of relief on hearing this woman is single. I can't explain why, but it's a feeling I recognize from a long time ago. *Is it hope?*

Zara seems to agree with Karina's perspective on sharing, as she offers to help Karina eat her Froot Loops anytime Karina wants to practice her sharing. It makes me proud, witnessing how caring my little girl can be despite not really understanding the meaning of the words.

Karina's comment affects me, too, not just the part that told me she was single, but the way she said it. It was the determination I heard lying beneath what she said, determination coupled with a hint of hope, and her apparent conviction that she will find someone—the right one. It sparks something in me. Suddenly, I feel a surge of confidence that I haven't felt in years, and for the first time in a long time, I feel almost optimistic.

I bend down to start putting the cereal boxes back on their shelves. Karina reaches over to help and Zara hands her a package, her eyes open wide, a smile like her mum's lighting her face.

Swallowing my guilt, I allow myself to think of the future, to think thoughts I know would make Trinity proud, wherever she may be.

You never know.

Maybe one day, I'll be capable of loving a woman again.

Maybe one day, I'll be healed by love, and not stay tainted by it.

The End.

Dear Reader,

Where to start? I'm not entirely sure, to be honest. I do know that Trinity and Hendrix's story might not be for everyone. And that's okay, I'm comfortable with that. As with *Call Me,* I took a risk and stepped out of my comfort zone to write another standalone novel with some controversial themes, separate from my *Pub Fiction* series.

I discovered that in North America, approximately 22% of new HIV infections occur in women (with the rate being closer to 29% for women ages 15 to 24). People I know have had friends and family members who have been personally impacted by HIV/AIDS, and I felt this was something I wanted to explore as a theme. Then, one day, Trinity popped into my head and wouldn't budge, and I knew that I needed to write *Tainted by Love.*

I also knew there would be a lot of research, tears, and some strong feelings over Trinity and Hendrix and a few of their decisions. Although their choices might not be what you'd choose, remember that there is an element of storytelling overlying the facts presented in the novel. These two are people in love, who made their own decisions and lived with the consequences. I consider this story to be a Happily Ever After in its own way, even if it might not seem that way to some readers.

Regarding the statistics, medical aspects and health-related issues, I am not a physician. I did my best with my research and was as truthful and accurate about life with HIV and AIDS as possible, but remember that this is a work of fiction and allow for that as you read. This is not meant to be medical advice.

Once again, thank you for giving my words a chance.

Lots of love. Play safe.

xx,

Gillian

More Information on HIV and AIDS

CATIE (Canada's source for HIV and hepatitis C information)
www.catie.ca/en/home

Canadian AIDS Society
www.cdnaids.ca

AIDS.GOV
www.aids.gov/hiv-aids-basics

The AIDS Network
www.aidsnetwork.ca

UNAIDS
www.unaids.org/en/regionscountries/countries/unitedstatesofamerica

WHO (World Health Organization)
www.who.int/features/qa/71/en

International AIDS Society
www.iasociety.org

American Foundation on AIDS Research
www.amfar.org

NAT (National AIDS Trust-UK)
www.nat.org.uk/what-do-we-do/nat

(RED)
red.org/what-is-red

World AIDS Day
www.worldaidsday.org/about

Acknowledgements

Once again, I have so many people to thank for taking this journey with me, especially with this story and its subject matter. I don't think I couldn't have done this one without them.

My amazing hubby and son—There aren't enough words that I could use to express how lucky and thankful I am to have you two incredible guys in my life. You are my light, and I love you both, so very much.

Paige—I literally could not have done this one without you. Thank you for being there and dealing with the special brand of crazy that came along with this story. Thank you for always talking me off the ledge, working issues out with me, and most of all for encouraging me and pushing me to write this story. I seriously love you and having you in my corner. I don't think "thank-you" will ever cover how grateful I am for you.

Toni—You are the best!!! I seriously would be lost without you. Thank you for always reading, giving me advice when I start to go crazy, for finding the little things, and for not only being the best PA ever, but more importantly, being my friend. I love you!

Jade—My Jade. Simply put, I fucking love you, and I'm so thankful for your perspective, advice and for making me rethink how I handled certain situations in the story. I appreciate your insights so much, and you made me cautious when I needed to be. Thank you for giving my story a chance.

Mandie—My newest beta, you were AMAZING! I loved having you on this adventure. Thank you for your honesty, for rereading over and over again, the late night messages, and, best of all, the friendship.

I adore you, and I look forward to the next! xoxox

Jelena—I don't really have the right words to express how incredible it's been getting to know you, and having you as a beta reader on this book. Your passion and enthusiasm were such a confidence booster, and I'll always be so very appreciative for all the feedback and support. I love you hard, lady!

Donna—Seriously, I feel you saved my sanity. Thank you for your honesty and for making me stick to the plan and for not letting me change a thing. Thank you for your kindness and knowing exactly what to say, and for making me feel excited about this story. But most of all, I need to thank you for your friendship; I cannot wait for the day we meet.

Sophie—OMFG! If you hadn't have stopped me, I would have given Hendrix the ending my heart didn't want him to have. Thank you for making me think about what I wanted for him, and for not allowing me to get in my own way. I seriously think you saved my ass on this one, and for that I'm eternally grateful. Xo

Shannon—Nugget!! Thank you for reading, and working through things with me over and over and over again. I've loved talking to you as if Hendrix and Trin were real (they are to me). Thank you for your honesty and feedback, and for being the *Shannon* for my Cannon. Xox

Kymmie—Again, thank you for being the voice of reason to my brand of crazy. For talking every bit of this book over with me, for helping me to get out of my head, and most of all, for pushing me to run with this idea when I shared it with you. Xox

Amanda—Lobby, thank you for taking the time out from being a new mom and giving me your feedback and for loving both Trin and Hendrix so easily. I always love hearing your thoughts.

Mom—I love you, I couldn't do this without you. Thank you for being my biggest supporter, for always being willing to help, for being willing to talk it all over with me when I get stuck, and for reading each story a million times. I'm so lucky to have such an amazing woman to call my mom. Xox

Dad—Thank you for always being so proud of your daughter who writes "smut". I'm lucky you're so open minded, and thank you for sharing my stuff on your Facebook.

River, Alissa and Cassia—Thank you ladies for being the amazing friends you are. For making me laugh, helping me when I'm stuck, and for being so supportive. I couldn't imagine not talking to you whores everyday! xo

Jen (ESM)—Here we sit editing book #5, and I can't believe we did it! Thank you for working on this specific book on with me, for questioning my research, and forcing me to double-check that I knew what the hell I was talking about, for making my words better and always pushing and challenging me to add that little something more. And for allowing SOME things to get past you and your Panda. I loved this crazy ride with you!! Xox

Doris—As always, thank you for reading over my words and picking up those pesky things I tend to miss. Xox

Deanna—Thank you for reading early on and always giving me good advice.

Freya—Thank you for giving me the feedback you did for *Tainted by Love*. Your help, guidance and opinions made my story better. For that I'm grateful. You're wonderful.

Brynne—Thank you for reading and helping to make this story better. I've loved chatting with you and look forward to returning the favour in the future.

Jenn and Laurie—Thank you for being there for me and reading my words, but, most of all, for being two of the bestest friends ever! Xox

Angie—Thank you so very much for reading *Tainted* over and sending me all those wonderful screenshots! I loved your messages, and think you're pretty amazing. I cannot wait to see you again soon. xox

Gilly's Gems—You guys are the best group of people! Thank you for supporting each of my books, and for always making me smile. Gilly's Gems is seriously one of my favourite places to be, and I thank you for that. We may be small, but we ROCK! I value you all so much and I hope to meet you all one day.

Ashley at Book Covers by Ashbee Designs—You continue to blow my mind with each cover and teaser you make. You are pure talent, my friend, and I'm so lucky to work with you. You seriously are awesome! I don't even have to say anything, and you just know, lol. Thank you for sticking with me, I look forward to many more. Cheers!

Between the Sheets Promotions—Thank you again for arranging an amazing blog tour, you ladies are incredible to work with.

Thank you to all the amazing bloggers for all helping to support and get my work out there. Everything you do is so much appreciated and I'm honestly very grateful. Thank you for taking a chance on me, and if ever I can help you in return, please contact me. xo

About the Author

I'm a wife, mother and a crazy Canadian living in Ontario with the loves of my life—my amazing hubby and sweetest little boy. I'm admittedly addicted to: my friends, red wine, and laughter. Also, I'm a devoted lover of alpha males and hot sex, all coupled with the perfect side of angst topped off with an epic happily ever after.

Follow Me Here

Website:

authorgillianjones.wordpress.com

Facebook Author Page:

facebook.com/pages/Gillian-Jones-Author/1493072067635651

Facebook:

facebook.com/gillian.jonesauthor

Twitter:

twitter.com/gillianJ_author

Instagram:

instagram.com/gillianjonesauthor

Goodreads:

goodreads.com/author/show/7144405.Gillian_Jones

Join my group Gilly's Gems:

facebook.com/groups/617265411707215

We talk books, eye candy and everything in between.

Books by Gillian Jones

My Mind's Eye

(Pub Fiction Book 1)

On The Rocks

(Pub Fiction Book 2)

One Last Shot

(Pub Fiction Book 3)

Call Me

48020788R00210

Made in the USA
San Bernardino, CA
13 April 2017